Epiphany Jones

ABOUT THE AUTHOR

Michael Grothaus is a novelist and journalist who spent years researching sex trafficking, using his experiences as a springboard for his debut novel *Epiphany Jones*. Born in Saint Louis, Missouri in 1977, he spent his twenties in Chicago, where he earned his degree in filmmaking and worked for institutions including The Art Institute of Chicago, Twentieth Century Fox and Apple. As a journalist he regularly writes about creativity, tech, subcultures, sex and pornography, the effects of mass media on our psyches, and just plain mysterious stuff for publications including *Fast Company*, *VICE*, *The Guardian*, *Engadget*, and more. He's also done immersion journalism at geopolitical events including the Hong Kong protests against Beijing in 2014. His writing is read by millions of people each month. Michael lives in London.

Epiphany Jones

Michael Grothaus

**ORENDA
BOOKS**

Orenda Books
16 Carson Road
West Dulwich
London SE21 8HU
www.orendabooks.co.uk

First published in the United Kingdom by Orenda Books 2016

A catalogue record for this book is available from the British Library.

ISBN 978-1-910633-33-5

Typeset in Garamond by MacGuru Ltd
Printed and bound by CPI Group (UK) Ltd, Croydon CRO 4YY

SALES & DISTRIBUTION

In the UK and elsewhere in Europe:
Turnaround Publisher Services
Unit 3, Olympia Trading Estate
Coburg Road,
Wood Green
London
N22 6TZ
www.turnaround-uk.com

In USA/Canada:
Trafalgar Square Publishing
Independent Publishers Group
814 North Franklin Street
Chicago, IL 60610
USA
www.ipgbook.com

For details of other territories, please contact *info@orendabooks.co.uk*

For m.e.

And for the figments that live in our heads at three in the morning.

1

The Dream

Tonight I'm having sex with Audrey Hepburn. Audrey's breasts are different from the last time we fucked; they're bigger, not as firm. There's a hint of a stretch mark on the left one. The leading lady is bent over, gripping the bedpost. Her pink panties are slid down and pinched in place by the fold where her legs meet her ass, so my rod has the most access with the least possible effort. She's looking back at me, eyes sparkling and fixed, with a slim PR smile. I'm going like a jackhammer, sweating, shoulders cramping, but her face is as placid as a sleeping bunny.

And I've got to slow down; it's only been three minutes. But who am I kidding? So I let it all out as I gaze at Audrey's face. And for eight seconds I'm calm, relaxed.

There's a loud crack under my foot. It's Emma's picture. My little sister. My sweet, dead little sister. My thrusting must have knocked it off the desk. I always turn her around when I do this. No matter how old the photograph is you don't want the image of someone you used to know watching you while you squeeze one off. The cracked glass has scratched Emma's face. She's now got a little white-cotton scar over her right cheek.

For the next three minutes I straighten the items on the desk.

Seven minutes after that I'm hiding all traces of fake celebrity porn from my desktop. Just in case my mom comes over.

Then, when I notice it's four in the morning, I get that guilt. *Why did I do this? I have to get up in three hours, for God's sake!* I tell myself I won't do it again. I promise. I pinky swear, you know?

And look, maybe you pretend you'd Never Do Such Things; that you'd never stoop so low as to jerk off to actresses whose heads have been pasted onto a porn star's body. But this is better than seeing prostitutes or shooting heroin. It calms me down. It's harmless. Besides, it's temporary. It's just what guys do when they're on a break from their significant others. And anyway, the best part of these late-night jerk-off sessions isn't even what came before, it's what comes next: the clarity that comes after the guilt fades; the realisation of everything that's wrong in your life and the vow you make to change it.

I need to lose weight. I need to be more outgoing. I need to save money. I need to get a better job. I need to, I need to, I need to.

This clarity is like the previews for next week's episode – the promise of new, exciting adventures to come. It's the trailer of what you can do to improve your sorry life.

But tonight the clarity doesn't happen. Just like the last few weeks. No big ideas. No Nirvana. My life feels like a rerun.

I know how tonight will end. I won't fall asleep for too long. When I do it will come again: that same dream I've had for the last three nights.

And yes, it is odd to have exactly the same dream night after night.

And no, I don't know what the meaning is.

When it begins it's black and I can't see anything, but I can feel my mind floating through the nothingness. Then, slowly, a figure fades in. It's a young girl. Fourteen, maybe fifteen. Her frame is petite and doesn't fully fill the light-blue dress she is wearing. Her face is small and round. Her hair, pulled back tight around her head, is black like a raven's folded wing. Her skin, white as cream. And curiously, her left ear is mutilated. It looks like a piece of her lobe was torn right off.

And for some reason, I know she is The Deliverer.

But I don't know what that is.

We're in a silverware factory, of all places. The factory is abandoned. Teaspoon after teaspoon rusts in boxes on roller conveyors. Forks dangle from strings overhead. Three furnaces fill the far corner of the room. Their mouths gape, revealing long-extinguished insides. Behind them, scorch marks on the brick walls. The floor planks are stained dark.

There's a hint of a cleft in the girl's chin and a slight tremble to her lip. The soles of her pale feet are black with dirt and dust and soot. She looks around frantically.

And I feel for this girl. She's terrified.

She's terrified because there are people coming. Bad people. I hear them outside, the people coming for her. Their silhouettes cast quick blue shadows as they dart past the windows, cracked and yellowed from chemicals and soot.

It's early evening. Outside, crickets scream in the tall grass. The strangers thunder at the tin sidings. They rip and howl and shout in bizarre tongues as they claw at boards nailed over a doorway.

And inside, this little girl, she just stands in place now.

And a voice is heard: 'An awakening is needed in the west.'

And the girl, she begins to cry.

Then they're in, the strangers. Faceless forms charge her. I know they'll kill her. I look away, there's nothing else I can do. But when I look back, the girl has grown. Now she is maybe twenty-something. And I would think her beautiful if she weren't so terrifying. Her smile is crooked and cold. Her eyes beget madness. She has a sickle in her hand. It's funny too, because it looks just like the Nike logo. And swinging this Nike Swoosh, she kills the first three men.

Swoosh!

There goes one head.

Swoosh!

Another.

Just Do It.

And as she's shortening people one by one, I start to focus on the dark hollow of the central furnace. I see something that leaves me feeling helpless and empty. I see myself hiding in the darkness of the furnace's belly. I'm curled up, naked and crying. I'm seventeen years old.

And I'm praying not to be seen.

2

Van Gogh

I wake feeling like I haven't slept.

The TV mutely plays an episode of *Mr Ed*. Wilbur and the talking horse are in astronaut suits. It's the one where Mr Ed tries to convince Wilbur that they can build a ship to the moon. And why not? If your horse can talk, it sure as hell can build a space shuttle.

I reach for a balled-up dirty sock on the floor and spy a lone yellow pill sunk into the carpet next to it. So I do have one left. I really should take it.

I really should do my laundry, too. Tomorrow. Both tomorrow.

I stumble into the kitchen and grab the box of cereal with a white cartoon rabbit on the front. The microwave clock shows just how little time I have. I spoon my breakfast into my mouth, but by the time I get to the museum I'm still twenty minutes late. The moment I step into the Grey Room my boss starts complaining.

'I need that Chagall done by eleven.'

'Sorry, Sir. I was jerking off till five in the morning,' would be the honest thing to say. But this guy, he probably hasn't got it up in twenty years. He wouldn't understand.

'Sorry, missed the bus.'

'Today is the last time you miss the bus. Understand? By eleven,' he orders and walks back into his office.

I turn on the Mac. It's got a grey desktop that perfectly matches the grey walls and grey everything else in this room. No wonder I'm depressed.

I'm a Colour Imaging 'Specialist' for the Art Institute of Chicago.

It's my job to make sure all the paintings you see in those art appreciation textbooks nobody could give a damn less about have accurate colour representation – so the periwinkle blues actually look periwinkle blue and the Venetian reds, Venetian red.

And let's get something straight about my title. There's nothing 'special' about me. Nowadays companies will throw 'specialist' or 'consultant' onto any job title. It's their way of tricking you into thinking you're important.

But a 'specialist' is one step above a peon and a thousand levels below anyone who matters.

Same thing goes for all you 'consultants'. Let's be real, you don't advise your company about anything. You're a salesman. You're Willy Loman and you've already got one foot in the grave.

'Hey, buddy,' Roland calls out before he's even in the room. 'Here're more negatives for that Chagall. Donald wants them by eleven, I think.'

No joke.

'Thanks,' I say, powering on the scanner. Roland looks like a failed male porn star: a little too old, a little too thin, a little too boney. Most disturbing though is that he shaves his arms every day. He does this so everyone can clearly see his stupid sleeve tattoo, which runs from his wrist to his elbow. And I swear to God, I've never seen him without his shirt sleeves rolled up.

'Hey, you want to see it?' Roland asks with the excitement of a twelve-year-old who's just found his father's nudies.

'They've brought it to you?'

Roland grins.

'I can't. I've got to get this done.'

Roland shakes his head. 'Check it out with me. It'll take five minutes.'

My sleep-deprived mind doesn't have the power to argue, so I follow him down the hall to his photo studio. What would normally be a thirty-second walk takes minutes because of all the plastic sheeting and disassembled scaffolding in the hall. This whole wing is a mess because of the renovation of the museum. The whole time I'm glancing over my shoulder to see if Donald is going to storm out and bust me. The whole time Roland keeps jabbering about 'It', his voice wriggling through the sludge in my head like a tapeworm.

And when we finally get to his studio there It is, on an easel, just like it probably was a hundred and twenty years ago. It's small: eleven inches by eight inches.

'Careful!' Roland shouts. He's caught a tripod I bumped into. 'That's ten million dollars right there.'

That's all I need. Donald would end me if I damaged a painting. The tripod, it's this old thing from the seventies. The MiniDV camera makes it top heavy. Its plastic legs are fractured in places. Anything heavier than the camcorder would snap it.

The way Roland is looking at me, he's wondering how I get through each day.

'Why don't you get the museum to get you a decent one?' I say.

'I've tried,' Roland answers like I shouldn't have even needed to ask. 'The renovation is cutting budgets from every department.'

The thing with Roland, he's friends with my mom, and that's where he gets it. Everything he says to me has a *'you should know this'* inflection to it.

Roland's desk is cluttered with fading flash screens, digital-camera card-readers, a week-old *Sun-Times* and books on outdated versions of Photoshop. But at least he's got a fairly new Mac. The one they make me work on barely gets by. Sticking out from under a pile of old prints is a *Hollywood Reporter* with a picture of Penelope Cruz on the cover. And out of the corner of my eye Roland is giving me a pompous smirk. He pretends to himself that he knows what I'm thinking.

Above his mess of a desk is a framed article that's clipped from the *Chicago Tribune*. In the article there's a photo. In it Roland stands next to Donald and the director of the museum. All three wear stupid Masters of the Universe grins. In the right-hand corner there's a picture-in-picture of the Van Gogh right next to Roland's ridiculous face. And, OK, maybe I am a little bitter. He helped the museum obtain the Van Gogh. It's on loan from the private collection of his old boss. It's why he got the raise over me.

Behind me, I can feel Roland staring. He thinks I'm envying him. But you know what? I have nothing to envy. I'm in that picture too. Go ahead, if you look closely enough, in the opposite corner behind the director's elbow, right there in the background, right where the caption starts you can see me behind the ' – IZED', hunched over my computer. The caption reads: 'PRIZED WORK COMING TO THE ART INSTITUTE. (FROM LEFT) DIRECTOR DAVID LANG, DONALD GENTRY, AND ROLAND PEROSKI.'

'It's the first self-portrait he did after he lopped off his ear,' Roland says, all high and mighty.

You can't tell that from the painting. It's a profile from the right. Van Gogh looks so sad. But at the same time, for someone who was so depressed he put a lot of colour into it. Bright specks of yellows, greens, reds and blues fill the painting. His hair is orange and his eyes a kryptonite-green. You can see the manic in them.

And here, Roland goes into bragging mode. He starts stroking the top of the canvas like it's a cat. 'The boss thinks this painting alone will attract an extra forty-thousand visitors in the next few months,' he says. 'So many museums wanted to get this piece, but none of them had the right connections. The real interesting thing is that...'

And I quickly lose interest. Lack of sleep makes my head feel so hollow my thoughts bound around the room like leaping sheep, before my eyes come to rest on his desk and the *Hollywood Reporter* with Penelope Cruz on the cover.

Maybe what I need right now is a pick-me-up. Maybe I can borrow the magazine and take a quick trip to the bathroom.

'Hey, buddy? Jerry? Hello?' Roland is saying. My thoughts snap back to him. He's still standing by the painting, absentmindedly rubbing his finger over the top of the canvas. You can tell Roland's an ex-Hollywood guy. He needs all the attention on him and his 'accomplishments'. When he doesn't have that, he's one of those guys that fake concern that because you aren't paying attention to him there must be something wrong with you. 'Hey, buddy, you OK pal?'

And that's when I think, fuck it, and decide to tell him about the dream. He's an artist after all. Maybe he knows what a silverware factory symbolises in dream-speak. But I might as well be talking to myself. Before I've hardly begun, Roland's solely focused on the painting again, a short stroking of just the same one-inch section of the top of the canvas, as if he's found an invisible pimple he's considering popping.

The painting isn't that big a deal, I yell in my head.

In my head I say, *No one cares about fine art anymore.*

In my head I say, *You're so full of yourself.*

So with Roland engrossed in his own glory, I edge over to his desk and take the *Hollywood Reporter* with Penelope Cruz and slowly roll it up and put it in my sleeve.

But with him stroking the canvas and me with my jerk material shoved up my sleeve, this is just getting awkward. So I say, 'Hey, what's with the camera crew outside?'

He says nothing.

I say, 'Roland?'

And he says, 'Oh, yeah – they're doing some story on how the museum's renovation is way over budget.' Then, as if starting to snap out of his trance, he says, 'Hey buddy, I should get started on this.'

And feeling the magazine rolled up in my shirtsleeve, I agree. I tell him I better get those Chagalls corrected, but he's already shut the door behind me.

Back in the Grey Room I'm all alone. Donald is at his weekly ten a.m. with the museum board. That gives me the privacy to lock the door.

And a little after eleven I give Donald the colour-corrected TIFFs. I tell him I'm going to lunch. I need to get out of this grey prison.

3

Figments

I grab my venti double latte and the *Sun-Times* and take a seat by the window. Today's headlines:

'Alleged Child Rapist Beaten to Death by Victim's Father'

'14 Die in Palestinian Suicide Blast'

'Archdiocese Settles in Sexual Abuse Charges'

'Kraft Lays Off Additional 6,000 Factory Workers'

And just as I begin to feel better about my own life, I catch something from the corner of my eye: the girl with the mutilated ear. The older, beautiful, terrifying version of her. She's standing on the sidewalk, just on the other side of the glass door.

But I blink and when I open my eyes again, she's gone.

And I guess this is as good a time as any to explain something to you. What I just saw, the girl from my dream, the one from the silverware factory, the one standing right outside the door just now? She wasn't real. She's just another figment of my imagination.

Look, to me this feels so long ago, and I still don't even remember half of it, but I'll tell you about it anyway. This was way back years ago when I was seventeen. This was the night my father and I were in the Explorer. But this was still five years after Emma died. Five years after I began to zone out on TV and movies. Five years of my mom and dad seemingly forgetting how to say her name. Five years of referring to her death only as '*What Happened*'. I mean, why talk about my little sister when you could just pretend she never existed?

Back then my dad was one of the most powerful public relations people in Hollywood. And on this night Dad and I were driving to one of his Hollywood studio parties. A wrap party for some forgettable film called ... well, I forget. Dad said he wanted me to meet 'the gang'. I think he just wanted to impress me. He knew how many movies and television shows I watched and wanted to show me that he was part of that world. Or maybe he was just trying to make up for not being around much. He and Mom didn't talk much after *What Happened*.

Most of the people at the party were behind-the-scenes guys: producers, executives, distributors. His group, the PR people, was there too, including an underling who worked for my father for years and who I'd never met. I can't even remember his name. And, of course, Roland, shaved arms and all, was also there – but back then he called himself 'Rolin'. He was the PR photographer at the time and believed that all photographers had to have cool names if they wanted the celebrities to trust them. In Hollywood it's not what you create that matters, it's the image you portray, and 'Rolin' with tattoos conveyed *serious artistic talent* levels of magnitude greater than 'Roland' from the Midwest.

'Hey, come here,' Rolin called over to my father and I when we arrived. He rolled up his sleeve. 'Check this out. My latest. Cool, huh?' It was da Vinci's Vitruvian Man on his inner forearm. He looked like he was skinned alive. Rolin's blood dribbled through where the ink had been injected earlier in the day.

I don't remember much else about the party, but my shrink says that's normal. He says, given after what happened next, it's reasonable for my brain to try to block memories from that night. It's my mind trying to save me from more hurt.

But I do remember what I wish my mind would let me forget. After the party, driving home through our subdivision, the Orange County air was warm and smooth as it flowed in the car windows. My dad seemed lost in thought, so I just listened to the crickets as they creaked and watched the curbs slide past, dipping and breaking every time there was a driveway. Suddenly there was a sharp swerve and a pop. I was jerked forward and the seatbelt snapped something in my chest as our vehicle stopped cold. I looked over at my father. The way the windshield was embedded in his skin, thousands and thousands of little shards of glass, his face sparkled like a mask of diamonds. I had never seen anything so magnificent. Then blackness crept in.

I woke to the horn. The windshield was gone. The steering wheel was in my father's chest. I remember trying to scream, but couldn't. Nothing was coming out. Someone was by the car. Blackness again.

'It doesn't look good,' a voice said when I woke at the hospital. I thought they were talking about me, but they meant my father.

Our car hit a large maple. The impact was so forceful part of the engine ended up in the back seat. I was the lucky one. Broken collarbone. Bruised arm. Three weeks of physical therapy. The next day, when I woke, my father was dead.

Maybe I looked like an asshole to all the doctors in the hospital because I wasn't all torn up and crying about things. But after Emma I had learned how to compartmentalise my hurt so well that I no longer remembered how I should feel when someone else close to me died. So I just lay in my hospital bed and held my mother's hand as she shuddered and cried.

The funeral came and went. I was given my father's gold watch to remember him by. It felt more like a retirement gift. *Thanks for your service, son.*

A few weeks later I met a girl. It was when, as usual, I went to a movie by myself. As fate would have it, Rachel chose to catch a flick on her own that day too. She was seventeen and had just moved to LA for a modelling contract with *Cosmo*. We hit it off right away, and though her work kept her busy, we were soon seeing each other. She was gorgeous: slim body, perky tits, anime-red hair and green eyes that would have matched the Van Gogh's eyes perfectly, now that I think about it.

One night Rachel stopped by while my mom was out grocery

shopping. I brought her up to my room and started to undress her. Truth be told, it was the first time I had ever seen a girl naked.

I can still feel how hard her nipples were, how soft her cheeks felt. Her hair smelled like Snuggles Fabric Softener.

I laid Rachel back on my bed and kissed her belly. She slowly arched her hips as I peeled off her mauve lace panties. I slipped a condom on and clumsily began thrusting.

She was so beautiful. Her little moans so comforting. Her breath on my neck so warm. She was perfect. Barely a minute had passed and I already wanted to cum. In her, on her – it didn't matter.

That's when Mom walked in.

'Mom!' I screamed.

'Jerry, what is this?' Mom yelped, her jaw long and her eyes wide in mortification.

And to Rachel, I yelled, 'Cover yourself up!' But she just lay there: legs spread wide, a perfect grin on her perfect face.

That's one thing about being a supermodel: you know you're so beautiful it just doesn't bother you if total strangers see you naked – even your boyfriend's mother.

'Oh, Jerry, oh Jerry,' Mom kept saying. 'What are you doing?'

To Mom I yelled, 'I didn't think you were home!'

And to the pillows on the bed I yelled, 'Rachel, get dressed!'

But that's one thing about being a bunch of pillows: they don't have to do what anyone tells them.

And just before I blacked out, Mom asked, 'Who's Rachel?'

Rachel, it turned out, was a figment of my imagination. That's the name my psychiatrist gave it: a 'figment'. A hallucination, a symptom of psychotic depression, maybe as a result of my father's unexpected death. Or maybe, my father's death, coming right after Emma's, was the thing that made me snap. Who knows?

Mom told the shrink how I had stacked the pillows like they were a person. Two duck-feather ones for the torso, decorative pillows from the couch for arms, a couple of body pillows for the legs. My mom feared the worst. But my shrink stressed that I wasn't schizophrenic. 'Psychotic depressives invent people to fill voids,' the shrink said.

What void? My mom didn't dare ask.

'Psychotic depression and schizophrenia are two different things,' the shrink told us. He said schizophrenia is a slow road into hell. It's not reversible. Psychotic depression is. 'With regular counselling from a mental-health professional and some Zyprexa we can rid Jerry of these figments,' he explained in his *Harvard Medical Journal* voice from behind a large oak desk. 'Your son will be good as new in no time.'

Mom looked like she really didn't believe it.

'Are you sure the medicine will make him OK?' she asked.

'If not, there's always electroshock therapy. That can help.'

'My poor baby,' my mom said, like the treatment was inevitable. Me, I was reading between the lines. I wasn't going to get laid by a supermodel any longer.

'And what other things should we keep an eye out for? Besides the seeing people?'

'As long as he stays on his meds, nothing major,' my shrink told her, like I wasn't in the room. 'Maybe some disassociation. Some minor anti-social behaviour. Perhaps a small inclination – less than one percent of psychotic depressives get this – but perhaps a small inclination to other rare disorders.'

'Such as?'

'Really rare stuff. An inclination towards things like Stockholm syndrome.'

My mom whimpered.

'Relax,' my shrink tried to reassure her. 'Just make sure he's never kidnapped and he'll be fine,' he winked. And to me he said, 'But seriously, be sure to stay on the medication or the figments could come back. And you don't want us to have to treat this with shock therapy.'

I took my meds religiously and saw the shrink once a month. I saw

Rachel less and less. Another difference between being a schizo and being psychotically depressed: you know your hallucinations aren't real once someone points the first one out. It makes them a lot easier to ignore. And though the medicine seemed to be working, my imaginary supermodel began to be replaced by very real stomach cramps.

'I want to try a new medication,' my shrink said the next time I saw him. 'It's off-label for this condition, but there's a lot of anecdotal evidence that it's helpful for treating it. It might even eliminate your hallucinations with little or no side-effects.'

Sounds great, Doc. What is it?

'Mifepristone.'

Aka RU-486.

Aka the abortion pill.

Don't ask me how the pharmaceutical companies figured that one out. Maybe some psychotic depressive was convinced she was pregnant, popped a 486, and suddenly realised not only was she never pregnant but that the father of her child never existed.

However they figured it out, they were right: the abortion pill not only kills babies, it kills imaginary friends as well. I never saw Rachel again.

A year after the accident my mom packed us up and moved to a teaching job at DePaul University. Her friends thought she was running from the memories of her husband, but Mom wasn't running away from anything. She hated Hollywood life. She was running towards the life she had always wanted. Sometimes we can only be free when the people we love are gone.

One day I came home to our new Chicago house to find Roland in our kitchen. His shirt was a hideous blue-and-orange Hawaiian theme and his goatee had started to sprout grey. Roland had left the studio and moved to Chicago to take a position at the Art Institute. Mom said he wanted to offer help in getting me a job at the museum.

'We have lots of computers,' he said to me, like I was some delicate flower.

Mom had told him everything.

'It'll be nice to get out of your bedroom, won't it, honey? Maybe get your own place with all the money you'll be earning?'

'Trust me,' Roland said, 'you're going to love the museum.'

I fucking hate the museum and I need to be back there in ten minutes – barely time to finish the paper. Like anyone else, the amount of love I possess for my lunch break is directly proportional to the amount of hate I possess for my job. I cherish this time. But just as I turn to the Celebrity & Lifestyle section he comes in.

The bum.

Besides his torn clothes and his dirt-marked face, he looks like an old version of Ernest Hemingway – or the Gorton's Fisherman. Silver hair peeks from the bottom of his knit cap, grey whiskers give him a rugged look, but it's his cool blue eyes that are the most striking.

Every once in a while he'll burst through the doors screaming about religion or philosophy, before someone offers him coffee to calm him down. I guess the regulars have found it's quicker than waiting for the Chicago PD to show up. Today he's unusually frantic.

'I seek God! I seek God,' he cries. 'Where is God?'

This sounds familiar.

'I will tell you,' he continues. 'We have killed him – you and I.'

Ah, Nietzsche.

'All of us are his murderers.'

Someone give this guy a coffee already.

'What was holiest and mightiest of all that the world has yet owned has bled to death under our knives.'

Personally, I think he just pulls this crazy act because he knows you can get a lot more out of people a lot faster by scaring them, annoying them, or making them feel like they're your saviour, than you can by sitting around asking them for a nickel.

Case in point: a kind-looking, balding man is bringing him a cup of Kenyan Select right now. 'It's OK. Calm down. Why don't you drink this and warm up?' the coffee-bringer tells the doomsayer. The bum takes it and stands between a set of tables and the snack counter, his body blocking the path of an alternateen barista with pigtails who carries a tray full of biscotti. Her shirt reads: ADMIT IT. YOU'D GO TO JAIL FOR THIS. As the barista awkwardly slips around him, carefully trying to balance all the biscotti on the tray, one falls off. The bum snatches it from the floor before the girl has a chance to see.

Now the bum's settled into a seat in the middle, at a little round table with a chequerboard. The barista, counting biscotti, eyes him suspiciously. The bum holds his biscotti in both hands, twitching his head left then right, like a skittish squirrel nibbling an acorn.

Choke on it, you freak. My lunch break is almost over and I didn't even get to finish my paper in peace. I put on my coat and leave the *Sun-Times* on the table. Someone else will get to finish it. As I walk towards the exit I pass the bum and intentionally check him with my body, knocking him back in his seat. *Fuck you*, I say in my head.

And just as I get to the door a lady screams.

I turn around and everyone is on their feet. Through their legs a mass of dirt-stained clothes wriggles on the floor. Then a break in the crowd reveals a black knit cap with silver hair sprouting from the back. The bum's face is turning an ever-darkening shade of blue. He's grasping at his throat. The motherfucker is choking on his biscotti.

There are eight people between me and the bum, but no one is doing anything. Admit It just rolls her eyes, wearing a face that says, *God, this is so inconvenient. I don't get paid enough to worry about choking homeless people.* Some guy near the back has started recording everything with his phone. Look for it on YouTube soon, no doubt.

And maybe the rest of the people don't know the Heimlich, but I'm betting no one else is helping him because they don't want to touch a creepy, worthless fuck of a man – worthlessness that might rub off on to them.

I can relate. To the bum, I mean.

Clawing at his throat, he's a minute closer to death than he was when the lady screamed, and still the crowd is acting like they're watching a one-man improv show.

And look, I don't know the Heimlich either, but I did bump him. So I push my way though and kneel at the bum's side. Then I do the worst thing possible. I do the thing the first-aid refrigerator magnets tell you never to do: I stick my fingers down his throat.

And there's a reason they tell you that. All I've done is lodge the biscotti further down. Panicked, I grab his coffee and pour it into his mouth.

And somewhere in the crowd a woman screams again.

Someone shouts, 'He's going to die!'

Someone shouts, 'His face is so blue!'

Someone shouts, 'Leave room for cream!'

And, leaning over the nearly dead bum with his mouthful of steaming coffee, I take my middle finger and jam it down his throat.

I thrust up and down, finger-fucking his mouth until the coffee has saturated the biscotti enough to break it in two. As I roll him onto his side the combined coffee and biscotti sludge slowly dribbles out of his mouth and down his whiskered cheek like a mini mudslide. Going back in, I stick all my fingers in his gaping, coffee-scalded mouth, past his rough, rodent-like tongue, till I feel the sewer-slime slickness of his throat and scoop out a clumpy mush of biscotti. I go in one more time, fishing for leftovers.

Then comes the gag.

And his warm, chunky, lava-like vomit flows over my hand.

He gasps for air.

'I'm not going to go to hell for someone as worthless as you,' I whisper under my breath, as I watch his sad face lose its blue. His whiskered cheeks softly pump up and down.

'Oh!' a woman exclaims. 'Oh!'

'Awesome,' says YouTube guy.

Then I guess the crowd realises they should do something so when they tell this story to their friends they can say they played a part. They help the bum up. They tell him he is so lucky. They tell him to view this as a new day, a new start.

I'm still on the floor, my hand covered with homeless vomit. No one wants to help me up.

My fingers are red and scalded. My heart is racing, beads of sweat dot my face, and it feels good when someone opens the door and the cold April wind blows in.

And when the door bangs shut, she's on the other side of it again – her raven hair hangs in wet strands before her eyes. Her pale skin is slightly pink from the cold. The place where her ear lobe should be drips with water from the shredded cartilage. And her green eyes stare at me. I mean, *right* at me. The words from my dream echo in my head: *An awakening is needed in the west.* Heat radiates from my skin. The little beads of sweat that dot my face evaporate. I'm dizzy and just want to close my eyes, but I can't look away from the girl. Those penetrating eyes. That mutilated ear.

Then a towel hits me in the face.

'Here you go, hero,' the alternateen barista says, moving between me and the door.

I wipe my hand clean of vomit and when I look up again, my dream figment is gone. It rains in her place.

4

Assassins

After you save someone's life, people don't just let you leave. When they think you're a hero, they want to be your best friend. They pretend like they care about you. They pretend to be interested in you because of who you are, not because of what you just did.

I sit on the steps outside the coffee house and let the drizzle fall over me. The barista takes a seat by my side. Her eyes are caked with eyeliner, the raccoon. Inside the coffee house a line has formed at the counter.

'On my break,' she says and lights up a cigarette.

I wonder if she's even old enough to be smoking.

'That was really cool what you did,' she says.

But my attention has shifted to across the street. I'm watching the figment from my dream as she stands behind a crowd of Asian tourists who're snapping pictures of one of the big lion statues that guard the museum's entrance. But then the Asian tourists, they see a WGN-TV cameraman shooting footage of the museum. It must be for their story on the west wing's renovation Roland mentioned. So the Asian tourists stop shooting the lion and start shooting the cameraman and a very bored looking reporter.

'I'm going to be a doctor when I'm older so I can do that stuff every day. Saving lives and shit every five minutes,' the barista says. 'What a high.'

'I don't think it's like that,' I say, thinking of every doctor I've ever been to. 'I think most doctors spend a lot of their time behind desks filling out forms.'

'I'm talking about being an emergency-room doctor,' she chides me. 'They're always running around saving lives every second.'

'I really don't think they are.' And I think of the night my father died. Across the street my figment is pacing in the rain and holding a flat newspaper under her arm.

'Don't you ever watch *ER*? It's exactly like that,' says the all-knowing seventeen-year-old. And I look into her raccoon eyes and consider trying to explain that TV shows only the exciting parts of life; that the boring shit that makes up ninety-nine percent of our existence is edited out. But it would just be a waste of breath.

Across the street my figment seems indecisive. When I look at her she looks away. I'm grateful for that. It's my mind trying to fight off my hallucinations. Still, it scares me that I'm seeing figments again so often. But it's my own damn fault. I've been so lazy about refilling my 486s. And my shrinks have made it clear: it's the medicine or shock therapy. And I'm not going to turn out like that. Tomorrow I'll go to my shrink and get a refill; maybe ask him to up the dose. For now I hail a cab. I tell the driver to take me to my place. I've got that one pill I saw buried in my carpet this morning. Donald will just have to believe whatever lie I tell him.

By the time I get back to the museum I'm over two hours late. I couldn't catch a return cab and had to walk most of the way. I'm freezing. The temperature has really dropped.

I run up the marble steps, hurrying to get out of the cold rain, which stabs like ice picks. Donald's going to kill me.

'Museum's closed, sir,' a security guard says, blocking my entrance.

Closed? It's three-fifteen. 'What do you mean it's closed?' I say.

'It's closed, sir.'

'Yes, I heard you,' I say, showing him my red museum badge. 'I work here. Why is the museum closed?'

'This is North Entrance,' the guard says into his walkie-talkie. 'I have an employee trying to enter. Yes, sir. Sir.' He holsters his walkie-talkie. 'Please wait here.'

Minutes pass and the rain continues to fall before Donald emerges from the emergency exit door. He waves me inside where a museum guard waits with two strange men; one is considerably taller than the other. The strangers don't have museum badges.

'It's OK, we just need to talk,' Donald says with a coldness that almost crawls from his skin.

The five of us walk in silence down two floors. The construction-lined corridors are practically deserted. The few people we do pass are silent. Some look scared when they see me with the two strangers. And then it hits me: these men are from HR. They're the guys employees here talk about in whispers. They call them financial assassins because their job is to roam around and find useless employees to lay off. Fewer employees mean more money for the renovation.

We enter a small conference room I've never seen before. The museum guard waits outside.

'Please sit down,' the tall financial assassin says.

'Why is the museum closed?' I say.

'Where have you been for the past three hours?' the short financial assassin says. He sounds like he's trying to channel Magnum, PI.

'Lunch,' I say, pretending I didn't take two hours longer than normal. 'Donald, what's going on?'

But 'Please just answer their questions' is all Donald offers.

'Do you normally take a three-hour lunch?' the tall assassin asks.

Mom will be so disappointed if I lose my job. She was so happy when I took it.

So I say, 'OK, look, I know I shouldn't have done it.'

My answer, it causes the two assassins to lean closer and Donald to look a little frightened.

I say, 'I'm sorry, but you're not gonna believe what happened.' And I tell them the events of the past three hours. I lie about the medicine though. They wouldn't understand. You tell someone you see things and they'll never look at you in the same way again. Hell, they'll find a way to fire you just because you're on psych meds. So instead I tell them that after the coffee house I had to go to my girlfriend's because she was feeling sick.

To Donald I say, 'You've heard me talk about her before. Harriett?'

But Donald just shakes his head. 'Why would you leave work for so long to visit a sick friend?'

'Please,' the short assassin says. 'Let us ask the questions.'

'*Girl*friend,' I say.

Donald looks at me like I'm a liar.

'Fine, *ex*. We're on a break,' my voice cracks. And I say that my *ex-girlfriend*, she gets scared when she's sick. Besides, I needed to wash up. And I shove my hand beneath Donald's nose so he can smell the dried homeless vomit that's crusted under my nails.

'It's not everyday someone gets to be a hero,' I say.

'Can we call your girlfriend to verify all this?' the tall assassin asks.

'No,' I say.

'Why not?'

'Because she's back at work. I dropped her off.'

'Where does she work?'

'The Water Tower Plaza.'

'What store?'

Fuck. I say, 'Auntie Anne's.'

'Auntie Anne's?'

'She likes pretzels,' I say.

And I can tell this isn't going well, so I take the pity angle. I say, 'Donald, I'm sorry, I shouldn't have been so long. It's been a hard day. Write me up if you want, but please don't fire me. And *please* don't contact my girlfriend. We're having enough issues as it is, OK?'

And then the outrage angle. 'Besides, these HR guys don't have the right to harass her.'

That's when the assassins look at Donald, who looks back at me.

That's when he says, 'These men aren't from HR. They're detectives, Jerry.'

Police detectives?

Donald says, 'They're *police* detectives, Jerry. The Van Gogh is missing.' His steel-grey eyes glaring. It's the first time I notice that his eyes match the walls of our office.

It takes me a minute to process what Donald has said. The short man folds his arms and keeps his gaze on me. I don't know what to say. How does a ten-million-dollar painting disappear from one of the most secure museums in the world?

'You think I took it?'

I sound guiltier than I'd like.

'You were the last one to see it before it disappeared,' the tall detective says. 'You told Donald that you had been in Roland's studio. You told him right before you went to "lunch".'

'That's not true,' I say.

Donald eyes me sharply.

'I mean, it is true that I said that, but I went to look at it *with* Roland. When I left he was still in the studio with it. He saw it after me.'

The detectives glance at each other.

'Look, check the fucking security tapes. We've got cameras everywhere.'

But then they tell me that for two hours this afternoon all the cameras were non-functional. They tell me this was due to the renovations – some electrical work. Then they ask how long I've known the cameras would be inoperable today.

'I didn't! I didn't know about the cameras, I don't know who stole the Van Gogh, and I wasn't the last one to see it.'

Then I yell, 'Talk to Roland, he'll tell you!'

And the police detective, the short one, he says, 'We can't.'

This is where they tell me how they found Roland in his studio. How he had a broken tripod leg shoved through his eye socket into his skull. They tell me how he's at Rush Memorial undergoing emergency surgery right now.

A moment of mute struggle passes through me. How do you react when you learn someone you've worked with, someone your father worked with before you, has been brutally attacked? I try to think of any movies I've seen that may give me some clue.

And look, I know this sounds horrible, but I don't feel anything over Roland's attack. That's just how it is. It's just how I am. But these guys, I can tell they'd expect anyone except the attacker to be all broken up about it – especially someone who's worked with him for years.

The three of them, they're waiting for me to react, to show sadness and fear and regret. To show innocence. So I put my face in my hands and soak up the smell of homeless vomit. I flick my tongue between my fingernails and taste the regurgitated-biscotti-stomach-acid mix. My tongue burns. My eyes water.

Then I pull my hands away, 'Not Roland. Oh my God, please, not Roland.'

And I let the vomit tears flow. I shiver. I shudder. I'm great. Donald even pats me on the shoulder.

'There, there,' he comforts mechanically.

I'll take my Oscar now.

For the next hour the detectives ask me about any bitterness over Roland's raise. They ask me to repeat my story again and again, looking for inconsistencies; hoping I'll slip up. At the end I'm so exhausted from answering the same questions over and over, from fake vomit-crying again and again, I can hardly stand. When I do, the tall one puts his hand on my arm. 'It's very important you didn't lie to us about anything just now. It would look bad for you. If you need to make any corrections, now's the time.' My thoughts turn to Harriett, but I remain silent. 'We'll have follow-up questions in the coming days after we verify your story,' the detective warns. 'Don't take any trips.'

'Why don't you go home and get some rest?' Donald says, as he walks me out. It's dark now and Michigan Avenue is black and shiny from the cold rain. A cab is waiting. 'It's been a hard day for everyone. Try to relax tonight. Go home and watch some TV. And take tomorrow off.'

Before I get into the cab I try to lighten the situation with a joke.

But here's the thing: even though the joke is stupid, Donald, who never smiles at me, lets out a laugh so theatrical I get the impression that he thinks if he didn't laugh I might hurt him. I also get the feeling that he only walked me out because he wanted to make sure I left.

A dim light shines from the distant downtown skyline through my living-room windows. I walk through the darkness into the kitchen and turn on the ceiling lamp above the table. I run the faucet and scrub the dried vomit from under my fingernails. That's when I'm surprised to find I'm weeping a little.

Who could put a tripod through Roland's eye? Why would someone? Then I think, what if they're some kind of art-museum serial killer and I'm next? And as I'm standing at the sink, scrubbing homeless vomit from beneath my fingernails, I suddenly get the feeling that someone's watching me.

But pangs of hunger quickly replace my paranoia and I grab some milk and a bowl of Trix and plop down hard on the aluminium kitchen chair.

I should call Mom. I don't like Roland that much, but he's been a good friend to her, especially after Dad died. I should call her; tell her he's in the hospital. I wipe my odd little tears away and take a spoonful of cereal into my mouth. Later. I'll call her later.

The crunch of the cereal echoes in my skull as I go over everything that's happened today. The sludge in my head hasn't left. It still feels like I haven't slept in weeks. And as I eat, gazing into the darkness of my living room, I still feel someone watching me. And then, with a spoonful of coloured children's cereal frozen in front of my gaping mouth, I catch two green eyes leering at me from the darkness.

Without taking my eyes off the eyes watching me, I grab a kitchen knife and inch my way into the living room just enough so I can feel around the wall and find the light switch. And that's when I see it.

The Van Gogh.

And what do you do when you find a stolen painting worth millions sitting on your living-room sofa? You lock the doors first of all, and then you close the blinds. Then you search your house for the person who put it there. Then a thousand thoughts fire through your mind like bullets. How'd it get here? I should call the cops. No, they'll think I stole it. I should call the museum. No, *they'll* think I stole it. I should sell it. No, I need to calm down.

I turn on the TV. I need to relax. No such luck. A reporter is talking about the stolen Van Gogh. She's on location, in front of the lion statue outside the museum.

On the TV, the reporter says, 'On loan from an unnamed benefactor...'

She says, 'Estimated value: over ten million...'

She says, 'Employee attacked in his studio...'

I am in so much trouble.

Then on the TV, the reporter says, 'Sources close to the case have just informed us that they may have a lead.'

And this is where I expect the reporter to tell me to wait just where I am. The police will be right over. Finish your Trix.

'Police are saying that they have questioned and released – for the time being – a "person of interest" in the case,' the reporter is saying. Then the image on the screen cuts to footage of the museum from this afternoon. You see a man with his fat wife and plump little Mexican children. They're standing in front of one of the big, green lion statues outside the museum. 'We shot this footage today for a story about the fifty-million-dollar renovation of the museum's west wing,' the reporter says. 'It's now thought that this was around the time the theft occurred.'

And on the TV, the Mexican family has walked out of frame and now we see a group of Asian tourists with cameras around their necks. And behind them...

'We've learned that, due to electrical work on the renovation, the security cameras were apparently disabled for an unknown amount of time this afternoon,' the reporter says. 'Authorities aren't yet sure if the thief knew of the lapse in security.'

Behind the Asian tourists stands a woman.

A woman with skin like cream.

And hair as dark as a raven's folded wing.

A woman with a mutilated ear.

The footage on the television, it shows the woman, the one from my dream. The one in the silverware factory. The hallucination at the coffee shop. The one who's nothing more than another figment of my imagination.

But it can't be.

Figments can't appear on film.

5

Occam's Razor

I covered the Van Gogh with a sheet and haven't looked at it since. Then I watched the news all night to see if there was any new information. And to see if they would play the footage again in which I saw my figment. But no subsequent story ever showed the same footage. Even if one had I'm sure she wouldn't have been there again. Once you've stolen a Van Gogh and you start seeing your imaginary friends on TV it's easy enough to connect the dots: I'm going crazy because I've come off my meds and now I've put someone in the hospital.

At seven this morning I stole my neighbour's *Tribune* from across the hall. The headline on the front page read 'MAYHEM IN THE MUSEUM!' Words from the article jumped out: 'PHOTOGRAPHER', 'CRITICAL CONDITION', 'CO-WORKER', 'PERSON OF INTEREST', 'STOLEN VAN GOGH.'

I threw it back into the hall.

At nine I called my shrink's office and got an appointment for three.

'I think I'm sick again,' I tell my shrink, before I've even sat down. I say I think my figments are coming back.

'Slow down, Jerry,' he says. 'What do you mean?'

And I suddenly wonder if my shrink watches the news. I wonder, how far does doctor-patient confidentiality go? So I lie and say that I was at the video store at lunch yesterday. I wanted to buy a DVD, only I had forgotten my wallet. When I left the store I saw one of my figments across the street. Then, when I got home that night, I discovered the DVD sitting on my couch.

I ask him if it's possible that my psychotic depression is getting worse. That instead of just seeing people who aren't there, is it possible that I am becoming them? Is it possible I have some kind of split personality and unconsciously carry out actions under their persona? Is it possible to do all this and not remember?

'Which of your figments did you see?'

I say, 'A new one. Not Rachel.'

'One you haven't seen before you were on the mifepristone?'

I nod.

'And when did you start to see this figment?'

'Several weeks ago,' I remember. 'Only I didn't realise she wasn't real. I saw her once on the sidewalk in front of the museum. Then sitting in the garden at the side of the museum. I thought it was coincidence when I noticed her in a few different places, but then I remembered that I dreamt about her years ago. That's when I realised I had gone off my meds. I knew I should have come for a refill sooner, but I kept putting it off. I thought she'd go away. But then I saw her at lunch and she felt more real than ever. And now the DVD...'

'Continue, continue,' he says.

I originally went to this shrink when we moved to Chicago because my shrink in LA recommended him. But for my tastes he's too talky. My old shrink would just prescribe medicine and be done with it. This shrink loves to hear about my feelings.

So I tell him how I've started dreaming this old dream about her. How in the dream she's terrified; how she fights off intruders.

My shrink listens and then says, 'Last time we spoke, a few months ago, you had just been turned down for a raise, am I right? This would be around the same time you started seeing this figment, correct?'

'Yeah,' I say. 'Maybe three weeks later.'

'Right ... two months ago was early February,' he says, watching me closely. 'Three weeks after that – well, Jerry, that's around Emma's birthday, isn't it?'

'March second.' I look away.

'You ever heard of Occam's razor, Jerry? It says that, all other things being equal, the simplest explanation tends to be the right one. Now, what's more believable? That you are suddenly suffering from split personality disorder and secretly stealing DVDs? Or that, because of the stress of rejection from not getting your promotion, the fact that you've gone off your meds, and the relatively close timing to your sister's birthday, your brain has had a relapse and started giving you nightmares and making you see a figment again? You know stress aggravates your condition. And as for this figment, this dream – is she like Rachel? Have you ever thought you touched her, talked to her, had sex with her?'

No, doctor.

'Our minds play tricks on us all the time,' he says. 'You know this more than most. I mean, Jerry, I buy things all the time and forget I've bought them.'

I didn't buy a ten-million-dollar painting and forget about it, I want to say.

'You've never talked much about your sister's death, but I think you should seriously consider how it's affected you.'

'I'm fine.'

'*Fine*, Jerry,' he says with a pause. 'The dream. Let's go to the dream. The girl in your dream is around Emma's age when she passed, right? This girl is scared as faceless invaders attack her, while you lie in the background, naked and helpless. Jerry, it seems like you're visualising what you felt like when Emma's leukaemia invaded her body.'

And I squirm.

'Though you were present, there was nothing you could do.'

Yes, I could have.

'You were in effect – as in your dream – naked and helpless. You were *only* a child. Are you hearing me? There wasn't anything you could have done.'

But I could have.

My eyes feel swollen. 'Could you up my dosage, Doc? Could you, just for a little while? Just until this thing passes? I got lazy. It was my fault. I got off the meds and I think I really need a top-up to get me back on track.'

'I really think the best thing for you,' he says, 'is to get out of your box. A little trip can do a lot of good. The world is a wonderful and amazing place. Go see some of it. Take a vacation. What about Heather? You two still seeing each other?'

'Yeah. Yeah, I'm seeing Heather tomorrow,' I say. 'Doc, I'll look into a vacation, I promise. But, in the meantime, could you just up my dosage a little? Please?'

'OK,' he says after a long pause, 'but I want to hear about your vacation next time I see you.'

'For curiosity's sake,' I say as he scribbles the prescription, 'let's say I was completely nuts. Let's say I did steal that DVD and not know it. You think a court would let me off due to my ... condition?'

'Of course they'd let you off,' he says, handing me the note. 'It's not like you tried to kill anyone, right?'

I step outside, where the cold bonds with my sweat and I feel like I've been dipped in an ice bath. My stress appears as rapid, clouded plumes of frosty breath, one after the other. Calm down, I tell myself. Think, I say. What's been done has been done. Roland is in the hospital; the painting is at my place. Roland can live; the painting can be returned. If this upped dosage can hold off any more hallucinations, maybe I can fix all this. Or at least prevent it from getting any worse.

I start towards the Walgreens a few blocks away, but each time I come to an intersection I get the feeling I'm being followed. But every time I turn around, all I see are the crowds of the city moving like herds. With the prescription in my hand, I think, *Just keep moving*.

But when I get to the Walgreens I turn around again and I distinctly see my figment half a block away. She doesn't seem to notice me though, which is my brain trying to fight off my hallucinations. I dart into the pharmacy and give my prescription to a young Asian woman who reads it, glances at me, and then turns to find the medicine. I breathe deeply.

Stress brings on my figments. Calm down. Calm down. This medicine will stop them – just like before.

But then a series of horrible thoughts occur to me. What happens if Roland dies? And what happens if this medicine doesn't help any more and my figments won't stop? Electroshock therapy? I don't know what would be worse: jail or being confined to a psychiatric ward my whole life, shuffling around, drooling, being a half-person. Are those really my only options? Back on the street the sounds of the city are hyper-loud in my ears. At the other end of the block is my figment, who turns and sees me. I turn around, pretending she isn't there. My feet feel weak. My stomach hollow. I feel a panic attack coming. I need to go somewhere quiet, somewhere safe. I need to go to someone who I can talk to, someone I can be honest with, someone who I know won't turn me in.

6

Joan of Arc

My mom lives in one of those big greystones in Lincoln Park. When we moved from Los Angeles she said she'd always wanted to live in a nineteenth-century house, but in LA, especially in my dad's LA – a world of parties and glamour – anything but chic modern would've moved you down in your social circle. LA wasn't for my mom. She didn't fit the lifestyle. She wasn't like my dad. He thrived on it. He drank it up and grew from it. Every year he added another ring of glitz and glamour to his trunk. But my mom, she was an intelligentsia at heart. She always thought celebrities were silly. She only put up with it because she loved my dad.

Roland suggested that my mom look in this area of the city. He grew up in Chicago and studied photography here before moving to LA. Whenever Roland came to our house in Orange County to see my dad, my mom seemed stressed. I got the feeling she never really liked him and didn't care much for his line of work. 'Photographs don't represent reality,' she told me once. 'They represent how something looks for one two-hundredths of a second. They only show you what something was for a fraction of a blink, not what that something continues to be. Yet everyone thinks the subject in the photograph is walking around, looking just as perfect, this very moment.'

But after my father died my mom and Roland bonded. It's because Roland decided to move back to Chicago. They finally had some common ground.

If you were sitting in my mom's house and didn't know a thing about her, you would swear she was religious. There are paintings of saints everywhere. Or, not saints, but *saint*. Singular. One saint.

My mom is probably the country's top expert on medieval French history and one of her pet subjects is Joan of Arc.

While other moms told their children bedtime stories about knights on quests to kill dragons and save princesses, my mom told my sister and I stories about Joan.

'Joan of Arc,' my mom would say, 'was the only person in all of human history, of either sex, to lead a country's army at the age of seventeen. She united France and stirred the hearts of old and broken soldiers to come to the battle lines once more, driving the English out of France.'

'But how'd she do it, Mommy?' my sister would ask. When my mom told her Joan of Arc stories, Emma was always curled up in her bed, next to mine, clutching her covers. 'I'm so glad she beat the English, but how?'

'You don't even know the difference between France and England,' I said.

'Shush, Jerry,' Mom protested.

'I do too! France is where they eat frogs and England is where Americans came from,' Emma squealed. She loved when she had an answer for something.

'Joan,' my Mom continued, 'believed she heard voices from God. She believed her voices were giving her orders about what to do, where and when to fight.'

'Were her voices from God?' my sister asked.

'Well, some said – mainly the English,' and she ruffled Emma's hair at this. 'Some said she was a witch. Others think she had a disease that made her hear things that weren't there. But all we know for sure is that a young girl did the most extraordinary things – things men with a lot more experience, education and skill – were never able to do.'

'But *how*?' my sister pleaded. 'Did she ever fall in love and get married? Did she have a dog? I bet she had a dog with her.'

Emma was allergic to dogs and always wanted one.

My mom smiled and touched Emma's cheek. 'No, she never got married, baby. And as far as we know, she never had a dog.'

Emma let out a little growl at this. 'If she didn't have a dog and if she was crazy, then how'd she beat the English? And why didn't she get married ever?'

'She was really ugly,' I told her, 'like you.'

'You're uglier,' she retorted. 'Why didn't she have a dog?'

My mom placed her hand on my sister's belly. 'I don't know why she didn't have a dog, baby.'

'Maybe she was allergic to them,' I taunted.

Another little growl from Emma.

My mom gave me a sharp look before she carried on. 'As for why she never got married, well, Joan was what you call a quester – a person who has a powerful sense of purpose – they believe they have to complete a great and important mission.' My mom's voice practically hummed as she said this. 'And questers – they live for their quests. They don't see any life outside of their mission. Their spectacular focus is what gives them their strength, but it's also what makes their life so singularly joyful.'

'So she never got married?' Emma asked, her heart clearly wounded.

'I'm afraid not,' my mom answered.

'Well, what happened to her?'

'THEY BURNT HER ALIVE!' I bleated out.

Emma shrieked.

'Jerry, that's enough,' Mom said. 'Both of you go to sleep. Now.' She kissed us on the cheeks.

When she turned out the lights and closed the door, Emma was the first to break the silence.

'Jerry.'

'What?'

'They didn't really burn Joan, did they?'

'Yes.'

'Why?'

'Because when you get older, you can't have heroic stories without a sad ending. People like the hero better if they die for something. That's just how it is.'

There was silence in the room for almost a minute.

'Jerry?'

'What, Emma?'

'I wouldn't let anyone burn you.'

'I wouldn't let anyone burn you, either,' I said.

I set the picture of Emma I've been holding back on the mantelpiece when Mom comes in.

'Sorry, dear,' she kisses me on the cheek. For a woman of fifty-five, my Mom is stunning. She could have been a model if she'd wanted. 'With the Joan lectures coming up at DePaul, I've been on the phone non-stop. How are you? What's new?'

What's new? I thought she'd already have some idea. I thought Roland would have called her to tell her where he was. I don't think he has any family left. I say the first thing that comes to my mind, like I'm on autopilot. 'I, uh … Heather and I, we might take a trip.' I feel confused.

Mom pauses a beat too long. 'Heather? That's … great, Jerry. What happened to Harriett?'

'What? No, Mom. She was before.' Mom smiles a reassuring look. She's only ever wanted the best for me. She's going to be heartbroken over what I've done. 'Mom, haven't you seen the papers? Don't you know what's happened?'

'I've been so busy I haven't paid attention to the news in days.' The phone in her den rings.

'Mom, I need to talk to someone,' I say over the ringing. 'I need someone to listen to me. Really listen.' The phone rings again.

'Of course, dear, but – I'm sorry. Let me just get that. I'll be right back.'

'Mom, I think I shoved a tripod leg through Roland's eye,' I practise in my head.

'It's the dean,' my mom says, peeking her head around the door. 'We had a conference call scheduled. Can you sit still for half an hour? Maybe watch some – maybe read a little? Then we'll talk?' Mom, she loves me but still treats me like a kid sometimes. She still thinks TV is a bad influence on me.

'Sure.'

'Thanks, honey,' she says and slides the den door shut. I take out my little opaque-orange bottle of 486s and swallow two of them. So far, so good. No figments.

On the television a young black man is telling a panel of judges that God didn't intend for him to win the singing competition, so he can leave with his head held high. The other contestants nod their heads in agreement – all certain in their belief that the supposed creator of the universe cares about television talent contests. I flip the channel, looking for something better to watch. I flip and I flip and I flip. And then I catch a glimpse of *her*. Jordan Seabring – my favourite actress. And when I say 'favourite', I mean the one I'd give my right hand to sleep with. Seabring didn't get her first role until she was eighteen, well after my dad died, but if she were in the game when Dad was still alive she's what he would have described as one of those rare, great stars that only come along once in a decade, the ones who capture the imagination of everyone from ten-year-old girls to eighty-year-old men.

Jordan Seabring has got this great doe-eyed innocent look in this movie. It's a look that says 'fuck me' without seeming too slutty. Her lips are plump and her breasts are even plumper. I'm not even into blondes either, but there's just something about her. If I had the choice of nailing Kate Beckinsale and Angelina Jolie in a threesome, or just one Jordan Seabring, I'd choose Seabring. I'd delete all my fakes just to nail Jordan Seabring once.

The shot on the TV is a close-up of her mouth as she takes a slow drag from a cigarette. Every little ridge that forms in her lips as she puffs is like a warm fold of a womb you just want to sink in to. Her mouth forms a perfect *O* as she exhales the luckiest smoke in the world, leaving an inviting dark centre between her lips.

And that dark, inviting centre between her lips, it's like a trigger. And I wonder if Mom still has that TV in her bedroom?

Why don't bedroom doors have locks on them anymore? I need to make this quick. When I flick on the television there's a commercial break. Next to the TV is a picture of me in my college graduation gown. I look so stupid with my crooked smile. A fat zit is immortalised on my eyelid. I didn't even want to do the dumb picture in the first place, because it didn't feel authentic. I never went to a real college with a real campus and parties and drugs and girls. With my condition my shrink thought it might be too stressful. I took online courses at one of those for-profit colleges for four years.

But Mom, she insisted my degree was an accomplishment. 'I'm so proud of you,' she said. 'No different than anyone else. Now let's go rent a gown and get your graduation picture taken.'

The reason I look like such an ogre in my graduation picture, the zits, the puffy skin, the yellow teeth, is because I was having a reaction to my meds at the time. The picture next to mine is much nicer. It's Emma at her third-grade class picnic. And you'd just die if you could see that big, Julia Roberts-like smile of hers in person.

I flip her picture around and rummage through my mom's nightstand looking for some kind of lotion – anything that won't be too sticky or smell too strongly.

I find Cocoa Butter Formula.

I find Makeup Remover.

I find Collagen Elastin Enhancer.

Jesus, doesn't she just have some old-fashioned Vaseline?

On the TV, the movie's back on. This is the scene where Jordan has to seduce the snooty businessman in the lingerie shop. It's pure gold. She struts around him, changing her outfits in every shot.

Come on, where's some fucking lotion? I open the bottom drawer.

Jackpot. A little tube of KY jelly peeks out from behind a stack of folded letters.

But then I think, *What's Mom doing with a tube of KY?*

And, against my better judgment, I push the stack of folded letters out of the way and that's when I see it. The thing that all sons dread: their mom's vibrator. This isn't just a little bullet one either. It's one of those big veiny things. The kind that looks like it fell off a small horse. It's got a ball sack you're supposed to fill with hot lube. On its side, next to one of its fat, wormy veins, the words '*El Captain*™' are embossed, complete with the little trademark symbol.

And I feel a little sick on the inside.

But on the TV, Jordan Seabring is in red lingerie and I think, *Screw it.*

I grab the KY. Jordan is bending over, pretending she has just dropped her bracelet so the snooty businessman has to take a nice long look at her ass. I take my cock out and splatter some KY on and start jerking. As soon as I do, everything that's happened – all my troubles – begin to slip away.

In my brain, dopamine is being released. Dopamine is a pleasure chemical. It makes your worries disappear. As the dopamine floods my neurons, it doesn't matter that Roland is in the hospital or that a ten-million-dollar painting is in my apartment. Even the fear of my figments returning doesn't bother me. Pleasure and excitement exist in this moment and nothing else. You know how it is. The longer you live, the more shit happens, the more you realise life is just about getting from one chemical state of mind to the next.

Jordan's character has gone back into the dressing booth. The snooty businessman's interest is piqued. Now she comes back out wearing nothing but hot pants, her arm draped across her breasts, covering her nipples. But as I stroke, *El Captain*™ explodes into my thoughts like a Fourth of July fireworks show. I try to shake the image of my mom's vibrator from my mind and refocus on Jordan on the TV but I can't get it out of my head.

El Captain™, my mom's big, fat, *veiny* vibrator with a pouch for synthetic semen. And briefly I see my Mom lying on the bed, opening her legs to let *El Captain*™ in. And that's when I lose control. My dick goes from hard to chubby in a second. And then on the TV the dressing room scene abruptly ends as the channel cuts to a regularly scheduled commercial break and an ad for dentures comes on.

Limp and unfinished, I wipe the excess KY from my dick. I turn Emma's picture back around and switch off the TV. I cap the KY and put it back in the drawer by *El Captain*™, that bastard.

That's when I wonder, *What's with the huge stack of letters?*

So I sit on the edge of the bed and unfold one after another. They're all love letters. They go back years. Some are dated. The one at the bottom of the pile – it's from a month before my father died.

'Jerry,' my mom says. She's standing at the bedroom door. 'Those are private.'

The nape of your neck... one reads.

'They're private, Jerry. Put them back.'

Will hold you once more...

With all my love...

'Jerry Dresden! Put! Those! Back! Now!' my mom orders through clenched teeth. 'You don't know what you're reading.'

Why is it that people always try to tell you that you don't know what you're talking about when you realise some horrible truth about them?

'There were things–' my mom says.

'You were cheating on Dad ... with *Roland*?' Not this. Not today.

'Jerry, there were things,' my mom says as she cautiously sits next to me, 'that were very wonderful about your father. He loved you two *so much*. But Jerry, when Emma got sick – your dad, he changed.'

I shake my head as if doing so can help me unlearn this horrible revelation. 'No, you two changed,' I yell. 'Both of you! You can't blame this on Dad! You two both stopped being there for each other.'

'For me,' I say.

Mom, she shakes her head. 'It was difficult, Jerry. Your father, he was convinced he was responsible for her leukaemia. To lose your child–'

'We didn't leave her in a park!' I yell. 'She died! She died and no one talked about her anymore!'

'He lost himself in regret,' Mom's saying more to herself than to me. 'He wasn't there for us like he should have been.'

'Don't blame Dad,' I warn, but Mom, she doesn't even acknowledge I'm speaking.

'His depression – he wouldn't let me help him.' And now it's like she's having this conversation with herself; trying to justify her actions; creating a narrative. 'Sometimes, sometimes I even think the car accident wasn't an accident–'

'Dad wouldn't drive into a tree!' I shout. 'I was with him, remember? You think he would have risked my life? The police said he must've swerved to avoid hitting an animal!'

But my mom, she just continues with her jumbled monologue, recounting past events everyone here knows already. 'He threw himself into work. His work at the studio took him further and further away. He was out of the country so much.' Finally she looks back at me as if she's suddenly become aware I'm in the room. 'Jerry, it's hard enough getting through the death of a child with your partner. Without him, it was unbearable. He wasn't there to help me through it.'

Then she says, 'Roland was.'

Roland with his sleeve tattoos.

Roland with his stupid goatee.

Roland with his tripod in his eye.

'After the accident, after we moved to Chicago, I tried telling you,' she sobs. 'Maybe not as hard as I could have, but I wanted to. It was just such a hard time for you with your problems. The porn. The hallucinations. I just wanted you normal again.'

'I am normal!'

'I know. I know, baby. Now you are,' she quickly patronises me. 'But I was afraid telling you would make you spiral and we'd never get you back.'

Mom, the way she's shaking, I haven't seen her like this since the night Dad died.

'And, do you still–?' I say, 'Are you and Roland–?'

'Roland and I are friends now,' she says with a pursed frown.

'Friends?'

'Baby, I want to be honest with you,' she pleads. 'Roland and I, I never wanted you to find out. Stress isn't good for you. You know that. The doctors always said so. I just didn't want you getting worse. Having to end up in shock treatment.'

She sits next to me and sobs. I almost feel bad for her. But through her muttering I hear a little slip, a little scrap of a feeling; an accidental truth.

And I say, 'Do you still love him?'

And my mom, she whimpers.

'Do you?' I breathe.

And she says, 'Every day.' And a little part of me relaxes, hearing her say that.

Then she says, 'He helped me so much after we moved to Chicago.'

'I was talking about Dad!'

Mom looks at me with guilt in her eyes. And me, well you know those times where you say something without knowing you were even going to say it? I mean, when words seems to come out of nowhere from your stupid little mouth? This is one of those times.

I say, 'Roland's in the hospital, you know? Right now. He's in the hospital.'

A look of caring-too-much runs across her face, but before either of us can say any more, the phone on the nightstand rings. Mom, she doesn't know what to say; me looking at her, her looking at me. In the space between us the phone rings again. Then again, and my mom answers. Her replies are short.

'Yes, this is,' she says into the phone.

'He's here with me now,' she says and looks at me.

'What do you mean?' And then, 'I don't understand.'

By the time she's hung up her face has gone white.

'Mom,' I say, 'I–'

But out of nowhere a flood of violence breaks across my mom's face. 'What did you do?' she screams, striking me with the palm of her hand. 'What did you do to him?' She howls and hits me again. And again. She cries and tells me that was the police. They asked if I was here. If I was calm. They wanted to come over and have a chat with her. Roland, it seems, has died.

The next hit draws blood as she scratches my face. I yell that I don't know what I did. I tell her that I've been sick again, that I've been seeing things. She doesn't care. Her eyes are full of rage. She hits me again and I slip off the edge of the bed.

And really, what do you do in a situation like this? I mean, you shouldn't exactly hit your mom back. I am getting the shit kicked out of me by a fifty-five-year-old Joan of Arc expert, though. So I reach for the nightstand to grab whatever I can get a hold of and swing it.

The slapping stops. My mom, she's recoiled in fear. When she removes her hand from her face a long red mark, a mark that's curved like a large banana, appears on her cheek. In my hand *El Captain*™ pulsates. His testicle sack full of synthetic semen jiggles. And I know this isn't the time, but I almost want to give it a squeeze, just to see how it works.

Mom, she slinks back to the bed, holding her face, sobbing. And in this moment, with her hair tangled in different directions and the age lines of her face made more visible by her crying, it's the first time I realise she's getting old, and I have a sudden overwhelming need for her to be young again and reading me a bedtime story about Joan of Arc.

I want to plead for her forgiveness, but I'm stopped cold when I catch someone from the corner of my eye. It's my figment. She's watching me from outside the bedroom window. My pills, they haven't worked.

And to my mom I say, 'I'm so sorry.' I tremble, 'It's not me. I'm seeing things again.'

But Mom, she just cries.

'I always knew you would end up like this,' she sobs and my heart sinks. 'I knew it and I let you down. I should have gotten you the shock therapy. You're sick, Jerry.'

'Mom–'

She won't look at me.

'Just go,' she says.

'Mom?'

Her face contorts in a ripple of pain. 'Go!' she shrieks.

And I want to scream 'But I need you!', but all I can do is place *El Captain*™, wobbling, on the nightstand and leave.

7

Spork

The street's elms and oaks rustle in the biting wind. A police car speeds past in the direction of my mom's house but the early spring night easily conceals me.

'Jerry?' a voice says from behind me. The voice, it doesn't belong to a person. It belongs to my figment. The one with the raven hair and pale white skin. I turn around and she's standing not two feet behind me. This is the closest we've ever been.

'Jerry Dresden?' it says. 'I need you to come with me.' Her voice, it has a hint of desperation.

I shut my eyes. I tell myself she's not real. Then I open my eyes and, just so she knows it too, I tell her, 'You aren't real.' Then I turn and walk across the street, averting my gaze, hoping my affirmation has done its job. And I think of bees buzzing around flowers on a spring day.

I think of colour-correcting a Renoir at my boring job.

I think of the latest superhero movie staring Hugh Fox.

My first shrink taught me that your mind can only consciously be aware of seven things at any one time. So if you're thinking about your mortgage, focusing on driving, listening to the car radio, tapping your finger on the steering wheel, chewing gum, concentrating on an itch in your side and feeling your foot on the pedal, it would be impossible to realise that the impacted wisdom tooth you have is bugging you.

'I know what's in your apartment,' it says.

I think of jerking off to Scarlet Johansson.

Halle Berry.

The Pussy Cat Dolls. All five of them.

'I know what's in your apartment,' it says again, 'and soon the police will too.'

I think of sperm. Conception. The womb. Birth. Childhood. Death. I think of Emma.

'You have no choice, Jerry,' it says. 'I know—'

'Of course you do,' I hiss, alarming an old couple that passes me. 'You know because you're me; I'm you.' I'm making a scene. I'm attracting glances. People see me screaming at someone who isn't there.

'You can't go home, Jerry,' it says. 'The police will be waiting for you.'

I turn and march up to myself (that's a little psychotic depression humour for you). 'Roland is dead,' I say, shaking. 'He's dead.' I muster a little laugh. 'Don't get me wrong, I didn't like the guy. He was fucking my mom and all, but we didn't have to kill him.'

'I didn't intend to kill him,' it says.

'What's intended is irrelevant when there's a tripod in the eye. And "didn't intend to" really probably doesn't matter when *murder* is involved.'

'I needed to know where you lived,' it says.

'You knew,' I yell. 'You are me! I'm arguing with myself. This is insane.' I reach into my pocket and pull out the opaque bottle of 486s.

'What are those?'

'These,' I say, uncapping the bottle, 'are what make you go bye-bye.' The two I took at Mom's house weren't enough to stop her from appearing so I spill half the pills into my mouth. I chew them around and the gelatine capsules burst like bubble wrap. The tiny beads taste bitter as I suck them down my throat.

Several yellow cabs drive past the intersection ahead. As I walk in their direction my legs get heavier. The new-dosage pills are potent and it soon feels like my head is a balloon trying to float away, but it's kept tied down to my concrete-block feet.

'So, why aren't you American?' I say. 'I mean, what's with your voice? And what's with the clothing?' The trousers she's wearing are men's trousers. Her shoes look like male hiking boots. A green hoodie completes her outfit. 'You're dressed like a dude,' I snicker. Over-dosing makes you slaphappy.

My figment, she doesn't answer. She's kind of fuzzy – everything is.

'You know, my last one was much better-looking than you,' I say. 'I mean she dressed better. Showed off her body. Great ass, you know? Don't get me wrong, your face is nice, but why'd I have to get one that looks like a tomboy who hasn't showered in a week?' She squints. I stumble and try to put my hand on her chest, but she quickly steps away. My head spins. 'My last one liked to fuck.'

As I reach the intersection my figment says something I can't make out. No matter.

'It's time for me to say goodbye to you now,' I say, flagging a cab. 'In thirty minutes you won't exist.' My brain throbs against my skull. 'Maybe less than thirty minutes.'

'You're insane,' my imaginary friend tells me.

'No, *we're* insane.'

A cab has slowed to a stop in the suicide lane. And as I step into the street I hear my figment's voice, or a voice inside my head – or both – yell 'lookout!' Then a truck whizzes by me. The mirror clips my shoulder and I whirl to the ground like a top. The cabbie rushes from his taxi and asks if I'm OK. 'Fool didn't even slow down,' he says but everything else that comes from his mouth sounds like the *Wa. Wa-wa-wa. Wa* that the adults speak in those *Charlie Brown* holiday specials.

I now realise it's possible that I might have taken a few too many pills; that I might not only kill my figment, but myself as well.

'I'm fine,' I shrug him off as he tries to help me up. My head thumps with pain. My figment, she's still standing on the side of the street in front of a diner, a look of relief pasted all over her face. 'I'm just going to go to that diner. Get some coffee.'

'That was stupid,' my figment says as I walk past her. 'Every child knows to look both ways before crossing the street.'

'I already have a mother,' I say. 'Hit her with a dildo right before I took these abortion pills.'

My figment looks disgusted at my recap of tonight's events, and that's before I wretch all over myself. The undigested 486s come out looking like the little yellow-and-white sugar sprinkles you put on cupcakes. Some sick dribbles down my front, but this doesn't bother my figment because it just squeezes through her fingers when she grabs me by my coat. Her eyes flash a wicked green in the streetlight. And for the first time I wonder if it's possible for my own figment to hurt me. 'I don't know what the matter is with you–' it begins, but I break her grip.

'Look you – me – whatever little neuron you are inside my head,' I say, thumping my finger on my skull. 'Please disappear, OK?' My voice trembles. I look up to the sky and, like I'm another contestant on a television talent show, I say, 'Please, please; just this once, give me a break.'

A look of, not compassion, but something akin to empathy shows on my imaginary friend's face. And I dare to hope the non-existent Big Guy in the sky is about to answer my prayers; that maybe this figment will dissolve in front of my eyes.

But no. No one dissolves.

No one is listening.

So to my figment, I say, 'Do me a favour. If you won't disappear, at least stay outside while I go and get some coffee. I don't need to look crazier than I already am.'

Inside there are two police officers sitting at the counter, eating steak and eggs. One of the cops turns. I guess he can smell the vomit. For a second I consider turning around, but I'm so tired, so dizzy. I need to sit. I try to ignore the policeman as best I can, so I look out the window and that's when I see the most curious thing. My figment, her lips are moving like she's having a conversation. She talks, then pauses for some invisible person to answer, then she talks again.

And I wonder, *Can figments have figments?*

I sit in a booth covered in cheap red vinyl. In the reflection of the silver napkin dispenser, the cop has turned back to his steak and eggs.

'What can I getcha?' an older waitress asks.

'Just give me a minute.'

'Whatever,' she says and plods away, her feet slapping the ground like pieces of meat.

My figment, I guess she's done talking to herself outside because she enters the diner. As she walks by the police officers she casts them a glance. The police officers, of course, don't glance back.

Then my figment, she slides into my booth without making a sound, as if she's weightless, which, well, I guess she is.

And I whisper, 'Please just go.' I feel like a little kid again, begging the bully to leave me alone. 'Go on, scram. Get out.'

Shoo.

But I might as well be talking to thin air. Which, well, again, I guess I am.

My figment, she says, 'What are you going to do, Jerry? You're the main suspect in a murder case now.' As she says this a woman in the opposite booth turns. I smile nervously and she goes back to her food. Am I acting both of our voices out loud? Am I playing one part and then the other?

I whisper to my figment, 'Once you leave me alone, I'll be able to figure out what I need to do.'

More and more my figment looks at me like I'm crazy.

'I'm going to drink my coffee, then I'm going to wait for my stomach to settle down and I'm going to take as many of my remaining pills as I can without throwing them up again,' I whisper. 'Then I'm going to go home – I'll go home and return the painting.'

'You can't go home to return the painting, Jerry,' my figment says, glancing over her shoulder at the police. 'They'll arrest you.'

'Just get out of my head,' I say, 'and everything will be fine.'

The grumpy waitress comes over again. Her nametag reads 'VERA'.

'Whatcha need?' Vera asks, pen ready, not looking up from her little white notepad.

'Just a coffee,' I say. 'Maybe some bread.'

'We don't serve bread,' she says. 'We serve san'wiches.'

'Fine. Just a bologna sandwich with ketchup then.'

Vera lets out a little 'All riiight' as she scrawls my order in short little lines across her pad. 'And what else?'

'That's it,' I say.

'I already got your order, big spender. What about you, girlie? What can I get for you?' And Vera, she looks right at my figment. She looks right at my imaginary friend; my psychotic delusion; the bane of my existence, and she asks it *what it would like for dinner.*

'Nothing for me,' it answers.

'Both big spenders, you two,' Vera says and plods away.

What. The. Fuck.

And my figment, she stares, trying to comprehend the look on my face. Her black raven's hair. Her mutilated ear and pale skin. The girl I've seen off and on for the last few weeks. The one I dreamt about years ago. The one I've dreamt about for weeks again. *She* studies *me.*

She tilts her head a little. 'Why are you staring at me like that?'

'How can that waitress see you?' I say, as if speaking for the first time. 'You aren't *real.*'

Then my imaginary friend, she says, 'Are you a fool? I'm as real as you.'

'No you're not.' And I pick up the little ceramic dish full of artificial sweeteners and, one by one, I toss the packets at my figment. To my amazement, they don't go right through her and hit the woman sitting in the next booth. A pink Splenda bounces off my figment's nose. And for the first time I notice a few blackheads on it. A blue Sweet-It hits her chest. And now I can smell the dank musk of the old hoodie she wears. A yellow Nutri-Sweet catches her in the eye.

'Stop it!' she shouts, rubbing her eye. It waters a little bit and a tiny stream flows down her cheek. Her voice rises as she asks what's the matter with me. This is when the woman sitting in the next booth gets up and leaves, but not before casting a nasty glance.

Vera returns with my coffee. 'Can't 'ave you two horsing around. Gonna have to leave if you do.'

I point to my figment. 'You can *see* her?'

'Oh, deary,' Vera addresses my figment, 'you like 'em weird, don't you, hun?' And she plods away again.

I look at the stream of water trickling from my figment's eye. And I think of every science show I've seen on TV. They all say water is essential for life. Without it, no organism can live. None can be real. So I set the sweeteners down and cautiously reach across the table and extending my index finger, I hover it in front of my figment's face. And in this position, I look like I'm ET healing Elliott.

My figment recoils, flattening her chin closer to her neck as she squints at my finger so close to her face. Then there's a jerk of revulsion as I dart my finger forward and dip the tip of it into the little stream of water on her cheek. She's practically cross-eyed as she follows my retreating finger with a drop of her tear on it. I press it between my thumb and index finger, spreading it over the ridges of my fingerprint. It glistens like dew. Then I bring the tear to my tongue and taste it. I taste my figment's tear and it's salty and warm.

My mouth gapes. 'How are you real?' I say. But instead of answering, my figment notices the woman who left the booth behind us is now speaking to the cops at the counter. The cops, they glance at us but my figment gives a big fake everything-is-fine-here smile and the cops return to their dinners.

Then pain suddenly shoots through my hand. My figment's pale white fist is on top of mine. It's clenched around one of those half-forks, half-spoons. She's jammed it right into the top of my hand. I didn't even see her pick it up, she was that fast.

And like a little girl I say, 'Ow! That hurts!'

And my figment, she says with a devilish tone, 'Do not scream, Jerry.'

She says, 'We do not have much time. I need you to come with me, now.'

She says, 'I do not know why you think I am not real, but I can assure you, I am as real as this pain in your hand. Do you feel that?' And she applies more pressure to the spork.

I wince a 'yes'. Now I'm the one who's eyes are watering.

'Good,' she says. 'My name is Epiphany, and I have been looking for you for a long time.'

8

Elmer Fudd

When you think something isn't real you just don't pay too much attention to it. But you sober up quickly when your imaginary friend stabs you with a spork. The shock, well it's like finding out angels are real. Or devils.

We've been walking in silence for a little over ten minutes, Epiphany and I. Epiphany, my not-so-figment. 'That's a weird name,' I say. She doesn't reply. 'Were your parents hippies or something?'

Since we've left the diner, Epiphany seems to have taken on more depth, more detail. Her body is small. Her pants hang loose around her hips; barely held up by a thick belt that could wrap around her twice. There's a small bulge of something in her left back pocket. She's no taller than five foot six. Her fingers are thin and long. Longer than mine anyway.

All my fear and anxiety have been replaced with an odd euphoria. Maybe it's from overdosing on the medicine; my body trying to get it to work its way out of my system. Or maybe it's because this is great news.

I say, 'You look more like an Amber, or a Lacy.'

I'm humouring her right now. I wouldn't have left the diner with her, but the cops took off as I was busy using a napkin to dab my blood from the spork attack. That's when it hit me: if she's real, I'm innocent.

She said we had to run an errand. Don't get me wrong, I had so many questions for her, but it wasn't the time. When your exoneration tells you to go with her, you go and you don't let her out of your sight.

At the Lincoln Park Post Office she removes the bulge from her back pocket. The package is small, no bigger than a pack of cigarettes.

The post office is closed but there's a drop bin next to the automated stamp machine. The sign reads 'Envelopes and small packages only. Last pickup, 8 p.m.' I look at my dad's gold watch.

'We have to hurry,' Epiphany says and taps the stamp machine's keypad a few times. On screen, the price reads: $37.46.

And, trying to sound light-hearted, relaxed, I say, 'Where are you sending that thing? China?'

She seems both annoyed and confused by my new attitude. 'You have a credit card. Give it to me,' she orders as if to reinforce who's in charge. 'I only have dollars.'

'I don't have one,' I lie, thinking the longer I can stall the greater the chance a cop will drive by. But Epiphany gets that look on her face. 'OK, OK,' I say, trying to rub the memory of the spork attack from my hand, 'Don't have a lot left on the account, that's all.'

'It does not matter, this is the last time you will be able to use it.'

And who the hell knows what she means by that? She's crazier than I am. As she takes my card, the package slips from her hand. I scoop it up and her body goes tense. I can't read the address. It's written in pencil on the brown shipping paper and the green glow of the stamp machine's screen isn't enough to illuminate it.

'Give it to me,' she says.

And I think: *Dr Phil.* I think: *Oprah.* I think of every bullshit daytime talk show that has ever interviewed the families of victims of a hostage situation. Because that's what this basically is, a hostage situation. The advice was: humour them. It was: show them you're their friend. It was: try to get them to see that you're on their side. Try to get them to think you're an equal partner, if possible.

So I say, 'Look, you need my help for something, right? So you're gonna need to trust me. I'll hold this while you pay for the stamps – with my card.' I tap my father's watch. 'You don't have a lot of time.'

I can't read the look on her face and a sudden fear grips me. I could never pull off confidence. What if I'm just pissing her off? What if she catches on to what I'm trying to do? And then I realise that the reason those shitty daytime talk shows are always interviewing the hostage's family and never the hostage are probably because the host's advice is horrible. The hostage is probably dead because of it.

But as I'm about to hand the package back to her she says, 'I need your PIN.'

Call it a trust-building exercise.

She enters my PIN and the mailing label rolls from the machine like it's sticking its tongue out. I gesture to the label. Then for the second time tonight Epiphany brings her hand over her ear like she's having a migraine or something, but it passes as quickly as it came. She looks at the package and considers me for a moment before handing me the label. And as I drop the package down the slot, in the green glow of the stamp machine, I think I catch a grin creep across her face.

Behind us on the street a car passes but it's just a minivan.

'I have a place to stay,' Epiphany says. 'South of downtown. We need to find a bus.'

'No problem. The fifty-five goes south. There's a bus stop just a few blocks this way,' I lie. I need to get her three more blocks, to the Clark and Division intersection. There's a 7-Eleven there and it always has police parked in the lot.

As we walk, the night is chill and damp and the streets are virtually empty. This neighbourhood is mainly residential and most people are already home from work, settling down to watch their prime-time imaginary friends. The only person I see besides us on the first block is a teenager jogging down the other side of the street.

Curiosity mixes with my attempt to keep Epiphany occupied so she doesn't realise we're headed in the wrong direction. 'You said you need my help. Why?'

'That's not for now,' she says, surveying the street.

We cross to the next block. Halfway down, on the opposite side a man walks with the help of a cane. Epiphany's eyes sweep the neighbourhood. Briefly I imagine she's a robot and her eyeballs are little cameras recording everything she looks at; like she's someone's creation just brought to life and doesn't fully understand the world she's been placed in.

Suddenly she seems distracted. Then I hear her whisper a name. I think she said 'Michael' but I can't be sure.

'You have a slight accent, you know?' I say. 'What is that? Polish? Russian?'

No reply. Her pace has slowed. On the other side of the street, the old man with the cane is walking faster than we are now.

Nervously I play with the little stab wounds on my hand. The lights of the 7-Eleven illuminate the night just a block and a half away.

'You said you've been looking for me for a long time,' I say, trying to sound cool and natural. 'I mean, I've only lived at my apartment and my mom's house. Haven't moved around a lot. How hard could it have been to find me? How long have you been looking?'

'Twelve years,' she answers.

I stop in my tracks. 'Twelve years ago I was still in LA.'

She holds my gaze.

'But, how old are you? Twenty-five? Twenty-six? You've been looking for me since you were a teenager?'

Over her shoulder I see a police car pull into the 7-Eleven. She turns to see what I've looked at, but the police car has already parked out of view.

'This is wrong,' she says.

'What? No,' I panic. 'The seventy-two bus stop is just up there.'

'You're lying,' she says, taking a step back. 'You said the *fifty-five* goes south.'

'No, I didn't,' I say with a guilty-as-fuck smile on my face. 'You mis-heard me. I said the *seventy-two* goes south. We want the *seventy-two*.' Another step back. She's not buying it. I say, 'Epiphany, look, calm down, OK?'

Don't panic, I think.

'You're lying,' she says again.

Dr Phil, I think. Show her we're on the same level. I put a hand on her shoulder in an effort to keep her calm. My mistake.

She recoils at my touch, then backs away and looks like she's about to bolt. So I lunge at her. But I forget how quick she can be and she slips from my grip and stumbles over the curb. Her feet tangle with mine and we both fall next to a bush on a small patch of lawn. Before she can move I grab her shoulders and crawl on top of her, pinning her.

'Don't touch me!' she screams.

And from across the street an old voice shouts, 'Who's there?'

On top of Epiphany, my hand slips from her waist to her thigh. I cover her mouth to stifle her screams as her fingers dig into the grass and her fists hit me with handfuls of soil.

But as she beats my face with dirt, I suddenly cry out. I roll off her as a white-hot pain spreads across the back of my skull. The old man from the other side of the street looms over me holding his cane like he's Babe Ruth waiting to hit one over left field.

'Get away from her,' he crows.

'Wait a second,' I shout. This time there's a crack as the old man connects his cane with my forehead. Blood trickles into my eyes.

'You OK, ma'am?' the old man says. Epiphany, she looks all red in my eyes; like a whipped animal, backed into a corner. I'm not sure she's even heard him.

'What's going on out there?' a gruff voice yells. I wipe the blood from my eyes. The voice comes from a kitchen window shining a patch of light onto the lawn.

'Rapist!' the old man shouts. 'I caught a rapist out here! Call the police!'

Epiphany's on her feet now. The old man is trying to reassure her everything will be okay. But she's looking wild-eyed; scared of me – like she's misjudged me. Then she hears the old man say 'police' again and looks even more scared. And despite the old man's reassurances that she is OK, she backs away and backs away again until the night's shadows envelop her pale skin.

'Wait!' I yell as I try to scramble after her. But the old man raises his cane and orders me to stay down. I kick him in the knee and he releases a sharp cry as his body crumples to the sidewalk.

'I didn't mean to – I'm sorry about that,' I stammer.

My head throbs. The old man looks at the blood on his cane. 'I got your DNA now, you pervert,' he says. 'Nowhere to run!'

Someone clearly watches too much *CSI*.

I look around in the darkness. She can't have gone far. I squint as I see a hint of something move. Someone has gone down the alley between two houses. But then behind me there's a click and something hard bumps my spine.

A gruff voice says, 'Don't move, you son of a bitch.'

So I don't.

'Now turn around,' the voice says. And when I do I don't see anything until I look down. A tiny, pudgy man holds some kind of pistol with a long barrel. His gruff voice doesn't match his frame. He's bald and so short he has to reach up just to put the barrel of the gun under my chin. He digs the pistol hard into the soft flesh under my jaw. I'm Bugs Bunny to his Elmer Fudd.

'You OK, fella?' Elmer asks the old man.

The old man props himself up on his elbow. 'Think I broke my hip.'

'Where's the girl?' Elmer asks.

'She ran away,' I say, calmly. 'It's not what you think.'

'Course not,' he says, pressing the gun under my jaw with renewed force. 'Never is. My little girl was violated by one a you years ago. I'm guessing he woulda said the same thing. Who knows, maybe he *was* you?' And he flips something on the side of the gun.

Safety is off.

All I can think is, *What Would Bugs Bunny Do?*

'Uh,' interrupts the old man, 'shouldn't we call the police?'

'The police aren't no good in situations like this. They couldn't help Patty,' Elmer says. 'It's best to handle this ourselves.'

'But still,' the old man protests from his supine position on the sidewalk and takes a cellphone from his jacket pocket. 'Perhaps ... let's just give them a call.'

Elmer shakes his head in frustration. 'What's your name?' he asks and his breath drifts into my nostrils. It smells like cigars.

'Tom,' I say.

When I get nervous, I lie. It's always been a protective mechanism for me.

'Tom what?'

'Uh, Cruise.'

'Tom Cruise?' he says.

I never said I was a good liar.

'Well, Mr Movie Star, I'm gonna make you a deal,' Elmer says. 'You're going to give me your wallet, and if your ID says you are "Tom Cruise", I'm gonna let that feller on the sidewalk call the cops. If, however, you're lying to me, I'm gonna shoot you in the knees.'

'Look–' I say. 'This isn't what it looks like.'

But Elmer shakes his head, 'Let's have the wallet. Slowly.'

With the barrel of the gun still pressed tightly beneath my chin I remove my wallet from my back pocket and place it in Elmer's pudgy little hand. He flips it open.

'*Jerry*,' he shakes his head. 'You lied to me. Now I'm gonna have to shoot ya.'

'Wait, wait!' I plead. 'Please. I must have grabbed my brother's wallet by mistake. We're twins.'

Elmer looks at the ID again. 'Jerry *Dresden*,' he reads. 'Don't brothers have the same last name?'

'He got married and took his wife's name.'

'Sir, *please*,' the old man interrupts again, 'let me just phone the police.'

But Elmer, he turns to the old man and yells, 'I say they never help!' And that's when I take my chance. I smack the gun away and lunge at his little body. Using all my strength, I lift him from the ground and toss him just like they do in all those midget videos you see on the internet.

'My other hip!' the old man shrieks as Elmer lands on him.

'I'm *really* sorry,' I wince.

But Elmer, he's like a goddamned prairie weasel. He's on his feet again and swinging the gun at me. His eyes are frenzied. The sound is so loud it sets my ears ringing and the blast is so hard it knocks Elmer back on his ass. I don't chance another bad shot and burst into a sprint as Elmer springs up again. A chunk of greystone explodes as I turn the corner of a house, dipping down its side-alley.

And I run and run and run some more. I jump fences and sprint across traffic-filled streets and through darkened yards. I move harder and faster than I ever have. I run with no destination in mind. I run for what seems like hours. And then I drop. My lungs burn and my legs feel like spaghetti. My right shoe is wet. I've pissed myself. When I finally catch my breath, I notice I'm in my neighbourhood. I almost cry. My apartment is just around the corner. A securely locked door. A shower. A quick wank. Sleep. There's nothing else I desire at this moment.

9
The Videotape

It's not until I'm right next to it that I notice what it is. I'm passing a brown Datsun that's parked across the street from my building when a squawk comes from it.

The squawk, it says, 'Car thirty-four, this is dispatch.'

Mounted to the dashboard are a CB radio and one of those heavy-duty laptops all police cars have nowadays. A portable police light sits on top of the glove compartment. 'Car thirty-four, where are you?' Squawk.

My building's door bursts open and someone hurries out. It's the tall detective who questioned me at the museum. I hesitate for a moment before I duck beside the Datsun's passenger-side door. I crawl onto my stomach and press my cheek to the ground as I peer underneath the car and watch a pair of slender legs approach from the other side. The driver's-side door opens and the car dips an inch closer to the ground.

'This is Ross,' the detective says from the driver's seat.

And the radio squawks, 'What's your status, detective?'

'We've searched the suspect's apartment. He's not here, but we do have the painting. We're going to need a forensics team down here right away. And could you have someone at HQ notify the museum?'

'Roger that,' squawk. 'Forens is inbound now.'

'Copy.'

'Detective Ross,' squawk, 'Officer Rogello wants to know if you've received his email.'

'Checking now,' he says and then laughs. 'Yeah, there's a shocker. Tell Rogello I got it.'

The car rocks as the detective shuffles back out. From peering underneath the car I see his feet shift on the asphalt. Then there's a rustle of hands in coat pockets and a spent match drops to the street. The smell of a cigarette fills the night air.

This is where I think, I can turn myself in. I can get off the ground and say, 'Excuse me, I'm the guy you're looking for.' Then I can explain how I didn't stab Roland in the eye; how I didn't steal the painting – how it was all done by my imaginary friend who turned out to be a real live person after all. 'I swear. My figment named Epiphany did this, Detective,' I'll say.

'Hey Fred,' someone shouts from a window. *My* window. 'You aren't going to believe this!' It's the second detective – the short one. 'The boys we sent to his mom's house, they show up and he's been there. He attacked her with a dildo! His own mom! With a dildo!'

'What the hell's with this guy?' Fred shouts back. From my vantage point underneath the car I see ash from Fred's cigarette drift to the ground. It lands and floats, hot and orange, in a little black puddle before the water drowns it.

'Wait, there's more!' the voice from my window shouts. 'There's more!' the voice shouts again like he's enjoying this. 'Just got a call from Mortimer. Responded to some guy who tried to make a citizen's arrest. Caught our boy trying to rape a girl up north.'

'Quit shouting and come down here,' Fred tells the voice from above.

'You told me to wait with the painting. You come up here.'

'Just lit one. Don't want to contaminate the scene,' Fred says. 'How do we know the rape is our guy?'

'The guy who tried to make the arrest,' the voice from above shouts, 'he got the perp's wallet! The ID in it says "*Jerry Dresden*"! This address and all!'

Fred takes a huge drag from his smoke.

'Forensics on their way?' the voice from above asks.

I guess Fred nods, because he doesn't say anything. 'Any sign of the videotape?' Fred asks next.

Videotape?

'Please,' the voice shouts back, 'he's destroyed that by now. I would have.'

But I don't have any videotapes.

Then the voice, it says, 'Hey, do me a favour?'

'What?'

'I got a USB thumb drive in the glove compartment; can you run it up here?'

'What on earth for?'

'You should see the amount of porn this guy has. He's got hard drives full of the stuff!' he shouts, and in spite my horrible predicament my sincerest wish at this moment is that all my neighbours are sleeping. 'I wonder if his girlfriend knows about all this?'

'Girlfriend, my ass,' Fred laughs. 'We just got an email from Rogello. That "girlfriend" who works at Auntie Anne's? The people who work there have never heard of her or of Jerry Dresden.'

Oh God.

'Then Rogello checked with our boy's boss at the museum and he said that most people there thinks he just makes up his girlfriends.'

I want to die.

'His boss says his co-workers have caught him in too many obvious lies about "her"', Fred continues. 'It's a running joke with them. Rogello checked it out with Dresden's mom. She even told him the same thing. She knows he just makes them up, too.'

Just kill me.

'How old is this guy? Twelve? What grown man makes up his girl-friends, has *this* much porn, *and* attacks his mom with a dildo?' the voice from above laughs.

Mortified isn't close to being the right word.

And yeah, I lied. I'm busted. But what did you want, the truth? That I don't have a girlfriend? That I'm not on a break from anyone and that I willingly *choose* to sit at home alone looking at fake celebrity porn? But what did you expect? I learned everything from watching sitcoms and talk shows and movies-of-the-week. I learned what was beautiful and what was ugly and how you should act in any number of situations.

I learned how to *feel* from these things. Larry Hagman. Ted Danson. Kirstie Alley. Roseanne. These were my fathers, my mothers. And they all took care of me half an hour at a time. Consider fake celebrity porn my own little version of the Oedipus complex.

I also learned a long time ago just to tell people what they want to hear. It makes it easier on everybody. But the thing about lying is that you need to have a good memory, and I don't. At work I told my colleagues I was dating Harriett, but at a shrink appointment I slipped up and told the doc I was dating Heather. Two-timing the world in your head is hard work. The next week I forgot which name I had told Mom. But she knew, too. She was just patronising me the whole time when she asked about my girlfriends.

'But come on...' a voice is fading back into my awareness. 'Bring my thumb drive up here. I want to grab some of his shit before forensics gets here.'

'You gotta be kidding me?' someone says. It's Fred.

'Come on, man. I didn't bust your balls when you took a favour from that prostitute we didn't arrest last week.'

On the other side of the car a cigarette hits the ground. It bobs in the black puddle for a second before it dies a cool death. 'Will you shut up?' Fred shouts.

'So just bring it,' the voice says.

Chicago's finest, ladies and gentlemen.

'Hold your horses,' Fred says, and the weight of the car shifts towards me as he leans across the passenger seat and opens the glove compartment.

The flood of embarrassment fades from my skin as a cold shiver runs through me. I'm going to be caught. Fred will peek out the passenger-side window and see me lying flat on the ground. He'll slap on the handcuffs and I'll be taken to jail. At the trial I'll tell them about Epiphany, how she was a real person for one day in my life. But the judge will call me a lunatic and a pervert and ask me how I could assault my own mother with a dildo. Then he'll order shock treatment and he'll send me to prison and that's where my hell will really begin. Hard-timers aren't kind to guys like me.

And I can't end up like that. I can't. So in the space of the time it takes Fred to close the door and his slender feet begin to move towards my apartment building, I make a decision that I've never imagined I would ever have to. When Fred enters my building, I slowly get off the ground and check to make sure the other voice isn't still by the window. And when I know it's clear, I don't run, I don't hurry. Calmly, I put one foot in front of the other, and like that I simply walk away from the Datsun and my apartment and my life.

Here's the thing about walking away from your life: It sounds all dramatic and final when you decide to do it, but it's a logistical nightmare. There are all kinds of things that you never realised you would need to consider. Things like, Where do I go? Where do I sleep? I've got no wallet and no money, how do I eat?

I wanted to go back to Mom's house, to apologise, to plead my innocence, to have some dinner, but the cops would've been there. The best I could come up with is this little park I'm in. It's far enough away from where everything that happened earlier went down so I don't think the cops would consider looking for me here. Plus it's dark and the bushes are large and do a good job of concealing me and keeping the wind off my back.

My father's gold watch says it's almost five a.m. and every time I close my eyes I hope I'll nod off into the sleep my body desperately craves. But my mind's on edge. My body's wired. Because out of everything that's happened in in the last twenty-four hours – Epiphany, Roland, my mom; Roland's tongue on my mom – the only thing I can't get out of my head is the videotape. The one the detective said they were looking for in my apartment.

And that's when it hits me that the videotape they're talking about is the one in the camera that I almost knocked over in Roland's studio. The one the insurance company required the museum to record on when any work was being done on the Van Gogh. If the cops are looking for it, it means it's missing, which means it shows Roland being murdered. Which means Epiphany is doing the murdering. Which means she took it.

And just then, just when I've connected all the dots, all the fruitless dots that don't count for anything because I let Epiphany get away, I feel a very cold, thin line form along the front of my throat.

It's Epiphany, behind me in the bushes. She tells me to remain quiet. No more talk, no more lies, no more distraction. One word and my throat gets slit. 'You touch me again and I do not run this time. Understand?'

And I feel a little blood dribble down my neck.

10

Sharks

There was this story I read in *Time* magazine. It was about a little boy. Timmy, I think. One evening around dusk, Timmy's swimming in the shallow Atlantic waters near Fort Lauderdale, Florida. He's splashing along having a great time when suddenly a shark swims up and takes a bite out of him. So Timmy, he starts screaming like crazy because his arm's shredded and there's blood everywhere. Hearing his nephew's screams from shore, Timmy's uncle rushes into the water. He's thigh-deep in the surf when he spots the shark approaching Timmy for seconds. And Timmy's uncle, what does he do? Does he pluck Timmy out of the water and carry him to safety?

No.

The uncle, he wades into the water and grabs the whole damn shark in his arms and wrestles it.

He wrestles it.

He literally grabs this six-foot eating machine from the ocean and throws it, fucking *throws it*, onto the beach. Its sleek grey body lands right where a stranger is walking along on his evening stroll. This stranger, he sees the shark – the poor thing – just lying like a big fish stick on the sand.

The shark's breathing becomes shallow as its black eyes stare at the stranger. Its eyes seem to say, 'I always thought a fishing hook would be the end of me.' This is when the stranger calmly reaches into his pocket. This is where he slowly pulls out a gun and points it at the shark – who at this point just has to be wondering if his day could possibly get any worse. The shark's big, black eyes stare down the barrel as three bullets are fired into its head.

Time called the uncle and the stranger heroes, but I couldn't help but feel for the poor shark. He was minding his own business – having some dinner – when he's plucked from his normal life and forced into an insane world with insane people.

I know how he feels.

I've been holed up with Epiphany in this shitty place for only an hour, but it might as well be a lifetime. We're somewhere on the south side of the city – the place middle-class white people go if they want to die. The street we're on is either called Windsor or Jacobson. The street sign was ripped from the ground, so I can't be sure which. This place, it's not even her place I bet. She's gotta be squatting. The outside of the building has a painted sign that reads 'Upholstery' in faded yellow letters with white drop-shadows. The furniture looks like it was found on the street. The ceilings leak and you can hear things crawling behind the walls.

At the park I checked my neck. The blood was from a little flesh wound Epiphany made to punctuate her point. She told me not to speak. She said she'd been following me since she saw 'the little man' who took a shot at me. She watched as I lay by the car listening to the detectives. She said she knew my plan was to get her to the police and that if I tried to do so again, I would fail. And then she used a leaf to wipe my blood from her blade.

As we walked south, taking back alleys and dark streets, Epiphany made sure I stayed in front of her. She never took her eyes off me. She said, 'If you try what you did before,' and produced the blade from her pocket.

It was a pointless threat. I wasn't going anywhere. I thought of nothing but the videotape.

We arrived here just before dawn. And look, I know what you're thinking. Why'd I go with her? To find the tape, sure. But why do I believe I can? My shrink told me that almost everyone today has something called 'sitcom resolution syndrome'. He said that people watch so many TV shows that their neural pathways get warped. They expect simple solutions to complex problems. They expect to be able to resolve all their dilemmas in twenty-two minutes, just like the characters on *Friends* and *Cheers* and *How I Met Your Mother* do. So maybe that's why I went: because television has made me believe my major life problems, like discovering where an imaginary friend is hiding the videotape that exonerates me for murder, can be solved in the time it takes to eat a TV dinner, *sans* laugh track, and not including commercial breaks.

In the place we're in, most of the windows are broken. At any given time a half-dozen pigeons are flying in or out. We're on the third floor and that's the good floor, believe it or not. The rest of the building is abandoned. The loft has three walls, which partition two small rooms. The first has an ugly corduroy couch that has been here since the seventies. There are holes bitten into it. The next partition creates the 'bedroom' – which can only be called so because of a blue floral mattress with deep-brown stains lying on the floor. The third partition contains what was probably a bathroom. Now there's only a hole in the floorboards where a toilet once stood. A rusty tap drips chocolate-milk-coloured water.

When we arrived, after I took the grand tour of the place with my eyeballs, I said, 'So whose place is this?'

And Epiphany, she shook her head.

I said, 'What are we doing here?'

Epiphany, she rubbed her temples.

I said, 'So, how long are we going to be here?'

Epiphany, she dug her pinky in her ear like she was trying to get a blockage out.

I said, 'So what's the game plan, Coach?'

'Shut up!' she explained. And then she said, 'I'm going to lie down.'

That's what she said. 'I'm going to lie down.' Like we're a couple who just got back from a tiring family reunion with in-laws we hate and she's *just got to get off her feet*. Like she didn't just bring me here by knifepoint. *I've got one of my headaches, will you take out the trash before coming to bed, dear?*

So Epiphany, she's been lying in the room with the mattress for the last hour. Me, I've been standing in the same place since I entered, part bewildered that she's secure enough in her situation over me to take a fucking nap, part looking around for where the tape could be hidden, and part afraid to move since any extra pressure might topple this building in an instant.

With all the loose floorboards and holes in this dump the videotape could be anywhere. But even while she's asleep I know there's no way I can search the apartment. So I sit on the shitty couch and I hear things stir inside. In the cushion something bumps against me as it moves from one location to the next. I try not to apply too much pressure.

Through a large gap that's rotted through the wall between this room and the next, I see Epiphany curled up, catlike, on the blue mattress with piss-brown stains. Her hands cup the side of her head, like even in her sleep she's still suffering from her headaches. Her little blade is clutched in one hand, between her thumb and index finger. It's pushing back her hair on that side, revealing her mutilated earlobe. And right where her feet meet the mattress, right next to a big brown piss stain, I notice an incision.

The incision, it's wide enough to slip a MiniDV tape though – the kind Roland shot his video on.

That's when it hits me. That's why she's so comfortable going to sleep and leaving me to sit here. She's not lying on the mattress like a cute little cat; she's Cerberus guarding a trap door.

Briefly, I consider taking advantage of this headache she's having. I think of pouncing on her and digging into the mattress for my freedom. But that's when reality sets in. She's little, but stronger than she looks. She's fast, too; I never saw that spork coming. And I feel the cut on my neck. What could she do with that knife if she really wanted to?

Out of nowhere Epiphany's eyes flick open and lock on mine. For a second I'm afraid that she knows what I've been thinking. She's creepy like that. And as she stares at me she just picks herself up from the mattress and enters the living room like she never had a headache at all.

'It's time to get started,' she says. 'We have a long journey ahead of us. We don't have a lot of time.'

Oh, but we have time for naps?

I say, 'Journey?'

She doesn't reply. She just stares at me like I didn't get the memo.

I say, 'Where are we going?'

And she says, 'Ensenada.' She says, 'We need to leave tomorrow morning.'

Ensenada? That doesn't sound like it's close.

'It's in Mexico,' she says.

Mexico.

'You can't be serious?' I laugh and begin to lose my cool. 'Even if I weren't wanted by the police, I couldn't get across the border without a passport. I don't even have my damn wallet anymore. It was taken from me when you flipped the fuck out last night. Remember?'

Epiphany sighs. She says, 'Watch your language, Jerry.'

Watch my language?

'Last night you lied to me, I reacted. It's in the past,' she says, like I'm the ex-boyfriend who can't move on. 'We need passports now and you can get them.' I'm about to tell her I don't know who she thinks I am, that I wouldn't know the first thing about getting passports, when she says, 'Your friend can get them for us.'

Now I know she's insane.

'I don't have any friends.'

This is where she steps closer and I see that little warning flash in her eye – the one she gets right before she stabs you with something. I'm not playing this well.

'I do have one ... friend,' I say. 'Maybe he can help us. But I would need things first – so I can contact him.'

'What do you need?'

'A lot,' I shake my head. 'I need to get on the internet. I need a computer.'

I expect Epiphany to say 'nice try', but instead she just walks towards the door.

'Where are you going?' I say.

'I told you we don't have a lot of time. I'm going to get your computer.'

I wait ten minutes in case Epiphany comes back, in case this is a trap. I mean she can't really be going to my place to get my computer. She can't be that stupid; the cops will catch her right away.

But after fifteen minutes I'm pretty sure she's actually left. I go to the bedroom and find the incision in the mattress, the one next to the big brown piss stain. And using both hands, I stretch it open until it's wide enough to fit my arm in. Then I plunge my hand inside. I blindly reach around the mattress springs and the stringy mattress filler until I'm elbow deep. I feel a tickle against my finger, but it goes away. I keep groping around the tightly coiled spring. And that's when the tickle, it comes back. And this time it doesn't go away.

The tickle begins to crawl along my forearm. Then it makes its way to my elbow, right by the mouth of the incision. It peeks its black, boney little head out. Its red rat eyes glowing rabidly. I cry out and the rat sprints up my arm and onto my neck. And me, I hurl backwards, shrieking like a little girl. The rat grips firm to my shirt collar, its claws pricking my skin, and squeals in unison with me as I grab its ropelike tail and fling it hard against the wall. It lands with a thump on the floor on the opposite side of the mattress.

I stand motionless as I wait for the rat to scurry at me, ready for round two. I can feel it orchestrating its best plan of attack. I wait. I brace myself. But after thirty seconds it still hasn't shown its hand. That's when I hear a light scratching. And cautiously, I peek over the other side of the mattress.

The rat, it's slowly dragging its body across the floor with its front paws. Its back legs refuse to move.

A twisted smile creeps over my face. Like it's one of my fake images, I picture Epiphany's face superimposed on the rat's ruined body. She's beaten, broken. And as I bring my foot up, I pause. Her whiskery nose twitches and Epiphany-rat, she says, *'Look at you. You couldn't hurt me if you wanted to. You're pathetic. See you in Mexico.'*

So I stomp as hard as I can. The rat's bulk cracks and collapses beneath my foot and when I lift my leg there's a little pool of blood forming below its body.

And I'm euphoric. I feel like this actually hurt Epiphany in some way.

But then I notice the rat's belly is still rising and falling in that pool of blood. It's eyes – they're still moving. It looks so afraid. Confused. Not understanding why its body won't work how it's supposed to. And I think of the shark, which makes me think of me, which makes me think of Emma in her hospital bed, her stomach rising and falling.

The rat keeps squealing in these short, painful bursts.

Suddenly, I so desperately want to end its pain, but I can't bring myself to fuck up killing it again. So instead I scoop the rat up in my hands. Its heart beats rapidly against my palm. Then I bring the rat to the broken window, its little red eyes looking wildly around, looking down at the street from the three-storey height.

I don't watch it hit the ground.

And under the rusty tap I scrub the blood from my hands in the chocolate-milk-coloured water. I scrub until my hands are raw. Until my skin splits. And even then I still feel the rat's heartbeat against my palm.

11

Horny Halfling

The sun has almost set when I wake on the mattress to find Epiphany standing over me with a white laptop. The mattress, it's the closest I've had to a normal bed in more than a day. It was too much to resist. Outside the window the sky is purple and in the far distance you can see the lights of Chicago's skyscrapers just twinkling on.

And how embarrassing, I'm the houseguest from hell. The place is more of a dump than it was before Epiphany left. The pool of rat blood is still semi-fluid. The mattress's guts are scattered everywhere, its tiny incision now a gaping hole. After my mercy killing I checked every conceivable place for the tape. I prised up floorboards. I pulled down decaying drywall. I even ripped the couch cushions open. But before I can begin to make excuses for the state I've left her shitty apartment in Epiphany hands me the laptop and says, 'The videotape isn't here, Jerry.'

'You're lying.' I take a step towards her. Mom told me never to hit a girl, but I don't think Epiphany counts.

'I'm not a fool, Jerry,' she says. 'The only reason you are so accommodating is because you've realised the videotape proves your innocence. It's the only card you have. It's why you haven't run to the police while I've been out.' She says all this in a matter-of-fact way. *This is just how things are.* 'You can't think I would have left you alone with it?'

I feel so stupid. 'Where is it?'

'Mexico.'

'Bullshit,' I say. And I'm about to say, *How would the tape get to Mexico?* But then it hits me. 'It was in that package I put in the mailbox.'

I feel sick. I had my freedom in my hands and mailed it away, International Next Day Air.

Epiphany studies me with her cool, green eyes. There's no gloating or pleasure when she speaks. 'I need you to help me, Jerry. The tape was the only way I could ensure you would. You'll go wherever it is.'

And I picture my videotape lying on the beach under the Mexican sun, sipping a Mai-Tai.

'I need you and you need the tape,' she says. 'If you go to the police I will simply disappear. You have no way of finding me. You'll sound like a madman, and, because of your condition, the authorities will think you are. You'll go to jail, Jerry.'

'My condition?' I say.

'You see things,' she says. 'You see people who aren't there. That's why you didn't think I was real.'

How could she possibly know that?

'The newspapers, Jerry. Your mom. Your doctor. The press has got to them all. They mention your disorder, your ... tastes.'

Then to underline her point about how fucked I am she hands me the *Chicago Tribune*. It's the evening edition. Looks like the weather is going to be cold; might snow. The Bulls won last night; that's good. Oh, and right on the front page, there's my name and face in black and white. The picture they've used, it's the one from my mom's bedroom, my online college graduation picture. The one with my hideous crooked smile and fat eye-zit. Even I have to admit that I look like a murdering rapist that would attack his mom with a dildo. I read how I've become the most wanted man in the city. I read how I'm on medication. I read how I stabbed a colleague in the eye. How I tried to rape someone last night.

And I think, *This isn't good.*

I think, *This isn't true.*

I think, *Couldn't Mom have given them a better photo?*

The look on Epiphany's face, it tells me, *There's no point in arguing.*

It tells me, *You're trapped.*

And it's right.

'You should get started,' she says and hands me the white laptop. It's not mine.

'Where's the power supply?'

'I could only get the computer.'

'You stole this?' I say, not quite sure why I'm shocked that the girl who put a tripod in an innocent man's eye stole something.

'Will it work?'

I open the lid. Someone was working on a spreadsheet when Epiphany nicked it. The battery level is almost full and it's picking up a Wi-Fi connection from somewhere. 'Yeah, it'll work,' I say. 'But I don't have a lot of time. Four hours max.'

'There's a bus leaving tomorrow morning,' she says. 'We will need the passports by then.'

'It's not like I'm ordering something from Amazon,' I say. 'This could take him a little bit of time.'

And Epiphany, she looks at me like she's about to say, 'This has nothing to do with South America, Jerry,' but then she recoils just a little bit. She swipes at her ear, like she's swatting an invisible fly away. It's not the first time I've seen her do this. I ask about it and she says, 'Just some ringing in my ear.'

'Ringing in your ear?'

'We'll need money for the trip,' she says.

I guess that conversation's over.

So I say, 'Don't look at me. I lost my wallet, remember?'

'There's a pawnshop down the street,' she says.

I look around her shitty apartment. 'I don't think we're going to have anything they want.'

Epiphany doesn't laugh. 'Give me your watch,' she says.

'No way,' I swat my hand over it. 'This was my father's.'

'All the more reason,' she says, as if that's a real argument.

And I know she doesn't mean to, but she inches up to me in a, well, it's almost a seductive way. Just like women do who know how to get what they want from men, without using tripods, or blackmail, or sharp little blades. And she inches up to me until we are chest to breast, and she takes my hand and turns it over in hers. Even though her fingers are long, my palms dwarf her hands. It would take both of hers to cover one of mine. And as she works at the clasp of the watch, I feel the warmth coming from her body.

Maybe it's because I haven't been this close to a woman in, well ... that's not important. But, her touch, truthfully, it arouses me a little. Her green eyes, from this distance they don't look so wicked as they do inviting. She looks me up and down. And my resistance, it stops when I feel the tips of her fingers tickle my wrist as she unfastens the clasp, then slips the watch from it. And as Epiphany takes a step back, as she goes all cold again, she walks out the door and says, 'Get started. We don't have a lot of time.'

Slam.

I look at my bare wrist and think of my dad. Then I think, No, just do whatever it takes to get to the tape. The watch was gaudy anyway. Big and gold and not my style.

There's a guy I know through a fakirs forum. And yes, that's fakir with an '*i*'. That's just how they spell it. Like you didn't know. This guy, he goes by the name *Horny Halfling* and he's regarded as one of the best fakirs around.

The way faking works is, first, you decide who you want to fake and what you want them to be doing in the picture. Let's say you want Jordan Seabring getting it up the ass. Now you need to find a body shot. Body shots come from regular porn pictures. Google 'tits' or 'fuck' or whatever and you'll find more body shots than you can imagine. So to create a fake of Jordan Seabring doing anal, you need to find a picture of some woman getting it in the ass.

Go ahead, write this down. I'll wait.

What's tricky is you need to find a body that's as similar to the celebrity's body as possible. If the actress is fair-skinned, putting her head on a tanned body wouldn't look realistic. If the actress has smaller tits, finding a body with double D's won't look right. In faking you want to make it look as real as possible.

After you find your body shot, you need to find a good headshot of the actress. Headshots come from scanned magazine photos or celebrity gossip sites. If you want a shot of the actress with her mouth open, so she looks like she's enjoying it, you want to stick to candids as most publicity shots are closed mouth or beaming, white-teeth smiles that a person wouldn't realistically be wearing if they were getting it in the ass.

Once a fakir finds the head and body shots, he works on joining them. Sometimes the fakir can just paste the headshot onto the body if the two are close enough in size, shape and skin tone. But the real champs – like Horny Halfling – they paste the head onto the body and repaint the entire image in Photoshop to make it look as uniform and lifelike as possible. And the best images are. You would swear they were real. I once saw a picture of Audrey Hepburn double-dicking at Tiffany's and there was no way I could tell it was a fake. Faking, it's more of an art than anything else.

Fakirs post their works to online forums where other fakirs critique them. The best fakirs rise to rock-star status in the forums. They have huge followings. They take the controlled fantasy that is Hollywood and present it to you in a more exposed, forbidden form.

I log into the New Fake City forums and send Horny Halfling a private message. After years of critiquing and requesting fakes from him, we've become friends. Not real friends, mind you. Internet friends. Common-interest friends. The only real-life things I know about him are that he also lives in Chicago and he learned how to fake while working the boring overnight shifts at Kinko's – that, and he's paranoid as shit and believes that the US government is part of some New World Order trying to enslave the lower classes.

Halfling initiates a direct IM session.

'You're not going to believe this,' he types, 'I think I just found out who killed Bill Clinton.'

'No one killed Clinton. He's still alive,' I type.

'That's a duplicate. An imposter,' Halfling types. 'The real Clinton was murdered in 1994.'

'Look,' I type. 'I don't have time right now. I'm on low battery. I need a favour.'

Halfling, he can go on these rants forever. He's one of those people who can suck you into his theories, because you just need to show him how wrong he is. We have that kind of relationship, the kind where we end up bickering about menial things and by the time we're done we're on the opposite sides of the argument from where we started.

'Look at his policy shifts in his second term,' Halfling types. 'No one changes like that. They killed him. Set up their own guy. Put a lookalike puppet in the White House.'

I type, 'I really don't have a lot of power.'

Halfling types, 'You know who else is running out of power? The middle class.'

I type, 'No it's not.'

'And it started when they killed Clinton and put a puppet in the White House and the country fell for it.'

'That's stupid,' I type. 'No one, NO ONE would be able to pull that off.' Then I add, smileyface.

Even though I have an overwhelming desire to correct him, I remind myself to keep it lighthearted. I still need his help.

Halfling types, 'You're right, it's only just ALL OVER the internet.'

'No it's not,' I type. Grumblyface.

'It's all over the sites I go to,' Halfling types.

And I type, 'I'm sure not everyone reads the sites you do.' And then I add, winkyface.

Winkyface.

'You're totally brainwashed, like the masses,' Halfling types.

No winkyface.

We're going to be here all night if this keeps up.

So I type, 'Look, you may be right. I read the same thing once on

Yahoo's homepage. But then it was pulled like they never wanted anyone to see it.' I type, 'I didn't want to believe it.' I type, 'It's just hard to accept...'

And Halfling types, smileyface. He types, 'That's how I first felt when I was alerted to all this.'

And before he gets carried away with his theories again, I type, 'I need a favour.'

'What?' he types.

'A big favour.'

He types a confusedface.

'A stick-it-to-the-man favour.'

And I ask if he still works at Kinko's? I ask if he still makes fake IDs?

'Of course,' he types. 'How do you think I make money? You can't make a living from being a corporate wage slave.'

So I ask if he could make some fake passports.

Halfling types, 'Easily.' Bigsmileyface.

He types, 'But you'll need to keep them in a passport holder. I can make them look like real ones, but they won't feel exactly real if you touch them. The card stock won't be perfect. They won't have the digital chips inside them.'

I type, 'Will that be a problem? If we're going by bus?'

He types, 'Where?'

'Mexico.'

He types, 'I don't think so. Buses don't have airport-like security. NAFTA made sure of that.'

I want to type that I don't think NAFTA had anything to do with transportation, but I don't.

And then Halfling types, 'We?'

And I type, 'Yeah, I'll need two. Is that OK? I don't have money, but I can give you my passwords to all the Adult Empire sites.'

'That's fine,' he types. 'But I'd do it for free. Anything that shows them they don't have all the power.'

And I type, 'Thanks.' Smileyface.

'So who's "we"?' Halfling types.

'Just this person,' I type, not knowing how much I should say.

'OMFG!!!' he types. 'IT'S A GIRL ISN'T IT?!?!?!?!?!?'

And I don't type back.

'Where did you meet one?' he types.

'It's a long story,' I type.

'Is she hot? Does she do anal? What are breasts really like?'

'It's not really like that,' I type.

'PICS please,' Halfling types.

And I type, 'I don't have pictures. It's not like we sit around photographing ourselves.'

And Halfling types, 'No, I need them for the passports.'

And this is why Halfling is important. Before I IM'd him, I logged into the museum's private intranet and I copied the picture used on my museum badge. I send it to Halfling.

'And I need one for your friend. The GIRL,' he types.

I type, 'She doesn't like pictures.' I type, 'I need you to make up a photo for her.'

And he types '...'

'Do you think you could do that,' I type? 'If I tell you what she looks like?'

'... Yeah ... I can try,' he types. Slantedface.

So I tell Halfling what Epiphany looks like. I put it in terms of things he can understand. I say she's got this actress's eyes, this one's jaw, this one's ear. But I delete that last part before sending. No one has Epiphany's ear.

'Sounds hot,' Halfling says. 'I bet she's awesome.'

'She's actually quite a pain,' I type.

He types, 'I bet she smells good.'

I never noticed.

He types, 'It must be so great to have someone around.'

No, it's not.

He types, 'To have company.'

Not hers.

He types, 'I'd kill to have a little attention from a girl. To wonder where you are at night. To wonder what you're doing.'

Not this kind of attention. Not this kind of wondering.

'What's her name? For the passports?'

And I type, 'I don't want you to use my real name.'

Halfling says no problem, he'll use his dad's name for me.

'The other name? Hers?' he types.

Bitch. Devil. Satan. Plague. Scourge. Nightmare of nightmares. All appropriate names, but all would look suspicious on a passport.

And as I'm going through curses in my head for Epiphany, the door to the apartment opens and the devil herself comes in with an orange plastic bag. The crinkly ones you get at grocery stores. I'm on the couch typing; the laptop's lid is back to her. I'm watching the screen, watching her watching me, wondering what I'm typing, if I can be trusted.

'The other name?' Halfling types again.

I'm wondering what Epiphany has in the orange bag. If it's just another thing to threaten me with.

Onscreen, Halfling types, 'What's her name.'

She's just standing in the doorway looking at me.

Halfling types, 'HER NAME PLEASE.'

And looking at Epiphany, I type her name. Then I delete it before I press send, and I type, 'Fanny.'

And on the screen, Halfling types, 'Old-fashioned, but great. She must be awesome.'

And I'm looking at Epiphany, wondering if that orange plastic bag is to put over my head. To cut off my air supply.

'You don't know her,' I type. 'She's not that awesome.'

And Epiphany, just when I think she's going to accuse me of trying to do something funny, trying to fool her; just as I think she's going to say, 'Don't make me suffocate you,' she reaches into the orange crinkly bag and pulls out one of those convenience-store sandwiches. The kind in the little triangular plastic cartons. The kind with the processed, wafer-thin ham and cheese that was probably made in some big factory eight months ago.

And Epiphany, she says, 'I thought you looked hungry.'

She says, 'I brought you food.'

And onscreen, Halfling is typing, 'You're probably right, man. Girls are a pain. We're better off without them.'

Epiphany, she says, 'I didn't know which you might like, so I brought you two,' and pulls out a roast beef with mayo sandwich.

'She's probably a total bitch,' Halfling types.

Well, I guess she's not all bad…

Epiphany takes out a bottle. 'And I got you water.'

'A fucking nightmare,' Halfling types.

She can be nice.

'Stupid broads,' Halfling types.

'And I brought you a sweet. For dessert,' Epiphany says and takes a heavily processed piece of freeze-dried chocolate cake in plastic wrap out of her bag.

And suddenly I feel a little bad about imagining her face on the rat's body.

'The downfall of mankind will be because of a woman like her,' Halfling types.

'She can be sweet, actually,' I type. And once again, Halfling and I end up on the opposite sides of the conversation from where we began.

As I eat, Epiphany just sits in the corner. I don't ask how much she got for the watch.

'I've arranged our passports,' I say and then realise, just a little bit, that I've said that like I'm looking for her approval. 'He's going to meet us at the bus station tomorrow.'

'You're wanted now,' she says, like she's not the reason for it. 'Can we trust him?'

On the laptop's screen, message after message appears. Halfling's on a rant now.

'Communism works in theory,' he types.

'We're all the next Rodney King,' he types.

'9/11 was an inside job.'

'Yeah,' I say, 'we can trust him.' He's as nuts as she is.

12

Stockholm Syndrome

I've been watching the laptop's screensaver display liquid light patterns for a while now. The pattern's tendrils of colours fade from purple to yellow, to green, and then start all over again. I'm lying on the couch, shivering. Cold wind whistles through the windows. I check my watch for the time, then remember it's been sold.

After working out the details with Halfling I lay down to get some sleep. So did Epiphany. She's in the bedroom, sleeping like a baby, that's how much she knows she has me on a leash. Her personality, if you can call it that, it's maddening, but at least I know what she wants me for now.

But part of me thinks, is the passport everything she wants me for? And how could she have known I would know how to get passports anyway? And why attack Roland? Just to get the painting to blackmail me to get passports? It doesn't make sense. There's got to be more to it than that. There's also that thing she said about looking for me for twelve years. Twelve years ago I was in LA. What would a teenaged Epiphany want with a teenaged version of me?

Fuck it. I'll go crazy if I keep thinking about this. We'll get up tomorrow, take our little trip to Mexico and I'll get my videotape.

I try for another twenty minutes to sleep but can't. I sit up and poke my head over the couch. Through the hole in the wall I see Epiphany curled up on the mattress in the next room. How can she sleep here? The whole building rocks with every gust of wind, like it's about to tip over. Plus it's freezing. At least the glow of the laptop's screensaver gives the illusion of warmth. And watching the coloured tendrils of light, I suddenly know what I need to go to bed.

I creep off the couch. There's still nine minutes of power left on the laptop's battery. Between Halfling's paranoid rants he managed to send me a new fake of some red-headed actress I didn't recognise. Halfling said she'd just been cast as the next Bond girl. The fake is soft core – just the actress, topless – but it'll be enough.

I peer through the hole in the wall to make sure Epiphany is asleep. 'I'm leaving,' I say.

No response.

Standing in the glow of the laptop I spit into my hand and begin to masturbate, but I can't stay hard. It's so damn cold in here. Plus, I have no idea who this redhead is. I've never seen her in anything. I've never heard her give an interview. It's hard to imagine her as a real person when I've never seen her body move or heard her voice speak. I spit into my hand and try again anyway. But my dick is like an uncooked Oscar Meyer hot dog.

Then I hear a muffled sound and glance over my shoulder. I have an audience, but it's only a pigeon that's returned from a late-night flight. Just in case though, just to make sure, I walk over to the wall and look through the hole into Epiphany's room. She's still asleep. A real asleep too, not one of those fake ones where people hold their breath to convince you they're so still they must be sleeping.

Her chest rises and falls ever so slightly. Her cheeks puff in and out with each breath. Lying there asleep on the soiled, shredded mattress, she looks almost sweet. Almost normal. She's using her green hoodie as a pillow under her head. The way she's lying, her blue T-shirt, it's caught up and stretched tight over her chest, so tight it looks like it could have been painted to her body. And yes, this is the first time I've noticed she has nice tits, OK? Small but pert. Think Natalie Portman in *Garden State*. The rain scene.

And looking at Epiphany in the T-shirt pulled tight around her body, well I suddenly feel very warm ... down there. And I'm shocked to see just how hard I am. Seriously, I'm stiff like a Maglite. And I remember the warmth Epiphany's body gave off as she removed my watch, the way her fingers tickled my wrist. I had goose bumps on the back of my neck. And even though she was taking from me, it felt *so good* to be touched by a human being. And sure, she may be insane, but who here isn't?

And look, I swear I've never done this before, OK? *I swear.* But don't even try to tell me you wouldn't do the same thing under the right circumstances. You know *exactly* how it is.

So I stroke my erection while I watch Epiphany purring like a kitten on her mattress. I stroke remembering how it felt when her fingertips trickled along my skin. I stroke and imagine her hand stroking me. I imagine her mouth waiting open for me. And when I cum there's a tingling in my penis I've never felt before. My load shoots with such force and volume I'm amazed it hasn't punctured another hole in the wall. I'm amazed it hasn't brought down this whole shitty building. And as I catch my breath, as I zip my fly, I continue to watch Epiphany sleep. My eyes trace her matted raven hair from her pale ear to her little mouth; from her hips to her fingertips.

And I think – I think I'm falling in love.

It's just past dawn and I've slept like a fucking baby. For ten minutes I've been lying awake on the couch, watching her. Epiphany, she's been sitting on the windowsill, back towards me, her legs dangling out onto the fire escape. She's been there since I woke up. She's wearing her green hoodie, her head turned to the side, looking at a black cat that's perched next to her.

Even though she's ruined my life I can't help feeling butterflies in my stomach. It's like I'm in third grade again; liking the girl who sticks bubblegum on my seat. Though in this case the bubblegum is a ten-million-dollar painting.

They call this *Stockholm syndrome*. And to be fair, I was warned about this.

Sitcom resolution syndrome, psychotic depression, Stockholm

syndrome. I'll just add it to the list of things to resolve with my shrink the next time I see him.

And I think, maybe this Mexico thing won't be so bad after all? It's like what a real boyfriend and real girlfriend do in a real relationship. A road trip full of bonding. Who knows, maybe she'll fall in love with me? Maybe she'll be sorry for everything she's done and want to have kids and stay in Mexico where we can live happily ever after.

And watching Epiphany sitting on the windowsill, I'm thinking of something to say, just so she'll acknowledge me.

Howdy?

No, too Western.

Beautiful day?

Too lame.

Top 'o the morning to ya?

Too Irish.

And as I've settled on 'Hi,' Epiphany's lips move. Her words are so soft I can't hear them. Then she pauses, looks at the cat, and strokes it again.

'Sorry? I didn't hear what you said,' I say from the couch. But she doesn't hear me. Then her lips move again and, again, silent words follow.

I clear my throat. 'What's that?' I say, louder. But Epiphany continues to speak silently while stroking the cat.

And it's quite big, the cat is. Larger than any cat I've ever seen. Its yellow eyes scowl at me when it catches me staring. And for a second I'm jealous. I want to be stroked by Epiphany.

'Epiphany?' I say, rather loudly this time, sitting up on the couch. 'Are you talking to the cat?'

The cat seems to take offence to this and jumps from the windowsill to the fire escape where it circles once before finding the stairs and disappearing.

It's only when the cat leaves that Epiphany seems to notice I'm in the room. She spins around on the windowsill and swings her legs back inside.

'The bus leaves in a few hours,' she says. 'We should go soon.'

And my heart flutters a little bit. She's talking to *me*.

'Hi,' I say.

No! Stupid! That was before.

I must look like a fucking idiot now.

So I say, 'Who were you talking to? Were you, were you ... talking to that cat?'

Epiphany, she finds this funny, and indeed, it's the first time I've seen her smile. Her smile – it's uncomfortable. Not uncomfortable in a fake-smile way, but uncomfortable as if it's the first time she's tried it. Like it's a new movement to her. And me, awkwardly I smile back, like I'm pleased I could make her smile. But my smile feels stupid, so I lose it.

'Don't be silly,' she says. 'Cats can't understand us.'

'Right,' I say. 'Cats *can't* understand us. So ... who were you talking to?'

Her smile breaks and she looks away.

'Listen,' I say, 'I'm going with you to Ensenada, right? So you need to start being open with me. Who were you talking to?'

She says nothing.

'And, I mean, what's in Mexico?'

Again, nothing.

'And, why Ensenada?'

And Epiphany says, '...'

And then, just as I think it's pointless asking anything else, Epiphany, she opens her mouth and actually speaks. And me, I stand in rapture, like I'm Moses on Mount Sinai listening to the voice of God.

And Epiphany sayeth: 'There is a person I need to find.'

That's it.

The end.

'And they're in Ensenada?' I say. It's like pulling teeth.

'I don't think so,' she says. 'But that's where I'll be told where to find them.'

'Told?' I say. 'Who's going to tell you?'

She doesn't answer.

'Is someone telling you to do all this?' I say.

Again, she's silent.

'Is someone *making* you do this?'

Nothing. Zilch. Nada.

So I try left field. 'The Van Gogh wasn't random, was it?' Epiphany stiffens. 'You said you've been looking for me for twelve years. Twelve years ago I was in LA. Twelve years ago Roland was in LA.' But something else was also in LA twelve years ago. 'Epiphany, do you know who owns the painting?'

And Epiphany, her mouth opens again. She says, 'A man called Matthew Mann.'

My heart skips a beat. 'Roland's old boss.'

Her face grows grim. 'He's much more than that.'

Is she a pissed-off actress? Did he reject her for a movie role?

'Is it Matthew Mann you're looking for?'

'If I find him,' she answers. I take that to mean 'yes'.

'And, if you do find him? What are you going to do?'

But I don't really want to hear the answer.

And Epiphany, she looks me right in the eyes. She says, 'I'm going to kill Matthew Mann.'

It's not what she says that unnerves me so much. I've told people I feel like killing someone lots of times. It's *how* she says it – totally matter-of-fact. No emotion, no anger, no rage. She said she's going to kill Matthew how most people say they're running out for some milk.

My throat tightens. 'Why?'

'Because she said I can.' And this Epiphany says like a little girl who's been told by a nanny that she's been a good girl and can have an extra cookie at snack time.

'She?' I say. 'Who? The person you were talking to just now?' Epiphany looks out the window, then back to me. 'Who? The cat? Who's told you you can kill Matthew Mann?'

And Epiphany, she crosses herself and says, 'God.'

13

Public Relations

Matthew Mann is the most powerful person in Hollywood.

Steven Spielberg, Tom Hanks, Harvey Weinstein – they can't hold a candle to him.

Matthew Mann produced four of the ten top-grossing films of all time – by the age of thirty-five. He started his own studio at the young age of forty. He's famed for turning nobodies into celebrity-gods you would just die to be like. He's created stars like Jordan Seabring, Timothy Edwards and Gwen Roberts. If you've seen any of the winning Oscar movies in the last five years, they've all been his. Last year, he produced three of the five Best Picture nominees.

He tops Bradshaw's list of philanthropists every year. Last year his charity gave over $100 million to fight disease and injustice across the world. He is a UN Goodwill Ambassador and has been invited to every Presidential Inauguration since Bush Senior. And in the last twenty years, he's never missed a Sunday Mass – not one. I know this, because until the day my dad died, Matthew and he were like brothers. They even looked like siblings.

My father came to Matthew's attention when he was a junior publicist at 20th Century Fox. At the time Matthew was directing *Revolution*, a historical epic about the American Revolution. Its stars were the dashing Robert Redstone and the sultry Vanessa Grey.

One of the best-kept secrets in Hollywood at the time was that America's sweetheart Vanessa Grey was a raving meth addict. She pounded the stuff down like it was water on the surface of the sun. Another well-kept secret was that, because she was a meth addict, she was losing her hair in chunks. She needed to wear wigs at all times.

One day overzealous paparazzi snuck into her trailer and photographed her *sans* wig. The next day the photo was in all the gossip papers in Hollywood.

Everyone at Fox was having an aneurism. *Revolution* had the largest budget of any movie in Hollywood history at the time. Audiences wouldn't show up on opening day – a mere three weeks away – to see an outed, balding meth addict playing America's first female hero. No one knew what to do. The papers said the film would be lucky to have an opening weekend of fifteen million. Vanessa Grey's career was all but finished and everyone in Hollywood blamed Matthew Mann for keeping Vanessa's condition under wraps.

It was my father who came up with the idea. He found a doctor who was willing to say Vanessa had cancer and had the doctor sell his story to the gossip papers. When the questions came flooding in, my father wrote a prepared statement for Matthew saying that Vanessa Grey had been diagnosed with leukaemia a year earlier, but had decided to fight it and not let it beat her or her career. He apologised for deceiving the public and her fans, but said he couldn't stay quiet any longer while this poor actress, who was bravely suffering so, was being libelled in the press with wild accusations of being a meth addict.

Next my father wrote a statement, which Fox released, saying their thoughts and prayers were with Miss Grey and that, because of her outstanding bravery, they would donate ten percent of every *Revolution* ticket sold to the American Cancer Society.

For the next three weeks the press regurgitated this story like the mindless drones they were, and by opening weekend *Revolution* had racked up the biggest premiere of any film in movie history. Matthew saw that my father had single-handedly saved, not only Vanessa Grey, but his film – and indeed, his entire career – as well. Soon afterwards my father went from being a junior publicist to the top public relations man on all of Matthew's films. And when Matthew formed Imagination Studios, he made my father head publicist.

Over the next ten years, Matthew and my father were practically inseparable. And, after Emma died, after my mom and dad stopped talking, it was Matthew who helped my father through his grief.

It was never really a secret that my dad blamed himself for Emma's cancer. He was a big believer in karma. He thought it was payback for using the leukaemia story to help market Vanessa Grey and save *Revolution*. But Matthew, he helped my dad see that karma didn't exist. He even got him started on the Bible to show him karma wasn't how God ran things. I don't think Dad ever really got into it, but it was because of Matthew's friendship that by the last year before his accident, Dad was starting to be his old, happy self again.

And after Dad's death Matthew and Roland had a falling out. Now I know why. He must have found out about Roland and my mom. That's why Roland left the studio. That's why Matthew stopped contacting my mom after my dad died. But Matthew, like a true Christian, he showed that everyone deserves a second chance. When Roland helped procure the Van Gogh he mentioned that Matthew had forgiven him for something. The painting was a sign of his forgiveness.

14

Road Trip

If there were ever a time that I wish Epiphany would start shoving tripod legs through people's eyes, this would be it. We've been on this damn bus for eight hours now. Epiphany is curled up, snug as a cat, sleeping in the window seat next to me. I'm cramped as can be. Buses aren't kind to people six feet tall. My knees are pressed into the hard back of the seat in front of me. Anytime the passenger shifts, my knee-caps want to burst. I wish I could get up and stretch but I'm afraid I'll be laughed at for what I'm wearing.

But then again, the people on this bus are the last ones who should be laughing at anybody. And really, out of all the buses in the world, Epiphany picked the worst one possible. The bus is full of guests headed for *The George Drudge Show* – the Jerry Springer of Southern California. The guests, they're all overweight, all entitled, and rarely stop screaming at each other.

'Yo brother's my baby-daddy and I'm gonna prove it to the world! Mmmhmm!'

'I'm gon' be so famous after this! I won't need you or yo' trailer home anymore!'

'Baby, I swear, your mom drugged me. *Twice*. Your sister, too. That's the *only* reason I slept with them. Please don't take the Chevy.'

What's worse is that two TVs hang from the ceiling down the middle of the aisle showing highlights, if you can call them that, of previous *George Drudge* shows.

This is television and real life blended together.

On the TV, a guest sits on the *George Drudge* couch. Below her a chyron reads: Chandice, Admits she eats her Kleenex.

A chyron reads: Rick, Says he doesn't trust Amy, that's why he watches her poop.

On the bus, someone shouts, 'I do dat, too!'

On the TV, a chyron reads: Selena, Admits she's obsessed with burping.

A chyron reads: Derek, Says he is proud to let friends piss in his mouth.

On the bus, someone hollers, 'You go boy!'

I don't know how Epiphany can sleep though all this. She's purring quietly, oblivious to everything. Her feet, covered in thick pink socks, rest against my thigh. Her white Converse shoes lie on the floor, each one facing the opposite direction to the other. She looks like a farmer's daughter with the dungarees and white T-shirt she's wearing. Her hair is bound in tight little knots that look like electrons surrounding the nucleus of her head.

And yes, all the clothes she's wearing were stolen – just like the painting and the computer and my life.

We were at the bus station on Holburn thirty minutes before departure. Horny Halfling was running late and Epiphany was getting nervous. She kept glancing around like a lost child, so much so that she was starting to attract attention.

'He'll be here,' I told her, a little surprised at how reassuring I was trying to sound. 'Why don't you go to the bathroom and wash up or something? Splash some water on your face, you'll feel better.' She gave me a hesitant look. 'I'm not going anywhere,' I said. And I wasn't. You know, the Stockholm and the videotape and all.

She went towards the bathroom, taking a round about way that brought her past the baggage drop. As the handler threw bags onto a trolley Epiphany snatched one without slowing. But suddenly she looked like she had another migraine and set the bag back down. Then her migraine seemed to pass as quickly as it came and she glanced at me, picked up a different bag and carried it off.

Then from behind me a voice said, 'Jerry?'

It was a curly-haired, red-headed kid. He couldn't have been older than seventeen. His face was covered in acne and his frame was so slim he had to have an eating disorder.

'It's me – Halfling.' His voice was squeaky.

'*You're* Horny Halfling?' I said. He blushed when I said his screen-name out loud. 'Sorry, it's just I wasn't expecting you to be so young.'

He brushed it off and glanced around.

Then a bit nervously I said, 'How'd you recognise me?'

'Um, your picture. The one you sent me for your passport?'

'Oh, right.'

'Yeah ... So, uh, where's this girl you're with?'

I nodded towards the bathroom.

'Oh, cool,' Halfling said, a geeky smile forming on his adolescent lips. 'It's hard to imagine that anyone who loves my work as much as you do would *know* a girl, you know?'

Hey.

'We're kinda short on time,' I said. 'Do you have them?'

Halfling looked on edge as he shuffled through his backpack. Epiphany had seen the morning's paper. I couldn't bring myself to look at it. She said a reward had been offered for information 'leading to my whereabouts'.

'I hope the passports didn't keep you up all night,' I said, wondering if someone as paranoid as him, if someone who seems to hate all authority as much as he does, would read mainstream news, and, if he did know I'm wanted, would he turn me in?

'Oh, hell no,' Halfling said, pulling out a Manila envelope. 'Work was dead. The passports were done and printed in a few hours. Spent the rest of the night looking at those sites you gave me. They're amazing. Haven't slept yet.'

The dark circles under his eyes; his tired expression; I wondered, *Was that how Donald saw me every day?*

Halfling is good. The passports look like the real deal. My museum badge photo fits perfectly. My passport reads 'Alan Jones'. But it's Epiphany's passport that shows why Halfling is considered the best of all the fakirs. He had to dummy her image from scratch, based solely on my description.

'Hers was harder than yours,' Halfling humbly said. The name on Epiphany's passport says 'Fanny Jones'. Her fake photo looks like a happier version of her. 'I used an image of Rachel McAdams from the 2002 *Perfect Pie* premiere for her eyes and forehead. The rest of her face is a mixture of Audrey Hepburn from *Roman Holiday* and Milla Jovovich from *The Fifth Element*.'

Halfling wasn't good at taking compliments and doubted his talent when I told him Epiphany's photo was spot on. He mumbled something of a thanks before saying, 'Remember, they'll both work fine as long as they aren't scanned and you keep them in their holders. The cardstock I used looks like an authentic passport cover, so a quick glance won't tip anyone off.'

'Well, I wish she wasn't in the bathroom,' I said, trying to sound as un-fugitive-like as a guy who's just collected fake passports can. 'You could have seen how well you did.'

Halfling fidgeted. 'Naw, it's cool,' he said. 'I don't like meeting people. I need to get going anyway.'

I shook his hand. It was like shaking a dead fish.

I followed behind him as he left to make sure I wasn't being set up. When I got outside, he hopped on an old bicycle and peddled away.

Back inside the bus terminal Epiphany came from the bathroom in her change of clothes and new hairdo, the stolen travel bag slung over her shoulder. Seeing her in fresh clothes made my soiled, three-day-old clothes even more uncomfortable.

'Couldn't steal anything for me?' I said. That's when she reached into her bag and took out a pair of purple ladies' sweatpants and a small yellow T-shirt with a picture of a blue My Little Pony on the front.

'I'm not wearing that.'

'Suit yourself,' she said, 'but I was told to bring it for you.'

By 'told to' she means God told her. When she explained at the apartment that God speaks to her, a smile didn't even break her lips. It's as if she thought what she was saying were the truest words ever spoken. She even said part of the reason she felt comfortable leaving me at the apartment when she went out to get the laptop and sell my watch was because she knew God would warn her if I tried to leave.

And there's a rule I have about dealing with people who think they talk to God – you don't. You just nod and smile. If someone believes they hear the voice of God, you're not going to argue them into seeing reason. This goes double for someone who's murdered a man.

So now I'm stuck on this bus and I'm wearing the My Little Pony T-shirt and the purple sweatpants. The pants only come down to my calves. When we boarded two sisters were arguing about who their father loved more – and they weren't talking paternal love. During the inevitable catfight their eighty-four-ounce Big Gulp spilled all over me. That's when Epiphany reached into the stolen bag and simply handed me the shirt and sweatpants. No 'I told you so'.

On the TV, a man dressed in a Cookie Monster outfit is sneaking up behind a guest. The chyron reads: Tina, Is about to confront her fear of *Sesame Street* for the first time.

A chyron reads: Jeff, Says he was once attacked by a dog who was the reincarnation of his ex-wife.

A chyron reads: Carla, Recently revealed she was born with two anuses.

Epiphany wheezes next to me. She looks so innocent lying there, sleeping. Her fake passport name makes her sound all squeaky clean – all old-fashioned. Fanny Jones.

Epiphany Jones.

Even though she's kidnapping me she's ... compelling. I've got all these questions about her. For starters, who would name their kid Epiphany? How can one girl be as hard as her? And there's something else I can't get out of my mind: if Epiphany is real and if I've never seen her before we met a few days ago, how come I dreamt about her all those years ago? How come I keep having that dream where she's in that silverware factory fighting off faceless attackers?

On the TV, a grown man is wearing a diaper. Below him a chyron reads: Edward, Wants a drama-free relationship.

I manage to doze off for a few hours. And yes, I dream of Epiphany. And yes, it is the same dream. When I wake it's past midnight and an interstate sign says we're in Oklahoma. All of the squabbling on the bus has stopped. Most of the people are asleep, but the TVs continue playing highlights on mute.

Epiphany's still purring away on the seat beside me, and when the bus hits a pothole her head bobs from side to side. She mumbles a little something as she presses her lips together.

What does someone like her dream about? Killing Matthew Mann?

I feel like I should warn him after everything he did to help Dad while Mom was busy fucking Roland. But how would I contact him? He's even more powerful now than when Dad worked for him. I'm sure his assistants get calls from people all the time saying, 'Yeah, I knew him. We're old friends. Can you put the most powerful person in Hollywood on the phone? He's gonna want to hear this pitch.' Besides, Epiphany may be able to get to someone like me, but Matthew has to be surrounded with some of the best bodyguards in the world. She'd never be able to get close to him.

On the seat next to me Epiphany's head continues to rock back and forth. Her beauty is almost evil. It's appealing like a Venus flytrap is. Even when she speaks her little tongue flicks quickly over her teeth, like she's the snake tempting you to sin.

But the thing is, right now, stuck on this bus together, I find it hard to take my eyes off those lips.

And maybe it's because of the time of night and the dim lights of the bus as it hums down the highway, but what happens next ... well, it's like I'm in a trance. My head bumps the window as I bend awkwardly over her. I inch my face towards hers until I feel her lower lip between mine. It's like a little, pink Gummy Worm. And in my head I see her in my dream, young and scared and crying, and I feel for her.

But as quickly as I bent down, I'm reversing back into my seated position, Epiphany's little blade against my Adam's apple showing me the way up.

'Never touch me,' her voice cracks. Her eyes are full of a controlled anger. 'Never again.'

'I'm sorry,' I say, blade pressed on my throat. 'I – I couldn't help myself.'

'You can always help yourself,' Epiphany breathes, keeping her eyes locked on mine. I'm too petrified to look away.

She withdraws the blade and turns to gaze at the blackness outside the window.

Me, I swallow and stare straight down the aisle.

And in the awkward silence, the *George Drudge* guests snore.

On the TV, a chyron reads: Marty, Says that time with the cat and Vaseline was a big misunderstanding.

A chyron reads: Leah, Says she found fingernails in her house that Gary can't explain.

A chyron reads: Patrick, Says his fear of corned beef is ruining his life.

And finally breaking the silence, Epiphany says, 'I know about your problem.'

Which one? I think.

'Not the seeing people problem,' she says. 'The other one.'

I hope she's talking about the Stockholm syndrome.

'The newspaper said you are a pornography addict.'

Oh, that one.

I'm too humiliated to speak. The woman blackmailing you, the one you just tried to kiss, shoots you down by holding a knife to your throat and then tells you she knows you love porn. Could this get any worse?

'I also know what you did looking over me last night.'

I squeeze my eyes tight. Every inch of my body goes beet red. I want to crawl into the crack between our seats and disappear forever. When that doesn't work, I look around for something to impale myself on.

'Hey, can I borrow that knife? You can pull it from my stomach when I've stopped breathing,' would be the logical thing to say. Instead, with my face buried in my hands, I squeeze out, 'I'm *so sorry–* '

'People never start with the intention of doing bad things, Jerry,' she interrupts. 'They start with small things, then it snowballs.'

Even with my eyes shut and my hands covering my face I can feel her looking at me. I bend forward, head buried into the seatback. Someone kill me.

'Before they know it, the bad things aren't bad at all; they're just normal. They're just life,' she's saying. I feel her green gaze burrowing a hole into the side of my head, but I can't bring myself to face her. 'Don't let your demons snowball, Jerry. We all still have a choice in what we do.'

15

Mexico

The ceiling ripples like the floor of an ocean. The sounds of my body hitting the tub echo under the surface. The madness is all above. But my peace is interrupted by a splash over my stomach. I break the surface, sucking a gulp of air, to find a soccer ball floating in the bathtub with me. I hop onto the bathroom's cracked, tiled floor and throw a towel around my waist. I spin the ball in the palm of my hand. Water sprays from it like one of those pinwheel sparklers you light on the Fourth of July.

A little voice shouts, '*Triste*, Jerry!' Ana Lucia is at the bathroom window. She's got a big grin that looks especially white because her face is covered in dust and sweat from playing in the street under the midday sun. I smile and hand her the ball. She says something I can't understand.

'No problem,' I say and watch Ana run towards the other kids as their game continues. I fill a little cup with water and swallow one of my 486s. In the mirror the cut on my neck from Epiphany's blade is nothing but a small pink line now. We've been in Ensenada for almost a week. The first thing we did when we got here was to buy clothes from a street market. The My Little Pony T-shirt I was wearing was attracting the wrong kind of stares from wrong-looking guys. Then we went to a store and stocked up on food. When Epiphany paid I saw that she must have gotten at least a thousand dollars for my father's watch. I asked if we should exchange it, but Epiphany said dollars go further here. Then she handed me fifty like it was pocket money.

It took her less than two hours to rent the place we're in. She found a guy, handed him some cash, and then we had it. It's not great, but it's a lot better than the shithole we were squatting in in Chicago. The roof is made of tin siding that makes a pleasant metallic sound when it rains. It's got a kitchen and bath and the bedroom has a bed and the living room has a few good-sized chairs where Epiphany usually curls up to sleep.

After what happened on the bus I didn't sleep for the remainder of the trip. I was so busy feeling humiliated that I didn't even worry about the passports when we came to the border. Turns out they were pretty much for nothing anyway. The customs officer that boarded our bus barely glanced at them. If you're white and American, Mexicans welcome you and your money with open arms.

When we arrived in Ensenada I asked for the videotape but Epiphany said I couldn't have it until she found whoever it is she's looking for here. I was too tired, still too ashamed to argue. When I woke the next morning she was gone. She didn't return until late that night. Since then, she's been in and out.

She doesn't seem as pressed for time here as she was in Chicago. And I don't see her much, which is a good thing. The horror of knowing she saw me masturbate to her still mortifies me. But really, she should have taken it as a compliment. No one masturbates to ugly chicks. If someone's masturbating to you it's like you've won a beauty contest.

At first I was sure Epiphany was avoiding me because of what happened, but then I began noticing how rough she looked when she came home – one time it even looked like she'd been attacked. Her clothes were covered in dirt and her arm had a long, bleeding scratch running the length of it. I asked her about it, but she waved me off saying she needed sleep. That night I heard her cry.

Maybe a saner person would keep pressing her, but I can't risk her getting angry and destroying the videotape – wherever it is. I already fucked up over the masturbation thing and I'm pretty sure Epiphany doesn't have a three-strikes-and-you're-out rule. It's gotta be two, at most. And after that she probably kills you.

Besides, I'm feeling better than I have in a long time. I know that's a weird thing to say considering my situation, but it's from being in a place where you can't read or speak the language. You feel better about yourself. It's because when you walk down the street you can't understand what anything says. The advertisements that tell you you're ugly because you don't use *this* whitening toothpaste or you're unlovable because you don't drive *that* kind of car can't penetrate your mind. The horror stories on the news mean nothing to you. With no TV or internet you spend your time thinking, walking, discovering. And cleaning. Cleaning has become a substitute hobby for me. It's therapeutic. When I'm scrubbing an oven, my mind is focused. When I'm scrubbing an oven, I manage to avoid thinking about my mom and Roland and being a wanted murderer.

And it's not that she's gotten any nicer, for the most part she ignores me (when I ask where she's going, her answer is always, *'Out'*), but being with Epiphany – with a real live person – has made me feel like I almost have a normal relationship. Almost.

Last night – I don't know, maybe I was coming on *too* strong. Maybe I was trying to be too nice because I wanted to show her I wasn't really a sicko who jerks off to people while they sleep. I told her she looked like she'd lost weight. Girls like to hear that, right? And that wasn't the Stockholm syndrome talking. She does look thinner, she needs to slow down and take time to eat. So I offered to cook dinner.

'What do you think?'

'I need to go out,' she said, throwing on her hoodie.

'Well, I'll have dinner waiting when you get home,' I said as the door closed behind her. In hindsight I probably sounded too desperate.

I spent the evening chopping vegetables, cooking pasta, grating cheese. I was excited at the prospect of having dinner with another person. The food was cooked; I set the table and waited.

And waited.

It was almost four this morning when she returned. She didn't even say anything; she just curled up on a chair in the living room and went to sleep.

There's a light rapping sound. 'Adios, Jerry!' Ana Lucia screeches when I open the screen door. She always makes sure to say goodbye after the game ends. This all started a few days ago when the soccer ball came through the bathroom window the first time. I was annoyed when she sheepishly came to retrieve it. The first thing I said was, 'I don't have a clue what you're saying, kid.' But when she smiled it reminded me of Emma's smile. Then she pointed to herself and said 'Ana Lucia' and then pointed to me and I said, 'What?'

Then she pointed at me again and I said, 'Oh. Jerry.'

'Adios, Jerry!' she says again as she turns to go, but I shout after her. 'Ana, wait!' And I grab a large chopping knife and split an apple in two.

'You need to keep your strength up after such a long game,' I find myself saying, handing her the halves of the apple. And the thing she does next just destroys me. She runs up to me and wraps her arms around my waist and hugs me as hard as she can.

But when I look down and pat her head, I see Emma. Emma's hugging me. She's nine years old and from the way she looks I can tell she has the cancer. Her thin, pale arms wrap around my waist and her big brown eyes meet mine. My eyes sting as I hold my dead sister again. I'm so sorry, Emma.

Emma, she releases me and runs out the door. The absence of her body leaves me feeling cold. Always cold. When she's halfway up the street, she shouts, 'Bye, Jerry!' and then smiles and runs. I want to tell Emma not to go. To tell her I'm lost without her; that I'm not a real person anymore. But when I wipe my tears away and open my eyes again, it's Ana Lucia I see trailing after her friends.

16

The Clone

Before I left I tried focusing on cleaning the oven, but with each scrub Emma burned more and more into my mind. It felt like I was suffocating. I needed endorphins. So I substituted the scrubbing with rubbing. I tried to focus on Sarah Michelle Gellar, Christina Aguilera, Jordan Seabring, but I couldn't hold their images in my mind. I gave up and decided to go for a walk. I ended up at this bar for a drink to calm myself. It's a shithole, but the sign on the window said, 'ENGLISH SPOKEN HERE'.

The Mexican bartender is speaking to some Australians. They're talking about a girls' orphanage here in town that burned down the other night.

'It is the talk of the city,' the bartender says, as the drunk Australians nod in sympathy. 'Over thirty girls lost their home. None were killed, thank the Lord Jesus Christ, but now they will have to be separated and sent to orphanages in other cities. No one place has the room to take all of them. It is like they are losing their families again. It is a tragedy.'

'Oi, right!' one of the drunk Australians says. 'A tragedy!'

I swirl the rum in my glass. It's a trip to Disneyland compared to my life.

Above the bar a TV plays an American station. A reality show is on. *Keeping Up with the whoever*. It's the first English-language show I've seen since the bus.

The thing about American television shows is that most of them are designed to be aspirational programming. That's a term coined by Hollywood in the 1980s. Aspirational programs are shows that dangle a carrot in front of the audience. They show us things we aspire to have one day: beautiful friends, money, cars, exciting jobs, exotic trips.

Think: *Gossip Girl.*

Think: *Sex in the City.*

Think: any stupid reality show about rich, beautiful people who are famous for doing nothing.

The reason aspirational programming is so popular is because viewers actually believe that one day they too will live lives just as exciting, sexy, loving, or rich as those of the characters on their television screens. It's just how we're wired; the desire that overrides reason.

But aspirational programming has a side-effect. The older you get, the more you watch, the more you realise that, no, your shitty life will never be as good as the people you are watching. It's constant, new dissatisfaction. This realisation eventually leads to depression because those aspirational shows you see, they aren't showing you what you could have, they're showing you what you'll never have.

And if you're me, seeing a show like this for the first time in weeks – after thinking about your dead sister, after getting shot down by the woman who's destroyed your life, and after losing your family and your job – well, it's an eye-opener to how silly you've been acting since a crazy lady kidnapped you, Stockholm syndrome or not.

It reminds you of everything you've lost.

And it makes you angry.

I've been such a fool pretending my situation has somehow improved in this little shitty town. I have forty dollars to my name. (Less. The drink cost me three.) I've been blackmailed. I have no home. No job. No proof of anything. Even the passport in my pocket is fake.

But what in my life isn't? Donald told the detectives that everyone at the museum knows I made up my girlfriends. On the surface they all pretended to be my friends, but behind my back they laughed. And maybe I did lie about Harriett, but they don't know what I've been through. And Mom, that look on her face – the shock and disappointment; the *disgust* – when she thought I killed Roland. The way she exiled me from her house, in an instant! Did she ever love me at all?

I'm pathetic; cleaning house, trying to win Epiphany's approval. Who gives a fuck if I jerked off to her? Who cares if it *disturbs* her? After all she's done, she deserves much worse.

The thing about anger: it gives you the clarity to examine your situation in new light; to look at things from a new, hyperaware perspective.

And maybe, just maybe, it gives you the drive to do something about it.

I'm surprised to find Epiphany home when I return. She's sitting at the little kitchen table with her hands folded. Her head is tilted and her lips are slowly moving.

You faker.

Her lips stop and she makes the sign of the cross.

You Joan of Arc wannabe.

'Talking to God?' I say.

'Praying,' she says, glancing at me before getting up and walking past me.

'PAY ATTENTION TO ME!' I scream. Epiphany's so startled she almost trips over her feet. Blood thunders in my head. She turns to face me and it's the first time I've ever seen shock on her face. 'I want the fucking tape and I want out.' My voice cracks and every part of my body shudders like I'm a cornered animal.

'Soon,' she says.

'Soon, bullshit!' I tremble. 'It's been a week. What the fuck are we doing here? I sit around doing dick all day while you're out doing God knows what.' My heart feels like it's vibrating. 'Where the fuck do you go? What the hell are you doing? Are you working the streets? *Epiphany*? Is that your fucking hooker's name?'

Her face goes cross. 'I don't like it when you swear, Jerry.'

And I literally spit on her. I spit on her and she recoils as it lands below her eye. 'Tough fucking shit, baby. I don't like it when you kill my fucking friends and frame me for their fucking murder,' I yell. 'So fuck what you don't like, fuck your voices, and fuck your God too.'

Before I know it I'm staggering backwards from the force of her slap. A slap! Like we're in a black-and-white gangster movie from the thirties! She presses me against the wall and slaps me again. 'Get the fuck off me, you crazy whore,' I shout as she raises her hand again, and I push hard and she's knocked against the kitchen counter.

Epiphany lets out a cry and brings her hand to her face. Behind her, the knife I used to slice Ana Lucia's apple has blood on it.

I take a deep breath. 'I didn't mean for that to happen,' I say.

Epiphany, she sucks the meaty part of her palm, looks at it, and then sucks it some more.

I say, 'Are you OK?'

'Fine,' she says and heads for the door without looking back.

'Wait, come on. I didn't mean for that to happen,' I say. 'Come on, where are you going?'

'To Momma's,' she says and slams the door.

Momma's?

Is that where she's been going all this time? Did she bring me all this way for a family reunion? The thought that Epiphany even has parents seems alien. It's easier to believe that she just hatched from an egg in a mental institution somewhere.

In the sink I wash her blood from the knife. Thoughts cloud my mind. That's when it hits me: who else could she have mailed it to? Her mom has the videotape.

I bolt out the door, hoping I'm not too late. I run south, glancing down all the little side streets. I catch Epiphany making a left on to a busy avenue a hundred feet in front of me. I sprint to catch up with her but pause when I reach the intersection. I can't let her see me. I only need to find where her mom lives. When Epiphany returns and goes to bed tonight, I'll sneak out and break into her mom's house. I'll get the tape and be done with all this.

Epiphany walks past a fruit-and-vegetable stand, where she catches a well-built man's attention. He's a good six inches taller than anyone else on the street. He wears a black leather jacket and has thick, dark hair and olive skin. He eyes Epiphany's hips as she passes.

And I think: *Trust me. She's not worth it.*

Epiphany turns around and the man in the leather jacket turns away. He grabs a tomato and squeezes it, hoping he hasn't been caught staring. She glances in my direction then abruptly turns down a side street. But as I pick up my pace my foot lands on something slippery in front of the produce stand and I skid into someone before crashing to the ground.

'Whoa! Slow down, friend,' a man says in an Italian accent. It's the guy who was checking out Epiphany's ass. He offers me his hand, which I take, after peeling a flattened tomato from the sole of my shoe.

'Really sorry,' I say as he helps me up.

'No problem,' he smiles. 'Just be careful, OK? Don't want to get hurt.'

The Italian notices that I keep glancing towards the street that Epiphany's turned down. The last thing I need is a guy thinking that busting a girl's stalker is his in with her. 'Sorry again,' I say as I start shuffling away. 'Late for a – late for work.'

I dart around the corner. There aren't many places to hide. All the shops' doors are shuttered. There are no alleys she could have ducked down. I jog to the end of the street where it crosses another even smaller street. Twenty more minutes of turning down countless streets and alleyways and it's become dark. I'm completely lost.

I've obviously gone from the bad part of town to the worst. Junkies are slumped in the shadows of alleys. Drunken men ramble incoherently. I'm relieved when I recognise a small bar on the corner. It looks like the one I was at earlier, but when I pass it it's not the same. On the next street a man in a doorway says something.

'Sorry,' I say, 'I don't speak Spanish.'

'Looking for woman?' he asks in broken English.

'Umm, yeah,' I say. 'She's pale, about five-six, black hair.'

'Good, good!' The man walks towards me and laughs. He slaps me on the back and shouts, 'I have blue! Katia!'

From the doorway the man was standing in a woman appears. She wears a yellow T-shirt and little green panties. Her hair is bright blue – a really bad dye job. She's all smiles.

'That's not her,' I say.

'For you: three hundred fifty pesos. Twenty minutes.' The man smiles. The girl bites her lower lip seductively. I gaze down the street. There are men in almost every doorway and girls in almost every window. The blue-haired girl's eyes sparkle as she glances towards my crotch.

'Sorry, wrong girl,' I say.

'Two-fifty pesos!' the man shouts as I walk away.

I continue down the street, carefully avoiding the men who roam like zombies, silently moving from one window to the next, trying to decide what girl to taste. A man on the corner mumbles, *'Coke? Guns? What you need?'* and I wonder where I am in relation to the apartment.

That's when I notice her.

Behind a plate-glass window is a virtual lookalike of Natalie Portman. Her face, her eyes, even the width of her shoulders – she's an exact match. I had this six-month stretch where I would only jerk off to images of Portman. This was before I knew who Jordan Seabring was. I had well over a thousand Portman fakes on my computer in every conceivable style and position: missionary, doggy, drill, bondage, rape, you name it. She just did it for me.

A large black man approaches me. He's shirtless and looks like he could give the Incredible Hulk a beating. 'Beauty, isn't she?' he says in a Jamaican accent. The Portman clone licks her lips. 'Rough day?' the Jamaican says sympathetically. 'Come in an' release that stress.'

The clone, she's wearing white sparkly boots and a short, pink latex skirt that she's slowly sliding her fingers into. Her dark nipples show through her thin, white top. She fucks me with her eyes.

'For you,' the Jamaican says, just like we're old buddies, 'two hundred pesos for the lay. One hundred pesos each for anything more *adventurous.'*

The clone, she pinches her nipples. 'I only have dollars,' I find myself saying.

I'm taken down a long, dimly lit corridor. At the end there's a crack of light spilling from the gap under the door where the clone entered to 'get ready'.

The Jamaican lays down some ground rules. 'Remember, twenty dollars for anything beyond a fuck. She'll tell me what you did, so don't lie to me.' His muscles ripple. 'I don't like liars.'

Salesmen are never as nice after you hand over the cash.

'When you're done, you leave this door.' His red, cracked eyes glare. 'You come back down the hallway an' go out the front where we came in. It's the only way out. She'll tell me whatever extra you owe me. If you fuck without a rubber, it's an extra twenty-five no matter what.'

Inside the girl is waiting. I glance at her before turning around to close the door. Taking a deep breath I turn back and give my best friendly smile. The Natalie Portman clone, she sits on a bed. It's small. A single. The sheets are stained brown and red in some places. I tell myself that's just the design.

'Hi, I'm Jerry,' I say, like we're on a blind date. She doesn't reply.

The clone starts removing her boots. I don't know if it's normal to stare, so just in case I pretend to find the room really interesting. There's a small sink in the corner with a dirty bar of soap. At the end of the bed there's a nightstand with a bowl of condoms sitting next to a little, pink lamp. On the mantel above a walled-up fireplace are various trinkets: bracelets, perfume, eyeliner, blush, panties, handcuffs, a dildo. The mirror has vertical lines drawn in lipstick. They're grouped into fives. The count reads thirty-two. The window is covered in black paint with bars on the inside.

The clone gets off the bed and walks towards me like she's about to take my order at McDonald's. She's lost that come-hither look that she displayed in front of her pimp, too. Now she's more like a robot. She moves, but there's no life. She rolls her hands. She wants my order.

'Uhh, I don't know. I'm new to this. What do you recommend?'

'The Big Mac is popular,' I expect her to say.

'English no,' the clone says and rolls her hands again. She takes her top off and presses her small tits together. And at this moment, something bugs me. She crawls back onto the bed and kneels. She brings her fist up to her mouth and mimics giving a blowjob. 'Like?' she says.

I don't know what to say. I feel like I'm thirteen.

As she moves around on the bed, going from spooning to missionary to cowgirl, I glance a burn on her calf, a heavily bruised inner thigh, a deep scratch on her back. I shake my head at all the positions, not because I don't want to do them, but because I wouldn't know what to do.

And, OK, look, busted. I've never actually had sex before. Not with a real person, anyway. I'm a virgin. I've never even dated anyone. My relationship with 'Rachel' and my hand are as far as I've gone. Judge me, laugh at me. Everyone else would. But, you know what? I've fucked hundreds of stars. Virtually anyway. I'm a master at what I do. I've taken masturbation to a level most could only dream of. The way I do it, it's practically a religion. And truthfully, I pity you a little. I do. I fucked Judy Garland a few weeks ago. She looked just as off-to-see-the-wizard as ever and she's been dead for forty years. How's the wife holding up?

In the room the clone keeps mimicking positions: piledriver, T-square, rimming, and I keep shaking my head. She interprets my headshakes as disappointment – as ever-increasing perversity. She gets off the bed and walks towards me, her little tits wobbling with each step. And something bothers me again. I don't know why, but it's her tits.

She glances into my eyes before turning her back towards me. Then, bending over the bed, she flips her pink skirt up and takes her left hand and spreads her ass apart. With her index finger, she points to her anus. And that's when I find myself nodding 'yes'. And that's when she doesn't look like a robot anymore. She shows emotion again. Not the come-hither seduction she displayed earlier, though. This time it's something – something that's not quite sadness. It's not even despair. It's the realisation that this is your life and you can't change it.

Kneeling over the bed the clone presses her face into the stained mattress and spreads her ass apart with both hands. And just for the record: I don't have an anal fixation. I don't. It's just your first time has to be way less embarrassing when your partner is looking the other way. You don't have to worry about any goofy virgin looks on your face.

Her body stiffens slightly as I unzip my pants. And even though I can't see them, in the back of my mind, there's still something that bothers me about her tits. Her small tits. I pull down my boxers and awkwardly kneel on the floor behind her. I'm harder than I've been in my life. Much harder than I am when I'm jerking off – even when it was to Epiphany.

The heat of her crotch flows over my balls as my dick pulsates an inch from her asshole. The Portman clone breathes shallowly. Will this hurt her? Do I care? And in my head I picture Natalie Portman in *Star Wars*. In *Where the Heart Is*. But this clone really reminds me of the way Natalie looked in *Beautiful Girls*. It was only her second film. Even back then, she showed such great range and she was ... only thirteen.

All her eyeliner. The blush on her face. Can makeup really make a girl look that much older?

No. No way. All the nights I lay awake fantasizing about fucking Natalie. This is as close as I'll ever get. How do I know she's really underage anyway? What is 'underage' in Mexico?

Fuck it. I grab her hips and the tip of my cock gently brushes against her anus. The side of her face not pressed into the mattress refuses to look at me. The heat from her is so inviting.

I can't believe I'm about to fuck Natalie Portman.

Her face tightens as my tip prods her opening. The mascara constricts around her eye.

That damn makeup.

'How old are you?' I say, still gripping her hips.

But she only replies with a broken 'please' and spreads her ass farther apart.

I shake my head. I asked. I did my due diligence. And the clone, she braces as I push against her anus. And a voice in my head says, *Don't let your demons snowball.*

I pause just for a moment before a loud crack suddenly breaks the seclusion of the room. I jerk backwards as the doorframe splinters. The Jamaican's muscles flex as he hurls me into the hall. 'You try to steal from me?' he shouts. A knife is snug in the waistband of his jeans. Behind him, in the room, the girl has scampered to the corner of the bed. She wears a look like she's the one being attacked. 'You steal from me?!' the Jamaican shouts again. The veins in his neck look like worms.

'What are you talking about?' I yell, scrambling to pull my boxers up.

'No one steals from me,' he rages and grabs the knife from his waist. The clone shrieks.

And this is when I discover just how fast I can run. I'm at the other end of the hallway before I know it. I turn the handle, but the front door doesn't move. I push and bang against it as the Jamaican barrels towards me, but it refuses to budge. And as I'm wondering how much it will hurt to be the Hulk's voodoo doll, I *pull* on the door and it opens, but my body jolts and my eyes go wide when I find Epiphany standing on the other side. She looks at me like she's not at all surprised to see me. Like we had split up to shop for groceries and now we're meeting in the cereal aisle.

I open my mouth but for the briefest moment nothing comes out.

Then I swallow and my voice is able to scream a single word. '*Run!*'

But instead of running, Epiphany, she puts her hand against my chest to stop me from leaving. And before I can push her away, before I can say anything, I feel the big hand of the Jamaican on my shoulder and the searing pain from his blade as it sinks between my ribs.

17

Names

I'm lying in an MRI machine. There's an identical one next to mine. The other MRI clicks and hums as its big magnets gyrate around its insides. As its sequence completes, the flat table in the centre of the machine slowly slides out.

The patient has a pointy snout. His head is flat and grey. A bullet hole oozing watery blood sinks between his big black eyes. Jagged teeth jut from his mouth; they're large, even for a shark. The MRI bed stops expelling the patient just beyond its dorsal fin.

'What is this?' I say. 'Where are the doctors?'

'Relax,' the shark answers. 'You were stabbed.'

'I know this place.'

'It's where the doctors first discovered her cancer,' the shark says, wiggling his head a little in my direction. The bullet hole goes deep. Salt water and blood mix inside it and flow like wine. 'I'd kill for a piece of cotton to plug this up. Maybe a cork.'

'You're the shark that attacked that Timmy kid.'

'I didn't attack anyone. It was simply dinner time.' His lifeless eyes make it hard to tell if he's looking at me.

'Is this a dream?'

'Of course it is,' answers the talking shark.

The room is so clean, so sterile. It gives the impression that nothing hostile can live in it; that what the doctors in the white coats find here, they can kill here.

'I miss her.'

'Let her go, Jerry. Live your life.' The magnets in his MRI kick on again. Slowly, the shark is drawn back in. 'I gotta go,' he says. 'More tests to be run.'

'Wait–'

'Can't,' says the shark. 'I don't have insurance and they charge by the minute.'

'But what does all this mean?'

'Sometimes a dream is just a dream, Jerry. It doesn't have to mean anything.' Then, as the MRI machine grows louder, the shark mouths something to me.

'What did you say?' I yell. 'I can't hear you.' And over all the noise, I think the shark says, *'Go find her.'*

My eyes open as I hear *'Go find her'* repeated. It's dark. I'm in bed at our place in Ensenada. Through the doorway a large, dark-skinned woman with faded red hair speaks to Epiphany. Epiphany, she glances at me and slips on a black backpack. Then I hear something I never thought I would come from her mouth. She says 'thank you' to the woman with red hair before glancing at me once more. And then she walks out the front door.

The redhead comes over and sits besides me on the bed. She feels my forehead. Her hand is knobby like the root of a sequoia. 'Take these,' she says and hands me two small pills.

'What are they?'

'You were stabbed,' she says. 'It's nothing serious. It's not too deep. But you have a fever. The wound is infected.'

I put the pills in my mouth and reach for the glass of water on the nightstand. A pain sears through my back. I reach around and feel bandages. The redhead brings the water to my mouth.

'It feels worse than it is. The wound has been cleaned. The pain will be less tomorrow, and less the day after that. Take your medicine.'

I swallow. 'Who are you?'

She doesn't answer until she's set the glass back on the table. 'Your friend calls me Momma. To most people I'm just LaRouche.'

'You're her mother?' A slight smile reveals a silver tooth. 'Where's she gone?'

'She had to take care of a few things,' the woman says, putting her hand on my shoulder, making me lie back.

'How'd I get back here?'

'We brought you. The both of us.'

'She trapped me,' I say as the memory of what happened returns. 'She fucking set me up.' Another shot of pain races through my back.

'Easy,' the redhead says. 'She didn't set you up. You were silly to try to follow her. She's been on this quest of hers for far too long. Someone like you couldn't track her without her knowing. Besides,' she eyes me, 'she didn't make you go to that pimp.'

I'm about to say, *'But I didn't intend to,'* then realise how stupid that sounds.

'She knew you were following her, so she doubled back and started following you. When she saw you enter the sex house, she waited until the pimp came back out. She led him to believe she was a prostitute and told him that you always skip out before paying for the extras.'

'What the hell is wrong with her?' I say. 'I could have been killed!'

'She only wanted to scare you. She didn't know the man had a knife,' the redhead says. She hands me the glass again and tells me to drink. 'Things went further than she would have liked.'

'Further than she liked? I got fucking *stabbed*,' I grit, 'because *she* blocked my way out.'

'Like I said, she thought you would only be beat. She wanted to teach you a lesson.'

Only be beat? Is this lady for real? A jolt of pain jumps through to my ribcage. I shift in the bed to take weight off my wound. 'Well, I know Epiphany pretty well,' I say. 'And I don't think someone like her should be teaching anyone anything.'

'Please,' the woman recoils, 'please don't call her that. It is a horrible name given to her by a horrible person.'

'What am I supposed to call her?'

'Hanna,' she says, 'Her name is Hanna.'

18

The Education of Epiphany Jones

'Hanna was brought to Ensenada when she was just eleven. It was my job to prepare and educate her. Her preparation was daily beatings. Her education: sexual brutalisation.'

That's how the origin of Epiphany Jones begins. LaRouche and I are walking along the port where cruise ships dock from places like LA and San Francisco. Once you get away from the shithole of a neighbourhood we're staying in, Ensenada isn't a bad-looking place. It's got palm trees, the Pacific Ocean – the whole nine yards. We watch the fat, white American tourists disembark, cameras around their necks, smiling. Not a care in the world.

My wound was inflamed when I woke this morning. LaRouche insisted I stay in bed, but I needed to get out. Epiphany hadn't returned and LaRouche, whether to keep an eye on me or to distract herself from worry over Epiphany's whereabouts, insisted on joining me.

'I was the mother at a local house not far from here,' LaRouche says, gazing over the Pacific. The sun is bright and the day is a far cry from the cold spring of Chicago. Every time she's in direct sunlight, her silver tooth twinkles just like the silver cross around her neck does when the sun hits it. 'If you want to break young girls, you first need them to trust you. The night they arrived I treated them to a homemade dinner and a movie on the television. I even tucked them into bed.' Her face grows sombre. 'But the next day you start with the verbal abuse – then the physical. By the time you brought the first man and locked them in the room together, they're already a fraction of their former selves. By the time you've brought them their ninth or tenth, they no longer exist as you or I do. They're just a shell.'

The wrinkles on LaRouche's face are set deep; too deep for her age. She can't be more than fifty. In the bright sun her red hair is a translucent orange around the edges.

'I don't understand,' I say. 'Epiphany's a hooker?'

'Prostitutes have a choice,' LaRouche says, 'slaves do not.'

'You're telling me someone abducted an eleven-year-old girl, brought her to Mexico, and forced her to have sex with people?' I say. 'No way. Wouldn't happen. It'd be all over the news.'

'Don't be so naive. Girls are abducted every day all over the world, Jerry. They're abducted for the sole purpose of being turned into a product – a marketable commodity like sugar or gold. Just because no one's reporting it, doesn't mean it isn't happening. The girl you went to last night: was she chained to her bed? You think she did that herself?'

'She wasn't chained,' I almost say. Then I remember the bars on the window. They were on the inside, as if they were meant to keep people in, not out. 'If Epiphany was brought here, where's she from?' I can tell LaRouche still doesn't like me using that name, but after all the bad shit Epiphany's done to me, calling her by a normal name would be like Batman calling the Joker 'Marty'.

'Russia, like most of the girls that were under my care.'

Care is a rather generous use of the term here.

'You're Russian too?'

LaRouche nods and knows I must be about to ask, because she says, 'My nickname was given to me by one of the girls. A girl from St Petersburg who spoke French.'

'But what's a Russian doing in Mexico?'

'I was trafficked, just like Hanna, when I was a young girl. My cousin sold me to a man in Omsk for fifty roubles. I was resold in Italy and again in Portugal. By the time I reached Mexico, I was worth a thousand times what my cousin sold me for.' LaRouche rubs her large knuckles before continuing. 'The work took its toll on my body. When I no longer made the traffickers money, I had only two choices: be left for dead on the streets, or become a madam.'

'But why didn't you just go to the cops?'

A glint of light reflects off her tooth when she laughs, like it's the most ridiculous question she's ever heard. 'This entire town is run by traffickers. Their connections cover Mexico, Europe, Russia, the States. And they aren't even the largest ring out there. You didn't go to the police because they were your clients, too. They received money and free use of the girls. They weren't going to stop anything. None of this would be possible if the right people didn't look the other way.'

LaRouche explains how the girls who aren't outright abducted are tricked into boarding a plane. They're promised jobs as nannies or waitresses in the States. The beautiful ones are led to believe a model or actress scout has 'discovered' them. They're promised a better life. An American life with a TV in every room and two cars in every garage.

She tells me how the exceptionally pretty ones aren't raped during their 'education'. They're saved and their virginity is sold for a hundred thousand or two hundred thousand dollars to rich US businessmen. She explains how the houses here, where the girls are kept, are just midway points before they're brought into the US where they'll fetch the most money.

The walk is making me tired and my wound is beginning to flare. I need to sit. The bar we stop at is this dingy underground thing. It's packed despite being the middle of the day, and when we enter everyone inside looks at each other like they're protecting a secret of something shocking that happened fifteen years ago. We order a few beers and some nachos from the bartender then find a seat near the door.

'Once we caught a girl who had fled from the man who purchased her. As punishment one of the runners at the time, a particularly cruel Italian named Nico, burnt her face with an iron. That night as I covered the wound with makeup, she told me about the man she escaped from. He was an American oil executive living in Mexico City. To everyone else she was his live-in maid, but every morning, after his wife went to work and his children left for school, he would enter her bedroom and bind her arms with padded rope so she wouldn't bruise. Then he would read her passages from the Bible before he raped her. He said she should be proud. She was saving his young daughters from his ungodly desires. As time went on, he invited his friends to join in. One day, a friend brought a large dog with him. They forced her to do the most humiliating things, Jerry. She was only fifteen.'

LaRouche's face is stoic. She fiddles with the silver cross on her neck.

'The next day Nico put the girl on the street again. But because of her burned face she only had one customer. Nico was furious. That night he assembled all the girls in the basement. He made the scarred girl bite the edge of a concrete stair. Then he kicked the back of her head. Her teeth went everywhere. I'd never heard someone scream like that before.'

I feel my teeth with my tongue and my stomach is suddenly sick. I look away from LaRouche, as if doing so will wipe the girl's image from my mind.

'Nico wasn't finished,' she says, meaning neither is she. 'He dragged the girl to the middle of the room and held her up by the hair. She was wailing so loudly. Her teeth were jagged and pointed in every directing. Blood poured from her mouth. Nico told all the girls to listen and watch. He said if any of them looked away, the same would happen to them. Then he slit the girl's throat. That's when I knew I had to get out.'

My stomach knots. 'This guy, this Nico, whatever happened to him?' I say. 'Did he get caught? Is that how you got out?'

LaRouche laughs. 'No one gets caught, Jerry. He runs the ring now.'

'So, what? They just let you go? Just like that?'

She shakes her head, like I'm just not getting it. 'All this – the girls, the smuggling, the payoffs – it's a business, Jerry. It may be all about sex on the client side, but on the distribution side it's all about profit. These men *owned* me, like a person owns a dog. In order to leave I had to pay back what they decided I was worth to them, and when you have no say in the price, they can set it as high as they like.'

'Then how'd you pay them back?'

'By helping arrange a sale,' LaRouche says. 'A powerful and wealthy man wanted a beautiful little virgin – a clean, untouched, child. He wanted her no older than twelve so she would last many years. He wanted dark hair and fair skin.' LaRouche's eyes appear to sink farther into her skull when she recalls this, and for a moment she's silent. 'I put the order out. Our people in Russia sent me photographs they took of girls on the street; girls at playgrounds; girls leaving school. When I saw Hanna's photo I knew she was the one. In the picture she was chasing a ball in a park. She was a fiery little girl with deep-black hair and the face of an angel. I placed the order for her that night.'

LaRouche finishes her beer and orders another.

'When Hanna was brought to me I didn't see a girl – I saw my freedom. The men who came by, they all wanted to sleep with her, but I couldn't allow it. I would make her watch, or make her love another girl, even force her into oral sex, but her virginity was top priority.'

When the barman returns with her drink, LaRouche goes quiet and doesn't speak again until he leaves.

'In spite of this,' LaRouche continues, 'I began to worry. It had been months and she still resisted whenever we educated her. Even the strongest girls could only hold out a few weeks before they accepted their fate. But Hanna, she was different. I started to believe she would never break. I began to fear for my life. If I messed up a sale, Nico would kill me without thinking twice – and he would make sure I felt pain before I died.'

LaRouche takes a sip of her beer, not so much because she's thirsty but as if she needs to collect her thoughts.

'One day, I called Hanna by name,' she says. 'She didn't reply. I called her again, but again she didn't reply. I grew angry and slapped her with a leather belt on the back of the head where her hair would hide any marks. She cried and asked what she had done wrong. I told her, "You must always answer me when I call you, Hanna", and I raised the belt again. It was then that she looked up at me, tears streaming down her face, and asked, "Who's Hanna?" That's when I knew she was broken. She had become the product the client ordered, ready to be delivered.'

An odd felling springs in my stomach. It's just a scrap, but even being so small I still recognise it as a hint of sympathy for Epiphany.

LaRouche takes a drink. 'So, I arranged the sale of Hanna to the man. He paid twice as much as any other girl had ever made us. Nico was pleased, and he thought I was used up anyway. Hanna bought me my freedom.'

'Why are you telling me all this?' I say.

LaRouche takes a long drink, sets the beer down and only answers when she is ready. 'Hanna is requesting something of you, so I thought you should know something of her. Sometimes people are misunderstood. Sometimes they're too aggressive. Hanna, in particular. She is so focused that she doesn't understand that the people she needs to help her might be more willing if they knew the maths – if they knew the reason for what she does.'

'Maths?' I laugh. 'There's nothing logical in what Epiphany does;' an ironic smile forms on my face. 'She's insane.' My wound flares and I realise how hot I am with fever. 'Don't get me wrong, it's a touching story. Really. Little Hanna is abducted, loses her mind, becomes Epiphany, and, twelve years later, believes that I can help her on some fucking quest. All of it's unfortunate, but none of that changes the fact that she's framed me for murder.'

LaRouche stiffens at how loud I've said 'murder', and I know that that tension in her eyes signals my best opportunity to get what I came for. 'There's a package she mailed you,' I say.

She doesn't reply.

'Listen to me,' I demand. My words come out with such force, LaRouche looks genuinely startled. I bite my lip before continuing. 'I get that you were a person who was stuck between a rock and a hard place. You had to do what you could to save yourself.'

LaRouche looks down at her root-like hands.

'But Epiphany killed a man I worked with because she was trying to get to me,' I say. 'She's framing me for his death. She's blackmailed me into coming here because she thinks she needs me for some insane mission from God.'

The harder I breathe the more my ribs hurt.

'Did you know that?' I say. 'You beat her so silly, she thinks she talks to *God*.'

And I would think that would underscore just how crazy this whole situation is, but LaRouche remains silent. So I say, 'I mean, why are you even helping her? Is she blackmailing you, too?'

LaRouche doesn't answer. Instead she rubs the cross hanging around her neck.

Then she says, 'We all need our chance at redemption for the sins we've committed.'

My jaw drops.

'You have to be kidding me. You actually *believe* God is talking to her? That this is your chance at redemption for all the bad shit you did?'

'Yes.'

My frustration causes my wound to burn that much more. 'Listen: God's not talking to her,' I say. 'She's fucked up in the head. You want to redeem yourself? Help me. Please.'

'Please,' I say again. Then I swallow and shallow my breath before I show all my cards. 'There was a videotape in that package, wasn't there?' And before she can deny it, I say, 'The one she mailed you.'

LaRouche begins to speak, but stops herself.

'I need that tape,' I plead. 'I *need* my life back.'

She still doesn't speak.

I say, '*Please.*'

Nothing. She just sits there.

I can't even breathe without hurting now. I feel tears coming. I grab LaRouche's hand. 'I just need the proof that *I* didn't do it. I won't turn her in. I won't tell anybody where she is. Please, LaRouche,' my voice trembles, '*please* let me have the tape. Please don't ruin another life to fix a mistake you made a long time ago. I never did anything to her. I don't deserve this.'

It takes me a minute before I realise how hard I'm squeezing her knotty hand. I release it and LaRouche takes a breath. 'I don't have it,' she says. And she can tell I'm about to lose it because she raises her palm, signalling me to hold on. 'She asked for the videotape back last night when you were passed out.'

I shake my head. 'Bullshit.'

'I'm telling you the truth, Jerry. She had me give it to her last night before she left.'

'Left?' I say. 'Left where? Where is she?'

She reaches into a small purse and slides something across the table. 'She's in Veracruz. You leave tonight.' And I see that the something she slid across the table is a ticket.

'No,' I shake my head. 'I'm not going anywhere else. No way,' I say, avoiding the ticket as if touching it would teleport me to Epiphany instantaneously. 'Why should I believe she's even brought the tape with her?'

Then LaRouche, she leans towards me. 'Look rationally at your situation, Jerry. You're in a foreign country, illegally. You don't speak the language. You have no money. You're wanted by the police in your own country. You're practically a trafficked person yourself.' She almost laughs. 'I'm sorry, but it doesn't matter what *you* believe.'

My whole body feels like it's being squeezed in a vice. I want to deny what she's said, but when I slump back in my chair my wound surges with fresh pain, as if reminding me, *She's right, Jerry. You're Epiphany's bitch.*

LaRouche says that I was meant to travel to Veracruz with Epiphany today, but something happened. Epiphany attracted the wrong kind of attention; she had to get out of town, but I wasn't in any position to travel. She tells me it's a long bus journey (*great*), and that Epiphany will arrive in Veracruz before I do. Epiphany will meet me at the bus depot and from there we'll meet with a man who will give us transport to Porto.

'Porto?'

'It's in Portugal,' she tells me.

LaRouche reaches into her purse again and hands me a large wad of pesos. She says it's the equivalent of two hundred dollars. On a note she's scribbled down the name of some medicine I should pick up to keep my infection in check.

She also tells me to buy some new clothes and a pair of sunglasses, 'Just in case.'

She tells me, 'Buy food.'

She tells me not to get off the bus until it reaches Veracruz. Not even to pee.

'Just in case.'

She tells me that, after I buy the food and the sunglasses and the clothes, I should meet her at the apartment. She'll have some euros to give me. 'That will make it easier when you reach Portugal,' she says.

I ask her why, *why* are we going to Portugal? How on earth does Epiphany think either of us is going to get on a plane with our fake passports? They don't scan. They don't even feel real. But LaRouche isn't bothered by those minor issues.

'Then at least tell me,' I say like I'm begging for bread crumbs, 'tell me why I'm here? Why did Epiphany drag me into this? It's not just for the passports.'

And for a moment LaRouche doesn't speak. Then, as if taking pity on me, she leans in. She leans in and says, 'Because, Jerry, Hanna believes you're the only one who can help her get to the person she's looking for.'

'Who?' I say, at the end of my rope. 'The man who abducted her? The man who bought her?'

I say, 'Nico?' and I sense the air in the bar stiffen.

'Don't say that name so loudly,' LaRouche snaps.

'Well, who?' I say. 'Matthew Mann?' and LaRouche doesn't budge.

'Who, dammit?' I practically yell. 'Who is Epiphany looking for?'

And a reflection of light finally gleams from LaRouche's silver tooth. 'Her daughter.'

19

Teeth

'Jerry, I promise I'll give you the tape after we reach Mexico. What? Oh, no, I meant Portugal,' Epiphany says in my mind.

I've been roaming the red-light district near the place where I got stabbed ever since LaRouche and I separated. I'm hoping I don't run into the Jamaican. Before I left the bar I tried to pry more information from LaRouche about Epiphany's daughter, but all she said was she'd already said too much, and that if I ever wanted to see that videotape I'd better get moving.

In my mind, Epiphany says, *'Jerry, I promise. We just need to go to Russia, and then it's all yours.'*

In the red-light district there are beautiful girls in window after window, but it's the men I'm looking at. The men that walk like zombies. The men who own the girls. The men who sell the drugs.

'Jerry, I swear. China is just around the corner...'

And finally I find him. He mumbles as I approach.

If I go to Portugal with Epiphany, what then? I have no guarantee this will ever end.

'Coke. Guns. Heroin,' the man mumbles.

'You see that glowing orb in the night sky, Jerry? Once we get there, I'll give you the tape. I promise with a capital P.'

No. The only way this is going to end is if I stop it.

'Coke. Guns. Heroin,' the mumbling man repeats.

'Gun.'

It's small and black and looks like a toy. The gun is wrapped in a brown-paper bag and slips easily into my back pocket next to the bus ticket and my fake passport. I spent most of the money LaRouche gave me on it so I can't afford to buy the medicine or the food or sunglasses or clothes. I've picked up a cheap postcard from a newsstand though. It has a picture of a beach and palm trees and says 'I love Mexico!' in red, bubbly letters.

It's nearly impossible to write a goodbye letter without sounding cliché, but I give it my best shot anyway.

> *Dear Mom, I know how bad things look. I know how everyone – even you – thinks I did it. But all I can say is, I didn't. And I'm about to get the proof I need. If I should fail, if something were to happen and you don't hear from me again, know that I'm sorry for everything. And know that I forgive you for not telling me about Roland. Love, Jerry*

> *PS: Is it possible Matthew Mann abducts and rapes little girls?*

I drop the postcard in the mailbox after I scratch the last line out, even though it's something that's been disturbing me ever since LaRouche told me about Epiphany. If what she said is true, could Matthew have been the one who bought Epiphany? He would have had the money to. Is that why she believes God says she can kill him?

I return to the apartment as dusk is settling over the neighbourhood. The dusty street is imprinted with marks from a soccer match the children played earlier in the day. A few of the kids are still outside, but most have gone home for dinner. I hope to see Ana Lucia. I feel like I should say goodbye, but she's nowhere to be found.

As I grasp the doorknob it occurs to me that I haven't thought of an excuse to tell LaRouche when she asks why I didn't buy the things she told me to. Too late now, I'll just have to make something up on the fly.

And through the crack in the door I see a red backpack and money scattered on the kitchen floor. Then my chest goes hollow. I open my mouth but no sound comes out. Blood drips from short ruts gouged into the edge of the wooden kitchen counter. LaRouche is on the floor, flat on her back, her red hair fanned around her head. Her mouth gapes open, clogged with blood, like it's a bowlful of tomato soup. Her teeth are cracked and jagged. Her lower lip, ripped.

I feel weak and stumble backwards to grasp the counter for support, but I pull my hand away as something pierces my palm's flesh. Embedded next to the bloody ruts gouged into the kitchen counter is a misshapen piece of metal.

It's shiny and small.

It's a silver tooth.

20

Headlights

A little girl. Pale skin. Raven hair.

A little girl. Pale skin. Raven hair. Talks to God a lot.

A little girl. Pale skin. Raven hair. Talks to God a lot, *and* has a sliced ear.

I'm sitting on the bus on its way to Veracruz imagining what Epiphany's daughter looks like. The best I can do is picture Epiphany shrunk. Mini-Me'd.

I'm trying anything to keep my mind off LaRouche's face. When I close my eyes I see her jagged teeth encircling that lake of blood in her mouth. Her gums were split open like the peel of an exploded orange where her silver tooth had been ripped out.

After I found her, after I grabbed as much cash as I could and threw it into the backpack, I ran to the bus station. I was on autopilot. The faster I ran, the more I sweat, the colder I felt. At first I thought Epiphany had done it, but LaRouche had said that she had already gone to Veracruz. It wouldn't make sense anyway. She was helping Epiphany and, if the two of them trusted each other as much as it seemed, Epiphany had no reason to kill her.

And her mouth – it's like what she described that trafficker doing to that girl who escaped all those years ago. LaRouche had said that Epiphany went early, without me, because she had attracted the wrong kind of attention. Did the traffickers see her? Would they recognise her? Do they know who I am? Is that why LaRouche told me to buy sunglasses and clothes 'just in case'? To disguise myself?

I look down the aisle and make my way again to the rear window.

About an hour ago we passed a car on the shoulder of the road. As we drove by it pulled back onto the highway behind us. It's been trailing back there ever since, its square headlights visible in the night as other cars overtake it, and then speed by us.

Back in my seat I swallow a couple of my 486s to suppress my anxiety and grab the bus company's generic tourist magazine from the sleeve on the seatback in front of me. The route map on the back shows Ensenada on the Pacific coast and Veracruz on the Gulf. I wonder where we are now, but when I look out the window all I see is the dark, purple sky over the cracked expanse of central Mexico.

I feel my forehead and it's warm with fever from my infection. I wake hours later. The large digital clock at the front of the bus says its half-past midnight. The desert is pitch black and inside little orange floor lights dimly illuminate the cabin. Paranoia compels me to check my surroundings. Across the aisle a little old lady snores softly. Her newspaper rests on the seat next to her. The back of a few heads sprout from seats closer to the driver. Behind me, there's another three people scattered throughout the bus – all sleeping. I peak down the aisle again to look out the rear window. There's still a car behind us, but it's farther away now. I can't make out the shape of its headlights. I can't tell if it's the same one.

The gun in my pocket presses against my thigh. I've never used one in my life before, but I'm glad I have it. If Epiphany is looking for her daughter it makes her even more dangerous. How many moms wouldn't kill to save their child? And she already has.

The bus jostles and I cry out a little as my stab wound hits the armrest. If my pain had a name it would be *Epiphany Jones*.

When I fall asleep again I dream I'm back in Chicago. There's a ticker-tape parade in my honour. The city knows that I was an innocent man framed for a heinous crime. The mayor and I ride in the back of an open-top car, waving at citizens screaming my name. 'At great personal risk, Jerry Dresden apprehended and brought to justice a most dangerous and wicked woman,' the mayor shouts. 'The videotape proved everything!' My mom and Donald smile at me from the car in front, and on a float behind us, Epiphany is tied to a stake. She's being burnt alive.

I wake to a growing fever and a new fear that's crept into my mind: What if the tape wasn't recording? Why should I believe *anything* Epiphany says? What if it's blank and she took it because she knew I would only come with her if I thought it proved my innocence?

A road sign says it's two hundred kilometres to Veracruz. It's now past eleven and the sun is shining brightly. There are more cars now behind us in the distance, some have round headlights, some square. I tap the woman across the aisle and gesture towards the newspaper she's discarded. For the slightest moment she looks at me as if we know each other but then she smiles, obviously mistaken.

I can't read Spanish but the pictures keep me occupied. There's an article that seems to be about jobs or the economy. A graph shows little Lego-looking workers with arrows going up or down next to symbols for the peso, euro, dollar and pound.

On another page is an article about the orphanage fire in Ensenada. A photograph shows a young girl crying as a medic treats her on-site. Another split-picture shows the orphanage before and after. Truthfully, the fire didn't make it look much worse than it already was.

Then I flip the page to find myself staring back at me. My graduation photo takes up four columns of text. Really, I should start a scrapbook. In the article, beneath my photo, the words 'Chicago', 'Van Gogh' and 'US' appear several times. I fold the paper shut, but for the remainder of the trip the old lady across the aisle casts inquisitive glances.

It's early afternoon when we arrive at the bus terminal in Veracruz. When we pull in I look back to see if any of the cars follow us off the main road, but they all drive past. The terminal is packed and it takes a while for the herd of arrivals to make their way through the exit gates. Outside the crowds mix with taxi drivers and a few policemen directing traffic. Some just stare into the flux of people who are coming and going. I don't see Epiphany anywhere. Back the way I came I notice two police who look a bit agitated and I think of the newspaper in my backpack that's now folded around the gun. Would Mexican police really be looking for me?

I flinch as someone grabs my arm. It's Epiphany. She's wearing this cute blue sundress, a wide-rimmed cream hat and white strapped sandals. The large sunglasses and yellow shoulder bag complete her look as American-chic tourist. And I remember what LaRouche told me: *Be inconspicuous. Be invisible.*

Her dress doesn't have any pockets. The videotape has to be in the yellow bag. In my backpack, I can feel the weight of the gun. But it's too crowded to do it here. Pull the gun now and the police would be all over me. Epiphany would have plenty of time to take off.

'Didn't Momma tell you to get some new clothes?' she says.

'Uh, yeah. I spent it on medicine,' I lie and jiggle the backpack. 'Antibiotics and all. You know, infection from *the stabbing*.'

Epiphany ignores my dig, instead explaining in her vague Epiphany-way why she had to leave early. 'I made a mistake,' she says. 'If I didn't leave town, I would have put Momma's life in danger.'

Too late, I think, and I almost feel bad not telling her what's happened to LaRouche. Almost.

Epiphany tells me we leave for Portugal tonight. There's a man we have to meet in thirty minutes to pay for our passage. Tonight he'll sneak us onto his boat. And nothing sounds worse to me than taking a cruise with Epiphany. I'd probably order the wrong thing at dinner and she'd have the maître d' stab me. And through all of her explaining her plan, she never once mentions my wound. She never once mentions setting me up; getting me stabbed.

And that fear, it creeps back into my mind. What if there's nothing on the tape? What if it's just a bluff?

But that's what the gun is for.

And relax, would you? I'm not going to straight up murder her. The gun's just here to give me some power over her; to make her give me the tape. I'm not a cop and I'm not an action star. The tape is the path of least resistance to proving my innocence. Let the cops find Epiphany after I've proved to them I didn't do it. My troubles end with the tape, but first I need to view what's on it. And if it is blank, well, then I guess I'll have no choice but to use the gun to take Epiphany by force.

So as Epiphany keeps talking about our itinerary, I wince and grab my back. 'I don't think I can go with you to meet the guy right now,' I say. 'I need to ... I need to sit.'

This doesn't fit into Epiphany's plan. She looks at me suspiciously, so I press my eyes closed and grab onto a railing. I make it look like I'm about to fall over. But Epiphany's not a fool. She knows why I'm here. Denying it would only make her more apprehensive.

So I say, 'I'm not going to lie to you. The second you give me that tape, I'm gone.' I wince as I take a deep breath. I bite my teeth together in a fake attempt to stifle another fake moan. 'But you have it, so I'm doing what you want.'

I'm not the best actor, but my fever lends credibility. My sweats are real. Plus my wound *does* hurt. Just not as bad as I make it look.

'I'm not much good if I pass out,' I say. 'Are you going to carry me to the boat?'

I give another muffled cry.

A cagey look sits on her face. And then Epiphany says, 'I didn't mean for that to happen.'

Stand back, ladies and gentlemen. That's an apology – Epiphany Jones style.

'I got these for you,' she says, almost timidly, and reaches into her yellow bag and hands me a bottle of co-codamol and another of ibuprofen. And if I weren't planning to rob her at gunpoint in a few hours, I'd be a little touched.

I wave her apology away like I'm a big martyr. 'Let's just do what we need to do. The sooner I can get back to my life, the better.'

But Epiphany, she looks like she's still on the fence.

So I say, 'I mean, I did just come all the way here on the bus. If I was going to take off I would have done it then. Besides, I hardly slept.'

Except when I dreamt about burning you alive, I want to add. 'I just need some rest.'

But she's nothing if not cautious.

'Fine. Here, look.' And digging in my backpack I pull out my bottle of 486s. I rattle them in front of her. 'You know I need these for my condition. Take them. I'll get them back from you when we meet tonight.'

And Epiphany, she finally says, 'OK,' and slips the bottle of 486s into her yellow bag. Then she pulls a tourist map out and marks a little circle on it by the docks. 'We're to be there at nine for transport to the boat. That gives us six hours. I'll meet him now to pay. You rest. I'll meet you back here in ninety minutes.'

I say, 'Thanks.'

And she says, 'And Jerry, if anything happens; if we can't find each other – be at the docks at nine. That's where your videotape will be.'

I follow the sightseers and the sounds of rumba music until I come to a large outdoor market. It's one of those markets designed to suck money from tourists who are killing time waiting for their cruise ships to depart. The magazine on the bus told me about this place. The stalls are full of prints of Mexico, ceramic plates showing generic images of beaches that could be anywhere in the world, and little bottles of sands labelled 'volcanic ash'. There are T-shirts, mugs and watches; key chains, pens, and shot glasses. If you can put 'Mexico' on it, it's sold here.

But what I'm here for isn't a souvenir. I'm here for the tourists carrying their MiniDV cameras around with them – the kind of camera Roland used to record his sessions on for insurance purposes whenever he photographed a painting. From the looks of it, I've got more than a few choices. And I mean, how hard can it be? I'll just wait until one of the tourists put their bags down to try on an authentic, indigenously carved tribal mask and then swoop in just like Epiphany did in the bus station in Chicago and grab their bag. Then I'll have what I need to view the tape.

And just as I pick my dumb, unsuspecting victim, shouts suddenly break through the crowd. I turn and notice a man. He's got dark hair and a black leather jacket. But before I can remember where I've seen him, the two police running from his direction slam into me.

And my heart, it sinks into my stomach.

And my head, it keeps screaming, *'No, no, no!'*

And the last thing I see before the two policemen force my face into the dirt is the man in the leather jacket, smiling.

21

Perro

Jordan Seabring is on a boat in the Caribbean. She's sunbathing in this little red bikini while her friends are in the water, diving for treasure. This is the movie that solidified her as the next Hollywood 'It Girl'. This is the movie that made her a household name. This is the movie that put her in the minds of men across the world. There's side-boob everywhere.

Seabring plays a total bitch who opens to taking chances when she falls in love with a lowly boat captain, who ends up having terminal cancer. We're at the part when she has to decide between playing with her rich friends in the water or helping the captain fix the boat's motor. We're at the point when she says – something dubbed in Spanish.

Then again, everything in this tiny jail is in Spanish. I'm sitting on a cell bench, shirtless and shoeless, being watched not closely at all by a lanky police officer who's reclining at his desk, engrossed in the movie on the black-and-white TV.

He is one of the cops who arrested me. When it happened I kept hoping to see Epiphany, of all people, in the crowd that formed. She would have been able to help me escape – somehow. In the cell, I look at the clock on the wall. She's expecting me at the bus station right now.

When they searched my backpack they found the gun wrapped in the newspaper. Because of that, in front of the whole damn crowd, they made me strip to my underwear and searched me. They took my fake passport. My pain pills. After they were convinced I didn't have any more weapons concealed in my anal cavity they let me put my pants back on, threw the newspaper on the ground and packed me into their shitty car.

The lanky police officer at the desk abruptly sits up as another officer with a large beer belly comes in. They speak quickly, glancing at me. Compared to the detectives in Chicago, these police seem so amateur. I can't believe they actually had the resources to track an American fugitive down.

The beer-belly officer says something else to the lanky one, who turns the TV off and then rubs his fingers together and presses a buzzer on the desk. The front door clanks open and a man walks in carrying my newspaper, which the police discarded. I can tell it's the same one because it's ripped from where they tore the gun from it.

The man who walks in is the same man who was smiling when he saw me get tackled; the familiar one in the leather jacket. He speaks briefly in Spanish to the officer with the big belly and then addresses the lanky officer at length. The officers grin at each other.

And now I know where I've seen this man before. I literally ran into him at the produce stand in Ensenada, the night I got stabbed. He's not a cop. You can tell that by the way he casually pulls out a large roll of euros, dollars and pesos, all mixed together, and bribes the two police officers to unlock my cell before they leave the room.

'You know what I love about this country, Jerry?' he asks in a thick Italian accent as he enters my cell. 'Money gets you whatever you want.' He speaks slowly, the way confident men do. The way men do when they know they're in control.

'How do you know my name?' I say, my mouth dry.

He smiles. 'Good, Jerry! Good! Right to the point! I like that in people. You're a busy man, I'm a busy man. Time is money, right?' He unfolds the newspaper. 'Your name is Jerry Dresden,' he says, paraphrasing the article. 'You murdered a co-worker and stole a painting in your home country.' His eyebrows rise, 'Very daring of you.'

My gut tells me, *You're fucked, Jerry.*

The Italian continues skimming the article. 'Unfortunately, the US authorities have had a break in the case. A young boy who was *threatened* into providing falsified travel documents to the fugitive – *that's you* – has come forward. From his testimony the police now believe the fugitive fled to Mexico late last week.' Another raise of his eyebrows. 'The boy had created two passports, but, given your psychosis, the police believe you only *imagine* you're travelling with someone. They are now working in conjunction with Mexican authorities ... ah, well, you get the idea.'

I sink low on the bench.

'Jerry, Jerry, don't look so down,' he says in mock sympathy. 'You've got a lot going for you. The Mexican police are a joke. They don't keep up on the wires. They don't know who they've got in their cell.'

'Then why did they arrest me?'

'Because I called ahead and told them to, of course,' he says, motioning with the wad of cash in his hand. 'I mean, how would it look if a foreigner like me abducted an American tourist in broad daylight?'

I say, 'I didn't do those things.'

The Italian, he paces around the cell. 'Jerry, you're not getting it. I don't care if you did or not. Do you know why I'm here?'

I shake my head, no.

'I'm here because I'm a businessman, Jerry.' He crouches in front of me. 'I need to protect my interests. My interests in Ensenada, my interests in Veracruz. My interests everywhere. You understand?'

I shake my head, no, again and the Italian stands back up. He takes off his leather jacket and folds it once before placing it on the bench. Even though he's got to be a good fifteen years older than me, his body is the image of a person ten years younger. His T-shirt is snug over his chest and his arms are firm and toned. As I sit, shirtless, my flabby belly forms a roll at my waist. *Pathetic.*

'The police in your country are wrong, aren't they, Jerry? You are travelling with someone. A woman named Hanna.' His pacing increases. 'Don't deny it, Jerry.'

And my stomach drops. My body goes cold.

'You're Nico,' I say.

Nico, the trafficker.

Nico, the teeth smasher.

Nico, he stops in place and smiles an ironic smile. 'See! I am right! How else would you know my name? I am flattered LaRouche spoke of me. Don't deny that either,' he adds.

I scratch the edge of the bench. Is that where he'll have me bite when he shatters my teeth?

'Focus, Jerry,' Nico says. 'I'm after Hanna, not you.'

'Why?' I say.

'Jerry, Jerry, Jerry,' he pauses and shakes his head. 'A long time ago she almost cost me a very large client. She caused them a lot of trouble and I had to do much work to keep their business. But, let bygones be bygones, right?' He pauses as if a memory has abruptly appeared in his head. 'Forgive me, I have lied. I did search for her for a while, but after a year, I gave up. I assumed she died on the streets. Where could she have gone otherwise?' Now he paces again and speaks without looking at me. The blood has drained from my skin. 'But as you know, Jerry, she came back to me. The stupid girl came back to Ensenada. And why? To burn down my orphanage.'

Orphanage?

'Oh, Jerry, you know as well as I do that it wasn't really an orphanage. It was a place where I could keep my newest girls without people thinking much of it. It's easy to pay off the police, but if too many people start questioning what parentless girls are doing together in one house – well, that wouldn't be good for business, would it?'

He pauses so long, I actually answer. 'No,' I say. His eyes crinkle and I realise it wasn't a question pause – just another confidence pause.

'I caught her red-handed,' he continues. 'She was running down the street, away from the fire and I grabbed her by the arm. We were eye to eye, and even though it had been over *fifteen years*, I recognised her right away. I never forget a girl, Jerry. Never. Lucky for her that fire truck came barrelling down the street when it did. It was either let go of her or be hit. And one whore isn't worth a man's life, is it?'

My mind spins as memories connect. I remember that night. When Epiphany came home she looked a mess. She had a long, bleeding scratch going down her arm. I thought she had been covered in dirt, but it was really smoke and soot.

'When I got to my orphanage the girls told me that a woman had made sure they all got out. They said she even went in to rescue a few of the youngest ones who were trapped upstairs.' Nico notices the astonishment on my face. 'I too wondered why. Why risk all those girls' lives? Just to get back at me? No. Hanna always was clever. She knew the news of an orphanage fire would spread quickly. She knew that the newspapers would follow up on what happened to the girls. She knew I would have no choice but to let them be split up and taken to real orphanages. She was saving the girls, Jerry.'

And if I weren't so scared right now, I'd be a little impressed.

Nico crouches by me. His face is flushed. 'You know what those girls would have been worth over the next ten years?'

I shake my head.

'Over four million US.' He takes a moment before he speaks again. 'So the next day I tracked Hanna to that street market. But then you ran into me and I lost her. You told me you were late for work, but it was obvious you were following her. Then, as fate would have it, a day later you shouted my name in a bar.'

My head sinks. 'You were there?'

He shakes his head. 'No, but saying my name is like calling the boogeyman, Jerry. I have eyes everywhere. You were with LaRouche.'

And I wince as her jagged, broken teeth snap into my mind.

Nico laughs. 'You saw her when I was done?'

I begin to breath heavily.

'You know, I didn't want to do that to her. I had to though. It took so much beating to get her to admit that Hanna was even back in this country, but then LaRouche just reached a point where she wouldn't tell me any other specifics. It was as if she thought we had reached maximum pain.

'Then I tried another approach: I asked her to tell me where the man was who she was at the bar with – but she lied and said that you weren't associated with Hanna. Of course I knew that was a fib. So I told her again to tell me where you were and she refused. So I changed the look of her mouth.'

'No, no, no,' I say under my breath.

'I did that because of you, Jerry.'

'Please,' I say, not knowing why.

'It takes multiple tries to knock all the teeth out you know,' Nico goes on. 'And with each try she gave up just a little more about you: that you weren't a buyer of Hanna; that Hanna has some kind of video-tape you want; and that you were heading to the bus station to journey to meet Hanna here.'

'Here, I have other *orphanages*,' he says grimly and pulls a thin little blade from his boot, and I begin to cry.

'I'm sure you can guess what happened next. LaRouche, being the dishonourable person that she was, was lying when she said you had already left for the bus station. I got on the road but then it occurred to me that maybe all that money in her kitchen was for you. Maybe you were coming back for it. Maybe you were taking the later bus. I've been in this silly country long enough to know there are three buses a day making the journey from Ensenada to Veracruz. So I waited on the shoulder of the road until the last bus to Veracruz passed and what did I see? You looking out the window at my car. Am I right, Jerry?'

I can't find the words to answer him.

He sighs and rolls his eyes, growing frustrated. 'Do you know how I got her mouth to fill with blood? After you shatter the teeth, you take a knife – like this one – ' he holds it to my mouth. 'You slice the tongue from the bottom, making sure you leave a little bit of flesh connected so it flops back but doesn't fall off. Here, let me show you.'

'No!' I scream, but already he's grabbed my head in his arm and with his fingers on his other hand he's spread my mouth wide and buries the blade underneath my tongue.

'Shh. Shh,' he says. 'You feel this?' The blade pokes the thin strip of flesh that holds my tongue to the floor of my mouth. 'This is where you cut. Then up through the bottom of the tongue. Then you push it down their throat.' The blade, it prods against the bottom of my tongue and I cry out as its tip pierces the flesh of my tongue's belly.

'Pleath!' I scream as sweat breaks on my brow.

'Jerry, don't distract me. I'd hate for my hand to slip.'

I try to freeze my face.

Then Nico says, 'After you're done with their mouth, you put your heel on their forehead so they can't turn over. They die from suffocating on their own tongue. The pool of blood is just for show.' He smiles.

My breath is rapid and shallow as he slides the blade from my lips and I taste the battery-acid tang of blood under my tongue. Spasms beat my insides. I keep seeing LaRouche's mouth in my mind.

Nico shows mock concern. 'Oh, don't cry,' he says. But I am. I'm leaking tears.

'Tell me where she is,' he says, 'so I don't have to give you a new mouth.'

And I spring from the bench. 'Police!' I shout. 'Police! Guard! Police!'

But Nico just laughs and starts shouting *'Police!'* with me. The lanky and fat officers come back into the room. They see me crying and look at Nico. But Nico walks over to them, takes out his roll of money and hands them more bills. Then, without warning, he grabs me by the back of the neck and pushes my face between the bars of the cell.

'That looks like a bad laceration,' he says and then I feel two thick fingers burrowing into the wound in my back.

I scream and scream as he thrusts harder and deeper. And the two police officers, they just leave the room as Nico finger-fucks the hole between my ribs.

The pain is unbelievable. White and hot, like a poker burrowing into my core. There are moments when time has no presence, when I hear nothing, not even my screams, and see only pale swirls of white. The pain is so great even death couldn't stifle it. I don't even know where it's coming from anymore. Am I on fire? Am I freezing in the cold depths of space? Has someone sent me to the bottom of the ocean, where the pressure is crushing my body from all sides?

'You see, perro,' someone breathes into my ear; my face is still stuck between the cell bars. 'Do you know what "perro" means? It's Spanish for "dog". You are my new dog. So you see, perro, money buys anything here.'

I drop to the floor. I'm wet all over. My head spins. Black-and-white spots muddy my vision, which is only slowly returning. Nico ... I think, yes ... it is Nico, he's wiping his bloody fingers on my pants. 'Every time you scream it will cost me money,' he says, his voice slightly delayed behind the movement of his lips. 'I have a lot of it, but I don't like spending more than I have to. It's bad business.'

I feel myself moving involuntarily. I'm sobbing uncontrollably, on the floor.

Nico squats next to me and I scream again.

'Shh. Shh,' he says. 'You want to keep your teeth, yes?'

All I can do is cry.

'Answer me, perro.'

Through my tears and blurred vision, I shake my head up and down, grunting a 'yes'.

'You want your videotape?'

Grunt.

'Do you know where Hanna is?'

'Yes.'

'Good perro,' he says. 'We both win. I need to make sure Hanna can never hurt my business again. You need your videotape. You will take me to her, I will make her give you your tape, and then you will leave. You can go back to your life, you can be Jerry again,' he says as I sob. 'If you refuse, perro, I will splinter your teeth.'

I begin to bellow so loudly.

'Relax, relax,' Nico eases, mocking sympathy for me. 'I won't cut your tongue. I won't kill you. I'll just leave this newspaper with our friends here and you can go back to your country and go to prison with a nice, gaping mouth.' He pauses to let a sufficient image of life with a hole in my face form in my mind. 'Or, you can bring me to Hanna.' Nico rises and puts on his leather jacket. 'Now, which would you like to do?'

Good perro.

22

Judas

I walk along the pier, like a zombie slowly shuffling towards its prey. And there is a hunger I'm feeling.

My flesh is blotchy and grey like the dirty dishcloth used to clean ashtrays in hotel lobbies. Plugging up my wound, a blood-soaked rag makes the back of my shirt stick to my skin. A rotting-meat smell radiates from it.

Still, I move without feeling, without pain even.

I shuffle past the mesh cages and wooden crates meant for holding crustaceans, past the nets and hooks the size of your fist meant for hooking marlins. Epiphany stands in the moonlight, just at the pier's end. Her little blue sundress looks almost black in the night. She's crammed her cream hat into the yellow bag that sits on a pile of lobster traps made of wrought-iron rebars and green plastic mesh.

After Nico picked me up off the cell floor; after the police returned and gave me my clothes; after Nico handed me a cup of water and my red backpack, saying, 'They're keeping your gun', I didn't *want* to come here – even if it meant not getting the tape.

What he had done to me, the pain I had felt was absolute proof – absolute truth – that nothing good comes in this life. It's a pain I will always remember. Not because it's memory will always linger in my body, but because it's a pain that wasn't contained only to me. It will grow and leap to another person, and soon Epiphany too will awaken to the fact that no, nothing good comes from this life. And, as Nico and me and the lanky officer left the jail, I wept for her.

I wept for her because I'm the virus that shows the pain where she is. And I wept for me too because you never want to believe you could be the Jew who gave up the location of other Jews to keep yourself out of the oven.

I saw what he did to LaRouche. Felt what he did to me. He did those things to both of us and we weren't even the ones who burnt his orphanage to the ground. What he'll do to Epiphany is going to make my wound-fucking look like a spanking.

Epiphany's pale skin glows in the moonlight. And I think, who is this girl who I've just condemned to unimaginable suffering? Epiphany Jones or Hanna? How can one person have such extremes? To me a devil but, to the girls she saved, an angel. Those thirty girls will have a small chance at a better life because of the risk she took. But then I think, it was a risk to the girls as well. This woman I'm about to betray is the greatest conundrum of my life. How could she have known the fire wouldn't kill any of them? And as I watch Epiphany breathe in a swath of night air in silent thought, I know what her answer would be. *My voices.*

In the cell, Nico pumped me full of the painkillers Epiphany got for me so I'd stop collapsing. The amount I took, all the little co-codamols and ibuprofens, I should be dead. Maybe I am.

In the cell, I showed him the tourist map with the docks circled. I begged him to let me go. I told him I'd just be a liability. I could barely walk after the finger-fucking he gave me. But he wouldn't go alone.

'She's not some dumb animal, perro. You don't survive for twelve years on the streets without being clever and aware. You already missed your earlier appointment with her. She'll be on guard. You don't show tonight, she'll know something's up,' he said. 'Besides, if you're lying to me, I'm going to take your nose.' He handed me a dirty rag. 'Now plug your hole up. I don't need you bleeding to death before we get there.'

In another time, in another life, who I see before me would be just an ordinary woman looking out on to a beautiful sea on a moonlit night. But in this life, on this night, I don't know who I'm looking at. A murderer and a saviour? How can one person be both? Why was Roland's life expendable, but the girls' lives at the orphanage valuable?

Is one life worth more than another? Is mine worth more than hers? Who is she to decide? Who am I?

I'm so close I can hear her mumbling to herself. Something's different about her. She's not on guard like she usually is. After I didn't show this afternoon, I'd expect her to be clawing at her skin – or mine. Any time before this she would know if I were within twenty feet of her. Now though, I'm close enough to reach out and touch her shoulder but she hasn't even noticed me.

And though my past pain and her future pain cause my empathy for her to grow, I know that I'm still going to go through with this. That hunger I feel? It's called necessity. It's called self-preservation. You'd do the same thing if you were in my position, so don't you dare judge me for this.

I clear my throat and Epiphany breaks from her mumbling and turns to me. Her mutilated earlobe glows like coral in the moonlight. I'm quiet for a moment. How do you begin a conversation with a dead person?

'What were you, um, talking about just now?' I say, hoping the night hides the grey of my skin, the emptiness of my eyes.

'A kiss,' she answers, letting the word float between us for a moment before it's carried off on the breeze. 'Where were you?' she asks, almost softly. 'I waited.'

And her eyes. There's something different with her eyes.

'I know,' I say. 'My – my wound. I laid down in a park. Fell asleep. Only woke up an hour ago.'

I can hardly bear to look at her.

'I'm sorry,' I say.

'It's OK,' she says. 'I knew you'd come.'

Over her shoulder, a quarter of a mile out on the moonlit Gulf, I see a three-storey freighter. Its hull is painted a dark red and 'THE CAPRICE' is written in white letters on the side.

'Is that it?'

Epiphany nods. 'The captain has arranged transport,' she says. 'It should be here shortly.'

In the distance the red light of a small tugboat moored next to the freighter blinks. I glance at Epiphany. What the hell is wrong with her eyes tonight? It's as if they don't belong to her. Like if you'd put your grandmother's eyes into Charles Manson's head, that's what they look like.

'You – you know, when you said we were taking a boat, I imagined it was one of those small fishing boats – like the one from *Jaws* or something.'

Epiphany looks puzzled.

'The movie?' I say.

She shrugs her shoulders.

Jaws. I see LaRouche, bloody mouth gaping open, jagged teeth pointing in every direction.

What's Nico waiting for? Is this part of his cruelty? To prolong the time I spend with the person I've betrayed?

Epiphany's new eyes look into my dead ones. 'I know this hasn't been easy,' she says, 'but we're almost done. It's almost over.' She turns towards the sea and I stand by her side. In the distance, the tugboat has just pulled away from the freighter.

On the pier, the moonlight casts soft, blue shadows over Epiphany's face. And it's then that I realise why her eyes look so alien. It's because that freighter is the last part of the journey that takes us to her daughter. Her eyes, it's not that there's something wrong with them – it's that they possess something they never had before. They're full of hope.

And out of nowhere there's an abrupt flash of movement in the moonlight. Nico, he steps from the shadows between two sets of crates. I must have made some sort of yell because Epiphany snaps around in an instant. Her figure is dwarfed by Nico's six-foot-six frame.

It begins quickly. He raises something in his fist and swings it at Epiphany. She tries to duck, but she's not fast enough. She's knocked to the ground before I can blink. She tries to rise, but Nico lifts his arm again. This time I can see the thing he swings is a sock with something heavy in it. I press my eyes shut before he hits her again.

My stomach churns and rolls around, like it's been cut loose from the rest of my viscera. In my mind, Nico's face warns, 'Don't interrupt, perro. I'll take your nose. I'll shatter your teeth. I'll dump you in your country and your wound won't be the only thing getting stretched in prison.'

When I open my eyes blood from Epiphany's skull falls in large drops onto the pier. She wobbles to all fours. Her eyes go wide as she sees I'm still here.

'Run!' she screams. That's when I feel the lanky police officer brush past me. Epiphany barely has time to register that I haven't moved before the officer boots her in the stomach. I snap my eyes closed again before I can see her fall for the third time.

And their viciousness, it's nothing like you see on TV. Seeing someone beaten in real life … it's the sounds. They aren't as pronounced. When Nico bludgeons her face, there's no THWACK or CRACK to go with it. You think, his strike *can't* be doing that much damage. There're no jarring jump cuts showing a close-up of the attacker sneering as his victim writhes in pain. There's no camera in the face of the beaten woman highlighting her tears and blood. And when you see her lying still, you think, You don't look like it hurt that much.

But you're wrong. It hurts more than is believable. You don't know how it is.

Even though it's just barely, Epiphany, she still moves. She manages to lift her head.

'Stay down, goddamn it,' I want to yell.

As the lanky police officer forces Epiphany's hands behind her back, Nico picks up the yellow bag. He digs through it until he finds a small, blue clamshell case. He flips it over in his hands, then tosses it to me. 'You're done here.'

The surface of my entire body is numb. I need to look to see if I've caught it. And though I don't feel it, there it is, this little thing, in my hands. Inside is the videotape with Roland's handwriting scrawled on it. I expect – *I hope* – to feel relief.

I don't.

The police officer, he's forced Epiphany into a bowing position – her knees under her chest, the left side of her face pressed hard against the pier. It's the same position I had the clone in. When our eyes meet, I expect hers to be glaring at mine with hatred. Instead they're empty. Lifeless. Like the shark's from my dream.

'You're done here, perro,' Nico repeats, surprised I'm not halfway to the bus station by now. 'Leave before I change my mind.'

I know I won't get another warning. I don't look at Epiphany again. I grasp the tape firmly in my hand and begin the long walk back down the pier. The sound of blood rushes through my head. I concentrate on the pain of my stab wound; on the feeling of the sopping rag stuffed into my grey flesh. I try to feel every millimetre of my body, soaking up every ounce of pain so I can focus on something other than what's happening behind me.

But then ... do you remember that rat I fucked up killing? Remember how its body was broken before I dumped it out the window? How I pictured Epiphany's head on it? How I wanted her just as broken?

Be careful, sometimes you get what you wish for.

And despite every voice in my head screaming, '*Don't!*' I turn back around.

The police officer is sliding Epiphany's blue dress over the top of her hips. He whips her across the spine with something that looks like a riding crop and, despite an effort not to, Epiphany cries in agony. And while she is being whipped again, Nico, he's pulling a strip of black electrical tape from a roll in his hand like this is just some common weekend housework. 'This is just the start,' he tells her. 'Enjoy it. It's the nicest thing that's going to happen to you.'

And I can't tell you why; I can only say that this is where I knowingly do the dumbest thing in my entire life. This is where I slip the tape into my pocket. This is where I pick up a lobster trap the size of a kitty carrier and hope my heart doesn't explode, because it's beating like a hummingbird. This is where I charge at Nico with the lobster trap and bring it crashing down on his head with all the force I can summon.

And all the force I can summon isn't much. Nico, he doesn't even get knocked off his feet. Hell, he barely teeters. What he does do is spin around and grabs my wrist in one hand while his other chokes my throat.

'Perro,' he says through gritted teeth, 'I liked you. I really did. You reminded me of myself – when I was a child.' His grip tightens as he walks me backwards. I think he's walking me backwards. I can't really tell. I'm feeling pretty lightheaded. It's hard to breath. 'But this is business,' he is saying. 'And you just broke the terms of our arrangement.'

And, still holding my throat, he grabs his little sock thing and whacks me in the head with it. And when he lets go, I have a falling feeling. Then I smack a surface, hard. And, as my view of Nico goes wavy, I sink into the cool Caribbean water.

23

This Is Your Life

LaRouche, Roland, my father – I envy them. They have no suffering. They have no pain. They got living out of the way. They'll never have heartbreak or loss again. They'll never have to go to a job they hate. They'll never fear anything else. When everything is said and done, the dead are the winners. You and me – we're the saps. We still have to get through each day.

Well, you do anyway.

I'm just about done.

They say before you die your life flashes before you in a split second. I guess this is my second.

Jerry, this is your life:

I was born in 1982 to Jonathan and Margaret Dresden. The birth was an emergency Caesarean section. And that little C-section should have been a big tip-off: life with this one isn't going to be easy.

But life for my family did move along uneventfully for the next three years. That's when Emma was born.

Emma, my beautiful little sister.

When I started kindergarten at six, I was a shy and introverted boy. While the other children became friends, it was quickly evident that I was *that one.* You know what I'm talking about. Every class has one – the kid no one wants to talk to. It doesn't matter why it's you. Once it's apparent that you are the one, everyone knows to stay away, lest they become *that one* through association.

Kids don't really bully you in kindergarten. They wait until first grade to do that. During break one fall day, Keith – a real alpha male, if you know what I mean – he snatched my GI Joe action figure from my hands. He twisted it at the torso until the little, black rubber band holding the Joe's hips to his stomach snapped.

'You,' Keith said, pointing to the dismembered Joe, 'unless...'

That was the day Keith first taxed my lunch money.

When I got home I ran straight to the backyard and cried. It wasn't only because of Keith, either. I wondered, was it normal to feel as sad and lonely as I did every single day? Was something wrong with me?

As I buried my broken GI Joe in the sandbox, Emma came scurrying around the fence with two Joe's in her little hand. She knew I had been crying, but didn't ask why. She just handed me one of the Joe's and asked if she could play with me. Her smile told me it would be the thrill of her day. So she played with Scarlet and I played with Firefly in the sandbox until the sun went down.

Being only three she could never realise how such a simple act had held me up that day, but I did.

Over the next four years, when the kids at school picked on me it was bearable because I knew that at three o'clock I would be going home to that glowing smile of hers. Anything bad in my life became tolerable because I had Emma. She was my friend when no one else wanted to be. And I loved her how a brother should: by ignoring her sometimes; by teasing her; by not telling her just how much she meant to me.

When I was sick she'd pick dandelions from the front yard and bring them to me. When I came home from school, crying on days the bullying was bad, she would run and hug me and ask me to play outside. And she never asked what was wrong. Not once. Even at that age she knew the bad shit should be left in the past so you could have room for the happy stuff in the present.

Every winter I counted the days until the start of Christmas break. For other kids the holiday break meant toys and hanging out with friends. But for me, I loved it because I would have two weeks of doing nothing but hanging out with my one and only friend. My one true buddy. The only person who I ever felt really loved me for everything I was and everything I wasn't.

Jerry, this is your life:

It's 1992 and Mom tells me Emma is sick with leukaemia. I expect Emma to be coughing and all snuffles and stuff. When she's not, I think it's no big deal – especially when Mom promises that nothing bad will happen to her.

Over the next year Emma tires easily. We stop playing outside. She asks me to stay in with her. She asks me to read to her while she lies in bed. And I do. Throughout that year, I read every book in the house to her. When we run out of kids' books I read her the Bible. When that is done I read the books in Mom's den. Imagine being an eleven-year-old and reading Nietzsche to your dying eight-year-old sister. After a while I don't think Emma even hears my words make sentences. She just wants the sound of my voice by her. She wants not to be alone. She knows she is dying.

Jerry, this is your life:

It's March 1994. I'm twelve, Emma is nine. Her bedroom has become the place where books go to die. They're stacked by the dozens in every conceivable location. Every book in the house has been read. Some twice.

Emma is white as a ghost tonight. I'm lying in bed with her, reading her one of Mom's Joan of Arc books. It's her favourite one. She has me reread a passage to her over and over and over again because, she says, 'They're the most beautiful words ever written.'

Her lips are pale, but they mouth along as I read:

'She was truthful when lying was the common speech of men; she was honest when honesty was become a lost virtue; she was a keeper of promises when the keeping of a promise was expected of no one. She was full of pity when a merciless cruelty was the rule, and honourable in an age which had forgotten what honour was; she was unfailingly true in an age that was false to the core; she was of a dauntless courage when hope and courage had perished in the hearts of her nation – she was all these things in an age when crime was the common business of lords and princes. And for all reward, the French King, whom she had crowned, stood supine and indifferent while French priests took the noble child, the most innocent,

the most lovely, the most adorable the ages have produced, and burned her alive at the stake.'

Emma reaches for my hand. I stop reading. She looks at me with her pale face and says, 'I wish I could be just like Joan of Arc.'

And I look at her and say, 'You are.'

Jerry, this is your life:

It's September 1994. Emma has been in this hospital for four months now. Mom and Dad rarely speak without fighting anymore. They're only civil when they're in front of Emma. I'm waiting in the hall for Emma to get out of an MRI scan. The room she went into is sterile and white like Cloud City in *Star Wars*.

Back in her room, I read. She's got so many tubes in her now I can't lie next to her anymore. I sit in the chair beside her bed and hold her hand with my left as my right one grasps tonight's reading. The nurses know our routine and bring any books they can find. But tonight all they could manage is a pamphlet on resuscitating a drowning victim. 'Optimal time to save a victim of drowning is in the first forty-five seconds,' I read to Emma as a machine helps her breath.

Outside the room, I hear my dad say, 'We need a miracle.'

Jerry, this is your life:

It's October 31st, 1994. I am that miracle. My parents tell me the doctors say I'm a perfect genetic match for something called a bone-marrow transplant. It's what I have in me that will save my sister's life.

Jerry, this is your life:

It's November 1994. It's been an unusually chilly fall. As the time to the operation approaches I get nervous.

It's two days before the transplant. Mom is at the hospital with Emma. I'm waiting at school for Dad to pick me up. He's running late because he's at a press conference for the foundation of a dead star named Audrey Hepburn. When my dad was my age, Audrey was his on-screen crush.

The other kids waiting outside for their parents ask why the teachers say I won't be in school for a while. I tell them. Then they tell me how some kid they knew had the same operation. They say how the doctors stick a straw in your legs and suck your bone blood out like it's a strawberry shake. They say how kids who have it done walk all wobbly the rest of their lives; how the kids who have it done never stop crying from the pain, even when they are old men. And as they walk all wobbly around me, screaming, *'It hurts! It hurts!'* I run. I run across the parking lot and into the woods. I run up into the Hollywood hills and I hide there, clutching my unwobbly legs.

I wake up, shivering. I begin to walk. I come home at four a.m. I come home to police in our kitchen and my mom frantic. I come home with pneumonia.

Jerry, this is your life:

The doctors, they tell my parents the thing about sleeping in nature is you don't want to sleep on the naked ground, even with a winter coat on. The ground is fifty-five degrees. You want to keep your body at ninety-eight point six. If you have to sleep outside, even if you have heavy clothing, put something between you and the ground – like a cut log, or even just prop your body up so there's space between you and the earth. That extra buffer keeps the ground from sucking the heat from your body. That extra buffer will keep you from getting pneumonia.

The doctors, they say I'm too sick now. My immune system is too weak. The operation would be too dangerous for me. They say, 'We'll have to postpone until the New Year.'

Jerry, this is your life:

Emma dies on December 24th, 1994. I stop reading after that.

Jerry, this is your life:

You never mention it to your mom or dad. You never talk to your family about how you killed your little sister. And they never blame you. Not to your face anyway. How can they? You were just a shit-scared, stupid kid. A cowardly little fuck. They can't blame you, so they fight with each other. At work, Dad volunteers for more and more assignments out of the country. Sometimes he's away for weeks. Mom, she loses herself in her lectures about a dead saint. She enrolls you at Sunday school because she's been told it helps with grief. But you don't show grief ever again. You turn to movies and TV. You veg out and slowly forget about everything one commercial break at a time.

Jerry, this is your life:

Your mother cheats on your father. Your father dies in a car accident. You become addicted to porn and television and go through life like a zombie. And it *is* an addiction – a cover for your misery – but you lie to yourself and call it a 'hobby'. You take a job you couldn't care less about. You lie to people about relationships you can't have because you're too apathetic to even try. You lie to them so they don't silently judge you behind your back like your mom and dad did. Each day is just another perfect example of the spectacular nothing that is your existence.

Jerry, this is your life:

You see people who aren't there. Until, one day, one of them is. And she frames you for murder and blackmails you into coming to Mexico. Then you're on a pier watching two men beat this woman in the warm moonlight. And before you know it, you're sinking in the water, waiting to drown.

Jerry, this is your life. This is your sad, pathetic life. It's so sad, it's flashed before your eyes in just half a second. Real lives – good lives – take at least a whole second.

My back gently hits the sandy bottom of the bay. The moonlight shines bright into the clear water, illuminating everything in a hazy blue flush. Shallow shadows ripple over the submerged masts of the pier; over the seaweed; over the fish as they slowly scatter from my faltering limbs. Down here, everything is calm. The madness is on the surface.

I release my final breath and my lungs burn as they flood with salt water. This is where I think, *'See you soon, Emma.'*

And this, this is where I see Emma standing over me on the sandy sea floor, shaking her head. Her arms crossed disapprovingly. 'Optimal time to save a victim from drowning is in the first forty-five seconds,' she says.

'This is for you,' I say to my figment of Emma. 'So I can be with you again. It's all for you.'

Emma shakes her head. 'No. This is all for you.'

A splash echoes from the surface and my figment of Emma dissolves in the water as the lanky police officer's body sinks, softly landing in her spot. Blood seeps from his neck in smoky plumes. They're almost relaxing to watch, the plumes are. His body sways gently with the current on the sea floor. Then, without warning, the officer jerks to life. His eyes go wide and his hands reach around his neck. That's when I see it: one of those big fishing hooks that are scattered around the pier has been pushed clean through his throat. And as he silently screams, he manages to rip the hook right from his neck. His mistake. Now the water has two holes to enter through.

'Twenty seconds,' Emma's voice says.

And me, I kick off the sea floor and aim for the wavy moon floating above me. My lungs are heavy and bloated. When I break the surface, I expect immediate relief, but I get nothing. There's too much water in me. As I paddle to the pier's ladder, black patches appear in my vision.

'Fifteen seconds.'

In the hospital room I read the pamphlet to Emma. *'A person can expel water from their lungs by forcefully falling over an object just below the diaphragm.'*

'Ten seconds.'

The water in my lungs makes my body dense as I struggle up the ladder. I stumble towards the closest mast and belly flop onto it. My insides shift. I vomit water. Collapsing to the ground, the rawest breath of air I've ever tasted shocks my lungs. It's what a newborn must feel when the doctor rips him from the womb and slaps his back. Lying on the pier, the moon above me, it's never felt so good to simply breathe.

Lying flat on my back on the pier, just behind me, just north of my head, I hear a struggle. When I tilt my head back I see everything upside down. The sky below, Epiphany pressed up against the ceiling of the pier with Nico between her legs. His fists are raised as if they're pummelling the night stars.

Suddenly a blinding light illuminates both of them. I totter to my feet as Nico shades his eyes from the light. Through my dizziness and black spots I manage to grab a heavy, rusted tackle box tucked between some crates. And as I approach Nico from behind I glimpse a long cut on the back of his neck. Epiphany must have tried to hook him, too.

Raising the tackle box, I hammer Nico's skull. On the second hit the box pops open, scattering lures and sinkers and bobbers everywhere. Then, silently, a steady stream of blood flows from underneath Nico's black hair. It's like I've struck red oil. Nico, in an instant his body stops moving. He just stands there and sort of sways. Then his body, it collapses to the pier like it's suddenly discovered gravity. His body, it lands next to Epiphany's, which hasn't moved since I crawled out of the sea.

And as the small tugboat moors to the pier, under a beautiful full moon on this warm Caribbean night, I stand over the lifeless bodies of two people I hardly knew.

Jerry, this is your life.

24

God

I'm in the hospital room with Emma. This is way before I acted like a stupid hero and tried to save Epiphany's life on the pier. This is before I became a murderer. This is seventeen years earlier. This is before I'm cruising across the ocean in a freighter ship. This is before I find out the boat I'm on is full of electronics and toys and contraband. This is years ago when I'm in the hospital with my dying little sister.

This is when I'm twelve. In the hospital room I'm reading *Siddhartha* to Emma. She falls asleep twenty pages before the end, but I read anyway. I don't want her to wake and not hear my voice. When I finish the book I look around for another one, but the nurses haven't brought us any in a while. So I pick up *TV Guide* and begin reading that. The next thing I know, Emma is shaking me.

Excitedly, she is saying, 'Jerry, Jerry!'

And you know how it is – waking when you didn't want to be caught sleeping. You pretend you weren't. You fake it and quickly start talking about anything. So I'm going on about a new mini-series that *TV Guide* mentioned. Emma, she's patiently waiting for me to stop babbling. Her skin has some colour to it and there's this serene smile on her face – the kind of smile that shows just lightly on the lips and around the eyes. I haven't seen her look this well in months.

'They made you go to sleep, Jerry!'

'Who?' I say.

'Joan of Arc!' she squeals. 'She was with two angels. They made you fall asleep so she could talk to me alone.' Emma squeezes my arm. 'Joan said don't be afraid. She said I was just as brave and strong as her. She said I only have good things to look forward to because God's waiting for me. And I told her I didn't want to leave you, but she said you've got your own path to go down.'

I'm speechless. How do you explain to a dying nine-year-old that something only feels real because she wants it so badly? How do you tell her a dream is just a dream?

I take her little hand in mine. 'That's great.' I smile as big as I can.

'She said I was *just* as brave and strong as her,' Emma repeats, keeping that serene look on her face until she falls back to sleep.

Now jump forward a year, this is after my sister is dead but way before the pier thing. This is when I'm thirteen and enrolled at Sunday school because my mom and dad don't have a clue how to deal with death and dying and everything that must be going through the head of their remaining child. This is when, even though your little, innocent, never-hurt-a-fly sister died from a cancer eating her body like fungus eats mouldy bread, the nuns expect you to believe that there really is a Christian God and everything that happens – all the bad shit happening to good people all over the world, and in your life – it's just all part of *the plan*. They talk like God is your agent and He's working all the time for you, but you just don't see it because your little, puny, mortal mind is so limited it can't comprehend His Glory.

This is when the nuns tell you: this loving God, this glorious, all-powerful creator of everything, this ultimate source of love and forgiveness, well, you want to be careful around him, though. Because, despite being pure love, this God who created and then killed your innocent, nine-year-old little sister, He still wants your undivided allegiance. You see, despite all the good stuff they say about Him, He also created a place of eternal torment. It's called Hell, and the people who fuck up, they go there and never see their loved ones again.

The nuns say, yes, the burning alive for all eternity is horrible, but the real punishment of Hell is being separated for all eternity from the little sister that you just lost. They say, look, if we go by averages, you've got another sixty years on this earth if nothing happens to you sooner – no accidents, or nuclear war, or cancer. Sixty years is a long time to miss your little dead sister, but just think of what it's like to miss her for eternity.

This is when you realise the nuns are not so much about helping with the grieving as they are about making sure they save your soul. They tell the thirteen-year-old boy who just lost his sister that he wants to be very careful now. He wants to make sure he never makes God angry so God never sends him to Hell. So he's not separated from his little sister forever. They tell you the way to go to Hell, if you're interested, is by committing a mortal sin. Then they list off all the mortal sins. All the seemingly arbitrary things you can do that piss off the caring, loving God in the sky so much that He sends you to the place of eternal torture He created.

This list is so long, I say, 'Give me the CliffsNotes.'

I say, 'What's the abbreviated version?'

I say, 'What's that main thing I should avoid if I want to see Emma again?'

The nuns, they say, 'Just one?'

'Just one,' I say.

They say, 'Murder.' They say just be sure I don't murder anyone and I should be good to go. No matter what, they say, never kill anyone. Even if it's an accident. There's no difference. Murder is taking away God's greatest gift and that pisses him off more than anything. You just can't imagine.

I say, 'Does that include suicide?'

They say, 'What do you think?'

I say, 'What about if you jump out at an old person, to surprise them and all, and they have a heart attack?'

They say, 'Did you cause it?'

'I guess, in that situation, I guess I did, yeah.'

They say, 'That's a ticket to Hell, then. Best avoid any surprise parties for old people.'

I say, 'What about animals? Do they count?'

They say, 'Are we talking something like a dog or more like a bug? A fly?'

I say, 'Either.'

They say, 'The jury's still out on that one. Just in case, don't buy any kind of mosquito spray or roach motels or fly traps.'

'Bacteria?'

'Just given their large numbers, there's like a million in a square inch, He'd probably consider that mass genocide. That's a ticket to Hell. No hand sanitisers.'

And the Christian nuns, they're so convincing. They're so brainwashing, the way they say everything to the vulnerable thirteen-year-old boy who just lost his little sister.

Even though you've never seen any proof that God exists, even though all the praying everyone did in the hospital clearly didn't do anything, their stories get you so paranoid and so fearful that it's always in the back of your mind that they might be right. It's always, what if they're right and I'm wrong? So no matter how shitty your life is, just as a backup plan, you remember you never want to commit a mortal sin to piss God off. Just in case the nuns who you've been told know everything, every truth, are right, and there's a God and a Heaven where you get to see your loved ones again.

And going on about your life, this stuff, you keep it in the back of your mind. It never really bothers you until you come close to breaking one of the Big Man's rules, even unintentionally. Then you get shit scared.

This is why I wanted to make sure the bum didn't die when I accidentally made him choke in the coffee house. Call it my safety net. My backup plan. Just in case the crazy Christians are right. It's not the pain and the torture that scare me, it's blowing my chance to see Emma again.

Now this is sixteen years after Sunday school. This is when I'm on the pier in the Caribbean and two people are lying around me all dead. One is just normal dead. That's Epiphany. The other is mortal-sin dead. Dead the way a guy gets after you hammer his skull with a heavy, rusted toolbox. If the nuns are right and there is a bipolar, really, really conflicted God and murder is murder no matter what, then I'm out of luck. If I was ever going to see my sister again, I'm not going to any longer.

And maybe that's why I feel so weird right now. Maybe that's why I'm in such shock. Or maybe this is just how someone always feels whenever they murder someone in Epiphany's defence.

Me, I'm looking at the dead man, I'm prodding his lifeless body with my foot, just checking, just making sure, but I'm the one who feels all dead inside.

Behind me, on the pier, a voice shouts, 'Jerry? Are you Jerry?'

It's the guy who's come from the tugboat that's just docked at the pier. He's got camouflage pants on.

He says, 'Are you Jerry or is that Jerry?' and points to the dead guy.

I say, 'I'm Jerry. That's the guy I killed.' Nico's blood puddles underneath his head the way balled cookie dough melts and spreads when you bake it in the oven.

And the guy in the camo pants says, 'I don't care about him then. I need to get you and her to the boat.'

'She's dead,' I say.

'No, she's not,' the guy says, his fingers pressed against Epiphany's totally dead-looking carotid artery. 'But she will be if she stays here.'

I don't say anything. Epiphany looks so dead.

'I'm the ship's doctor,' the man in the camo, the man who looks more like a soldier, says. 'We need to get her there.'

And I look towards where 'there' is: the little tugboat that came from the freighter. The soldier doctor, he first throws Epiphany's yellow bag into the tugboat and then he makes for her body and beckons me to help lift her. And I do, in the end. But first I do the most unusual thing. Before I help the man carry Epiphany to the tugboat, I reach into Nico's pockets – the man who I just murdered – and I steal his money.

And, as we speed over crests of surf towards the freighter, I watch as Nico's body shrinks in the night until it and then the whole pier are engulfed in darkness.

25

Lost in Translation

Shadows grow and lean and shrink along the walls, bending when they meet the metal frame of the bunk. Sometimes the shadows spin clockwise; sometimes they swing side to side, like a cross.

When we docked with the freighter there were a few crewmen who met us and helped the man in camo pants drag Epiphany on to the deck. They brought us to this cabin. We've been here ever since. In a way it reminds me of the Grey Room back at the museum. Except for the bunk bed, the sink and a toilet, it's bare. The walls are an ugly marine green, the paint is peeling. The only thing that connects this cabin to the rest of the world is a small circular patch of sky that shows through the porthole. On a thick black wire a light bulb sways from the ceiling.

This is now three days after we got here. The freighter has long since left the pier and Mexico and my murder victim. According to Sarge we're somewhere in the middle of the Atlantic. That's his name, Sarge. The guy in the camo pants. He really is the ship's doctor. The first night aboard he spent most of it with us, making sure Epiphany was stable. He put ice around her head and gave her several shots of something. Then to me, he said, 'Take off your shirt. I want to look at your wound.'

So I did.

'This'll go easier if you talk. If you keep your mind distracted,' he said and gave me some kind of shot into my side. He said, 'Your latissimus dorsi is punctured.'

'My what?'

'A big muscle that covers part of your back and ribs.'

'Oh.'

'That's gotta hurt.'

No, it doesn't. Not now. Not the way my mind is. Shock is a great painkiller. It works like any addiction, I guess. It distracts you from the agony you feel.

'You've got quite an infection. I'm going to need to sew you up. So talk to me.'

'How do you know her?' I said, looking at Epiphany all passed out, looking all dead still.

'I don't,' Sarge said. 'The captain does. I just look after the boat's crew. I don't ask questions.'

I said, 'Must be a big crew. It's a big boat.'

And Sarge told me that ninety-five percent of the boat is storage. It's cargo crates. It's consumer products. It's electronics and toys and cheap souvenirs and clothes made in sweat shops bound for America and Europe. He said there's only a dozen or so crew on the whole ship.

I said, 'Are you American?'

'I used to be.'

In my back I felt the needle threading in and out of my skin.

'Where's the captain?' I said. 'The guy that knows her.'

'He'll be along later. Someone's got to steer the ship, right?'

'Yeah,' I said, immediately not remembering what I was replying to.

'Do you speak Russian? Like her?' he said.

'No. Why?'

The needle pricked my skin.

Sarge said, 'The captain, he speaks Russian. And Spanish and Arabic. I don't suppose you speak any of those?'

'No.'

'Well, I'm going to have to translate then,' and he looked at Epiphany, 'since she can't.'

Outside the cabin door a few crew walked by. One of them had a PSP, the other had a toaster.

Sarge, he said, 'Yeah, we dip into the cargo sometime. There's plenty of stuff to go around. The companies aren't going to miss one or two items. Besides, you can only look out at a beautiful sunset over the ocean so many times before it gets old.'

On the sink Sarge laid out three syringes.

'OK,' Sarge said. 'The hard part is over.' And he ran his finger over my stitches, testing their strength. 'But you have an infection and a bad fever. You need sleep. Your body won't heal if it doesn't sleep. I'm going to give you some shots. Some are for pain, some are for infection, and some are to knock you out.'

I looked at him and he said, 'Don't worry. I'll keep checking on you. It's not like there's a lot to do on this boat anyways. And we have eight days before we get to Portugal.'

So now this is three days, no, probably four, since we've been on the boat. It's hard keeping track. Epiphany stirs on the floor in the corner of our cabin. She hasn't woken since we've been here. We had put her in the lower bunk but she kept rolling out. The second time she hit her head. Since then, I've just left her on the floor.

And from the floor Epiphany, her eyes closed, she begs, 'Please!'

In her mind, she's still on the pier. She yells and, as if on cue, the light on the thick black wire hanging from the ceiling sways, fuelling the repeating cycle of shadows clawing and scratching their way like demons towards her body.

When I sleep, I have nightmares. I dream the dream of Epiphany in the silverware factory. When I'm awake, I'm never quite sure I am awake. I feel like I'm a figment of a figment of a figment. And it's all because of her. All because I've killed a man. *For her.*

And in the corner of the room, right by the sink, I think I see something. Or someone. She's just there for a moment. Rachel with her anime-red hair. But when I look again, she's gone.

Today I finally get a visit from the captain, though the way he looks at me I suspect he's checked in on me when I've been out. He and Sarge show up at noon. Well, I think it's noon. Outside the porthole the sun is high in the sky over the ocean.

Abdul, he's this dark-skinned Arabic guy. He enters the cabin, looks at Epiphany, then says something to Sarge in what I assume is Russian.

Then Abdul looks at me and Sarge translates, 'He says it's good to finally see you on your feet.'

'Uh, thanks,' I say.

'He wants to know where LaRouche is,' Sarge says.

'She's dead,' I say, and Sarge just looks at me.

'Let's not tell him that.'

And whatever Sarge does say to Abdul makes him look satisfied, like everything is A-OK.

'Can you ask him if I can walk around? Get some fresh air?'

'Unfortunately, that's not possible,' Sarge answers without asking Abdul, as if the two of them already spoke about this.

Abdul says something again and Sarge says, 'He says that he expects your friend to be better by the time we reach Porto and he expects you to let LaRouche know how well the journey went, because she's given him a lot of money and he would like business from her in the future.'

And part of me feels like I didn't get the memo on something.

Sarge translates that Abdul has to go back up to the helm, but one of them will bring food around later in the evening. And, as Abdul steps out of the cabin, he picks up something that they obviously left in the hall on purpose, as if they weren't sure they were going to give it to me. Then Abdul, he hands me Epiphany's yellow bag, which Sarge grabbed from the pier.

When Abdul leaves I say, 'Why didn't you tell him LaRouche is dead?'

Sarge looks around all frustrated for a second. 'Jerry, I don't know who LaRouche is, but I know he really likes her. I know she's given him business in the past. He wants to retain that connection. Abdul isn't the kind of guy you want to make angry. He's not the kind of guy you want to give bad news to.'

'I thought this boat shipped toys and electronics and stuff?' I say.

'It does,' Sarge says. 'But it also smuggles whatever Abdul wants. Like drugs or guns, or you and her. I don't ask questions. I just look after the crew.' And he leaves, locking the door behind him.

So here we are. A few days left to go. Me, locked in this cabin with the dead-looking but alive Epiphany. Me, the murderer. And again, in the corner of the room, I think I see a red-headed model ex-girlfriend. I think I hear a voice.

I dig through Epiphany's yellow bag. It's got her trainers, her Fanny Jones passport, some euros, and a notepad with Abdul's name and an address in Spain scrawled on it. For some reason she's also got a torn-out clipping of the photo of Donald and Roland and David Lang with me sitting in the background. It's the one from the *Chicago Tribune* article in February. The one with the picture-in-picture of the Van Gogh painting. I fold it back up and stick it back in the yellow bag. I keep digging. Finally I find them beneath her folded-up hoodie. My 486s. I swallow three. All I want to do is get knocked out again. I want to sleep forever.

26

The Autobiography of Epiphany Jones

I wake to a dull sound. *Thump. Thump. Thump.* It's pitch black and I can't tell where it's coming from. My body feels strange – like it's moving. The sky from the porthole is now non-existent. *Thump. Thump. Thump.* I search for a light, but I immediately stumble to my right. Only the wall keeps me from falling over. I straighten, but now I'm stumbling to my left. *Thump. Thump. Thump.*

It's not until there's a quick flash of a sphere of light that I'm even sure I'm still in the cabin. I stumble to the porthole. Outside it's as black as it is in the room. Then lightning flashes again and I see the rain is horizontal. The sea churns as if it's flagellating itself in punishment for some watery sin.

Making my way back towards the bunk, I trip and land face down in the dark. It's Epiphany's body I've fallen over. Even when she's unconscious she's trying to kill me. I scoot against the wall below the sink, right next to Epiphany. Why get up when you'll just fall down again?

And rocking on the floor in the darkness, I still hear it.

Thump. Thump. Thump.

As my eyes adjust I see that it's Epiphany's head that's making the noise. It's knocking against the wall. *Thump. Thump. Thump.*

I place my hand on the back of her skull to steady it. There's a soft lump the size of a tennis ball beneath her hair. And every time there's a flash of lightning I see just how badly the attack left her.

Her arms are covered in dried blood and long, thick scratches.

Flash.

A bruise on her calf isn't even blue; it's black like ink.

Flash.

There are circular marks on her neck where Nico grabbed her throat.

Flash.

The palm of her hand has a blister where skin has been scraped off, and her fingers are curled, as if she's grasping an invisible hockey puck. Even her breath is rattling, like something inside got crushed.

Call it what you want: regret, Stockholm syndrome redux, but in the cabin in the dark I find I've taken Epiphany's hand in mine. My thumb gently rubs back and forth across a long scab on her wrist. A fleck of the scab breaks and fresh blood dribbles to the surface. I wipe the blood, smearing it. The streak runs vertically across the long scab, forming a cross.

The look in her eyes before the attack – the hope she showed on the pier – I can't recall the last time I had that look. Hope is the best feeling in the world. Hope is what gets you out of bed in the morning. It's what gets you through your shitty job. It's what makes you believe you can save your marriage or beat that disease. Hope isn't the cure for your problems, but it's something almost as good: it's the belief – the blind faith – that you will overcome them.

And I look at the bloody cross I've made on Epiphany's wrist and wonder how some people can believe so completely. How do they have that blind faith? What does it feel like to believe some big, ever-silent guy in the sky is lovingly watching over you? How can someone believe He's giving them orders?

I run my thumb back over Epiphany's bloody cross, smearing it. No. If He does exist, He's an angry God. He's distant and apathetic and doesn't care about your pigeon-shit life.

And then I feel it in my back pocket, sitting here on the floor. It's been there since the pier. In the dark I take the videotape out, and when lightning flashes I can see the label. A ghost's handwriting reads, '*Work: Van Gogh, 1889. Donor: Mann.*'

Then through the porthole, lightning flashes again. Once and then twice. And then in the darkness of the cabin my heart skips a beat. I don't know how long she's been awake, but even in the darkness those green eyes burn like emerald embers. And for the rest of my life I'll know those eyes left me one heartbeat closer to death.

I shove the tape into my pocket with my pills, which rattle a bit as Epiphany struggles to sit up enough to lean her back against the wall. Her hair is all matted against her face. She's a wreck. Beaten and scratched, red and swollen. But those damn green eyes could still slice right through you. And watching her green eyes watching me, I wonder how she'll react to my betrayal on the pier. I wonder if she's seen the tape.

'Why did you change your mind?' she says.

Her question catches me off guard so much that I blurt out the truth. 'LaRouche told me you're looking for your daughter,' I say, my voice faltering. But the thing is, this is the first time I've realised that's why. 'I had a little sister and if I could have her back nothing would stop me either.'

Epiphany doesn't reply, but even in the darkness I swear I see the glow of her green eyes flicker. And for a few minutes there's a silence between us that I can't endure. So I find my voice and I tell her how I found LaRouche murdered; how Nico tortured her into telling him where we were going – all in retaliation for the orphanage. I tell her about getting arrested and how Nico gave me no choice. I tell her how I crawled out of the water. I tell her how I murdered him.

'Murdered,' I say, my voice shuddering.

I wait for her to reply, but she remains silent.

I wish I could go inside her head, hear her thoughts. 'How old is she?' I say.

Epiphany, she takes a moment before answering. 'Twelve now,' she says and falls quiet again.

Epiphany and I – we're no longer captor and captive, tormentor and tormented. It's hard to see your devil as separate from you once you've learned of its pains. Her daughter is only three years older than Emma was when she died.

And then my heart sinks again. Your worst regrets will always be for the things that you can't have anymore because *you* fucked them up.

Looking at Epiphany looking at me, I tremble. 'I *killed* man,' I tell her again, in case she doesn't get that, for some people, killing someone is a big, horrible deal.

I say, 'No more lies or half-truths.'

I say, 'You haven't told me anything about you. I don't know why we're here...'

I say, 'You need to be honest with me. About everything.'

'*Please*,' I tremble.

And I don't know if someone like Epiphany is capable of compassion, of mercy. Maybe it's because of the pain in my eyes, or because she remembers how she felt the first time she took a life. Or maybe, maybe it's that she's like me, and after everything that's happened she needs someone to talk to too. Whatever the reason, she finally answers my prayer. This is where I get the autobiography of Epiphany Jones.

She was born just outside of Moscow in a village whose name she can't remember. The only image she holds in her head is of a young woman who was probably her mother. She sees this young mother screaming as her daughter is pulled inside a car. From the back seat, Epiphany looks through the car's window and sees her mother being beaten by a man. The man gets in the car and they pull away, and the last image Epiphany has of her mother is her, lying on the ground, not moving. Epiphany thinks she is ten at the time.

For the next three weeks she is kept in a damp cellar somewhere in Moscow. There are adults who run the place. They feed her. They beat her. And when one of the men tells one of the women that he wants to break her, the woman stops him. 'No. This one is a special order,' she says. That night Epiphany wakes, chained on her cot, to the man rubbing himself at her bedside. His cum lands in gooey strands in her hair. If Epiphany remembers correctly, this is her birthday.

After a month, Epiphany is brought out of the cellar. She's taken upstairs, where a large suitcase is open on the floor. She's told to lie inside it. She's zipped up, nice and tight, and carried out to a car where she's put in the trunk. She's certain she'll never see light again.

It's who knows how long, and Epiphany is taken out of the trunk.

She's unzipped and the air has never smelled better nor has the sky ever looked so beautiful. She's somewhere in Italy, she thinks. That day, money changes hands, and Epiphany is given to new people. That night, a large, blonde Russian lady holds Epiphany while a black man fucks her in the mouth. Epiphany is beaten on her stomach and back when she vomits over the man's penis. During the beating, the woman tells the man, 'Careful, avoid the face.'

After a week the blonde woman and the black man buy her an ice cream in a park. Then they walk until they come to a train station. They board the train like they're all one big, happy family. On the train they give Epiphany a magazine and make her sit by the window. The magazine is in a language she doesn't know, but she recognises movie stars in the photographs. After three hours on the train Epiphany has to pee so badly, but they don't let her leave the seat. An hour later she wets herself.

The train arrives at some city where the air is warmer and the smell is salty. Epiphany asks if this is Spain. 'No,' they answer. The blonde woman and the black man part ways. Epiphany remembers the black man giving the Russian woman a large sum of money. She doesn't know how much, but it's more than she's ever seen.

The black man takes Epiphany on to a big boat with the letters 'PORTO' written on the side. She sees other girls her age on the boat, but none of them are allowed to talk. She is kept in a storeroom below deck. The black man occasionally comes to her. He makes her hold his testicles while he masturbates. One day she refuses and he punches her in the stomach. He tells her this is nothing compared to what the other men on the boat would do to her. 'They all think you're the prettiest, but your purity is worth too much. This is the least you'll do in return for me keeping them away.' He places her hands on his testicles. They are hairy, like a stuffed animal she used to have.

Time on the boat seems endless. Then, one day, she's brought above deck. They're docked at a port and before them a large city stretches into the distance. Epiphany's heard that the other girls have been herded into crates and moved onshore already. When she hears English she asks if they are in America. 'Close,' the black man says. 'This is America,

Junior.' He has an envelope full of cash. 'You're a special delivery,' he tells her. 'Stay quiet at customs.'

After the black man hands the envelope to the customs officer, they board a bus. The ride is long. Epiphany asks where they are going. 'The other side of this damn country,' the black man answers.

A day later the black man is shaking hands with a woman with red hair. She looks empty and broken. 'This is the one,' the black man says, pushing Epiphany towards the redhead. 'She's pure.' The redhead admires Epiphany and then takes her into a bathroom and inspects her genitals. Outside again, she thanks the black man and tells him she'll take the girl.

The first night Epiphany feels safer than she has in a long time. The redhead insists Epiphany calls her 'Momma'. And indeed, this first night, Epiphany almost feels as safe with this woman as she did with her real mother. But over the next week Momma starts to change. She yells more. She begins to hit her. One week, a young blonde girl, hardly older than Epiphany, is brought into her room, followed by Momma and a man Epiphany has never seen before. The young girl is bent over and tied to a desk as the man drops his pants and has sex with her from behind. The girl, she screams like a dying animal.

Week after week, this happens again and again. Epiphany is never raped, but she's forced to watch the rape of other girls. Sometimes she's forced to kiss and touch other girls while a group of two or three men watch. Other times she is forced to rub men and let them cum on her. When she hesitates, even a little, she is beaten – always with Momma in the room; always with Momma saying, 'Never in the face.'

This goes on day in and day out, until one week ... one week something changes. One day, Epiphany remembers Momma calling a strange name and being upset when she doesn't answer. That's the day she realises she doesn't know her name anymore – if she ever had one. But this week she remembers well for another reason. It's the week she first hears her voices. In the beginning, she thinks the walls have gotten thinner, but then she hears the voices even when there are other people in the room. The other people, they can't hear anything.

'Only two today,' the voices say one morning. And during that entire day Epiphany is only made to see two men. Sometimes the voices, they repeat nursery rhymes to her to help her go to sleep. Sometimes they tell her who is outside her door. Or they tell her to be careful that day. The voices, they speak in Russian.

One day Momma brings a girl of about fifteen to Epiphany's room. A client follows. The client orders the older girl and Epiphany to make love while he masturbates. During it Epiphany hears her voices say, 'You need to be strong now.'

Epiphany, she stops touching the other girl and sits up and, for the first time ever, she speaks back to her voices. 'What's about to happen?'

As she asks this, the client loses his weak erection. He becomes enraged. He screams that they don't stop until he finishes. He begins hitting the older girl in the face. He just keeps pounding her and pounding her. And, the longer he pounds, the harder it is to recognise that what he is hitting *is* a girl's face.

Epiphany is screaming so loudly, but she doesn't realise it until Nico bursts into the room. It's the first time she's ever seen him and already she knows he is a very dangerous man. Nico, he grabs the client by his hair and swings his head against the wall. There's a loud crack as the client's skull hits the concrete and his body crumbles to the ground. Two Mexicans enter the room. Nico looks at the client and the girl, who barely has a face anymore, and orders the Mexicans to dump both of them in the river. That night Epiphany's voices say, 'They are moving you soon.'

Two days later Momma enters her room. Momma is holding a pretty pink dress with white stockings and shiny black shoes. She tells Epiphany that she must put these on. She must look her best.

Momma puts Epiphany in a car. Not in the trunk, or even the back seat. It's a special day and Epiphany sits in the front between Momma and Nico while they drive to the expensive part of town. They stop in front of a hotel called the Royal Meridian. The lobby is what Epiphany imagines a king's palace must look like. Nico presses the button for the thirty-seventh floor. Outside room 3702 a man answers the door.

He shakes hands with Nico and smiles at Momma. His face is pleased when he looks at Epiphany.

The hotel room is even nicer than the lobby. Only an American could afford this, Epiphany thinks. And as Nico and Momma and the man discuss things, from the room's floor-to-ceiling windows, Epiphany admires the view of the ocean and the ships and the little cars driving on the long streets below. And Momma, she clears her throat and motions to Epiphany to come sit by them.

'And how will you get her across?' Nico asks.

'My company's Gulf Stream,' the man says. He *is* American. And the American, he looks at Epiphany and takes in her features. She takes in his as well. He's tall and in his late forties. Bushy eyebrows rest like caterpillars above tiny wrinkles around the eyes. His brown hair looks as if it has only recently begun to go grey. 'What's her name?' the American asks.

Momma is about to answer, but Nico interrupts. 'Anything you want it to be,' he smiles.

'Does she speak English?'

'She understands it.'

'Well,' says the American, looking at Nico, 'this is for you. Two hundred and fifty. Count it if you like.' Nico nods and he does count it. 'And this,' says the American, 'is for you.' He hands a slender box to Epiphany. The box is covered in black felt. Epiphany opens it. A long string of white marbles connected by a silver chain lie inside.

Nico and the American shake hands, then he and Momma turn and walk out of the room without looking at Epiphany again. The American picks up a glass on the table and pours red wine into it. He turns to Epiphany. 'This should make it easier for you,' he says with a kindly smile. Epiphany takes a sip and is surprised to find it sweet and delicious. 'Do you like movies?' the man asks her. Epiphany nods, and the American smiles. 'Well, I'm in the movie business and I think we are going to be very good friends.'

And that's how Epiphany Jones came to America. And in America she was kept and raped for years. Then one day she got pregnant. But the man who bought her was a good Christian. He insisted the baby be born. And when it was, the baby was taken from Epiphany before she could even hold it.

In the cabin, my mouth has gone dry. The Gulf Stream and the pearls; the good, Christian American; tall; wrinkles; grey hair; makes movies; hands over two hundred and fifty thousand dollars like it's nothing: Matthew Mann.

If Epiphany realises I've connected the dots, she doesn't let on. She tells me that, after she finally escaped, it took her twelve years to track Momma down. By that time the guilt was eating LaRouche alive and the fact that God was speaking to Epiphany was evidence of a chance of redemption. She told Epiphany that her daughter had been given to the traffickers to be kept until she would be old enough to be 'useful' to the client. The client got a discount on future purchases and the traffickers were guaranteed continued business from them.

Momma told Epiphany that the client has a storehouse of sorts in Spain, where he keeps the best girls he's bought safely out of the way of prying eyes. It's looked after by one of Nico's grand madams. There the girls live a relatively 'nice' life compared to most trafficked women. They're kept at this house until they're transported to locations around Europe, where they'll be treats for select guests at extravagant parties – orgies for the elite.

'Why not just go to the police?' I say. 'Why not tell them what happened?'

But Epiphany says what LaRouche said when I asked her the same questions: because these people are just too powerful. Money and girls buy anything. 'If the police ever did ask them questions about my daughter, they would simply kill her and dump her body somewhere, and it would be as if she never existed.'

Besides, who would believe a person of Matthew Mann's standing would be capable of something like that, I think.

Outside the porthole the storm has lessened. Dawn will soon break through the early morning's grey clouds. Only now, in the creeping light, do I notice just how much the retelling of her origin took out of her. Epiphany winces as she tries to keep herself propped up against the wall.

I say, 'Do you want me to help you into the bunk?'

'Tomorrow, maybe,' she says as she slides back to the floor. She closes her eyes and presses her lips together in an effort to suppress pain occurring somewhere in her body. If her pain had a name, it would be *Jerry Dresden*.

I watch her stir. She's caused me pain. I've caused her pain. Where does this all end?

Then suddenly her eyes spring open and catch me staring.

'I gave you to Nico,' I blurt, an involuntary confession.

I say, 'You're like this because of me. Why aren't you angry?'

And Epiphany, her eyes flutter, struggling with some new *Jerry Dresden* somewhere. 'I've known you were going to betray me since I arrived in Veracruz,' she says.

I shake my head, not so much in disagreement as in pity. 'How could you possibly know? I didn't even know.'

'My voices told me your betrayal–' she says, abruptly breaking off and squeezing her eyes shut, '– your betrayal, it was necessary.' She breathes as the pain passes. 'It was the only way to get you on the boat.'

It's like I'm beside Emma's hospital bed again, listening to sick people talk about how angels visit them. Only this time I'm Judas to Epiphany's fucked-up Jesus.

And then lightning flashes and on the bunk I see Rachel looking at us, the light bulb swaying from its wire in front of her.

There's silence in the room and I hear Epiphany say, 'Are you seeing one of them now? Your figments?' And when I look at her in the dark, despite her condition, she looks almost sorry *for me*.

'Yeah,' I say.

'What is it like?' she says, as if it's obvious to everyone in the room that the voices she hears are real but the figments I see are just a delusion in my mind.

'It's a lot like watching TV,' I say. 'You see people in your living room but you know they're not really there.'

Rachel, she grins at me in the dark. And, not wanting to talk about it, I say, 'And you? What are yours like?' And Epiphany, she's quiet for a moment, then she tells me the conversations are one-sided. She can't talk to them like I can talk to my figments. Sometimes, a painful headache or a ringing in her ears precedes them. Sometimes, even when she prays for weeks, begging them to contact her, they never do.

The voices, she says they'll give her a warning sometimes, or they'll tell her something will happen. But they're rarely specific. 'I would never neglect anything they told me. Everything has a purpose,' she says and glances at her cut and bruised arms. 'Even this.'

I shake my head. 'You keep saying "they"', I say. 'I've heard you mention "Michael" before–'

'The archangel.'

Well, if you could talk to angels, he'd be the one you'd want.

'But you said God talks to you–'

'Angels are God's voice.'

An answer for everything.

Epiphany clenches her teeth in response to another rush of *Jerry Dresden*, and I look for Rachel on the bunk again, but she's gone.

There's a moment's silence when the only sounds are the rocking of the ship. And then Epiphany, she asks about it – the big pink elephant in the room. 'What's in your pocket?'

'Just my pills.' I reach into my pocket then pull them out instead of the tape. I rattle the bottle in front of her. 'I got them from your bag when you were sleeping.'

'Oh,' she says and looks a little confused. Her eyes wince and she rubs her brow. 'On the pier...' she rubs the back of her head again. 'On the pier, Nico ... gave you the videotape...'

'A lot of good it did me. I lost it when I was pushed into the water,' I lie and give the best disappointed grin I can muster. 'See what I get for helping you?'

And Epiphany, ever so briefly, she looks almost sad.

'Jerry...' she pauses.

'Yeah?'

'Jerry...'

'Yeah?' I say again.

She winces.

'I still need you...' she says, but suddenly her words become a deafening scream. She lurches back in the lower bunk, grabbing her skull as she cries out. Her screams, it sounds like she's on fire. It sounds like she's Joan of Arc being burned alive at the stake.

27

Reason

Abdul's cabin is packed full of the normal legal stuff all the other crew members are nicking from the ship's inventory: digital cameras, iPods, toasters, DVDs, faux-leather shoes, Dust Busters, dress shirts still wrapped in plastic. But then there's the other stuff. Samples of the illegal smuggling stuff: the AK-47, the Armalite AR-10, the six-pack of grenades, the big bricks of white stuff wrapped in plastic wrap. I'm looking around making sure there're no girls tied up in here.

How I got here is Sarge had rushed into our cabin within moments of Epiphany screaming. He had heard her cries all the way down the hall. As soon as he entered, Epiphany collapsed and fell silent. Besides attending to Epiphany – giving her a shot of something, shining a flashlight into her eyes – he had his hands full when Abdul arrived, constantly translating what Abdul, who looked increasingly angry and concerned over Epiphany's state, was saying and then translating what I told them about how Epiphany got into this condition.

Every answer I gave to Sarge – 'We were just talking then she started screaming' – caused Abdul's glaring at me to deepen, as if I were full of shit and were holding a pillow over Epiphany's face that very moment.

Sarge tried to explain to Abdul that the most likely scenario was a blood clot from the beating she took. One that had shifted in her head. He told Abdul the best thing anyone could do, now that it looked like she had stabilised, was to give her peace and quiet and get to Porto as soon as possible so we can get her to a hospital. And glaring at me, Abdul seemed to like that idea – keeping her safe from *me* – so he

ordered that I should stay in his cabin as he's at the helm speeding us
towards Porto as fast as possible.

So in Abdul's cabin Sarge is sitting on the couch across from me,
something that looks like a rocket-propelled grenade launcher resting
right behind him, pretending he's not seeing any of the illegal arms or
drugs or stuff. I know if I would point them out he would say, 'I don't
ask questions.'

So I say, 'Um, what's with Abdul?'

And Sarge, he says, 'What do you mean?' like Abdul is the most
ordinary guy ever.

I say, 'Why does he care about her so much?'

Sarge stifles a laugh. 'He doesn't. He cares about getting the freight
he's paid for safely from one location to the next. It's just business for
him.'

And, looking at all the guns and explosives and stuff that Sarge
doesn't see, I suddenly get the feeling Abdul is another Nico, but with
a Rambo complex. It's all just business and anyone who gets in the
way of it needs to be taken care of. And I think about the last thing
Epiphany said before she started screaming like she was on fire. She
said she still needs me.

And suddenly the plan in my mind, the one where Epiphany just stays
all unconscious and I walk off the boat when we get to Portugal and fly
home with the videotape proving my innocence, doesn't seem as cut and
dry as it did a few hours ago. I get the feeling that, if Epiphany wakes
up, she could tell Abdul to walk behind me with the rocket launcher
pointed at my back until I do everything she wants, and he would. And
if she doesn't wake up he'll make sure I stay on this boat until she does.

The boat rocks a bit and a Russian-made anti-tank mortar rolls out
from under Abdul's bed. And on the floor by it I see a Braun Citro-
matic Juicer, new in its box. I see a Sony DVD player. I see a Panasonic
NV-DS27 MiniDV camcorder. The boat rocks again and the mortar
returns to where it came from.

'She thinks she hears voices from God,' I say, not wanting to think
about the free-moving explosives. 'That's schizophrenia, right?'

'Could be,' Sarge says.

'What else could they be? The voices, I mean.'

Sarge shrugs. 'Trauma. A way for the mind to deal with horrible things. Trauma victims sometimes hear voices. It gives them a sense of power in a situation where they're otherwise helpless.'

I say, 'Is that common?'

'Common? No. But it does happen. Usually to victims of extreme abuse.'

Abuse. And as if on cue Abdul comes in and says something in Russian to Sarge.

To me, Sarge says, 'Excuse me. I'm needed elsewhere.'

Abdul follows him out the door, but before he closes it he turns around and looks me in the eyes, then motions around to all the explosives in the room and, interlocking his fingers together like he's praying, he violently separates his hands, saying, 'BOOM!'

I get it.

As the night goes on Sarge is back and forth between the cabin I'm in and Epiphany's. He says no news is good news when I ask if her condition has changed. While he is out I take some more 486s. Until now, until all this happened, I never realised how they do more than help me stop seeing figments. They've helped calm the swirling mass of fear and emotions rocking around inside me. And though I'm not quite there yet, I can feel that merciful apathy returning. The pills, they help me sleep through the night, despite the explosives rattling all around.

In the morning Sarge comes in and tells me that Abdul is going to be at the helm all day; that we've made good time and we're arriving in Porto tonight, where we'll wait off coast for the evening before it's our turn to dock. He says, 'Abdul asks that you stay in this room for just a little longer.'

And I think, Well, I'm sure he asked nicely, so OK.

Sarge leaves, but even knowing Abdul won't be stopping by, it's still not until the afternoon that I get enough courage to open up the Panasonic camcorder under his bed. And, as I put the tape in, part of me doesn't want to see it – Roland being murdered – but part of me needs to. But when I put the tape in, the camera doesn't turn on. Its battery hasn't been charged. That's when I look at Abdul's laptop with its satellite internet dongle sitting on his small desk. That's when I find the FireWire cable in the box.

So, against my best possible judgment, I find I'm not only opening the arms smuggler's new camcorder, I'm using his laptop too. I plug in the camcorder with the FireWire cable. And being at a computer again, it feels like I've found a long-lost friend. I'd almost enjoy it if my heart weren't beating so fast.

I click the QuickTime icon on the desktop and wait for the feed to open. It's like waiting for porn to download – it never happens fast enough. Then the lights on the camcorder's buttons blink on and suddenly the QuickTime window on the computer jumps from black to blue, then to a fuzzy peach. On the screen the fuzzy peach becomes the hand that's just turned the camera on...

And from down the hall, I hear a voice. I hear footsteps coming this way.

I hide the camcorder behind a three-pack of dress shirts still sealed in plastic and hit QuickTime's pause button, then open Firefox to hide the player's window.

Sarge comes in and frowns when he sees I'm browsing *Chicago Tribune*'s website. He gives me a look that says, *I think we both know it's not a good idea to be using Abdul's laptop.* But instead of saying that, he says, 'That can wait. Believe it or not, because I can't, your girlfriend's up and she's asking for you.'

My heart sinks when Epiphany says, 'Hello.' When Sarge said she was up, I thought he meant barely lucid, laying-under-the-covers 'up', not sitting-in-her-bunk, legs-crossed-Indian-style, lightly-sipping-soup-from-a-bowl 'up'. Now it's going to be harder to slip away when we dock. Between us the light bulb sways, illuminating her green eyes.

'What happened to you?'

'I've never spoken of my voices in detail to anyone before,' Epiphany says. 'I think I was punished.'

'Sarge thinks you had a blood clot.'

Epiphany just shrugs like that's obviously ridiculous and takes another sip of her soup. She doesn't beat around the bush. From Portugal we go to Spain, she tells me. Thirty miles south of Seville is the storehouse Nico owns. It's there where Epiphany thinks her daughter was taken twelve years ago. It's there where she thinks her daughter is being kept now.

I think, going from Portugal to Spain – what could possibly go wrong? We'll probably just meet more of her friends. You know, more totally safe, laid-back, non-dangerous psychopaths like Nico and Abdul.

She notices the dissent on my face but doesn't give me a chance to speak. 'Before – before I was punished,' she says, 'you told me the videotape was lost. When we get my daughter I promise–'

And look, I no longer care about turning Epiphany in to the cops. Everything we've done to each other over the last few weeks – you can't find two other people who've fucked each other over more. And it's not that I feel completely sorry for her, but I mean, how badly do you need to be beaten to forget your own name? What length wouldn't even a sane person – someone who hasn't been abused their whole life like Epiphany has been – what length wouldn't *anyone* go to to get their child back? I've lost my simple assumptions of right and wrong after everything that's happened since going to Mexico.

Besides, I've got the videotape. It will exonerate me; it'll be enough. I don't need Epiphany. After I show it to the cops, if Epiphany can get to her daughter and disappear before they find her – if they even try to – that's fine with me. Just so long as she never interferes with my life again. But I'm getting out now while I'm still alive. I'm not going to be bullied or threatened or manipulated into going on any more fucked-up road trips with her.

So I shake my head and say, 'You don't need me. You never have.'

'I do, Jerry. My voices, they've never been wrong.'

The light bulb hanging from its wire sways. I take a breath. 'But what can *I* possibly do?'

And maybe this is the first time it registers with her: *What can this loser possibly do for me?* She looks at me almost pleadingly. 'They didn't tell me *why* I need you, only that I *do*.' She sees the disbelief in my eyes. She believes the videotape is lost, and without it, she knows there's no reason for me to help her. She says, 'Jerry, please, if this were your sister...'

'She's dead,' I say, losing my temper. 'She doesn't exist anymore. I still do! But if I keep following you, I'll end up just like her; or maybe I'll end up killing someone else.' And when I say that, my eyes sting. 'I can't do that again.'

'But they told me,' Epiphany stutters, desperation showing on her face. 'They told me I need you, Jerry. *They told me*.'

And I break my rule. The one about not arguing with people who think they talk to God. I foolishly believe reason will overcome faith. '*They* told you you need me?' I mock. 'But *why* would they tell you *I* could help? You must have some idea? I can barely show up to work on time – when I had a job, that is. I'm not a guy who gets things done. I'm a guy who goes to a shrink and has to take abortion pills just to get through the day because he sees people who aren't there, for God's sake. I'm not someone who is clever or strong or dependable. So why would they tell you I can help? The *only* connection I even have to the man who bought you is that my dead dad worked for him years ago.'

Epiphany's eyes furrow when I say this. It's the first time I've mentioned knowing that Matthew Mann was the person who bought her in that hotel room in Mexico.

I say, 'I met Matthew less than half-a-dozen times. I haven't seen him in over a decade. He wouldn't even know who I am anymore. I don't know where he is and I wouldn't know how to get a hold of him if I did.'

Epiphany, she opens her mouth to speak, to lie, to manipulate.

'No!' I yell and swing my hand in anger. It hits the light bulb hanging from its wire, which spins away in pain. Shadows dance back and forth across the cabin. 'I *killed* a man for you. I didn't mean to, but I did. And I've got to live with that.' The tears in my eyes feel like they're about to pop. 'I'm messed up enough as it is. I can't do this anymore.'

Epiphany, again she tries to talk, to confuse me with more lies, but I don't give her the chance.

I say, 'I understand how horrible it must have been all those years, but I didn't do anything to you. I didn't abduct you. I didn't beat you. I didn't spend two hundred fifty grand on you, Matthew did. So give me one good, *logical* reason why your damn voices would say *I'm* the one who can help you?'

There's silence between us as the swaying light throws shadows around the room. Long shadows. Thin shadows. Demon shadows. And as the light sways and the demons grow, shrink and grow again, Epiphany's emerald eyes flash. Her voice is cold and unforgiving.

'Because the American who purchased me for two hundred and fifty thousand dollars in Mexico wasn't Matthew Mann. He was your father.'

28

The Murder

The world splits. A huge chasm rips the Heartland of America open. North and South are separated. The Atlantic is divided and the Iberian Peninsula comes dangerously close to leaving Europe. I'm back in Abdul's cabin watching a globe once bound for some eighth-grade geography classroom totter, cracked and broken, on the floor. If I hadn't stormed out of Epiphany's cabin I would have two murders on my hands.

It's too much. She's *completely* mad. She's desperate. She'll say anything. Worse, she thinks I'm totally stupid. Like Mom and I wouldn't have known if Dad was hiding a little crazy girl at our house. And I guess that two hundred and fifty grand he used to buy her was from that currency press he had sitting in our living room that we never noticed!

She's lying. She's trying to confuse me. She's taking advantage of my sympathy for her. Back when I tried to kiss her on the bus – she knew I had Stockholm syndrome. Maybe she didn't know the clinical term, but she knew she had me, nonetheless. She knows I'm off balance – it's why she was asking me about my figments. This is just more of her manipulating and lying and thinking I'm so stupid I'll believe and do anything she says.

I pace Abdul's cabin. Out of all the explosives in here, I'm the biggest bomb waiting to blow. I think I hear someone at the door. Let Epiphany come. She'll learn the hard way that enough is enough. I run my fingers through my hair. My body shakes in anticipation of the door opening.

But it doesn't. I pause to catch my breath, to collect myself.

I'm getting off this fucking boat. I'll swim to shore if I have to. And then I'm going to the police with the tape. The tape, let her refute the tape. Video doesn't lie.

I take a breath and grab the laptop. I'm about to X out of the Firefox window when I notice a small headline in the *Chicago Tribune*'s recent news ticker. It's an article about the Van Gogh. It's been returned to the museum and is scheduled to go on display as originally intended – albeit under tighter security.

I click on 'Related Stories' and find the article from February in front of me. It's the one about the acquisition of the painting. The one with the photo of Roland and Donald and David Lang – smiles all around. Smiles on all but me anyway. There I still sit in the background, hunched over my computer – one two-hundredths of a second of my life frozen in time. That moment seems ages away now.

In the 'Free Events Chicago' sidebar my mom's Joan lectures are listed. Above the listing is a small picture of my mom standing next to a painting of Joan of Arc. The photo was taken after I was kidnapped. She's smiling, but not with her eyes. It's one of those smiles you wear when the guy with the camera orders you to. But behind that forced smile you give to the world, your life's really in pieces. And I wonder if she's received my postcard yet.

I remember Mom telling Emma and I that she loved Joan's story because hers was one of the few lives that were recorded under oath during two separate trials – one condemning her, the other exonerating her. Experts like my mom could look over every detail of Joan's life as if they'd been there. Mom told us that at her first trial many people believed Joan was insane. Scholars have said that troubled people like Joan see signs that aren't there. They need hope, they need purpose, or they can't deal with everyday life.

Even today a number of experts have tried to explain Joan's visions and voices in neurological terms. Some think she had something now known as Ménière's disease: a neurological condition that affects the ears. The primary symptoms are ringing in the ears and migraines

– both of which Joan suffered from. Some even believe she had tuberculosis – an insult if you believe she's a virginal saint – but a disease that, in extreme cases, can cause the sufferer to hear voices.

Voices.

Ringing in her ears.

Migraines.

'Occam's razor,' my shrink said. 'All other things being equal, the simplest explanation tends to be the right one.'

And what's more plausible? That Dad wasn't the man Emma and my mother and I knew; that he bought kidnapped girls for ridiculous sums of money we couldn't afford and then raped them; that one of those girls talks to God and, years later, He's telling her that I can help her find her daughter? Or, like Sarge said, Epiphany is so traumatised, the voices she hears are her mind's way of helping her feel some control over her situation? Hell, it's even possible that she got tuberculosis from one of the men she was forced to service.

And then it all snaps into place. I remember the torn-out photo of Donald and Roland and David Lang and the Van Gogh that I found in Epiphany's yellow bag when I was looking for my 486s.

Epiphany must have seen the photograph in the *Chicago Tribune* from February. She tore it out. She saw that the painting was donated by Matthew Mann and read about Roland's connection to him. She couldn't get to someone like Matthew, but she could get to Roland. So he became the target of her revenge. After she attacked him it didn't quench her pain. Her warped mind needed a new plan. It needed a new person to hold power over, because she couldn't get to the guy who hurt her. So again she saw the same clipping of the photograph hanging above Roland's desk and she must have seen me sitting in the background, and Roland, he could have told her I was Jonathan's son. That's when her mind created what she needed it to in order to feel a sense of hope and purpose again.

And I need to see it for myself. I need to tell Epiphany that I've seen exactly what happened with my own eyes.

On the laptop I click the QuickTime window to the front of the screen.

No commercials, no coming attractions.

The show starts now.

The window jumps from black to blue, then to a fuzzy peach. A hand moves away from the frame and a person appears.

His orange little goatee with white sprouts of hair.

His pock-marked face.

His yellow teeth.

'This is April fourth,' Roland says in close-up. His voice is weak. When I left his studio that morning, he was as peppy as could be. 'Photographing Van...' The audio cuts out for a moment as he reaches around the camera to adjust it. He comes back into frame and you can hear his voice again: '... camera I am using today to photograph the work is a Nikon D1 with the SB-28DX speedlight hot shoe flash.' Roland gets smaller on the screen as he moves closer to the painting. You can almost see his whole body now. 'Painting is on aluminium easel, with rubber guidings,' he says about seven feet from the video camera's lens.

Minutes pass as Roland adjusts the lighting in his studio. Then, from an off-screen source, extra light floods the room for a second. Someone's opened the door to the studio, entered and closed it behind them. Roland looks towards the off-screen door and all the colour drains from his face. He's silent for a good ten seconds. Granted, the tape isn't the best quality, but in those ten seconds I could swear I see his orange goatee sprout a few more threads of white.

His voice shakes. 'What are you doing in here?'

The voice that answers, you can't make it out. The mike on the camera is unidirectional; it only records sounds in front of it and right now Epiphany is behind the camera.

Show the devil. Just one shot. One frame. That's all I need and I'm free.

'I swear I don't know,' Roland pleads, an answer to some unheard question.

There are muffled sounds for the next thirty seconds. During this time, Roland cries. As he's crying, something small and black flies into frame, something no bigger than a quarter hits him in the face, causing his whole body to jerk unnaturally, as if the object was much larger.

Roland briefly muffles his tears as he listens to someone speak. 'Why?' he says as he breaks down again. For another twenty seconds Roland just stands there on screen next to the painting and shakes. He looks like he's going to wet himself.

Then the entire video image, it shakes a little, then stops. Roland, he pauses for a moment before begging, 'Please.'

And then the video image, it quakes strongly as everything on the screen wobbles from side to side. And even wobbling, you can see just how white, just how ghost-like Roland is now.

'Please,' he sobs.

And as Roland screams, the Van Gogh and everything else on screen suddenly slides frame left as the image falls on its side. Then the video image, it flickers a few times before cutting to the default blue status screen.

And the last thing you hear is Roland shouting. He's shouting at his attacker. He's shouting their name. He's begging for his life.

Jerry! Jerry! Please, no! Jerry! No!'

29

Rape

'Jerry! Jerry! Jerry! Give it to me, Jerry!'

'Fuck my ass.'

'Harder, Jerry! Harder! Make me hurt!'

I've got Epiphany bent over the bunk. It's like I'm drilling for oil. I want her to crack. To bleed. I want to give her pain. I want to cum rivers in her ass so she'll leak for the rest of her life. And when people ask her what happened she'll say, 'I messed with Jerry Dresden.'

You would do no less if she fucked up your life.

'Is that all you've got?' she grins.

She says, 'Your dad was *so* much better than you.'

And before I can even cum my dick is limp in my hand. Look at what Epiphany's done to me. I'm in front of a computer with an internet connection – the first one I've had in weeks – all the porn I need is just a click away and I can't get her out of my head. I can't even revenge-fuck her in my mind right.

My whole body feels like it's broken.

After I watched the videotape, after I boxed up the camcorder and pieced together the globe I punched, Sarge stopped by. He said he was just checking in, but he acted weird. I wondered if he had talked to Epiphany; if she had told him I was being less than cooperative. And I wondered how long it would take both of them to tell Abdul, who will no doubt then have no problem making me do whatever his little smuggled princess wants.

Outside the porthole the lights of Porto flicker in the night. Late tonight we'll be docking. We'll be docking and I've got nothing. Epiphany owns me. She's never going to let me go.

I look at my limp dick in my hand, chubby and covered in saliva. I begin to sob.

'Get a hold of yourself, Jerry,' a voice suddenly says.

My eyes go wide. 'Rachel?' My model ex-girlfriend figment is sitting on Abdul's bed.

'Put you dick back in your pants and let Epiphany have it,' she says.

'I'm stressed,' I say to myself. 'This is what happens when I get stressed.' I reach into my pockets.

'What are you doing?' my imaginary ex-girlfriend asks.

I pull out my little bottle of 486s.

'You don't need those,' Rachel says.

'But I do. I'm seeing things again. I'm going crazy,' I say.

'Look at you, Jerry,' Rachel shouts. 'Your whole life you've always done whatever other people wanted you to. Everyone walks all over you. Be a man. Take a stand.'

'A stand? Like what?' an exhausted smile of utter disbelief breaks out on my face. 'I thought I had her, but this whole time, she's had me exactly where she wants me. Roland was screaming *my name*. I know he was screaming for the last person he saw. He was screaming for help, but the tape makes it look like he's screaming *at* me. Like I'm there killing him. Epiphany's the devil; she's a master puppeteer. She's taken *everything* from me without breaking a sweat.'

'So you're just going to sit here, watch your little movie and pretend to revenge-fuck her in your mind?' Rachel scoffs. 'Do something *real*, Jerry.'

'Real?' I say. 'What could *I* possibly do to *her*?'

And looking past all the obvious guns and explosives in the room Rachel nods towards my dick that's still hanging out of my pants.

She says, 'Show her she hasn't cut your balls off.'

I say, 'How?'

She says, 'Give her her worst fear.'

I say, 'What's that?'

She says, 'That little revenge fantasy in your head?'

I say, 'Yeah?'

She says, 'Make it real so she never fucks with you again.'

The hall is empty and when I enter Epiphany's cabin she's just getting dressed. It's the first time I've seen her standing since we've been on the boat. The blue dress she wore in Mexico is slung over the bunk's frame. With one hand she's holding her cargo pants up. They're still unbuttoned. I can see her underwear through her fly. They're maroon.

'Jerry?' Her long-sleeved T-shirt hugs her chest.

My skin burns. I can't go home. I can't see my mom. I can't be innocent. It's all because of you, I think.

You even took away the one pleasure I did have in my shitty little life.

I can't jerk off because of you.

In my mind, Epiphany cackles, *Your dad was SO much better than you.*

The bitch. The liar. If her voices were real they would have warned her about this, the false prophet.

And standing before her, her pants still unbuttoned, she's staring at my crotch.

Oh, how embarrassing. I've forgotten to put my dick back in my pants.

Fear spreads on her face.

There are no rewards. No punishments. No voices. No God.

'Jerry – '

No one judges you at the end of a tunnel.

I toss the tape into her hands. It takes her a moment to register what it is.

'You said–' The caught look on her face, it's almost enough to make what I'm about to do seem excessive. Almost.

'I lied. Just like you,' I say. 'All that's on there is Roland shouting my name. You aren't in the footage at all. You've known that all this time. The tape was nothing but a lie to trap me into following you.'

Epiphany speaks quickly, the way the guilty do. 'I've never viewed it. I was only told to take it.'

'By your voices?' I yell so loudly that Epiphany cowers.

'Jerry, please. I'll go back with you after we find my daughter–'

'You mean, after looking for your daughter *for twelve years*, you'll go back to the States and tell everyone you were the one who killed Roland?' I say, incredulously. 'You'll give up your daughter again and go to jail?'

'What happens to me doesn't matter,' she breathes. '*She's* all that matters.'

'Quit lying,' I sneer. And before this goes any further, before she can con me into anything ever again, I grab her by the back of the neck. She's still weak from Nico's beating. From lying in bed most of a week. Her unbuttoned pants slide down to her knees as I force her over the lower bunk.

'Jerry!' she screams into the mattress.

'*Show her she hasn't cut your balls off*,' Rachel says from the corner of the room.

Epiphany, bent over, face-down in the bunk, I cross her wrists behind her back, holding them together with one hand.

I put my knee on the back of her thigh to keep her from kicking.

My dick, hanging out of my fly, it wiggles against the inside of her leg.

I press my other hand into the small of her back to keep her from rolling over.

And into the mattress, Epiphany bellows, 'Don't become your father!'

She bellows, 'Don't!'

She screams, 'Don't, Jerry!'

And I say, 'I can't.'

I say, 'Because he never did any of those things to you.'

And I reach between my legs and grab my limp dick and push it back into my pants and zip up my fly.

It's cold in here. No one likes shrinkage, you know?

Then I reach into my pocket and pop my bottle of 486s open and, lying on top of Epiphany on the bunk, I pull her head back by her raven hair and force the contents of the entire bottle into her mouth. As she struggles against my weight, I hold her mouth closed. I hold her firm on the bunk and try to remember how long it took the pills to affect me that night in Chicago when I swallowed half a bottle. Five minutes? But Epiphany's much smaller than I am and in less than two minutes she's stopped struggling. When I push her to the floor she barely squirms. The green fires in her eyes have clouded over.

As I walk out the cabin door Epiphany just looks at me all paralysed-like.

Rachel says, 'My way would have been more fun.'

And within minutes I'm at the rear of the ship. There's one crewman out here, but he's across the deck playing with a remote-controlled car once bound for a toy store in America and doesn't notice me in the dark. I double-check that the roll of Nico's cash is snug in my pocket. The yellow lights of the city twinkle in the distance. I lean over the railing, waiting for my heart to catch up with my plans. The sea is dark like oil. 'I can't do this. I can't. What if there're sharks?' I say to myself.

'*No*. Take charge for once, Jerry. You have to do this,' Rachel demands.

And as I press my eyes shut and blindly jump into the night, I pray that this swim goes better than my last.

30

Portugal

Traveller's Tip: When a shark attacks, it strikes from the bottom. It rams you with its snout. While you're stunned, it swoops back around and takes a bite. And when it has you in its jaws it's easy to panic, but you must stay calm. The only way you're going to get free is if you point your fingers like they're a gun and jab them into the shark's eyes. You jab and you jab until it releases you. Then you just pray you can make it to dry land.

I know this because I read it in that *Time* article and it was all I could think about as I swam to shore. And being at night, not being able to see what could be in the water three feet away made it that much worse. But it turns out the only thing I had to worry about was my tongue. Sucking salt water for an hour makes it swell.

Traveller's Tip: After you jump ship and finally make it to shore you'll be more tired than you ever thought possible. Swimming a mile isn't your afternoon walk. Not one muscle in your body is at rest when you swim. And as you get close to shore, as your feet meet the sandy ocean bottom, it feels like you've swum past the stars and landed on the moon – that's how tired you are. The first thing you'll want to do is sleep. But you can't. Not right on the beach anyway. You need cover. Thankfully the locals have lined the beach with purple-and-yellow-striped huts. I crawled into one and was out before my face hit the sand.

I woke, my tongue still numb from the salt water, to a drone of voices. I peeked out of the hut. It was morning and the beach was packed with locals. Fat locals, thin locals. Locals with iPods and books and inner tubes. The freighter, now visible in the daylight, had moved to the port a mile down shore.

Traveller's Tip: When you land on strange shores there is one thing you can always count on: the younger locals will speak English. They'll speak English because they've all grown up watching Hollywood movies, just like you.

I stopped a teenage couple on their way to the water. 'Ith thif Poro? Wfher can Iffind anth infernef caffé?'

'*Desculpe*?' they said.

'Ith nefd anf internef caffe. Internef!'

They looked at each other. 'Sorry,' they said. 'Do you speak any English?'

'I thpeak Englith! Wfher can Iffind anth infernef caffé?' Fucking salt water.

Eventually they understood and told me that the beach I was at was in a suburb of Porto and that any internet cafés would be in the city centre.

Traveller's Tip: You get to an internet café. You set up a new email address. Hotmail. Yahoo. Gmail. It doesn't matter. You set up a new email address because you don't know who is tracking your old one. The cops. Angry mercenary smugglers. A girl who talks to God. You set up a new email address and then you search for a place to stay. Hostels are no good. They're likely to be full of Americans. And who knows if they follow the news? Who knows if they'd recognise you? So you need to find a site that has rooms to rent from the locals.

Traveller's Tip: Find a currency exchange. Don't worry about the exchange rate if it's blood money from the guy you killed. And don't act surprised when you give the lady on the other side of inch-thick bullet-proof glass the dead sex trafficker's wad of pesos and she hands you back almost ten thousand euros. That's just how you roll, big spender.

Traveller's Tip: Find a Gap. Even foreign lands have them. Buy pants and shirts and some new shoes. Buy a wallet for all your money, high roller. A backpack. A watch.

Traveller's Tip: Find a bookstore. The one I stop in is called Livraria

Lello. But you find your own. There's something magical about this one. A winding, red staircase that looks like it was created by dripping wax from giant candles connects the first and second floors. Large iron lanterns hang from struts on the walls and the roof has a massive, stained-glass skylight that bathes the floor-to-ceiling oak shelves in multicoloured rays of light.

Pick up an English-language guidebook. In my case it's a guide to Porto: it's history, language, culture and customs. At the beginning of every chapter they have these Traveller's Tips.

Traveller's Tip: Portugal is a culture that respects hierarchy.

Traveller's Tip: Loyalty to the family comes before other social relationships, even business.

Traveller's Tip: The Portuguese are a people who retain a sense of formality when dealing with each other, which is displayed in the form of extreme politeness.

The bookstore owner sits behind the counter.
'I WOULD LIKE TO BUY THIS BOOK PLEASE,' I say.
He shoots me an odd look.
I say, 'HOW MUCH IS IT PLEASE?'
But the owner doesn't understand what I am saying even though I spoke slowly and clearly. He's old. Maybe seventy. Probably doesn't know a word of English. His younger assistant comes over and says, 'I help you buy.' She tries to take the book from me, but:

Portugal is a culture that respects hierarchy.

I just got here. I'm not going to start breaking any rules. I don't need any more trouble. The old man is obviously the top dog. I'm sure he should ring me out. I ignore the girl as best I can. I won't even look at her. So the old man saunters up to the counter and pats the girl on the hand. No doubt he's telling her this foreigner respects tradition; he understands our ways.

'THANK YOU VERY MUCH,' I say. 'HAVE A GOOD DAY.'

Traveller's Tip: Money talks. When I return to the internet café I have an email from a woman named Diana. The apartment she has for rent isn't far from the bookstore. It's on a narrow, hilly street above a café with yellow walls. It's not much, but it'll do. There's even a small fireplace. The lady wants to copy my passport, but I can't exactly explain that I've had my fake one confiscated by corrupt cops in Mexico after I ran from the house of a former sex trafficker I'd just found murdered, so I offer her twice what she was asking and pay for two months on the spot. The passport isn't a problem after that.

Traveller's Tip: Setting up a temporary life is exhausting.

I unpack my new backpack and shower. The TV only has one channel and it is all in Portuguese so I shut it off and crawl into bed. And for the first time since any of this happened, I have a place to myself again. I am free from Epiphany.

Traveller's Tip: It's all gotta catch up with you sometime. When it does, just cry and cry and cry. Let it all out, you big baby. You don't need to pretend that you're not worried that some of the people you talked to today weren't real. You're fucked up. You're out of medicine. All that time you were swimming, your imaginary ex-girlfriend swam right besides you saying, *'Quit worrying about the sharks! Swim! Swim!'* like she was coaching Michael Phelps.

Necessity always comes first. You knew giving up your meds was the only way you could incapacitate her, but now you need your medicine or you'll go crazy. Your figments will cause you to. Accept that and plan for the next step. Know that this is all temporary. Know that this all is going to end the way it began. You just need the courage to do it.

31

Caged Parakeet

It's been two days since I jumped ship. My figments are getting harder to ignore. When it's not Rachel, it's LaRouche. The dead mix with the never-real. Their appearances are accelerating. I even hear them talking to me before I'm fully awake – they must start in that moment before your body's alarm clock goes off.

The guidebook says Portugal is a very Catholic country. Even if I could somehow break into a pharmacy I doubt they'd have the abortion pill here. But even if I could get the pills, what then? Live on the run forever? Maybe if I was stronger, but I'm not. I'm me.

And flipping the pages I find what I'm looking for: how to end all this.

'Jerry, do you know where my soccer ball is?' someone says.

It's Ana Lucia.

I say, 'No. No. No. You aren't–'

'Real? But I was real in Ensenada,' she laughs. 'Wasn't I?'

A cold realisation grips me. 'Get out!' I yell.

'But I came for my soccer ball,' she says.

Spasms ripple in my head. 'You weren't real?'

'Who's real? You?' she cackles. 'Or are you the Madman, Jerry? Are you Nietzsche's Madman? Are you mad, Jerry? And what about Epiphany? She's coming to kill you, you know.'

And I yell again and hurl my guidebook at her and, in an instant, she's gone, replaced by a crack in the windowpane.

I feel like I weigh a ton, like the air around me has been replaced by mud. I sludge over to where the guidebook landed and turn to the page

I was on. She's right – I'm right, I mean. Epiphany must be on her feet by now. She must be looking for me. Hunting me.

But suddenly a little spring of hope erupts in my stomach. If Epiphany was right about her daughter being in Spain, maybe she's on her way there already? But even if Epiphany did go to Spain, Abdul has probably been sent to look for me. I'm sure she had no problem wrapping him around her little finger.

I turn back to the guidebook and dog-ear the page with the answer on how to end all this. The only sane way, anyway. My chest sinks at the inevitable. But I get off the bed. There's still right now, before the inevitable comes to pass. And right now I'm hungry and I've got thousands of euros burning a hole in my pocket.

Portugal's economy is one of the worst in Western Europe. That's what the guidebook says. In older cities like Porto most of the young look for jobs elsewhere, in Lisbon or Spain. The ones who don't leave Porto choose to live in the suburbs by the ocean, leaving the city centre to a much older and poorer crowd. That makes living cheap. Even after paying Diana double rent for two months I could live here for a year off the blood money.

A waiter asks me a question in Portuguese. In the guidebook I flip past the dog-eared page to the translation pages. I'm at the café below my apartment. The table is shaded by an awning and a warm breeze flutters past. I point to the Portuguese word for eggs. 'Double,' I say, then look at my little Porto book and say *'Duo, par favor.'*

An old man at the table next to me lets out a little laugh. He puffs on a large stogie. His silver-rimmed glasses reflect the bright morning sunlight as he turns to me and says, 'You told him you wanted two eggs, when you meant you want two servings.'

Embarrassed, I flip though my book searching for the right words, but the old man reaches over and places his broad hand on my arm.

His skin is like leather, darkened from years in the sun. The hair on the back of his hand has gone white and stands out like rice in a patch of black earth.

'Please,' he says, 'allow me.' And without taking his hand from my arm he calls the waiter back and rapidly speaks in Portuguese. The waiter shoots me a quick grin and runs back to the kitchen. 'Now,' the old man says with a smile, 'you'll get what you want: two orders of the best eggs in Porto.'

'Thanks,' I say. 'I've never been good with languages.'

'You tried,' he says with a wink and brings his stogie back to his lips.

I eat my breakfast slowly as my eyes roam. Sometimes they rest on the back of the old man's head. The little hair he has left hangs in thin, white strands across his skull. They blow and interweave over chocolate skin spots.

Across the street, on the ledge of a second-floor window, a large orange-and-white cat meows at a caged parakeet. Below the window a girl coos at the bird. Her hair is anime-red.

Rachel, she blows me a kiss.

I force myself to find an elderly couple that sits a few tables away the most interesting people in the world. I've seen them talking to others so I know they're real. They wave at the old man, who says *'Bom dia'* and waves back. And that's when I notice another girl. I didn't see when she arrived even though I've been scanning the crowd most of the morning on the lookout for Epiphany or Abdul.

The girl, she sips coffee and eats what looks like a little upside-down custard cake as she scribbles on a white notepad. Her brunette hair is tucked over her right shoulder. Her lips are plump and her arms are thin – almost gangly. She looks up from her writing and catches me staring. She glances at my guidebook and gives a gentle smile. I ignore it and she returns to scratching on her notepad.

An influx of paranoia comes over me. I raise my hand. 'Cheque, please,' I embarrassingly say in English. This is when the old man with the leather hands and silver-rimmed glasses turns around and speaks to the waiter again. The waiter nods, then smiles to me as he walks off.

'If you eat here again, you pay for that meal. This one is on the house,' the old man says. I try to protest, but he stops me. 'Please Jerry, my name is Paulo. This is my café and what I say goes.'

My heart stops. 'How do you know my name?'

'Forgive me,' he laughs. 'You are letting the flat upstairs, yes? My friend Diana owns it. She likes to bug me in the morning and gossip.'

My insides churn. He knows Epiphany. Or Abdul. Or Diana knows them. Or they all know each other and they're all in this to trap me.

No. Snap the fuck out of this, Jerry. Get a damn grip. He's just a nice old man. There are still some of those in the world.

'Thanks,' I say, trying to smile. 'The eggs were amazing.' And they were. They were some of the best eggs I've ever had.

'I'm glad,' he smiles back.

See? There's nothing to be paranoid about.

I get up from my table and walk the five feet to my apartment's entrance. And from the corner of my eye I see the pretty girl with the notepad reflected in a window. She's stopped writing again and watches me unlock the door.

Nothing to be paranoid about at all.

32

Bela

When I get out of the shower and dress it's the first time I notice how baggy my pants are. I didn't even try them on when I bought them. I just went by my usual waist size. I take a long look in the mirror and notice my potbelly is almost gone too. All the running; all the craziness; I must have dropped fifteen pounds.

'Looking good, Jerry,' a voice says.

I put my T-shirt on.

'Come over here and fuck me.'

I count the money in my wallet.

'This time your mom won't walk in on us.' And I make the mistake of looking in the direction of her voice. Rachel, she's laying in my bed with her ass in the air and her tits on the sheets. 'Just hit it baby. Remember how it felt? A velvety tunnel of love?' She laughs. 'Don't get me wrong, you sound like a fourteen-year-old virgin when you say that, but it's sweet anyway.'

'Not real,' I say to myself.

'What's real anyway?' she asks, wiggling her ass. There isn't a single hair on her pussy. 'Reality is only in the mind. And you, baby, have one hell of a mind,' she grins. 'It'll feel *soooo* real. You know it will.'

But I grab my keys. Out on the hilly streets I stroll past a flower stall, past a wine shop, past a shop selling cheap souvenirs. I walk with no direction in mind. When I hear her voice again I begin to hum. I hum to drown her out.

'Baby, I'm still here,' Rachel says, now dressed in the most form-fitting, low-cropped jeans I could ever imagine. I cross the street and she follows, skipping by my side.

I shake my head and walk around her. I hum.

'Fine, baby,' she says. 'I tried to give you a good send-off. She's going to find you, you know. She's going to kill you.' And Rachel, she starts singing '*la la laa la,*' in tune with my humming.

I pass a bus stop; pass a bakery selling sweets that look like they're dipped in orange wax; pass a church whose walls look stained with olive oil. I walk and I walk and I walk, all the time hearing Rachel sing. It's relentless, this noise only I can perceive. I find myself back in front of the bookstore. The one where I bought the guidebook.

I sit on the curb. I grab my ears.

Traffic is heavy. What would I need to do? Just walk out a few feet? *'La la laa la, la la laa la.'*

That's all – a few feet.

I stand.

And then–

'Do you like my flowers?' a voice asks.

And, as if on cue, the *la la laa*-ing is gone.

'What?' I bark, expecting to see Rachel, but I turn to find the pretty girl from the café standing in front of me, her arm outstretched.

'My flowers. Do you like them?' the girl from the café asks slowly, pausing a little too long between each word. 'The flowers, no?' Her little plump lips almost comically bellow in and out as she speaks her *o's* and *w's*.

And, yes, now I notice that she is indeed holding some yellow flowers. Sunflowers, I think.

'What I would like to know is: I ask, do you like my flowers?' she smiles as she asks the same question a third way.

I furrow my brow. 'No,' I say.

'Excuse me, please,' she calls after me. 'You are American, no?'

I turn back. 'Why are you talking to me? Are you another one? Or did Epiphany send you?'

The girl, her head bounces up and down a little as she replays in her mind what I've just said. It's like she's following one of those dots above the words in a karaoke song. 'I do not know that word – *iffany,*' she finally answers. 'But you are American, no?'

In a nervous sort of way, in her style of pausing a little too long between words, the girl, she says, 'I saw you talking to my friend Paulo at the café. He said you are a nice person. My name is Bela and these flowers are for you, if you like. I am hoping we can be friends and you can help me learn better English.'

Seriously, that's what she says. Just like that. Right to the point. No beating around the bush. No hiding *why* she wants to be friends. No pretending that she doesn't want something in return. I haven't had conversations this direct since I was four.

And she stands in front of me, arm straight, sunflowers in hand, and waits. Her smile, it fluctuates between nervousness and hope. And as she waits for my answer, in the silence between us, there's no *la la la*-ing or imaginary supermodels offering forbidden fruit; there're no dead madams or imaginary Mexican children. There are just some sunflowers grasped in an outstretched, slightly trembling hand.

And standing there, this girl, she casts furtive glances at me.

And as it looks like her arm is about to give out, I take the flowers. 'My name's Jerry,' I say.

For the rest of the afternoon we walk the streets, just me and Bela – figment free.

Bela, my odd little tour guide. 'The city enchanting, no?' she says. A two-storey bridge that looks like it was designed by Eiffel spans a wide, flowing river that divides Porto. On the south side is the wine-makers district, and on the north, in Porto proper, is the main city. It's a city of hills and churches; of narrow streets and cafés. It's a city that looks like its being born again from the inside out. From the outside the buildings look old and dilapidated, but in any number of them, when you peek through open doors, you see carpenters hard at work.

Sometimes we talk, sometimes we move silently, side by side. Bela moves like an old lady: feet together, cautious little steps, elbows at her sides – as if she doesn't balance properly she'll tip over. When she asks, I tell her I'm in town on vacation. She tells me she wants to move to America one day. She points things out as we walk and says their names in English, but she always adds a 'no' on to the end. Her *no's* mean *yes*.

'Apple, no?'

'Grandmother, no?'

'Cat, no?'

We're waiting at a crosswalk for the electric sign's red man to go green when Bela tells me that she's seen me before this morning. She was in the bookstore when I bought the Porto book. I'm listening to her but there are no cars coming so I begin to cross. And that's when she rebukes me. Right out of nowhere. 'We are not to cross until it turns green!'

She does that sometimes. She has these little moments where she'll snap at you.

'The man is not green!'

So, as we wait on the corner of the street with no cars for the red man to turn green, Bela says that when she saw me again at the café she thought it might be a sign that we're supposed to be friends.

And me, I get nervous now when people speak of 'signs'. So I change the subject. I say, 'Porto is a pretty city,' not so much because it is but because it sounds like something you should say.

'Eet is,' she says. 'What else have you been?'

'At the beach,' I say, not correcting her pronoun error, 'then the bookstore. Besides those, I've just been sleeping in my apartment. Haven't seen much else.'

'So lazy,' she shakes her head.

See what I mean? Who says that to someone they've just met?

But then she adds, 'I see,' and nods. 'The shore and then the bookstore.'

I grin and she asks me if her English was incorrect. 'You rhymed, that's all.'

'Rhymed?'

'You know – *rhyme*.'

Bela stares blankly.

'See you later, alligator? After a while, crocodile?'

'Ah! Yes. *Rima*.'

At eight o'clock she checks her watch and says she must go. She needs to be at work in an hour.

'Where do you work?'

'The bookstore. That is why I saw you before, and again today. The first time you would not let me transaction your book. My father. He has a bad back, no? You made him get off his seat and do it. You should be more considerate.' Scold. Scold.

'I *was* trying to be considerate,' I say. 'The guidebook said you people have a *hierarchy*.'

'And you were screaming at him to buy your book. Very rude.'

'I was *enunciating*.'

'And then you even screamed when you left.'

'I was telling him to have a good day!'

Then Bela, she furrows her lips, like she's considering what I've said. Like it's dawning on her that, from my point of view, I wasn't being a dick. And as she looks like she's about to apologise for snapping at me, she says, '*I-er-archy*. I do not know that word.' She shrugs, 'But it is always good to be considerate in a country that is no yours, no?'

Groan.

Moving on, she says, 'We put out new table displays at night. Yes, I must go to work. We all can't be American tourists.' But this time she lets out a good-natured laugh that almost sounds fake, but the crinkles around her eyes tell me it's genuine.

And as I watch the crinkles go flat again, I suddenly feel a little, well, *something*. I don't want her to leave. I mean, what if my figments come back?

'Now, Jerry,' she says accentuating the -*ry*, 'I will see you tomorrow, no? We will continue our walk then?'

'OK,' I say.

'Good,' she says and quickly kisses me on both cheeks. Her kisses, they feel like little, moist doughnut holes. 'Ciao. Oh, and don't tell my father about the flowers. They were for the shop,' she laughs like a child who's gotten caught doing something naughty but knows they won't be punished. As she begins her old-lady's walk, she turns back briefly. 'See you later, ally-gator,' she smiles. 'Rhyme, no?'

The way she says it makes me laugh. She waves goodbye and I turn to walk in the other direction. Then I remember she hasn't told me where we'll meet, but when I look back, she's disappeared.

And look, if you were in my position, you'd worry too.

But ... these flowers. She's got to be real, *no*?

I run back to the apartment. Like if I keep moving my figments won't have a chance to catch up with me. When I get back Paulo is still seated outside, glass of wine in hand, puffing on a cigar. I suddenly feel stupid carrying a bunch of sunflowers and dump them into a trashcan before Paulo can see. The night breeze blows his white strands of hair. It's good to see the face of someone who I know exists.

'American or Canadian?' he asks.

'American,' I say. 'Why do you ask?'

'My friend Diana joined me for dinner tonight. She said a man had called her asking if the flat was still available. When she said it was taken he asked if an American had rented the room. Her brother rents a room in the city centre, too. Earlier today he received the same call.'

A chill runs through my body. Epiphany does have Abdul looking for me. 'What did she say?'

'Told him "no". Can't be too safe, can you?'

'No, you can't,' I smile, hoping my look comes across as one of mild amusement. I wish Paulo a good night and unlock the door leading to the stairs.

'Bela is a pretty one, isn't she?' Paulo says.

'You've seen her?' The words slip from my mouth before I can stop them.

Paulo gives me an odd look. 'Watched her grow up across the street where I used to live.'

A thin layer of anxiety sheds from my skin. 'How'd you know I was out with Bela?'

'Those were her flowers you threw away, right? She loves sunflowers.' I feel bad, like I should have a really good explanation for ditching the flowers, but then Paulo says, 'We're men. We're not supposed to like flowers.' Then he gives me a wink and says, 'After you left today she asked if you came here much. She was so excited to hear a native

English speaker. I hope you don't mind that I told her you were renting the room?'

I tell him no, of course not, and wish him a good night, then make my way up the dark stairwell leading to my apartment.

And when I open the door Epiphany's in the living room. She waits, wraith-like, in the dark to remind me what a silly boy I've been. How I've been a child out playing in the world of adults today, like I have any say over my life.

But she's wrong. I did have a say. I could have ended all this today, but instead I walked around town with an odd girl who gives flowers to strangers.

'My voices require a sacrifice, Jerry,' Epiphany says, holding a little sickle in her hand. It's not one of those long, Grim Reaper sickles. It's more like the sickle in the Soviet flag. The kind she had in my dream. 'Your throat, Jerry. They require your throat.'

'Epiphany, look–' But I'm frozen as she glides towards me. Then I'm on my knees. I'm crying.

She holds the sickle above her head, ready to swing.

'Please,' I say.

'Sins of the father, Jerry.'

'Please stop this,' I tremble.

'Then say it.'

I gaze into her face. She's so calm. The sickle is held motionless, its orders to strike on temporary hold.

'No,' I shudder.

She sighs. 'I gave you your chance...'

'Please...' I beg.

'...and you didn't take it.'

And as she swings the sickle at my throat I scream all the things you believe are false but you secretly fear anyway. 'My father! My father! He did do all those things you said he did! He's a rapist and a liar and a devil!'

And like that, Epiphany is gone. And me, I'm left kneeling on the floor, sobbing.

It's who knows how long before I can pick myself up. The heaviness has returned to my body. I make my way to the cracked window where I threw the book at Ana Lucia. Outside, Paulo's seat is empty. The café's lights are off for the night. I walk through the apartment and check the back window. Moonlight splits the cobblestone alley as cats scamper from shadow to shadow. My face is clammy with cold sweat and looks yellow in the reflection of the glass.

'People like heroes better if they die for something,' I told Emma once. But I'm not a hero and I'm going to die anyway. It's only a matter of time. Epiphany *is* out there, somewhere, hunting me. This has got to end. And I open the guidebook to the dog-eared page with the answer about how to stop all of this. The only sane way, anyway.

I read:

The American Embassy in Porto. Address: R. Barão de Forrester, 4400 Vila Nova de Gaia, Portugal. Hours: Monday through Friday 8:30 – 17:00. Closed weekends.

I read:

Services: Visa renewal. Lost passport replacement. Legal advice (US Citizens only).

I read:

Safety: If you are a US citizen and have been the victim of a crime, or have any information about a crime, the American Embassy is fully staffed with legal counsel, government advocates, and officers of the International Criminal Police Organization (INTERPOL).

33

Scrabble

M-E-D-S. Seven points.

It's half past three in the afternoon when I wake up. I saw Epiphany two more times last night – once at the kitchen table playing Scrabble with Emma. She was helping her spell 'mifepristone'. Even with all the money in my pocket, I don't have a chance at a normal life without my meds.

And I wonder, do they give you medicine in jail?

I get out of bed. I don't even shower. If I do anything but go to the embassy, this will become something I'll always do the day after tomorrow. I leave everything in the apartment – my clothes, my backpack, even the guidebook – I just rip the dog-earned page from it. The page with the address that starts the next chapter of the rest of my life.

I'm glad Paulo isn't sitting outside. I'd use talking to him as an excuse to let this go another day. And in another day Epiphany could really be waiting for me in my apartment. I start up the hilly street, my mind as unstable as my ankles on the bellies of black cobblestones. I reach the bookstore and see Bela through the window. She looks frustrated with this old lady of a customer who has a big loaf of bread for hair. She's arguing with Bela. Bela probably snapped at her like she tends to. Bela's jabbing her finger into her palm in an attempt to convey some point to the old lady. I smile at the scene of it all. Part of me feels like I should go in and say hello, but I continue on. The embassy closes in an hour.

And maybe I'm not totally fucked. I'm turning myself in and that has to count for something. INTERPOL, they'll question me and then they'll bring me back to Chicago, where I'll be handed over to the detectives. I'll stand trial for a murder I didn't commit, but at least I'll be safe from Epiphany. And anyway, don't they have to prove I killed Roland beyond a reasonable doubt?

I can still tell the cops what happened – the whole truth and nothing but the truth. I can tell them about Epiphany and her abduction. I can tell them about how Matthew Mann rapes little girls. And the footage – there's always the television footage from outside the museum. The footage that I saw Epiphany in real life on. I can have my lawyer play the footage in court and say, 'That's her. That's the girl who really killed Roland.' And won't that be enough?

D-E-L-U-S-I-O-N-A-L. Eleven points plus fifty-point bonus for words of seven letters or longer. Sixty-one points.

I make my way up another steep hill towards a bell tower. The bell tower is at the opening of a large plaza. I scan the buildings. The embassy should be right here.

'You're going the wrong way, Jerry,' Rachel says. She's wearing this killer tank top that's so thin you can see her perky nipples right through it. 'You're turned around. The embassy is back the other way.'

'Shut up,' I mumble. 'You're just trying to confuse me.'

'Why would I confuse you? We're one, remember?'

'You don't want me to go.'

'That would mean *you* don't want *you* to go,' she smiles. 'Turn around, you should have gone right at the bookstore.'

'Of course I don't want to go,' I snap. 'I didn't want any of this. But this is the *only* way. I can't be a fugitive any longer and I can't wait around for Epiphany to find me or for Abdul to show up with his favourite rocket launcher. And even if neither of these things happen, I'll still go crazy without my medicine. Case in point.'

'No offence,' I add.

'Whatever,' she says and starts her damn *la la laa*-ing again.

A group of college kids walk in my direction. Rachel's singing is so loud I have to shout to hear myself when I ask if they know where the American Embassy's at. They point me in the direction I came; the direction Rachel was telling me to go. They tell me I should have made a right at the bookstore. On the bell tower's clock it's almost four-thirty.

I run back the way I've come, down a hilly street, and almost trip over a black cobblestone. I pause to catch my breath, but hear Rachel's incessant singing, so I run again.

And maybe you think I'm a coward, but turning myself in is the bravest thing I've ever done. People in real life, when something bad happens, they don't turn into action heroes or detectives, like they do in the movies. In real life you take the path of least resistance. You do the easiest thing that ensures your survival. It's always about necessity. It's why the starving steal food. Why the desperate resort to violence. And why the cowardly take money from the man they just killed.

'Jerry?' a voice calls. 'Ola, Jerry. You exercise, no?' I've reached the bookstore again. Bela is wearing glasses that give her a studious look.

Panting, I say, 'What? No, I was just–' And once again Rachel has vanished like she was never there. 'I – I need to go to the embassy,' I say. 'Passport issue.'

'OK,' Bela says in her round way. Her head bobs a little. Either she didn't understand what I've said or it doesn't interest her in the least. 'I am off my shift now, you see?' And she waits for my acknowledgement.

'Uh – I see.'

'I am to meet my friend Kate. You will like to come, no?'

I'm not sure if that's a question or an order.

'I would,' I say, 'but I need to get to the embassy.'

And here she gets the word. 'Ah! *Embassy*. Surely they are not open today, no?'

The thing about travelling is that days and dates blend into the background until you no longer notice them. I look at the torn guidebook page in my hand. Hours: Monday through Friday 8:30 – 17:00. Closed weekends.

'What day is it?'

'*Sabado*. Saturday.'

I'm a D-U-M-B-A-S-S. Twelve points plus fifty-point bonus. Sixty-two points.

'So, you will come?' Bela's face is expectant.

'I–'

'It is because,' she interrupts, letting out a little laugh like she's confiding a dirty secret, 'I do not like her, you see? She drink a lot and say stupid things. She speaks like she know everything all the time. But I promise Kate I go. And if you come, we can make excuse to leave if she get too stupid, no?'

And in the silence between us she waits for my answer. And well, that's the thing: there *is* silence between us again. There is no more Rachel or humming or singing.

Look, we all use people, right? You may say you don't, you might even believe it, but deep down you know you do. I've got to put jail off until Monday now and that means, provided Epiphany lets me live through the weekend, I'm going to have to deal with all these damn figments until I can get arrested and get my 486s back in the States. But until that happens – well this Bela girl – she's like my own personal 486.

So I smile. 'Sure. Where to?'

'Irish people love to travel. We love it. That's why you'll find an Irish pub in any country you go to. In Ireland I...'

Don't shut the fuck up? I think. This Kate girl has been rambling on for hours, telling one 'me' story after the next. She and her friends are in Portugal on a round-the-world trip paid for by Mommy and Daddy. In just an hour she's managed to tell us her entire life story – an amazing feat considering she's had seven beers.

'Ay!' Kate shouts to a group of people who've just come up the stairs. All four are Irish and for the next hour they all yap as much as she does. And I feel bad, for Bela. I can tell when she's only pretending to follow one of their stories because they're speaking too quickly for her. She laughs a little too loud at the jokes they tell and does so a moment after everyone else laughs. The Irish are hard enough for me to understand, but for her they must be near impossible.

One of the Irishmen, a particularly short one with a bad comb-over, asks Bela if she's ever been to Dublin. But Bela laughs, faking understanding, like the question is the punch line to a joke. There's silence at the table as the Irish cast blatant smirks at one another. Then Bela's face goes beet red. The Irish's smirks turn into laughter. The comb-over leprechaun raises his eyebrows, 'Speak English much?'

S-H-E-S-P-O-R-T-U-G-U-E-S-E. Seventy points.

'Who needs a refill?' I say, silencing them. Everyone at the table blurts out their orders and begins taking money from their pockets. 'No, it's on me,' I say. I'm not being nice. These guys are all dicks. I just have more than nine thousand euros to burn through before I turn myself in Monday morning. 'Except for you,' and I pluck the five-euro note from the comb-over's hand. I turn to Bela. 'Want to help me?' She slides out of the booth, her hair subtly draped in front of her face to hide her embarrassment.

'Hey, Bela!' Kate shouts after us, 'Grab a game while you're down there! Bela – a *game*. G-A-M-E!'

I groan and Bela blushes and gives a weak smile. 'I do,' she says.

Downstairs the bartender sets the drinks on a tray. He says something in Portuguese. 'Twenty-nine euro,' Bela translates.

'Glad you're here,' I say, giving her a little smile. 'Or else I would have been here all night trying to guess what he was saying.' She bobs her head up and down, afraid to answer. I give the bartender thirty euros and ask Bela if she'll collect the change. 'I'm going to pick out that game. Something that will distract them from talking so much,' I wink.

Bela returns a self-conscious smile and nods. I'm not sure if she totally understood me. 'OK. I bring these drinks up.'

'Won't be too heavy? I can help – '

'I OK. I have,' she says softly.

I walk across the bar to a table that has several board games: Monopoly. Guess Who? Trivial Pursuit. Jenga. Checkers. Ah, perfect–

I hurry to catch up with Bela, who's near the top of the stairs, balancing the tray in her hands. 'Look what I've got,' I smile.

But then Bela, she snaps at me. Me, the one who did her a favour by coming here. Me, the only one who has been nice to her the whole night. 'I do not want to play that game!' she says.

I only grabbed it because I thought it would be the one that would require the most concentration from the leprechauns – so they'd all have to shut up and speak slower – so Bela could have a chance at understanding them.

'It's a fun game,' I say defensively, my feelings hurt; my intentions missed.

'No! I said I do not want to play that game,' she snaps again.

My face flushes. 'I just thought–'

'No!'

When we return to the table I sit away from Bela. The way I feel – I was trying to do something nice, you know? And she rebuked me like I was a child.

As the night goes on the drunken Irishmen apparently think the object of Scrabble is to make as many lewd words as possible. I can only tolerate their annoying laughter so long. And Bela and I, we aren't saying anything to each other anyway. I soon tell everyone I need to get some sleep. Even my figments are preferable to how I feel right now.

As I get up from the table the leprechauns shout their drunken goodbyes. And Bela, she furtively waves her hand. 'Good-bye, Jerry,' she says, timidly.

'Bye,' I reply sharply, without looking at her. And walking home, instead of worrying if Epiphany is around the next corner – instead of feeling fear – I feel something that stings much worse. Something I've felt all my life.

I feel A-N-G-R-Y.

I feel U-N-A-P-P-R-E-C-I-A-T-E-D.

I feel M-I-S-U-N-D-E-R-S-T-O-O-D. One hundred and eight points, triple-word score.

34
The Mountain

There's a light rapping at my door. The clock on the nightstand says it's 7:15.

I didn't sleep much. After I left Bela at the bar Rachel walked me home. I had to put up with her and Ana Lucia all night.

'You going to get that?' Rachel says.

On the door, the rapping becomes louder.

'I need my medicine. You aren't– '

'– *real*,' Ana Lucia says. She's showing Rachel soccer tricks. Bouncing the ball on her knees. 'Yeah, we get it.'

The rapping on the door becomes an outright knock.

And for a moment I wonder if it could be Epiphany or Abdul. But then I think, Why would they knock?

'You gonna get that or what?' Ana Lucia says.

'Shut up,' I say, and the knocking on the door stops.

'Whatever,' Ana Lucia says, balancing the soccer ball on her forehead.

I scramble out of bed and crawl for my boxers, which lie on the floor. I open the door and light explodes from the hall skylight. I shut my eyes in defence.

'Ola. Hello,' a little round voice says sheepishly.

When I crack my eyelids I see Bela standing in front of me, her hand reaching into her blue-jeans pocket. She's wearing a turquoise shirt that reads '*Everyone Needs Music*' in an elfish-style font. Her eyes give me a once over and the edges of her nervous lips curl slightly.

'Bela...?' I say and glance back into the room. Rachel and Ana Lucia are gone.

Bela, she pulls a single euro from her pocket. 'Your change. From drinks last night.' And she holds the silver-and-gold coin in her extended arm. Her little feet in their black loafers fidget on the floor. 'I forgot to give to you last night, you see?'

Her lips twitch ever so slightly and her eyes shift furtively as she waits for my reply.

And I take the coin.

Apology accepted.

Both of us, we stand in the doorway, each unsure of what to do. 'What's that?' I finally say. She has a small, grey backpack stuffed full.

And Bela, she says with a smile, 'We go to the mountain today. Today, we climb.'

The mountain she's referring to is nothing more than a really steep hill. It's been a winding, four-hour drive to get here. Bela owns this white, two-door Ford and drives it as if she doesn't realise other cars use the roads too. More than once the vehicle in front of us pulled over to let Bela fly past.

As we drove out of the city we followed the river to the shore and then went north past the port where all the freighters dock. From my view in the passenger seat I saw Abdul's boat cruising out to sea – its big 'CAPRICE' letters visible in the bright sun. It had been four days since I jumped ship and I guess that's too long for someone who has illegal arms to get to mercenaries to wait around, even if Epiphany wants him to. If he was leaving maybe Epiphany has given up too and gone to Spain already. And as Bela turned the car to head inland I felt a bit of relief come over my body.

Bela held a perpetual smile on her face as her hair whipped back in the breeze as we raced though the countryside. The longer we drove the less traffic there was, which allowed me to concentrate on things besides images of flaming car wrecks and tangled metal. Seeing Abdul's boat go, knowing Epiphany's minions weren't following me anymore, felt like a reprieve. For the first time in weeks I didn't think about the future and allowed myself to relax in the present.

'We will conquer this mountain today, no?' Bela said when we arrived and she drew her hand across the hill's base as if she expected me to faint at the sight of it. I almost laughed, but the resolve on her face stopped me. This was important to her.

'Shall we get started?' I asked.

Bela smiled, a little unsure of what I'd said. I'd spoken too fast.

'After you,' I said and pointed the way.

'Yes. After me,' she said with determination.

We've been hiking for forty minutes now. Bela's back is wet through her turquoise shirt. The sun is as high as it will be in the sky today and I notice that I'm sweating as well.

I watch her hips, the way one glute tightens while the other leg takes a step up. I see the way she pulls her hair to one side to let the breeze cool the back of her neck. And I can't help but marvel at this peculiar girl who seems to be able to keep my figments away. Maybe the compounds in the 486s originated from the sweat dripping down the back of her neck? Maybe if I go to a pharmacy in Portugal, I'll see little Bela-shaped pills in two rows of eight, sealed in foil packets? *Bela*™, the once-daily tablet from GlaxoSmithKline.

'What?' I say, suddenly realising Bela's stopped walking and said something.

Oh, God. Did she see me staring at her ass?

My throat dries. 'I mean, want me to carry the backpack?'

A slight grin breaks her lips. 'I'm not a weak girl now,' she says, turning back towards the summit. 'I'm a climber. Come on, we climb.'

We reach the top in another twenty minutes.

The breeze blows in hard spurts up here. Bela drops her backpack on the ground; it lands with a muffled thud. Her shirt is stained with sweat marks that outline where the straps were. Just below her breasts there's a little damp spot that saturates '*Everyone Needs Music*'.

Looking back to where we've come from, I can see her point of view more easily. From up here this hill does make you feel like you've climbed a mountain. Portugal stretches before us. Cattle graze on farmland in the distance. Brown mountains break the horizon.

Bela spins, taking in the views from every direction. Then she stops and places her small hand on my forearm. She squeezes and says, 'Can you believe? I have climbed a mountain!' And she says this almost with a child's wonder and amazement – completing an easy task that they believe to be much harder than it is. 'I am so proud of this accomplishment.'

'That's great,' I say, and find I'm skimming the top of her hand with my thumb. I feel Bela's body freeze for a moment before she removes her hand from my arm.

It takes Bela five minutes to spread out everything she's brought. There are two bottles of red wine (*'Port wine from Porto, you see? No?'*), a large loaf of bread, three different cheeses and a sausage. She's even brought placemats (*'Portuguese always eat with placemats'*). After we gorge ourselves, I lay back and watch the bright, puffy clouds float over our heads.

'No nap yet,' Bela says and slaps my leg playfully. She's making an extra effort to keep her snapping under control. 'We are here to work.' Bela reaches into her bag and pulls out a notebook. Tucked inside is a single piece of A4 paper.

It's written in English.

'What's this?'

'It is my *rezoom*,' she says.

I say, 'Résumé?'

Bela blushes. 'Yes. My res-oo-may. You help me with it, no?'

I shrug and begin to read it out loud. 'Personal Information. Name: Anabela Filipa Oliveira. Address: R. Cedofeita–'

'Not aloud,' she says. 'You will embarrass me.' Her face has already flushed. As I scan the first line again I feel her eyes on me. She's looking for any warning that I'll laugh at what she's written.

And now I get it: Scrabble – her reaction wasn't random bitchiness. She snapped at me because she had already been embarrassed by her

English that night and didn't need any more jokes at her expense for misspelling words. How did I not see that?

On her résumé her work experience lists two jobs, one in a call centre selling mobile phones, and the other in Livraria Lello, the bookstore.

About myself:

I was born in North of Portugal in the second biggest city: Oporto. It is located next to sea (Atlantic Ocean) and it has also a river (Douro). At the age of 18 I went to study to other Portuguese city, called Braga, Journalism. Now I am in a bookstore saving funds so I can continue my studies in politics field in Estates United, I hope.

I am an active person, I believe, and I easily make friends. I like to laugh. I am very expressive and I like to meet new and different people as well as cultures.

'Bad, no?' she asks. Her eyes fidget. 'It is first draft, you see? And I hope you will help me. I want to move to United States and hope to get into masters.' Her eyes scuttle more, avoiding mine. 'It is silly, no?'

'It's ... perfect,' I say, touching her hand. This time it remains still.

My eyes open. I'm on my back. The wind blows hard and the sky is a deep purple. Except for Bela, I'm all alone and the silence is wonderful. Bela is nuzzled at my side, her back towards me. Wisps of her hair blow in my face.

Why don't I see my figments when I'm with you?

Before we lay down, Bela hadn't taken my 'perfect' at face value and made me correct the mistakes on her résumé. She told me how she dreams of going to America to become a political journalist. She spoke deeply of how words can change the world. How thoughts and ideas can have physical effects. Then, after more wine and bread, with full bellies we lay back on Bela's mountain for some rest.

Now, as the blue-grey clouds move at a turtle's pace in the purple dusk, as I feel Bela's body rise and fall with each breath next to mine, I find it hard to believe I'm here after all the horrible places I've been in the last few weeks. In the breeze and fading sunlight the grass breathes and heaves like a living being. I get up as quietly as I can and stretch like a cat. Despite the lumpy ground, I haven't felt this good after a rest in a long time. It's the first time in days that I've slept without nightmares or woken to figments. I walk around our little summit and watch as the last remnants of the sun sink behind distant mountains. I turn to find Bela sitting up with her eyes closed and her hands folded.

'My mother always taught us that when you fall to sleep and wake up in nature, to pray and give God thanks for not only your safety, but also for such a beautiful bed to begin with,' she says when she opens her eyes.

I hear 'God' and I think 'Epiphany'. I think 'Nico'. I think 'hell'. I think 'eternal separation'.

Bela is waiting for me to say something.

'I don't think I believe in God.'

She smiles. 'It doesn't matter. He believe in you.'

Ordinarily if someone said this to me, I'd dismiss it as a bottled reply. But Bela – she says it in such a matter-of-fact way. She says it like one would say, '*The sun has just set*' or, '*We are on top of a large hill.*' It's just a fact. It just is.

'Well, if God is real, do you think he holds a grudge?' I say, not so much to her, but to the hills and mountains surrounding us.

Bela stands and takes my hand. It's small and warm. 'People make mistakes. Look at me – my horrible res-oo-may,' she laughs. 'But people made big and small mistakes. It's we who can't forgive ourselves. We make our own hell. Not God. He will forgive us anything. Don't listen to Bible or Pope or religion. God is only goodness.'

And she says this with a confidence that would make Jonathan

Edwards burn his theological writings. But I wonder, do dead little sisters forgive as easily?

Bela can see I'm lost in thought. She squeezes my hand and smiles warmly. 'Come now,' she says. 'We have a long journey down our mountain.'

35

Virginity

She pats my hair as I lie on top of her, trying to catch my breath.

What *was* that? The noises. The squishy sounds like two wet fish slapping against each other. The hair – *her* hair – that gets caught and pulled under elbows. I was so damn hard. Your hand, it can't make you feel like that.

Screw what Rachel says, it really is like this warm velvety tunnel. And man, that didn't take long at all, but I'm really, really exhausted. Bela says something to me in Portuguese and closes her eyes. Sleep is coming for me so quickly, but I'm afraid to let it take me. I'm afraid to see Bela gone when I wake up.

It's now a few hours later. Bela is lying next to me. She hasn't taken off. She's smoking a cigarette. Her little mouth blowing perfect rings of smoke. 'That's it?' she says in flawless English. 'What are you, some kind of virgin?'

I wake for real now. Bela is lying next to me. She hasn't taken off. My heart skips a beat as I slowly remember why she's in my bed.

I just lost my virginity.

And it's different than all the porns make it seem. There's something ... extra with real sex. The cover is pulled down around Bela's waist, exposing a breast. Her nipple is almost smooth and flat now, like a melted pink Hershey's Kiss set on top of a water balloon covered in skin. Bela's eyes open ever-so-briefly. She runs a finger across my lips. A smile shows on her mouth as she drifts back to sleep.

It's dawn when I wake again. The sunlight is beginning to spill through the bedroom window. Bela sleeps on her side – her back towards me. I slip out of the bed and grab my khakis from the floor. The crinkled guidebook page with the embassy's address is in the front pocket. Out the window I see Paulo helping his staff set the tables for the day. It's Monday. The embassy will be open in a few hours. In the bed Bela's stomach expands and contracts with each breath. She sleeps so soundly.

And what do I do about you? I think. The taste of her skin dawdles on my tongue.

It's Monday. Go to the embassy and turn yourself in like you planned. Do it before she gets up. Do it before Epiphany finds you.

'Jerry?' Bela says in her soft voice.

And a panic suddenly grips me. *I need to talk to her.* You never need to talk to your porn when you're done with it. She's lying there, looking at me. What do I say? What's she thinking? What if I wasn't good? *Did she just look at my penis?* Oh my god, what if I'm not big enough? Was I the worst she's ever had? How many *has* she had?

'Come back to bed,' she smiles. 'It early.' And she stretches her hand towards mine. My fears evaporate at the sound of her call. I drop the khakis and the crinkled guidebook page and I gravitate to her like I'm a skydiver and she's the earth. As I take her hand, as I climb into bed, she wraps my arm around her waist. She's so warm. So real. The embassy can wait one more day. Besides, if I went right now I'd just walk in there with a big I'm-not-a-virgin-anymore grin on my face and they wouldn't take me seriously. Tomorrow. I'll go tomorrow. For now all I can think about is last night.

The drive back from the mountain took longer than the drive there. I had told Bela how much her driving scared me, so she made sure to go turtle's-pace slow. On the way home we never spoke of her dropping me off at my place. When we arrived she parked and got out of the car with me. The air was chilly. She pulled a leftover bottle of wine from her backpack and said, 'We should finish, no? You help me with my resoomay, now I help you with your Portuguese.'

So we went up to my place and Bela tried to teach me her language.

'*Vinho,*' she said and pointed to the wine bottle.

'Ve-no,' I said.

'V*inho*,' she repeated, smiling.

'You know, this isn't going to work. I can't speak any languages.'

'What is English?' she shot back. '*Eu sou uma mulher*,' she pointed to herself.

'E-su-uma-muller,' I pointed to myself.

'I am sure that is not the case, no? You don't look like a woman,' she laughed. Her eyes, they glistened like wet crystals. She pointed at me. '*Tu és um homem*.'

'I'm a man,' I guessed.

'Very good!' she said, taking a large drink. 'Now, what else would you like to learn?'

'CanIkissyou?' I mumbled.

'I am sorry,' she said with a slight grin, 'I can not follow your words that quickly.'

My face went red and my self-consciousness turned the rest of her teaching into a less playful lesson. A bottle of wine later I still couldn't speak one word of Portuguese. But Bela, she was having fun anyway. I could see it in her eyes.

'Wine makes me warm inside, but skin cold on outside, no?' she shivered. 'May we light your fire?'

I lit the fire and we sat down on the back windowsill and looked out into the chilly April night. For minutes neither of us said a word, we just watched cats scurry from shadow to shadow on the cobbled street below. Then, through glassy eyes Bela said, '*Gostei da nossa conversa de hoje*.' I shrugged and she placed her hand on my arm and said, 'I am sorry. Our Portuguese lesson already ended. It is easy to slip into mother tongue, no? I said, I enjoyed our conversation today, on the mountain. It was nice.' Then she cast a glance away from me like she'd suddenly become embarrassed.

'It was nice,' I said.

And her eyes caught mine again and after a moment she said, '*Não tens de perguntar se me podes beijar*,' and she sat there waiting. I thought she'd accidently slipped back into Portuguese again, but she didn't correct herself. She just held her gaze on me.

And though I had no definitive way of knowing what she'd said just then, the way she timidly cast her eyes down, the way a little drop of wine reverberated on her lower lip – well, sometimes we say things in hard-to-interpret ways because we don't know how to come right out with it.

I kissed her little round lips. They tasted like plump grapes. And as I stroked her face and kissed her mouth, all inhibition suddenly left us both and she climbed on top of me and I peeled off her turquoise shirt. As we stumbled to the bed the shadows and light from the flames of the fireplace danced across her breasts. And her breasts, they weren't at all what I was used to looking at. The breasts in my porns were usually perfect spheres with rock-hard nipples. Bela's nipples were soft and slowly tightened with caresses; her breasts were supple and natural and gave slowly when I kissed them. Her stomach had the slightest hint of a paunch – just a little bit of baby fat that was the most erotic thing I've ever felt. And her pubic area, far from being the hairless, slick wax land of the porn actresses, had a little nick and a few red razor bumps where she shaved. Our movements were awkward at times. Our bodies made embarrassing and occasionally funny noises as we joined. But it was wonderful.

When Bela got out of my bed that first morning, when she said she had to go to work, I thought that what had happened had been an anomaly. I thought it was a slip-up on her part due to all the wine we drank. But she left my place for work and when her shift ended she came back that night. She came back *to me*. And lying in bed that second night we cradled and touched each other all over. We whispered to one another, our faces just millimetres apart, and we felt the other's breath warm us like a heavenly steam.

The second morning-after was worse than the first. Better, I mean, but still worse, you know? I started to feel something I never had before. In bed, next to her, the world was made of nothing but us. But when she left for work that second morning-after there was some kind of new pain in my stomach, like the earth had split and one half of it had floated away. The pain was worse than the fear of going to the embassy. Worse than even Epiphany finding me. A pain that would only be quenched when Bela's half of the world returned.

Today is *17 AV.* That's seventeen days After Virginity, for those of you keeping track. I can't go to the embassy anymore. Everything's changed – even my figments. The longer I'm with Bela, the more some kind of anti-figment latency carries over when we're apart. After the first night, the next day I did see Rachel, but she just stood across the street and didn't bother me. Later in the day I saw Ana Lucia, but she too left me alone. Since then all my figments have completely disappeared. Even my dreams of Epiphany in that silverware factory come less and less. When I do have them, it's only partially. Only the beginning where she's a young girl, alone and afraid.

This afternoon I met Bela when she finished work. As we wandered up and down the narrow side streets we passed a sex shop. Bela laughed at the peculiar toys in the window: the sex swings, the cock harnesses, the nipple suction tubes. Her laugh has the infectious curiosity of a child. She pulled me inside *'For fun, no?'* and we strolled the aisles and she giggled at the awkward instruments – much to the annoyance of the tattooed and pierced man behind the counter, who knew we had no intention of buying anything.

There was the life-sized dildo shaped like an arm that ended in a clenched fist. There were the anal beads, the whips, the tittie-tassels and cock rings. Then there were the videos, some were pure fetish: animals, midgets, men with vaginas (manginas – a word Bela found hilarious). And of course, there were the leaked celebrity sex tapes.

As we browsed I was more embarrassed than she was. For me, this stuff was always something you never mentioned except anonymously online. In the outside world it was things you would refer to as shameful – no matter how much you enjoyed seeing them used in videos. But Bela, she snickered with hand over mouth at everything and was glad to have a partner in her criminal curiosities.

'Pulp Friction!' she laughed and squeezed my arm as she read the title of a sex tape with an Uma Thurman lookalike on the cover.

We're in bed. Bela's head is on my chest. Her pubic hair is damp as her crotch nuzzles my thigh. She gently purrs as I stroke her hair. I lick my lips, still feeling her taste on them. Is this what it's like for normal people? Is this how nights are spent; not in front of a computer, but wrapped around someone you never want to let go of?

I kiss her forehead and a small trickle of bitter reality manages to enter my mouth. Sure, it's been sixteen days now, but where *is* this going? What am I doing? I can't believe someone like her likes me, but does she even *know* me? I mean, she knows me, but she doesn't know what's happened. She doesn't know I'm wanted for murder. This little sheltered romantic bubble can't last forever. It wouldn't be fair to her. I'm going to need to tell her the truth.

From underneath the covers, Bela raises her arm and makes a fist. She twirls her forearm, wrist locked tight, and playfully makes a little monster noise. She laughs and her eyes glisten. 'The fist, no? From the shop?'

I smile. 'Yeah, the fist,' I say.

'What are you thinking?' she says.

I don't want to lie, but I don't want to lose *this* to the truth. Not yet. So I change my thoughts quickly. It's an automatic response I've picked up after years of deceiving others. I tell Bela that, as a child, my sister and I used to love to make jack-o-lanterns on Halloween. We'd carve two each and give our pumpkins one scary face and one silly face.

'Jacklantern? What is that?'

'Pumpkin carving.'

Bela just furrows her lips.

'Don't you carve pumpkins on Halloween?'

'No,' she says. Always short and to the point when appropriate. Then she lets out a little laugh. 'A pumpkin is just a vegetable, no? Why do you carve vegetables?'

'We carve *pumpkins*,' I say, giving her a squeeze, which she quickly uses to nuzzle into me, 'because, traditionally, they're meant to ward off evil spirits. You give your pumpkin a scary face and leave it on the porch so ghosts and goblins don't come around.'

Her look tells me she thinks I might be pulling her leg. But then she smiles and says she would like to make a 'jacklantern' too. 'To protect against ghosts and goblins and,' she locks her wrist again and waves her clenched hand in my face, *'the fist!'*

36

Jack-o-Lanterns

You would know better than me, but I guess Bela and I had 'that' conversation today. That conversation I'm assuming all couples have when they've been seeing each other for a while. 'Where's this going?'

Bela didn't phrase it like that, but as we were having coffee at my place after lunch she was being unusually quiet. When I asked her what the matter was, she kind of snapped at me. It took me a while to coax out what was happening. 'You just say when we meet that you are here on vacation, no?' Then it hit me that I'd been here for over three weeks now. 'And when does that vacation end?' It's questions like this that make me admire her so much. Questions where you lay your feelings on the line and hope that the person you're asking doesn't run over them with a dump truck.

I've lied to Bela once and only once. Last week she asked what I did and I told her my father died (which is true) and that he left us a lot of money so I don't need to work (not exactly true – being a Hollywood PR star might be high-profile, but the pay is lower than you'd think). I didn't know how else to explain the money, though. But she smiled and took what I said at face value and it killed me inside.

So now, when I tell her that I'm staying as long as she's here, it's not a lie. I mean, besides the phone call to Diana after I arrived, there's been no other signs of Epiphany looking for me. Abdul's boat left long ago. The police have no way of knowing where I am. And as long as I'm with Bela I don't see my figments. I don't need my medicine. I *could* make my life here.

Bela's sombre mouth grows into a big smile. 'I like that answer,' she says. 'Yes, I like.' Then she gets up from the table as if talking any more about it might change something. 'Okay, I go to my father's now. We move books to the store. Only a few hours of work today,' she smiles and leaves me with a caffeinated kiss.

Paulo greets me as I step out into the afternoon sunlight. I want to do something for Bela and ask if he can give me directions to the nearest farmers' market. He tells me if I cross the Ponte de Dom Luis there's one on the other end of Vila Nova de Gala. After getting lost more than once I finally reach the market. I search the stands for fifteen minutes with no luck. Then I find a stand with two young men behind it. They've got three pumpkins. One has a crack and has started to soften. Though the remaining two are small, they'll have to do.

As I reach into my pockets for my wallet, out of nowhere there's a loud crash. I turn in time to catch a glimpse of a figure in hunter-green pants darting out of sight past a stall twenty feet from where I stand. Several boxes of watermelons have splattered to the ground and the stall-keeper's swearing after the culprit. I quickly pay the two men for my pumpkins and leave before anything happens to them.

I stroll back home and the weight of the pumpkins feel good as I balance one in each hand. When Emma and I used to carve ours I'd go for the traditional jagged mouth or missing tooth face, while Emma would always try something more artistic – like a cat's face or a flower. I wonder what face Bela will carve into hers?

I turn down a tiny street. Varying objects hang from the small balconies on the worn buildings. On one drapes the red-and-green Portuguese flag. Another balcony has today's laundry. A third, a cage with two blue parakeets. Fado music escapes from the building with the worn red paint.

I'm about to pass an alley between two of the buildings when I'm stopped in my tracks by a flood of cats that suddenly charge from it. Brown ones, black ones, calico ones. I've never seen so many together at one time. I glance down the alley to see how many there are but besides the discarded construction materials and trash that lines the entrance, the rest of the alley is too dark to see into. Wooden boards crisscross the buildings' roofs on either side, blocking any sunlight.

But then, as my eyes slowly adjust to the alley's darkness, I see it, just barely, skulking in the dark. Its shapeless form obscured by shadows could be anything: cats piled on top of each other; a cat the size of a person. But before I can make out what I'm looking at, before I have a chance to move, the object comes right at me and I'm grabbed and pulled into the alley. One of my pumpkins hits the ground with a soft, hollow crack. I stumble forwards and catch the other inches before it meets the same fate. The shadowed form scurries past me in the dark, blocking the exit.

'I found her,' a voice says.

And if my pumpkin had a face, it would be one of shock.

Epiphany stands before me, framed in the light of the alley's exit. She's wearing hunter-green khakis and a black, long-sleeved T-shirt. A little blood seeps from her lip where a scab has broken.

If my pumpkin had a face, it would be one of irritation.

'She's in France,' Epiphany says.

If my pumpkin had a mouth, it would say, 'I don't care.'

'Jerry,' she says, as she prowls towards me, 'she's in France!'

I hold my pumpkin close like it's a football and charge my shoulder into her breast. For all I know this could be the last pumpkin in Portugal. No way is she gonna take *this* from me too. Epiphany stumbles back and hits the alley wall. I set my remaining pumpkin safely on the ground behind me.

If my pumpkin could talk, it would say, 'You've got a good thing now, Jerry. Leave Epiphany behind.'

Epiphany looks as if she hasn't eaten or slept in days. Her eye sockets are sallow. Her arms are thin. And even though it's been almost a month since she was attacked at the docks, she has marks that look fresh.

If my pumpkin could talk, it would say, 'Leave thoughts of returning to Chicago behind. You're happy for the first time in your life. You have Bela. She'll make you whole again.'

It would say, 'It's time to fight for what you have.'

'What's happened to you?' I say, extending my palm so she knows to remain still. Epiphany looks at her hands as if the answer is written on them. Her knuckles are scabbed with freshly dried blood. 'He found me, but it doesn't matter– '

'Who found you?'

'Didn't you hear me?' she shouts. 'Matthew has her in France!'

I raise my other hand to calm her. 'I thought she was in Spain?' I say in a way that can't be taken as anything but an accusation of her increasing instability.

'He moved her to Cannes!' she shouts like a lunatic. 'I arrived too late. He moved all of them already!' She's hardly comprehensible now. She's babbling about some 'awakening'. Saying we have to get to Cannes before the film festival starts. It's in two days. We need to leave now.

And again she says, 'He has her.'

She says, 'In Cannes.'

She says, 'The awakening.'

If my pumpkin had a face it would be one of pity – almost. Doesn't she even remember me drugging her? Doesn't she remember me disappearing from the ship?

'It's been over three weeks since I left you on the boat,' I say. 'Do you know that?'

But she only repeats, 'The awakening ... In Cannes ... He has her.' Her voice fluctuates between a loud whisper and a shout and she stumbles towards me like a beggar and clutches both of my shoulders. 'Matthew is going to give her to monsters at his party. That's why God told me to bring you! Don't you see?' Her nails dig into my shoulders. 'I can't get into it on my own! But with you! Matthew knows you! He knew your father! Your father, Jerry! We can get to her before the monsters!'

And I find myself laughing at the ridiculousness of it all. '*That's* why you did all this to me?' I pry her hands from my shoulders and push her back against the wall. '*That's* why you killed Roland and ruined my life? So I could be your date to some fucked-up party?'

If my pumpkin could talk, it would say, 'Be careful.'

Epiphany shakes. Her green eyes flare at me from behind dirty raven's hair that's folded in clumpy strands across her face.

I think of Bela to calm myself. And one last time, I try reason. 'Even if any of this was real, it wouldn't work. I haven't seen Matthew since my father died. He probably doesn't even remember me. There's no way he's going to let me into some exclusive party of his.' The tears in her eyes pop and stream down her face. 'But even if he would,' I say, 'I'm not going with you.'

And my pumpkin – if it could talk, it would shout, 'Look out!'

Epiphany springs at me, slamming me against the opposite wall. Another scab on the side of her lip breaks and blood flows together with the water from her eyes. 'Your father did this to me! You owe me this! You owe me my life and my daughter's life! Your father's sins–'

'Enough!' I shout through gritted teeth. 'My dad was a good man! He had a hard life. He lost his daughter and his son got fucked up and maybe he wasn't there for me or my mom like he should have been, but that doesn't give me one reason to believe anything you say.' My breathing is heavy and I'm surprised to find I feel like I could cry too. 'You went to get Roland to force him to take you to that party, didn't you? Because he knew Matthew. But you lost it. You killed the man who could have helped you more than I could. Well, I'm not going to let you kill me, too.'

And my pumpkin, it would warn, 'Stop while you're ahead.'

'I've met someone,' I say. 'For the first time in as long as I can remember, I'm happy. I'm alive. I've wasted the last fifteen years of my life walking around like a dead person and I'm not going to do it anymore. I'm staying where I am. I don't care who thinks I killed Roland.'

It would say, 'Shut up, Jerry.'

I say, 'The only thing that matters is Bela.'

I say, 'You can't control me anymore.'

My resolve is palpable, and as Epiphany realises she's lost any power she had over me a shudder reverberates through her body. 'I can't get close without you,' she cries. 'You owe me. You owe me–'

'Nothing,' I say. 'I owe you nothing.'

Epiphany shakes her head in short little sways. When she speaks her voice has a grimness to it that I've never heard. 'They're going to rape her, Jerry,' she says clutching her fists in the air. 'She is what I was – the prized virgin. And they're going to *fuck* her and not care when she cries out. That will just make them *fuck* her more. She'll be raped and beaten and made to do the most humiliating things. She'll be a shell of a person.' She's trembling so much she drops to her knees. 'Please, Jerry. She'll end up like me.'

It's the first time I've ever heard Epiphany use the word 'please'. And shuddering on the ground before me, she cries. She leans into me and wraps her arms around my legs and cries. 'Please,' she begs again. But there's no warmth in her embrace – not like with Bela. Epiphany, she's a husk with nothing inside. She's a fake person. Just like I was.

I place my hand under her chin and raise her face to mine. And I look into those horrible green eyes. 'I'm not going with you,' I say.

'But you're meant to,' she says quietly. Hollowly. And slowly her arms unwrap from my legs. She beats her fists against my hips. Even when they pick up speed they're still just hollow punches. She's tired and worn down. She beats her fists against me, mumbling about my father and God and fate, until I push her to the ground. And as she struggles to grab my ankles, anything to keep me from leaving, I kneel at her side and tell her that God has never told her she needed me. God has never spoken to her. The voices she hears, it's just because of the horrible things that happened to her.

'Everything you believe is wrong,' I say.

Epiphany cries into her hands.

'The people who did all this to you,' I say, 'they fucked you up. Matthew fucked you up. LaRouche did. But you ruined my life for no *real* reason, and I don't owe you a thing.'

I grab my pumpkin from the ground.

'Goodbye, Epiphany Jones,' it would say.

And, as I turn the corner and leave Epiphany crying on the alley floor, she shouts empty words.

She shouts, 'You're meant to help me, Jerry!'

She shouts, 'You owe me!'
She shouts, 'You'll regret this!'

I took bus after bus, crisscrossing the city, in case Epiphany tried to follow me. I was stupid. I shouldn't have mentioned Bela. If her life was in danger because of me...

Bela is already at my place when I return. She notes that I look dirty. 'Well, that's what happens when you go to the pumpkin patch,' I say and pull the pumpkin from behind my back.

When we carve it that night, she's meticulous. Like everything else, if she's going to do something, she wants to do it right. It takes her an hour to make the mouth. When she's done we put a candle in it and she asks what we do with the guts.

'You can cook them,' I say, 'and eat them with the seeds.'

'Or,' she says, grabbing a handful of the orange insides, 'you can throw them, no?' And she shrieks as a stringy wad of pumpkin flesh hits me in the face.

When I get out of the shower there's no light in the bedroom except that which comes from the pumpkin we placed on the nightstand. Bela is in my bed already, naked under the covers, propped on her elbows admiring her work. She ended up going with the traditional gap-toothed pumpkin mouth, but its eyes are made of stars. I admire Bela admiring her work and lean down to kiss her bare shoulder.

'Is that a birthmark?' I say, noticing she's got a small brown splotch the size of a dime where her hairline meets her neck.

And as if it were a mosquito, she swats her hand over the mark and rolls onto her back. 'All Portuguese have them,' she blushes.

And this is when I realise I'm in love with her. She seems so strong. She knows what she wants, and what she believes in she never doubts. But she's also vulnerable. She has her own insecurities, like everyone else.

As I smile at her in the glow of the pumpkin light, she pulls the covers aside.

'Keep me warm, alleegator.'

She's taken to calling me *'alleegator'* when the mood strikes her.

I drop my towel and slip into bed. As I lay on top of her, she takes my face in her hands and kisses me. Then, running a hand down my back, she says, 'I tell you about my mark, now you tell me about yours.' She gently caresses my stab wound. The last time I checked it in the mirror the stitches had dissolved and it had closed up but the scar was still red and jagged, like it's Epiphany's attempt at pumpkin-carving me.

I smile as best I can at a bad memory and look into Bela's eyes – they're a wonderful blue with green flecks. 'Can I tell you about it another time?'

She understands and kisses my mouth. 'Of course, alleegator.' And that understanding, it makes me want to tell her how she saves me from my figments; how she, and she alone, can single-handedly reverse the tide of my life.

'Come here,' I say and flip onto my back. Bela nuzzles her body into mine and before long her breath has gone into the regular rhythmic wheeze she makes when she sleeps.

I wake to a scream. My scream. The candle in the pumpkin on the nightstand has melted away into a little pile of wax. In the dark I reach next to me and place my hand on Bela's warm back. I slip out of the bed and creep over to the window. Moonlight illuminates the street below. The café's awning is retracted and its outdoor tables and chairs are folded against the wall.

'Sometimes a dream is just a dream,' a shark told me once. But this one ... Epiphany held Bela's limp body as a wine boat ferried them down the Douro. I screamed from shore for Epiphany to give Bela back, but she remained silent as she shuttled Bela towards the Underworld.

Bela stirs in the bed. I creep across the floor to the kitchen and scan the alley from the back window. My heart stops as I see Epiphany outside. The moonlight dances across her as she stumbles around the alley. Then another woman rushes up to her and wraps an arm around her neck. The other woman is holding a bottle of wine. I look closer and see that the first woman isn't Epiphany. It's just two drunk friends walking home after a late night.

'The biggest regrets in your life will not come from the things you did,' my shrink once told me, 'but from the things you didn't do.'

If Epiphany were to ever harm Bela ... I could have ... in the alley ... I could have taken care of her – made sure she couldn't hurt me or anyone I love, ever again.

But no, that's fear talking. She hasn't done anything to Bela. Bela is with me. She's safe. And Epiphany, she said the festival starts in only two days. She'll have to be on her way to France soon – where she'll either save her daughter or be killed trying.

I slip back into bed and cradle Bela in my arms. I taste her skin on my tongue. I smell her hair on my nostrils. In the darkness the pumpkin grins over us and I foolishly hope that it does have the power to ward off ghosts and goblins and all kinds of evil, because I can't escape the fear that in the same city there's an angel in my arms and a devil on the streets.

37

Vikings and Fairies

The clock on the nightstand reads 13:01. Can it really be one in the afternoon already?

I wasn't able to get to bed until almost daybreak. I kept thinking of everything Epiphany told me in the alley: her daughter being moved to Cannes; Matthew somehow finding her in Spain.

If she's right about any of this, Matthew will be in Cannes for the film festival. Epiphany said it started in two days. She won't stick around here. She'll rush there to make that party. And Cannes is a pretty long trip from Porto; she'd need a few days to get there if she weren't flying – and she can't. Her fake passport isn't authentic enough to get her on a plane. She'll need to take a bus or train. Which means, if she's going to make it, she has to be heading there now. Epiphany's 'you'll regret this' was nothing more than an angry, empty threat.

I hear Bela moving around in the kitchen. She's singing a song in Portuguese. If I am going to make a future here, with her, I need to do this. I slip out of bed and enter the kitchen. Bela's at the sink. She's got an apron tied around her and her sleeves are rolled up to her elbows. Her hair is pinned up. I put my arms around her waist and pull her close, kissing the birthmark on her neck. 'Good morning.'

'Good *afternoon*, alleegator,' she replies.

Fruits and vegetables of every kind lie on the counter: red and green peppers, melons, onions, cucumbers and some gourds I don't even recognise.

'That's a lot of food,' I say, squeezing her tight.

She turns in my arms so we're face to face and places her hands on the back of my head. 'I make you surprise,' she smiles.

'Making me lunch?'

'You get up too late for lunch,' she quips. Then she kisses me softly and tells me not to come back until dusk.

'Making me dinner then?'

Bela squirms free from my arms. 'Don't ruin surprise!'

'Bela,' I say, not knowing exactly how I'm going to phrase it, 'I wanted to talk...'

But she's engrossed in our dinner preparations. 'Out!' she says, working with her back towards me. 'We talk later. Not nice to ruin surprises.'

I kiss her behind the ear and she shrugs in fake irritation. In the reflection in the window I see her smile. It's best to leave, however. I could use more time to think about how I'm going to tell her.

'Good afternoon, my friend,' Paulo says as I leave the apartment. He's sitting in his usual chair outside the café. 'I know what you're thinking. "*Does this man never leave his seat – or his cigars?*"' and he takes a big puff from his stogie. 'That's the beauty of being your own boss and living a simple life. You can do what you like. And I like to sit and people-watch and smoke my friend here.' He admires the stogie's glowing ember.

'Sounds like a good life,' I say.

'And you, my friend, where are you off to today?'

'I don't know, actually.'

'Good then,' Paulo smiles. 'I need to walk to the hardware store. You can help an old man get there – if you don't mind?'

Paulo walks with the help of a rather odd cane. It's carved with images of carnations painted bright red. 'I injured my leg badly many years ago,' he says as we stroll along the river. Out of politeness I don't ask how, even though I'm wondering. I don't know much about him. Even though he's talkative, he's the type who's private about his past.

As Paulo espouses the joys of owning his own café, I watch small boats glide back and forth, transporting large barrels of wine down the river. Paulo speaks of the pleasure he receives from chatting to the regulars; of waking early in the morning, before dawn has broke, to help the young baker he employs knead the dough.

I listen with polite interest and in no time we're at the hardware store. 'Well, my friend, thank you for accompanying me,' he says and shakes my hand with both of his. 'What will you do now?'

'I don't know.' I raise my eyebrows. 'What do you recommend?'

Paulo shrugs. 'Go back to the river and take a ride on a *rabelo*. You think you're strong until you try to steer one of them.'

I shiver as I recall my dream about Epiphany ferrying Bela's body.

'Maybe I'll go to the beach,' I say.

'As you wish,' Paulo says and climbs the store's steps – foot, cane, foot, cane. When he reaches the door he turns back and says, 'Oh, I almost forgot. A man came around this morning. He spoke Spanish. Asked if anyone had rented the place upstairs in the last few weeks. It seemed like he was looking for someone.'

A chill shoots down my spine. But Abdul's boat left weeks ago. Could he have returned with Epiphany? 'Looking for someone?' I try to say casually. 'Sounds like a guy who's looking for his cheating lover.'

'Could be,' Paulo says, with a slim smile.

I fidget a little. I don't want Paulo thinking the wrong thing and I don't want anyone telling Bela what's happened but me. 'It's–'

'Jerry,' Paulo stops me, 'I'm just an old man who likes to people watch. But I've been face to face with horrible men. You're not one of them. I know because Bela wouldn't be with you if you were. So get that look like you're worried that I think you are off your face.'

I relax a little and nod my head.

'I told the man that a German couple had been renting the room and that they ate at my place a few times, but they left days ago,' Paulo says. 'When I told him I knew the landlord and could get him a good deal on the flat, he left.' Paulo turns towards the store. 'Anyway, I better get inside,' he says and continues his ascent up the steps, foot, cane, foot, cane.

'Paulo?' I call after him.

'Yes?' he turns.

'Do you think ... It's just ... I'm not familiar with–' and I say it out loud for the first time, '– with love. Can people still love you even if they find out you aren't ... perfect?' When the question comes out, I feel so silly. It makes me sound like I'm a fifteen-year-old boy.

And Paulo, he descends the steps of the store all the way – cane, foot, cane, foot – just so he can place his hand on my shoulder and look me in the eyes. His silver-rimmed glasses shine in the sunlight. 'Jerry, you are looking at a man who did some bad things in his day. I was scared to death, too, but I told my wife about them and she still loved me until the day she died. Not because she agreed with or even fully understood what I did, but because she knew people never stop changing. A man could be a devil one year and a saint the rest of his life. It's the change and the growth that make people good, not the stuff in their past that keeps them bad. I see Bela every day with you. She's just like my wife.'

I sink my eyes to my chest before looking at Paulo again. 'Thanks,' I say.

'Don't worry about it, my friend. Now go on a walk or a boat ride. Just please, don't go home yet. Bela made me promise to keep you out of the house until later,' he winks.

'I know,' I say. 'She's cooking me a big dinner.'

'*You* know?' Paulo laughs, 'She came to the café this morning and begged me to give her all of my vegetables!'

I avoid the boats and the river and I spend my time walking around the centre of Porto waiting for nightfall. I find Epiphany creeping into my mind more than I like. I hear her scream, *'You'll regret this!'* over and over. On more than one occasion I see her out of the corner of my eye – standing on the side of the road or sitting in a café – but on a second glance it always turns out to be my mind playing tricks on me;

it's always someone who barely resembles her and my mind fills in the gaps with what it fears the most.

More than once I get the urge to run home and check on Bela, but I resist. Paulo's café is always packed and the only door to my apartment is right beside it – and it's locked. If Epiphany were to try to get in she'd have to break down the door in front of a dozen diners.

I walk down Avenue da Boavista, past a concert hall that looks like a huge, white monolith carved at irregular angles from a building-sized meteorite. I follow da Boavista past Parque de cidade and find myself at the beach where I first came to shore. Abdul's freighter is nowhere to be seen. The man who spoke to Paulo really was someone else.

As the sky turns a glowing red I head home. And it's funny: this little apartment feels more like a home than any place I've ever lived. And I don't kid myself – I know it's only because Bela will be waiting for me. She'll be waiting with the dinner she's worked on all day. I'll open up to her and then we'll eat and we'll make love and she'll help me forget my shitty past. But how much do I tell her?

'*Everything*, Jerry,' my own voice answers. 'She deserves to know everything.'

As I approach the apartment Paulo isn't sitting outside. Then I remember it's Sunday. The café closes early on Sundays. Paulo's probably in bed already. But then I notice the apartment lights are out and, though the windows swing open, there's no noise coming from them. No pots clanking or plates being set. And then I see it – the flutter of a shadow. And from the bedroom window I catch a glimpse of someone peeking out, but they pull back before I can make out who it is.

That's when the cold terror sets in. That's when I hear Epiphany in my head again shouting, '*You'll regret this!*' That's when I realise I've underestimated her. She found me in Chicago, she followed me in Mexico, and just yesterday she pulled me into an alley. She could always be near and I would never know it.

You'll regret this!

'Bela!' I yell as I run up the stairs. At the top the apartment door is ajar.

'Epiphany!' I yell. 'Bela!'

The living room is empty. A faint light shines from under the kitchen door.

You'll regret this!

My heart beats wildly as I swing the kitchen door open.

Bela stands at the counter holding a glass of wine, a large smile shining on her face. The room is bathed in an orange glow. The glow comes from vegetables. Dozens of vegetables: cucumbers, gourds, tomatoes, there's even an onion – all carved like mini jack-o-lanterns. Each vegetable wears a different face. Some of the cucumbers are carved length-wise and have wide smiles and tiny eyes. The tomatoes sport round eyes and lopsided grins. A cantaloupe has slanted eyes and a jagged mouth.

'Surprised?' Bela says.

'I don't know what to say,' I breathe, frozen in place, my heart still thumping in my chest.

'I make Jack Lanterns for you.' Her smile is broad as she places her arms around my neck. Her touch melts me. 'Because you liked them as a child.' And she kisses me. 'And,' she adds, holding my gaze unflinchingly, 'it is because I love you, you see?'

Since Emma died no one has told me they've loved me in any convincing way – not even Mom. To hear those words again, it makes me feel like I've been living without oxygen for the last sixteen years. The words, they give me breath. I tell Bela I love her and we kiss this long kiss, like we're both trying to crawl into the other to be kept safe and secure and together for all time. And in that kiss a whole future – a whole world is created. I will never leave Bela. I will follow her anywhere. I will father her children. I will die for her. I would even kill for her.

I gaze into her blue-green eyes. Her pupils are dilated large and they have a glassy look.

I say, 'You're a bit drunk.'

She laughs a little laugh. 'Yes, my alleegator.'

'And what happened to dinner?' I smile, holding her in my arms.

'We have wine,' she answers, 'and some bread. And if we get desperate, we can eat our Jack Lanterns.'

Bela squeals a little as I collapse onto her. Our bodies are wet with sweat and our chests heave in unison as we catch our breath. 'We gave them a show, no?' she smiles exhaustedly.

We moved most of her jack-o-lanterns into the bedroom after we finished the wine. The pumpkin on the nightstand we carved the night before looks like he's a proud father now, surrounded by all his little, glowing children. Bela kisses my mouth and gets out of bed. She walks in the dark, the light from her jack-o-lanterns dancing over her body. Her little paunch glistens with sweat. Her nipples are soft once again. When she walks past the glow of a cantaloupe I spy where my hands have left a bruise on her hip.

'I will turn on the television, no? And we can lie and watch TV with the vegetables,' she smiles.

I nod a 'yes' and fluff our pillows. Bela turns the knob on the little black-and-white TV. It looks like it's from the early eighties – there's a hardwired aerial sticking out. All the channels are blank but one. There's an ad for diapers on. Bela climbs back into bed and nuzzles into my arms, stretching a leg across my torso.

On the television a little eight-year-old boy speaks in Portuguese to his mom. I think he's telling her that his little sister needs changing.

Bela laughs a short little laugh. 'It is great to be a child, no? They ask for what they want, directly, and expect to get it,' she says. 'We forget how to do that as we grow up.'

'I want you,' I say.

And she looks into my eyes and says, 'You have me, alleegator,' and pauses before adding, 'and my vegetables.' And she lets out a little squeak and squeezes her leg more tightly around my torso.

We lie in bed surrounded by burning vegetables and watch a movie I've never seen before. It's definitely a B-movie, probably from the 1930s, and most likely from Britain. There are no recognisable stars. It's dubbed in Portuguese and the plot, as far as I can tell from the bad sets and costumes, revolves around a race of Viking-like aliens trying to move into a forest inhabited by fairies. The Vikings are big and brutish and played by tall or fat actors. Small actors, mostly women but also some children, play the fairies.

Bela is engrossed in the story. I'm taking greater pleasure from watching her watch the movie than I am from the movie itself. 'They are like veekings, no?' Bela asks without taking her eyes from the TV. She hasn't noticed I'm not really watching. Then in a serious voice she adds, 'I hope the fairies win.' And just as two big Viking-creatures have a group of fairies surrounded the movie is interrupted for a regularly scheduled commercial break. Bela squirms at this and kisses me on the chin. 'Good, no?'

I smile and nod my head.

'I hope to see a fairy one day,' she says.

I playfully poke her in the stomach and begin to say, 'I don't think fairies exist–' but she covers my mouth with her hand before I can finish.

Bela considers my face for a moment. Then her eyes go soft and she blushes before she even begins to speak. 'I don't want to be another person who stops believing in the small things,' she says. 'Gypsies, God, miracles and magic.' She removes her hand from my mouth and kisses me. 'And, as silly as it sounds – love.' I squeeze her thigh when she says this.

'My grandmother always said to me this,' she continues as she places her hand on top of mine, 'just because you do not see fairies dancing on the lawn does not mean they are not there.' She pauses, giving me time to let this resonate. 'And as silly as that may seem – even if it is wrong – what harm does it do to believe?' She takes my face in her hands so we are eye to eye. The little green flecks in her beautiful blue eyes sparkle. 'What good is one more unhappy person going to do for this world?'

And maybe it's the wine, or maybe it's because I love her and she loves me, but I believe her words are the truest ever spoken. I'm actually choked up. But Bela, she takes my lack of reply as disagreement. Her face blushes more as she begins to fear her thoughts might have turned into a lecture. 'But I am being silly, no?'

'No,' I say as I roll on to her. I stroke her lips and I make sure I can see every little green fleck in her blue eyes before I speak again. 'That's not a silly thing to believe at all.'

Before the movie is over Bela is asleep in my arms. The movie ended, by the way, with the fairies and the Vikings moving in together and learning to live in peace. Bela will be happy to hear that.

In the bedroom a solitary green pepper remains lit. A little drool escapes Bela's plump lips and collects on my chest. I feel our hearts beat in unison, as if with each beat they're trying to reach the other.

Between the fright I had when I came home and Bela telling me she loves me, I didn't have the energy left to bring it up. But now that she loves me – *me!* – I don't doubt what Paulo said about her understanding. And as I hold Bela in my arms, as I watch the last flame in the green pepper extinguish, I think about what Bela said about believing and I wonder what she'll say tomorrow when I tell her that I knew someone who thought she heard voices from God.

38

Tampons

The TV plays an episode of *Mr Ed*. Wilbur and the talking horse are both in astronaut suits. And even dubbed in Portuguese, I know Mr Ed is trying to convince Wilbur that they can build a rocket ship to go to the moon. The clock on the nightstand reads 6:07 in its red stick digits. Some of the tomatoes have begun to turn to mush, but most of the other vegetables scattered around the room are holding up well. Their insides are charred, but their structure is sound. Instinctively, I rest my hand on Bela's back, only to find she isn't there.

'Bela?' I get out of bed and turn off the Portuguese *Mr Ed*. 'Bela?' I repeat.

'In here,' says a soft voice, sheepishly.

The bathroom door creaks open and Bela peeks her head out. Her long brunette hair dangles to the top of her breasts.

'What are you doing?'

'I am having woman problems,' her face flushes.

Woman problems? Oh. *Woman problems.*

'I need a *tampao*,' she says. 'I will get dressed and go to pharmacy.'

I tell Bela there's no need. I'll run to the pharmacy and get her *tampao*. I dress as Bela throws on one of my T-shirts. It hangs to just below her hips. She walks me down the stairs and from the front door points to the street that I need to turn on to find the pharmacy. Then she wraps her arms around me and gives me a big crawl-into-you kiss.

'Good morning, you two,' Paulo says. He's sitting in his usual captain's chair, stogie in hand and the morning paper resting on the table.

'Ola, Paulo,' Bela smiles at him, a little embarrassed. Paulo gives me a quick wink. Bela flushes and gives a little mock shiver. 'It is cold and I am half-naked, no?' she giggles. 'I go back inside.' She kisses me quickly one more time and says *adeus* to Paulo. Her bare feet pad up the stairs as the door closes.

'Looks like you two are doing well.'

'Yeah,' I say, knowing the hardest part is still coming. When I return I'll tell Bela everything. There'll be no lies, no omissions – something that would have seemed impossible a few days ago. But now that I know she *loves* me...

'Thanks for the talk yesterday,' I say.

'That's what friends are for,' Paulo nods, taking a big drag on his stogie and blowing out a swathe of smoke. 'You know, I saw something interesting a couple of hours ago.'

'At four in the morning?' I give him a mock grin. 'Don't you ever sleep?'

'From nine at night until three in the morning like every other old man.' Paulo smiles. 'But no, on Mondays my fish delivery arrives by five in the morning so I make it a point to get to the café early.' Then he tells me that at slightly past four on his way to the café he saw a woman standing on the sidewalk across the street gazing at my apartment. He could have sworn she was talking to herself. 'She had dark hair – black as the night. I think she was the girl that man was looking for the other day.'

'I don't know, I see a lot of drunk people around here late at night. Only the other night I saw two drunk girls in the alley behind me,' I say, wanting more than anything to believe I'm right. 'Where'd she go anyway?'

'Not sure. One minute she was there, and then I turned around to unlock the door and when I turned back she was gone.' Paulo takes a long drag from his stogie and some ash falls onto his newspaper. He wipes it off and the ash smears a headline that has the word 'CANNES' in it.

'What's that headline say?'

Paulo squints. 'The Cannes Film Festival Starts Today.' He takes another puff from his stogie. 'You know, if you and Bela keep getting on like this you're going to have to learn Portuguese, right?'

I nod; only this is the first time it's occurred to me. Paulo offers me a coffee, but I decline. I want to get to the pharmacy and back as quickly as possible. The sooner I do, the sooner I can tell Bela everything and we can begin to get on with our lives.

When I find the pharmacy it's not even open yet. The hands of the plastic clock sign on the door point to seven o'clock. As I wait, my mind reels with what Paulo said. Even if it was Epiphany she obviously didn't know I was just across the street; she would have confronted me if she had. Besides, the newspaper said the festival starts today. Epiphany's got to either be in or on her way to Cannes. She's not going to risk her daughter's life to keep trying to get me to come with her.

After what seems like forever the green neon cross above the pharmacy flickers to life and a middle-aged man unlocks the doors. When I bring the tampons to the counter he gives me a sympathetic look that doesn't require any translation.

But, I don't know ... a future of early-morning tampon runs and learning another language doesn't seem bad at all. Not when the future's got Bela in it.

Paulo is slumped in his chair when I return. His stogie is barely gripped between his two fingers and his mouth hangs open, a loud snore escaping it. I open the lower door leading to the stairs. On every other stair is one of Bela's jack-o-lanterns. She's relit all the candles in them. I follow the vegetables like they're a treasure trail and step through the apartment door that's held open by the cucumber with the wide smile.

In the bedroom the curtains are drawn and I almost slip on a mushy tomato that Bela's placed on the floor. She's lying on her side, her right arm folded under her head. The cover drizzles her sleeping body. The halo of the relit pumpkin outlines the curve of her hips; the dip of her waist; the slope of her chest. I place the tampons on the dresser and gently sit on the bed beside her. She's put perfume on. I softly kiss her ear, her neck, her shoulder. The taste of her skin is like a drug. My lips find hers and I kiss them. I kiss them as my tongue slips past her teeth and meets with hers.

But she doesn't kiss back.

'Bela?' I place my hand on her shoulder.

I say her name again.

And again.

She doesn't answer.

And this is where I notice the marks on her neck. The small bruises. The skin burn.

This is where I grab her shoulders and shake her.

This is where I scream her name.

And this, this is where my future dies.

39

Carnation Revolution

This is the split second when you wake up. It's the most perfect second of your day. It's the second when your mind is absolutely free from any thought. During this second, you have no worries; you have no fears. This eye-blink of unconscious ignorance is absolute bliss.

And this is the second after that. This is the second when your mind boots up and you realise you're living a nightmare. Pain, loss, agony, grief; they're all waiting, ready and willing, to begin where they left off.

Before I open my eyes, I know he's still here. I can smell his cigar. I'm crumpled on the bedroom floor. A pillow is under my head. If I look to my left, in the bed, I'll see a sheet covering Bela's body.

I was screaming but couldn't hear a sound. Bela's body – I shook it and shook it and shook it. I begged her to wake up. I screamed that I had so much to tell her, as if the dead would return if they knew they had conversations left to be had. Then someone was trying to pull me away from her. Their touch felt like the cold hands of the doctor clawing you from your mother's womb.

'Stop, Jerry. Stop,' someone was saying. They reached under my arms and clasped tanned hands around my chest. My fingers felt like roots violently ripped from Bela's flesh as those hands dragged me away.

Things happened so quickly then. My sister materialised and dematerialised in the corner of the room. Then Rachel did the same thing. And my father, too. And Ana Lucia. They all kept popping in and out of existence like electron bursts in a quantum field. The only constant was Paulo, holding me as I struggled in his arms.

I pick myself up. I'm at the kitchen table now. How I got there, if I walked or floated or was carried, I don't know. I feel like I'm moving through time in violent spurts – like jarring jump cuts from a Godard film. Paulo pours me a cup of tea that he's made. The window is open. I wonder why he's opened it. I feel like a ghost, not part of this world anymore.

Jump cut.

Maybe it's a second later; maybe it's an hour. I don't know how long I've felt his eyes on me. A moment ago his cigar was almost full-length, now it's reduced to half. Then the teacup in front of me sits empty, but I don't remember drinking it.

'I didn't do it,' I hear myself say. But those words, I don't even believe them.

Jump cut.

If I had told Bela everything sooner ... maybe she would have wanted to run with me. Maybe she would have left me. Maybe a million other things would have happened, but all the possibilities end with her being alive.

'I know you didn't,' Paulo says, glancing towards the bedroom – the place my eyes fear to follow. 'But who did?'

You'll regret this!

Jump cut.

How long ago did he ask me who did it? 'The devil,' I mutter. 'The girl you saw this morning.'

Paulo runs his hand through his thinning hair and takes a drag from his inch-long cigar. 'I've got to call the police.'

Jump cut.

'Jerry,' a soft voice says suddenly.

'Bela?' I stir. A cold chill comes over my body as I catch my breath. Oh thank God for nightmares! They make waking all the more joyful. I look towards the bed but find Bela's motionless form still covered by sheets. I settle back into my chair, hopes and dreams, fears and reality confusing my mind. Ten hours ago we were lying there beside each other. Happy. In love. Alive. I begin to cry. I want to crawl under the sheets and lie next to her; die there, with her.

Jump cut.

Paulo's cigar is stubbed out on a plate. Both his hands are on my shoulders. 'I will be back shortly, OK?' he says. He pauses long as if I had the voice to reply. 'Jerry. Listen to me. Jerry. Say your goodbyes, Jerry. It's important to make peace. You understand?' I shake my head but can't bear to look at him. I'll break if I do. Paulo, he releases my shoulders and ... jump cut.

I don't know how long I've stood in the bedroom's doorway. A minute could be an hour. Paulo left years ago.

'Bela?'

I wait for a reply. I wait and hope the sheets will rustle and she'll get up and ask me why I'm crying. 'I was just in a deep sleep,' she'll say. 'Come to bed, lie with me.'

But the body beneath the sheet doesn't move. It doesn't say anything. It's an empty vessel; no more a person now than the pumpkin that watches over it. And without removing the sheet I lie down by this vessel and ask a favour.

I say, 'Please, God, please. It's too much.'

Give me a stroke. Stop my lungs from taking in air. If you make the oven spark, so the apartment catches on fire, I swear, I'll just lie here. I won't even scream, I promise. Just please, if you do exist, do something. End me.

And I wait for a haemorrhage or the fire, but I get nothing.

I look at the pumpkin on the nightstand and recall the knife Bela used to carve it. A quick slit of the wrist would allow me to bleed to death. A small jab of the femoral artery would get me there quicker.

I pull the sheet from her face. The dead, they always look like they're sleeping.

I say, 'Don't be mad at me.' Silent tears stream from my eyes. 'Please, baby, don't be mad at me.'

And I tell Bela everything that I should have told her earlier. I tell her how I killed my sister and how my dad died and how I grew up stuffing my mind with television and movies and porn to block the pain. I tell her about my figments and about the woman who killed her.

I tell Bela that she was my first – 'I was a virgin till I met you.' And I tell her she's only the second person in this entire shitty world who's ever loved me. I drop tears on her face as I tell her no one regrets the things they've done as much as the things they didn't do.

And I tremble as I tell her the last truth I have left to tell. 'You're dead because of me.'

I kiss her lips, but there's no warmth in them. They feel like cold strips of steak fat that have been stretched over a mannequin's mouth. 'I love you, baby,' I say and kiss her cheek one last time. But instead of the normal sweetness of her skin, I taste the bitterness of perfume applied too heavily.

'I am sorry for interrupting,' Paulo says, 'but you need to get going.' He's standing in the living room, leaning heavily on his cane. I didn't even hear him come in. He holds a paper bag in one hand. His eyes, I only begin to see now, burn with their own grief. He had told me he watched Bela grow up across the street from him. This must be like losing a daughter.

I look at Bela for the final time then pull the sheet that begins the eternity of our separation over her head. To not really anyone in the room, I say, 'I'm going to kill myself.'

And then Paulo, he does the most unexpected thing. He hands the man who's just said he's going to kill himself a brown paper bag. Inside the bag is a revolver. 'Why wait any longer?' I expect him to say.

'Jerry, forty years ago Portugal was ruled by a dictator. Every person hated it. Everyone complained behind closed doors. Publicly, fear kept us in line. But finally some people decided to do something about it. I was one of those people.' Paulo glances at the brown bag. 'I was in a militia that orchestrated guerrilla warfare. We hunted the PIDE – a kind of secret police that terrorised anyone who wanted political freedom. I *killed* people for what I believed in to make the future of my country better and safer for all.'

I don't know if I'm hearing him right. Paulo killed people?

'When I told my wife what I did, she was horrified,' he shakes his head. 'But she loved me anyway. She began working towards the results I was trying to achieve, but her ways of achieving those results were different. She marched in Lisbon in what is now called the Carnation Revolution. One day she, along with many others, protested outside the PIDE headquarters. That's the day PIDE officers went to the roof and started shooting into the crowd. Four people were killed, one of them my wife. We had only been married for seven months,' Paulo pauses, his voice momentarily lost. 'The world remembers the Carnation Revolution as a virtually bloodless coup. Our country was so happy to be free from dictatorship it didn't even pursue the PIDE officers who shot into the crowd. Our new leaders *reasoned* it was time to move on. I couldn't. I tracked two of them to Spain.' He pauses, as if choosing his next words carefully. 'Force *is* necessary when you can't get justice any other way.'

'I don't know how to find her,' I tremble. 'I wish—'

'You *find a way* to find her,' Paulo says resolutely. 'Wishing is futile. Every day I sit at my café and I think about my wife. I *wish* she were never taken from me. But nothing, *nothing*, can bring the dead back to us.'

I watch Paulo as he speaks. Everything seems just a little too far off, just a little out of reach, like I've been shoved into the wrong end of a giant telescope.

'I need to call the police,' he's saying. He's got one hand on his cane and the other on my shoulder. 'Jerry, listen to me. It's obvious you aren't here legally. They aren't going to look kindly on that. I've talked to Diana – my wife's sister. I've told her everything. Let us deal with the police. You need to go, now. The longer you wait the less chance you have of finding her.'

I open my mouth to say something but nothing comes out. And as I leave Paulo and Bela and the apartment forever, I stroke the barrel of the gun. 'Sometimes a death for a death *is* the right thing,' a voice says in my head.

The only thing is, there's no note, no sign, no indication of *who* should die for Bela's death. Epiphany and I, we're both her murderers.

The sun is too bright. A father walks with his beautiful daughter. Lovers make out under a tree across the avenue. Two grandparents swing their grandson by his arms. The whole street looks like one big pharmaceutical ad – everyone is happy, everything is perfect. The world shouldn't look like this. Not today. Not after what's happened.

I finger the gun in my khakis. Maybe if I do it in the middle of the road? Cars will be forced to stop. People will be forced to pay attention. If I take someone with me, I bet I'll even get in the newspapers – maybe some magazines. If I clean out the whole street, I bet we're talking TV movie. I could reach the widest audience possible then. My character could scream: *'Why didn't you hurt with me? Why didn't you tell me how to stop the pain?'*

Paulo, he told me to find her. But I'm just me. I don't know how. There's no sign pointing to Epiphany Jones.

And I hurt so much. I want it to stop.

I step off the curb when someone grabs my arm. A snap of air whips by as a little car spits past where I would have been walking. The man who stopped me, his eyes are big and black and proud. 'Fuck you,' I say. His long face becomes confused. 'Fuck you!' I scream. My saliva dots his skin.

The happy happy people on the happy happy street have all begun to stare. I'm acne on the complexion of their product-perfect day. The grandparents pull the grandkid close. An ice cream vendor is frozen mid-scoop. Across the road a group of beautiful young people furtively glance at me as they kiss and hug goodbye.

But when they part, a woman remains behind.

Her smile is kind, her frame small, her hair thin. And I know if I could see her eyes up close, they'd be blue with green flecks.

She waves me over.

I stumble across the street. Tears of joy flood my eyes.

'Hello, alleegator.'

My entire body trembles with sublime weakness. I drop to my knees and wrap my arms around her waist. I press my face into her stomach. I say, '*Bela.*'

Her little giggle. Oh, I can hear it! My heart, it beats in these large, slow pulses. It rejoices in oxygen again.

I weep with relief and squeeze her thin legs hard. I kiss her waist. I bite her hip so I can feel she's real. She strokes her fingers through my hair and purrs, '*My little alleegator.*' And I look into her eyes. Blue with green flecks. She caresses my face and I lean my cheek into her soft hands just as she pressed her ear into my kiss on the day she was irritable with me for discovering her preparing the vegetables.

'I don't want to be another person who stops believing in the small things,' she says. 'Gypsies, God, miracles and magic.' She smiles and pets my head. 'And, as silly as it sounds, love.'

'I know, baby,' I say, my face smeared with tears, 'We talked about this remember? It doesn't matter.' A tiny laugh escapes my mouth. It's a laugh of relief; of joy; of a second chance at a new future. 'You're *here.*' Salty tears slip into my mouth.

'My grandmother always said to me this: just because you do not see fairies dancing on the lawn does not mean they aren't there.'

And my heart takes a deep, slow beat, as if realising something in Bela's words that my mind refuses to. I bury my face into her stomach and sob, 'I remember.'

'And as silly as that may seem – even if it is wrong –' she continues, 'what harm does it do to believe?' She takes my chin in her hand so I'm looking into her eyes. 'What good is one more unhappy person going to do for this world?'

'I remember, baby,' I say again as she smiles down on me. And her lips, they bellow briefly, in a round little way, the way they do before she begins her last words. My chest constricts as air is forced from my body.

'OK,' she begins...

'No, no, no,' I tremble, spasms rippling through my soul. 'Please. I can't make it without you.'

'I go now,' she smiles at me. 'See you later, alleegator.'

'*No! Please,*' I beg. I hold her tight. I'll pin her to this spot. I'll never let her go again. I'll never hurt again. I won't allow it. I *will* her to stay with me.

But it doesn't help.

My arms ensnare nothing but air. I look like a human basketball hoop kneeling on the sidewalk. On the street the pharmaceutical characters are at a standstill. The grandparents clutch their grandson. A shop owner is on his cordless calling the police. But it doesn't matter. I'll have shot myself by the time they get here.

And out of everyone staring at me there's this young kid who stands a little closer than anybody else. He's got a balled-up piece of newspaper in his hand and wears a playful grin. He can't be older than five. The world is still good and beautiful to him. God is loving. His parents are caring. Bad guys always go to jail.

The pure pools of his eyes stare into mine as his amusement grows at my frozen basketball-hoop body. Then with the flick of his wrist he sends his balled-up newspaper sailing towards the day's perfect sky, where it appears as if it could be a piece of broken coral floating in a calm, blue sea. Then the balled-up newspaper, it completes its arc and begins its descent towards the earth where it, much to the boy's satisfaction, drops between the rims of my arms. '*Dois pontos!*' he shouts.

And feeling the gun in my pocket pressed hard against my thigh, I gaze at the balled-up newspaper resting at my knees. I watch it unfold, blossoming like a flower in a time-lapse video. Black-and-white letters bud into florets of words until one headline – one sign – stands out. It's the only sign I've ever needed.

'The Cannes Film Festival Starts Today.'

40

Cannes

This is me, forty-eight hours after leaving Porto on a train.

This is me, faking my way through life again.

This is me, standing on the Promenade de la Croisette, pretending everything is just great.

A fifty-foot Jordan Seabring looms over the Croisette, Cannes' main boulevard, which has the beach and boardwalk on one side and the most expensive hotels in Europe on the other. On the banner, Jordan is wearing a surprisingly conservative red dress and holds a 3D-generated creature – something of a cross between a porcupine and a snail – in the palm of her hand.

Every building on the Croisette is plastered with more of these massive banners promoting the summer's sure-to-be blockbusters. There's the grim and gritty superhero movie about the alien from another planet staring Hugh Fox; the vampire-romance with the pretty-boy actor; the final part of that geek-turned-mainstream fantasy trilogy.

The Croisette crawls with stargazers and hopefuls. The people who look rich are most likely the poor ones – having spent their savings trying to impress the truly wealthy who are here. Desperate people stand on corners asking total strangers if they have an extra ticket to spare for this event or that showing. And everyone here, *everyone*, speaks English. You don't come to the festival if you can't speak English. English is the language of Hollywood. Even the gypsies that come from all over Europe to pickpocket the people here speak English.

Just past a huddle of street vendors hawking DVD movies and

glossies of the stars I find a semi-classy shop where I buy some off-brand shoes, shirts, pants and a tux.

This is me, knowing I need to fit in.

As the clerk wraps up my new clothes, I flip through the Cannes edition of *The Hollywood Reporter* someone has left in the shop. The cover article is about the film that's opening the festival: *The Princess of the Sands*. It's an animated CGI film about an Arabian princess named Houda who discovers a race of creatures living below the Sphinx. Her evil half-brother, the king, has enslaved these magical creatures. Jordan Seabring voices the princess. This is Hollywood's sex kitten trying to appeal to the under-twelve crowd.

Growing up, reading about the festival in *Entertainment Weekly*, everything looked so magical. The palm trees, the red carpet, the fancy limos. I believed the fantasy that the festival was about celebrating the best of film. But my father explained that Cannes is really about the backstage deals. For every film that's in competition there are a thousand films being viewed privately in hotel rooms, and on yachts, and on portable DVD players between courses in fancy restaurants.

The public face of Cannes is about the big-name stars and the best of 'art cinema'. It's about Hollywood telling the world that film is noble, that film is profound. But the private face of Cannes is all business. It's a marketplace. It's about sales. It's about desperate directors trying to get a meeting with a big producer so they can sell the film they mortgaged their house to shoot. It's about fading stars trying to be photographed to get back into the public's eye. It's about young and beautiful women prowling the large hotel bars, hoping to catch the attention of someone important who will invite them to an exclusive party. And at these parties, these young and beautiful women, they'll do anything to become the next big starlet – the next Jordan Seabring.

And it's at one of these hotel bars where I know I'll find Epiphany. If Matthew really does have her daughter, she'll need to find someone with a way into his party.

I pay the clerk when he's done wrapping my clothes. Everything's designer imitations, but it still costs me almost a thousand euros. But

I won't get into the hotel bars if I don't look the part. Everything in Cannes during these three weeks is about image.

Outside the Carlton Hotel life-size statues of two of the characters from *The Princess of the Sands* flank the doorway. One is Jordan Seabring's princess; her large eyes and wrist-thin waist sure to give eight-year-olds eating disorders for the rest of their lives. The other statue is the princess's evil half-brother, the king. He's got a triangular grin and barrel chest and holds an Arabian sword in one hand and a football-sized red jewel in the other.

The Carlton is the hotel where my father always stayed. Matthew wouldn't be here but some of his lower-downs might be, which means Epiphany could show.

This is the best plan I've got. This is my version of Paulo's, 'You find a way to find her.'

The concierge tells me with a hint of snideness that he's sorry, but the best rooms have been booked for almost a year – just after the last festival ended. 'You understand.'

Meaning, if I really was important, I should know that.

So I put two hundred euros on the counter and the concierge takes the bills, folds them and puts them in his pocket.

He says they do have a single room left. It's small and is only on the second floor. No bigger than a closet, really. Desk. Bath. DVD player. Normally it's for the help working night shifts. 'You understand.'

I place another hundred euros on the counter that disappears just as quickly.

He says that, at this late stage, however, the room is as much as their normal single-bed suites. That is, four thousand for the week. 'You understand.'

I hand the money over.

He raises his eyebrows. 'And the name? For the register?'

'Jerry Dresden,' I say. And I spell it for him. 'Give it to anyone who asks, got it? Anyone.'

'I understand,' he says.

This is me, breaking down again. It happens as soon as I'm in the room. Just like I did on the train coming here this morning. I break down and I cry. I hurt so bad.

Then I take the gun out of the paper bag Paulo gave me. It's the kind that you need to pull the cock back on. Like one of those Wild West Howdy Doody guns. It's got a barrel chamber with six bullets in it.

And Paulo's wrong. This is revenge, not justice. Justice would have been Epiphany going to France – on her own – without murdering Bela.

Justice would have been everyone leaving everyone else alone.

In my mind I can still hear Bela's little giggle. I can still feel her hands on me.

What was she thinking as Epiphany strangled her? Did she know what was going on? Did Epiphany tell her that she was my punishment for not going to France; for not believing in her voices? And as she died, was she angry at me?

With the gun in my hands, I know Bela would be angry at what I'm about to do.

But she's dead. And the dead don't see. They don't feel.

This is for her memory. It's to show Epiphany she can't take an innocent life. That she can only push the weak and cowardly around for so long before they push back.

41

Bullets

'They put you on a boat and knock you out. You wake up at the party on some island off the coast, and the only way they let you leave is by knocking you out again.'

'I've heard if you've never been in a picture with a twenty-mil opening day, there's no way you'll be invited.'

'I've heard it's thrown by Matthew Mann.'

In all the swanky hotel bars, Cannes' most exclusive party is talked about in whispers.

'How would Mann afford it? I heard all the glasses are made of diamonds and the plates are solid gold. The guests get to keep them, too.'

'I heard guests have to sign a non-disclosure agreement!'

'I heard you go to bed one night and you wake up the next morning with the invitation laying next to you. No one knows who delivers them – or how they got in to your room.'

All anyone knows for sure is that the party hasn't taken place yet. No one wants to risk saying they were there to a person who's going and knows it hasn't happened. The good news is that means Epiphany is still in Cannes. No doubt she's heard the same whispers and is waiting until she can meet someone who's going. The bad news is I've been going from hotel bar to hotel bar for two days and haven't spotted her.

It's the fifth day of the festival and the city is in full swing. The Carlton bar is crowded when I return at quarter to midnight. I've wasted the last four hours sitting in the Majestic, hoping Epiphany might show there.

However Bela did it, whatever *it* was, it's wearing off. I've started to see my figments again. On the walk back I saw Ana Lucia dribbling her soccer ball. Rachel called me from the beach. She said, 'You haven't fucked until you've fucked in the sea under a full moon.'

The Carlton's waiters in their white coats double in the large mirror lining the back of the bar as they dash from table to bar and back, ushering drinks to all the Very Important People. The bar is packed with beautiful girls. These are the girls who emptied their bank accounts just to get to Cannes. Girls who spent every last penny on the dress they're wearing now. And that dress, it's the same one they'll wear every night of the festival because it's the only one they could afford. It's the dress that perfectly shows off their young bodies. The dress which will, they hope, persuade a producer to sleep with them and then offer them a role in his next film.

I'm at a small table near the back. At the table next to mine are five loud Americans, all dressed in suits, drinking and laughing. All but one of the men looks to be around my age. They laugh extra hard when the older man tells a joke. The older man, his beard is perfectly manicured, like his suit and his eyebrows and his nose hair.

'Look, Frank,' the manicured man says to one of the younger guys, 'This is your first year here, right?'

Frank smiles too big.

'A little word of warning,' the manicured man says. 'If a beautiful woman hits on you – it's really a man. For some reason Cannes really brings out the transvestites.'

'It's true,' chimes in another American. 'Just ask Mark!' Laughter erupts.

'It was one time, and anyone could have made that mistake,' a red-faced Mark says.

More laughter.

Across the bar another group of beautiful girls enter. They scan the room, look chronically dissatisfied, and leave as quickly as they arrived.

'Sorry, sir. Busy tonight. What would you like?' a waiter who has appeared out of thin air says. I give him my order and he glides back through the crowd. That's when I notice a redhead facing the bar. And for the next few minutes I watch this redhead as she refuses drink after drink. The redhead, she's wearing a shimmering blue dress with silver heels. She's wearing a black choker around her neck. She's wearing her hair over her ears. And of all the girls in this bar, I immediately know she's unique. Of all the girls in this bar, I immediately know it's her that doesn't belong.

'Hey, I can get any *woman* I want,' Mark bleats out at the American table, silencing his teasers. 'Just don't tell my wife.'

'Deal!' says the manicured man. 'The lonely girl at the bar – that one with the beautiful red hair. She's been casting off men all night. You get her and I'll trade rooms with you. You can have the penthouse. You don't get her and you're buying drinks for everyone the rest of the trip.'

And I, along with the Americans, watch as Mark makes his way to the bar and tries to chat the redhead up. We watch as Mark touches her arm and she recoils. We watch as the bartender delivers the drinks and Mark picks his up to toast her but she doesn't touch her glass. We watch as Mark places his hand on the redhead's cheek and says, 'Hey, loosen up.'

And we watch as this girl with the beautiful red hair who doesn't belong here digs the heel of her silver shoe into Mark's foot and grabs him by the tie, causing him to spill his drink all over himself. We watch her lips say, 'I said, leave me alone.'

And the reason this girl doesn't belong is because she isn't here to sleep with a producer, or get a movie part, or find a rich husband. No, the reason this girl doesn't belong is because her name is Epiphany Jones and she believes she's on a mission from God.

Back at the Americans' table, over his colleagues' laughter Mark mumbles that the redhead was clearly wearing makeup to cover a bruise on her cheek (*'probably a hooker'*).

'Next time I won't keep you waiting so long, sir,' the waiter says out of nowhere. I swear, he's a damn ninja. 'Here's your Coke, triple rum.'

If you're about to take a life a little liquor never hurts. I swallow the glass in one gulp. And as I wait for the alcohol to take effect, underneath the table, I fidget with the revolver. I spin the chamber around and around as I fixate on Epiphany, who's facing the bar again.

I rehearse it again in my head: Walk up behind her. Say, 'This is for Bela.' Shoot her in the head. Watch people scream and run. When the police show up, fire my remaining bullets into the air so they're forced to shoot me.

'Another drink, sir?' The ninja waiter says from out of nowhere, startling me. And I accidentally eject the gun's chamber, spilling its bullets to the ground.

The ninja waiter, he sees something small and shiny hit the floor. 'I've got it, sir.'

'No,' I shout, immediately afraid that I've been too loud; that Epiphany will turn and see me and run.

'Of course, sir. Sorry, sir.' And the ninja waiter evaporates into the crowd again. Epiphany is still at the bar, her back towards me.

Beneath the table, hidden from view, I finger the chamber of the gun. I finger three empty slots where bullets should be. As I bend under the table, I snatch two bullets from the floor and quickly jiggle them back into the chamber. My fingers crawl along the floor for the last bullet, all the while keeping Epiphany in my line of sight from just underneath the lip of the table. Then I glance and see the last bullet laying by my shoe. But when I glance back towards the bar Epiphany is gone. I jump straight up in my seat. But Epiphany hasn't left. She was only blocked by a crowd of people who have moved on.

At the next table, the manicured American looks my way. His face furrows a little before he turns back to some inane story one of his lackeys is telling. I make sure that Epiphany isn't going anywhere before I bend underneath the table to snatch up the final bullet, but my movement is too awkward and my foot pinches it against the ground and sends it spinning across the floor until it hits the leather loafer of the manicured man. My eyes go wide. And as the manicured man bends down to see what the little gleaming piece of metal is by his shoe, I slam the chamber of the gun shut. Around his feet, the manicured man walks his fingers awkwardly across the floor. And, bent low under the table, head cocked sideways, he squints as he catches me in his sight. His jaw drops a little.

'Is this your bullet?' I expect him to say.

I turn to the bar. Epiphany's still there. My heart pounds. My ears hum. This is it.

'Jerry?' a voice says from the next table. It's the manicured man. He's lost interest in what's hit his foot and straightens himself. 'Jerry *Dresden*?'

'Uh ... yeah?' I say, my arm suddenly powerless to raise the gun.

The manicured man gets up from his table and walks to mine. 'God, you're his spitting image.'

I stare blankly, unlike the lackeys at his table whose eyes all burn with jealousy.

'Sorry,' he says and extends his hand. I fumble with the gun underneath the table, quickly flipping it from my right hand to my left. 'My name is Phineas Quimby. I worked under your father for over eight years.'

I take his hand in my gun-free one. Not a stray hair on that beard of his is out of place. 'I'm sorry, have we met before?' I say, glancing at the bar.

'Only once,' he says. 'Sadly, it was the night of your father's accident. Your dad brought you to that wrap party.' And then he waits as if I'm supposed to react a certain way. When I don't, he goes on. 'Your dad was a legend. Any problem Matthew would throw at him he would spin it and turn it to pure gold. He was the best of the PR people.'

Then he sits at my table without asking and says, 'What are you doing in Cannes?' And then waits again, looking like I'm supposed to answer in a certain way.

'Just about to kill someone. Can we talk later?' would be the honest thing to say. 'I'm just here for pleasure,' I say, peering past his shoulder. Epiphany still has her back towards me. She briefly talks to another man before sending him away. Underneath the table, my gun hand shakes. Then, without warning, a pain explodes in my head.

And then I see Bela. She's lying naked on one of the bar's tables, bruises around her neck. She lies lifeless as Phineas tells me he's still working for Matthew; he's got my father's old position. He's here supporting Jordan Seabring and *The Princess of the Sands*.

On the table behind him, Bela's dead body smells of generously applied perfume.

I tell myself it's just a figment, and Bela's naked body disappears and Phineas is saying, 'You liked her, huh?'

I loved her. Wait, how could he –

'Jordan Seabring,' he smiles a broad, knowing smile. 'I know how much you liked her.'

How the hell would he know that? She wasn't even a star when my father was alive.

But Phineas's mind reading takes a back seat as I fight fresh figments of Bela.

Now Bela is at the bar with Epiphany. They're having a drink.

At my table, Phineas carries on telling me how he owes his whole career to my father. 'He brought me into Matthew's inner circle. I'd be a nobody without your dad.'

Up at the bar, Epiphany sets her drink down and puts her hands around Bela's neck. Epiphany laughs as Bela struggles in her grasp. And I know it's just my stupid mind playing with me, but I so desperately want to run over to the bar and save her.

'What?' I say as Bela vanishes again.

'I asked how long you're here for?' Phineas says.

'Not too much longer.' Under the table, I feel to make sure the safety is off.

Phineas takes a small pad of paper from his jacket pocket. He shouts to his lackeys for something to write with. They all glare at me then fall all over themselves to be the first to give Phineas what he wants. To beat the others someone tosses a pen, but it hits Phineas's hand and lands on the floor. And as he bends to pick it up, leaving the view of me wide open, Epiphany turns from the bar and our eyes meet.

My body tightens. A cold sweat breaks out on my forehead. But, to my surprise, Epiphany doesn't run. She looks at me for a moment and then starts sliding through the crowd towards me.

'Are you staying here?' Phineas is saying. 'Give me your room number. I'd like to meet to catch up in private when I'm not babysitting these yahoos.' And if I weren't fixated on Epiphany in her stupid red wig, I would see the yahoos pout, their eyes filled with resentment.

I flip the gun back into my right hand, my eyes locked with Epiphany's, ready to spring from the table. But before I can, Epiphany stops. Her mouth hangs open a bit as if she's just been punched in the stomach and gotten the wind knocked out of her. Her eyes, they look almost sad.

'Well,' Phineas says, following my line of sight, 'this is the second night I've seen her here. You're the only one who's caught her attention.'

Yeah, lucky me.

Now Epiphany begins backing away, then turns and pushes through the crowd until she reaches the exit.

'Guess she likes the chase,' Phineas quips. I slide the revolver into my pocket and tell him to excuse me. And as I get up from the table and begin to push through the packed crowd I feel Phineas tug at my arm and ask for my room number again.

I make it to the bar's exit just in time to see Epiphany running through the front doors of the Carlton, just past the big cartoon mannequins. Outside, the midnight air is warm. The floodlights bouncing off the hotel exteriors are blinding but I keep her in my sight. The bulk of the gun in my pocket bruises my thigh with each stride as I burst after her. She darts down the wide sidewalk then makes a quick left onto a smaller street. The street's empty. I close on her, my stomach in knots, blood pounding in my ears. The heel of her silver shoe snaps, sending her towards the ground. I lunge and grab her red hair but the wig comes off in my hands. She tries to scurry to her feet. I lunge again and grab her real hair and drag her into an alley.

I pull her by her raven hair until she falls to the ground. Her white face is blushed red. Her chest is winded. Smudged makeup reveals a scratch on her cheek. My heart wants to explode.

'I didn't kill her,' she breathes, struggling to get up.

'Bullshit!' Spittle flies from my mouth and I realise I'm heaving tears. 'You took her from me! *Her perfume* ... you put her perfume on her so I would think she was waiting for me.' I pull the gun from my pocket. My arm trembles as a cold strain floods my chest.

'Jerry, no...!'

'She didn't do anything to you! I was out of the apartment. You could have taken me. Why didn't you take me? Why did you have to take her!' The way I'm shaking, if my hand touched the ground the quake would split the Earth in two. 'She had so many plans. She had a father too. Did you know that? She had a father. And you killed her.'

Epiphany puts her palms up for me to stop. 'I didn't, Jerry,' she desperately lies. I move towards her until the gun is an inch from her snow-white skin. Spasms run across her face. Sweat makes her mascara bleed. 'I didn't – '

I shake my head and wipe tears on my sleeve. *Then how do you know she's dead?*'

I cock the gun and Epiphany's eyes go wide as she realises how this is going to end. She lowers her hands halfway – a way of telling me to *just calm down'*, a way of saying, *'we're all friends here'*. And, as tears pour from my eyes, Epiphany stammers her last lie.

She says, 'In the bar ... when they warned me about the gun–'

Looking into the barrel of it, she says, 'My voices–' then shifts her gaze to my eyes.

She says, 'My voices, they told me how much you are hurting.'

And I say, *'Stop with the voices.'*

And I fire into Epiphany Jones' snow-white face.

42

Gypsies

In movies the term point-blank is thrown around incorrectly all the time. Point-blank actually refers to a shot fired from within one to two metres of the victim. When you shoot someone within inches of the face, as I just did, it's called a contact shot. A contact shot will produce what's called tattooing – a distinctively patterned wound from the powder burns that spray the face.

The sound of a gunshot has nothing to do with the mechanics of the bullet. The bang comes from gases that are released during the shot. In a contact shot the body will act as a suppressor for the muzzle blast, trapping the propellant gases under the skin, causing it to bubble up, thus muffling the sound of the shot so that even people walking on a busy boulevard forty feet away can't hear it.

Now, what's meant to happen when you shoot someone in the face at any range is the bullet leaves the barrel of the gun. It enters the victim, ideally between the eyes, travelling through the skull and that lump of grey matter we call a brain. Then the bullet, it exits the back of the head, taking a large chunk of skull and skin and mush with it.

Think JFK.

Think MLK.

Think Honest Abe.

This person you just shot, they're supposed to collapse lifelessly to the ground. All thoughts, all memories, all pain and all joy, gone from them forever.

That's what's meant to happen. But guns, they act differently when you fire them at Epiphany Jones.

She's still standing. Her eyes squeezed tight. Her breath held. Her whole body rigid like a bronze statue as she stands braced for impact against the half-inch shard of metal that's supposed to end her shitty life.

One second passes. Two. And she opens her eyes a little. Three. She exhales. Four. She says, 'God,' and crosses herself. I flip the chamber open. Five. There are only five bullets in the revolver. The one that should have gone into Epiphany's skull is lying somewhere on the floor of the Carlton's bar.

'Not God,' I say, snapping the chamber shut, 'luck.'

And maybe she's convinced I'm right for once, because she doesn't give me a chance to take another shot. With the broken heel of her silver shoe she kicks hard against my shin and grabs my wrist. And she slams my hand against the alley wall until I drop the gun. She's relentless with her kicks and I stumble from the alley, tripping over a curb, landing in the middle of the street.

She kicks off her snapped heels and races barefooted down the street then turns onto the main boulevard. I grab the gun and sprint after her. I weave between the nightlife lovers and the celebrity seekers that fill the Croisette. A mass of people huddled around a DVD stall selling two-for-ones slows my pursuit. I push though them and run into the street. A black Benz blares its horn as it swerves to get around me. Epiphany is just twenty feet ahead of me on the sidewalk, and I'm gaining on her. Suddenly the mirror of another car hits me as it tries to swerve around me on the street. I leap back onto the sidewalk into the thickened crowd again. Then I realise it's not just the crowd, but one of the roving bands of gypsies that have slowed my pursuit.

The gypsy and her children, they circle around me. The gypsy mother lifts her baby to my face and mumbles something about food. The longer the gypsy blocks me the smaller and smaller Epiphany gets down the boulevard. So I wrench the baby from the gypsy's arms.

And I dropkick it.

And from behind me, someone yells, 'My God!'

Someone yells, 'That man just punted a baby!'

Someone yells, 'Nice range!'

And I probably forgot to mention this before, but the gypsies that come from all over Europe to festivals like this – my dad told me all about them. They'll roam around in packs, a mother and her gypsy children. The mother will always carry a baby wrapped in a blanket in her arms. As she carries this baby, she's followed by her other little children, who weave through the people on the crowded sidewalk. The mother gypsy, she'll hug her baby tight, whispering prayers in its ears. And the other children, they'll wait for a cue from their mother. They'll wait for a cue from their mother because, that baby she's holding? It's not real.

My father explained that what these gypsies will do is find a crowded area and ask people in broken English if they can spare some change to help feed the children. When no one offers any money, the gypsy will scream and scream until she's attracted a lot of attention. Then she'll toss her baby into the air. And the onlookers, they'll all stand dumbfounded as this small baby sails through the sky.

While this is going on, while everyone's attention is on the baby, the gypsy's children will deftly pick the pockets of the onlookers. They do this in less than five seconds. And as the baby lands on the ground or is caught by a Good Samaritan, the onlookers will breathe a collective sigh of relief when someone shouts, 'It's just a doll!' Everyone will slowly depart, crisis averted. 'The woman is mad,' they'll say. They won't realise until much later that their pockets are lighter.

And across the street a man has his hands stretched towards the sky. 'Mine!' he calls, like he's Shoeless Joe Jackson waiting in the outfield. And soon three men are on me. Two wear tuxes. The third looks like paparazzi. They're forcing me to the ground, and as a hand presses my head against the sidewalk, I gaze down the boulevard, my view all sideways. Epiphany has disappeared.

'Someone call the police!' a man is shouting.

'Oh, take his picture, darling. The help will never believe this!' a woman says.

Across the street, Shoeless Joe catches the baby to loud applause. He beams like he's single-handedly won the World Series. But, 'Wait!

Wait!' he says. 'It's not real!' And he gives the baby a squeeze and it squeals like a dog's toy.

The men holding me down, they apologise. They help me up now. The anger on the boulevard turns towards the gypsy.

'You should be ashamed!' someone says.

'Get a job,' another shouts.

But the gypsy, she just gathers her real children and walks away. Their pockets stuffed full of wallets.

Rachel is in my room when I get back. She's sitting in a chair by the window. But she has the decency not to say anything other than, 'How could you let her get away?' When I open the bathroom door, Ana Lucia comes running out. But she disappears just as quickly. It's when I leave the bathroom that I find Bela lying naked in my bed.

In my head I keep hearing her say, '*My alleegator.*' So I cry.

Then my phone rings.

'Jerry?'

'Who is this?'

'It's Phineas, Jerry. We met in the bar. Your father's friend.'

I don't say anything. Bela's in my bed. Her mouth gaping open and eyes wide as she's invisibly strangled.

'Jerry?'

'Yeah.'

'Are you OK, Jerry?' His voice seems distant. 'You ran out so quickly, I wanted to make sure everything is OK.'

'How did you get this number?'

'The concierge,' he says. 'I mention I work for Matthew and doors open. His name carries weight here.' The way he says it is like he's expecting me to chuckle.

'So are you OK, Jerry?' he says. 'I'm up in the penthouse if you want to talk.'

'What do you need?' I say.

It's a moment before he says, 'There's an event tomorrow night at the Martinez. *The Princess of the Sands* party. I thought you could come. I haven't seen you since the wrap party and it would be nice to catch up with my old friend's kid.' Then he adds, 'You remember that party? Your dad had that special present for you?'

I remember the party but I haven't a clue what present he's talking about. The only thing I ever got from my dad was his gold watch.

'Sure,' I say. 'That's fine.'

'Great, Jerry. I'll have someone drop an invite by your room.' Then he adds, 'You with anyone here? You need another invite?'

I look at the bed and Bela has disappeared. 'No,' I say.

'OK, Jerry. No problem,' he says, like that's the wrong answer. 'Sounds good.'

We hang up and half an hour later someone slides a green envelope under my door and I go to bed but I don't sleep.

43

Memory

I'm standing in a roped-off area outside the Martinez Hotel. This is eighteen hours after I fucked up shooting Epiphany. I clutch the piece of parchment from the green envelope that's the fancy ticket to *The Princess of the Sands* party. Fans, barricaded from the guests attending the party, scream endlessly. Celebrity after celebrity walks from limo after limo into the hotel. With each additional celebrity, the fans' shouts increase.

There goes Brad.

Screams.

And Gwyneth.

Screams.

Ah, and here's Tom.

And a girl on the sidelines – she *faints*. The celebrities, they're like Greek gods in front of adoring legions of soldiers. There goes Zeus. Here's Hades. Ah, Persephone is wearing a lovely laurel, isn't she?

It's different watching the celebrity procession in person than it is on television. You see what the cameras don't show you: everything is orchestrated. The agents treat their celebrities like children. One scolds, 'No dammit, not yet! Angelina hasn't cleared the walk yet and we need all the cameras to be on *you*! Wait! Wait! OK, *now*!' Another one shouts at an up-and-coming child star, 'It's no good just being seen! You *need* to be *photographed*! If you don't make it to the glossy pages, your career is dead before you turn thirteen!'

A security guard asks to see my ticket. 'OK, you go in once the As are done,' he says.

A is for A-listers.

The celebrities keep coming. Megan. Julia. Natalie. Jennifer. And I've jerked off to them all. Standing over my keyboard, I've fucked them every which way and they don't even know it. Then a large white limo pulls up. A valet opens the door and Matthew Mann gets out. It's been more than a decade since I last saw him. He's gotten fat, sloth like. His hair has gone grey, but his veneers are still whiter than the flashing of the cameras.

And he's the reason I came to this stupid party. Not for what he's done. Not for knowing what he does to little girls. Not to bust him. No. If he's here, I'm betting Epiphany will show. I left my gun back in the room. Security is too tight, but I'll use my hands if I have to. I'll grab her by the neck and wring the life from her pale little face. I'll grab a chair and bludgeon her to death while all the stars look on. *'Luck doesn't save you twice,'* I'll say.

Matthew extends his big, fat, sausage fingers into the limousine and a slender, tanned hand takes his. And then out comes the belle of the ball. The hottest It Girl in the history of Hollywood. And the crowd screams like it's one massive animal. It's in ecstasy.

Jordan Seabring drifts up the red carpet as flash after flash after flash explodes from cameras. Shouts boom from the audience. *'I love you!' 'Marry me!' 'Oh my God! Oh my Gooooooodddddd!'* And Jordan, she looks perfect. Her wavy blonde hair shimmers. Her strapless black dress shows off her Cs just the right amount. And in the eyes of the crowd, with every flash Jordan becomes more beautiful; more important; more of who to aspire to be.

But as powerful as Matthew is, few of the screaming fans recognise him. Matthew knows this. But it doesn't matter. Not to someone like him. The people with the real power in Hollywood don't need to be recognised. They *make* the celebrities. And they know each star is just a cog in the wheel. *A brand*. Each star will be replaced when the time comes. They'll be replaced with the younger, the more beautiful. But people like Matthew – they'll be around until the day they die, celebritising the world as they see fit.

After Matthew and Jordan slip inside the golden doors, the crowds disperse. Everyone who walks in now is the Unphotographed – the people who don't matter. And as the crowd thins, I expect to see Epiphany left standing behind, but she's nowhere to be seen.

'How do you like the party?' a voice says from behind me.

'The Bellini is good,' I say, holding up the same glass I've had for twenty-five minutes.

Phineas smiles. 'Yes, these parties are all the same, aren't they?' He pauses for a moment, then confides, 'You know, for the last ten years, Matthew just arrives at the parties for the press photographers? As soon as he gets in the door, he goes right out the back.' Phineas laughs. 'But that's what he has me for. I'll tell the reporters he had a wonderful time dancing with the star of whatever film until the early hours.'

All around us celebrities and Hollywood hacks talk and laugh and smile. And still they all look like they're acting. Just past a waiter who's dressed as a porcupine creature from *The Princess of the Sands*, an agent is saying to his seventeen-year-old Disney star, 'The goal is when someone types the letter of your first name into Google, you're the top auto-suggestion that appears.'

He's saying, 'The goal is to Tweet one sexy picture of yourself to your followers each week.'

He's saying, 'The goal is to get more "Likes" than Facebook has users.'

Always keeping an eye out for Epiphany, I say to Phineas, 'I remember my dad saying this world really wears on you. After the first month in, it loses its shine. The mystery and sparkle are gone.'

'Your father was an intelligent man,' he says, 'He knew there were better things than this.' Then he looks at me for a moment. 'How was the redhead? She looked like fun.'

'I lost her in the crowd,' I say.

'That's a shame,' he says. 'You said you're here alone? Lots of pretty women to be had.'

'Yeah,' I say. But I'm only looking for one.

And Phineas looks like he's contemplating me, like maybe he's annoying me, so I say, 'Look, thanks for the invite. I'm sorry I didn't remember you.'

'That's OK, Jerry. You were just a kid the last time we met. You had to be, what? Sixteen? Seventeen? It's a rough age and, well, that night was a rough night.'

'Yeah,' I say.

'How much of it do you remember? I spoke to your mom a few times after the accident and she said you were having difficulties.'

'I remember enough,' I say sharply. 'The wrap party. The accident.' And I feel bad how that came out, so I say, 'Sometimes I think how differently my life would be if he hadn't died. Like I wouldn't be where I am right now if he were still around.'

Phineas puts his hand on my shoulder. 'Your dad would be so proud that you're right here, right now. He spoke so highly of you. He hoped you would follow in his footsteps.'

I open my mouth, but no words come out. Dad was distant after Emma. I always wondered if he were mad at me for it. But to hear he spoke proudly of me ... it makes me even angrier at the lies Epiphany told.

As the night goes on, I have a few drinks. Since Mann left I know Epiphany isn't going to show, so I try to make the best of it. I try to ignore the occasional glimpses of Bela I see in the crowd. Phineas introduces me to more and more stars. He asks me how my mom is. He tells me old stories about my dad's greatest PR coups and how my dad always had a crush on Audrey Hepburn.

And when a waiter dressed as one of the porcupine creatures from *The Princess of the Sands* stops in front of us, his quills momentarily blocking us from most views in the room, Phineas grabs my arm and leans close. 'Here,' he says and slips me a bar-coded bracelet. It's black and looks like the ones you get when you're admitted to hospital. 'This is for a much better party tomorrow.'

I realise it's the coveted invite to the party only spoken of in whispers.

'Why are you giving this to me?'

'Because you are your father's son and he was a good man to me. I can see you miss him like I do. And,' he looks into my eyes, 'unlike everyone else in this room, your goal of coming tonight wasn't to find a ticket.'

No, I think. It wasn't.

'Now, each bracelet gets two people in,' Phineas speaks quietly. 'The address on the other side is where you're to go. A car will pick you up there and you'll be driven to Matthew's private villa in Antibes.'

'Phineas!' a voice cuts through our hushed conversation. It's a voice that I immediately recognise. It's a voice I've heard in countless movies.

Jordan Seabring, she stumbles over to Phineas and gives him a big hug. 'P!' she says tipsily. 'How's my favourite publicist?'

'Enjoying the party, though not as much as you,' he says with a good-natured smile.

'Oh, P!' she laughs.

And after Bela, I'd like to think I wouldn't act like this, but I do. Maybe it's because I'm American and celebrities are our gods. Or maybe it's the too many Bellinis I've had. When Jordan notices me my body stiffens and I poke my chest out and suck my stomach in. In this moment, I wish I were better looking than I am. I wish I were funnier; more charming.

'Miss Seabring,' I say with bullshit confidence and I extend my hand, 'I'm a big fan.'

She smiles with an 'of course you are' look and takes my hand. And when she does, something in me remembers the wrap party the night my dad died. But then I'm back at the current party looking at her plump lips and her round breasts and her windswept hair and she's looking at me, and then she says, 'Little J?' And she turns to Phineas. 'Little J?' she asks him. He nods. And then the biggest movie star in the world slaps my outstretched hand away and wraps her arms around me. She kisses me on the cheek, her fake breasts crushing against my chest.

'I believe you two have some catching up to do,' Phineas smiles, and gives me a wink before he trots off.

'I can't believe it's you,' Jordan says and pauses for a moment to take my features in again. I begin to ask her what she means, but she just says, 'Come on,' and takes my hand and leads me through the room. And as we pass Natalie, and Brad, and Tom, they all give looks that say, 'What's *that* guy doing with *her*?'

We reach the balcony, where I see the moon shrink a little, jealous of the competition. 'Some privacy, please,' Jordan says, and all the people go back inside without saying a word.

A light breeze blows in the night. Ten storeys below us people scurry like ants on the Croisette. Out to sea you can just make out where the evening sky ends and the Mediterranean begins.

'This is wild,' Jordan says. 'It's been, what? Twelve years?' And in the moonlight with the plump lips and the cleavage spilling from her dress and the windswept hair in the breeze, Jordan looks like she's just pried her way from the pages of *Maxim*.

But if you think you know what this is like for me, being alone on the balcony with the most desired woman in the world, with an actress I've fantasised about for years and masturbated to enough times to populate the planet ten times over, you'd be wrong.

Talking to Jordan is like picking up a seashell on the beach and putting it to your ear, expecting to hear the sound of the ocean, but what you get is some slug that tries to make your cochlea its new home. I can't get a word in. Her questions are all rhetorical. She talks only of herself; of how people love her and want to be just like her. She talks of how many hearts in Hollywood she's broken and how she believes the more heartache you cause people, the more desirable you must be. And after each and every thing she says, she pauses, like she's expecting me to clap or congratulate her or something. I'd call this conversation the dullest I've ever had, but a conversation only exists when both people are allowed to speak.

I listen to Jordan's boastful crowing and it contrasts so starkly with Bela's round, meaningful words with the little pauses in between. And an unpleasant feeling creeps into my gut. Suddenly I'm so ashamed of how I reacted to her. How I puffed out my chest and tried to impress her.

'But I think I've finally found true love,' Jordan yaps. 'I mean, he's the world's biggest star. He makes forty million a picture, did you know?'

Did know, couldn't care less.

I glance inside to see if Epiphany has somehow made it into the party. Killing a person with my bare hands would be preferable to spending any more time with Jordan.

'It started off as just another publicity move,' Jordan explains, not realising I don't give a damn. 'I was piggybacking off his success, but then – then it kinda became something like love, you know?'

Love. I'm familiar.

'I mean, I won't fuck a producer anymore just to get the part, unless it's a really, really big part...'

But as she prattles on, I notice something, first in her voice, and then by the lack of lustre in her eyes. She's speaking to me in the way most people have an internal dialogue when they're trying to work out the discrepancies between what they expected something to be and what it actually is. And then I realise that what she's said – it's not boasting or ego. It's her talking to someone on the outside about the life she wished Hollywood would be and the reality that it is. And I pity her. She's so moulded by what the fans demand. By what the studios demand. By what her handlers demand. Even when she laughs, it's a hollow laugh.

'But, you know,' she says, 'I owe everything to your dad.'

I really wish people would stop blaming their shitty lives on him.

'I was an extra – a nobody,' and she looks at me conspiratorially, 'and you, well, you *were* a virgin.'

I'm sorry, what?

'We were at that wrap party – do you remember?'

No, I don't.

'That horrible movie?'

Nope.

'That utterly forgettable piece of celluloid? It was that first movie I was an extra in. And, God!' she laughs as she gazes over the balcony. 'Do you remember? The whole damn movie took place on one set! It was supposed to be some kind of–'

And my heart stops when she says, '– silverware factory.'

Jordan, she turns and places her palm on my cheek. She caresses it. 'And your dad, your sweet dad. He came to me and said that if I took care of *you*, he'd make sure I'd have a role in Matthew's next production.' She presses her body into mine. 'You were so nervous when you found out I was going to fuck you,' she says, twirling a bit of my hair around her finger. 'You looked like you were going to cry.' She strokes my cheek, then laughs. 'And then you came so quickly! A two-minute fuck for twelve years of fame! I was going to fuck you again even, in case the first time was too short for it to count as part of the deal.' She puts her hand over her mouth. 'Oh! My! God! But do you remember that horribly skinny girl who burst into the room? She looked terrified when she saw us! She ran out as fast as she came in and you – you ran out after her! And I was going to fuck you again! Just imagine!' she laughs. 'You know how many men would kill for a fuck from me now? And I was going to give you two!'

And as I feel like I'm about to have a heart attack, Jordan takes a long sip of her Bellini and looks back over the Mediterranean.

'Oh dear,' Jordan says as she casts her gaze from the sea back to me, 'that was the night your dad got into his accident, wasn't it? It was so horrible! I was so afraid I wouldn't get my end of the deal. But Phineas, kind, kind Phineas honoured it when he took over for your dad.'

Memory. It's a funny thing. Just because we can't recall things, we believe they've never happened. We think we've blocked out the pain of a sister's death, but if by chance we come across her old photo on our mother's mantelpiece, we want to burst into tears. When we see children playing soccer in the streets, the regrets of long-ignored mistakes rise and beg forgiveness in the present. And when we meet our father's old colleague we suddenly realise how important it is to hear that Dad was proud of us.

They're such imprecise instruments, memories. Some are just

habitual, like storing enough about Photoshop in your brain to get through your shitty museum job. But others ... other memories are spontaneous. They're the kind that suck up your imperfect perceptions and impressions of the world. They're the kind that are brought to the front of your mind when it benefits you and shuffled to the back when their recall would do you harm. But even these can be summoned in sudden, painful flashes. Sometimes it's a father's gold watch or the long-forgotten theme song to an old TV show that summons those flashes. But sometimes, just sometimes that flash requires an unbelievable story from an international sex symbol.

But I was a virgin until ... until Bela, you believe.

No, Jerry, your spontaneous memory answers, *you weren't.*

Memories. Your head doesn't have enough room for all of them at once. When some come up, others need to get pushed to the back. Your thoughts become clouded.

I feel sick. I'm going to fall over. These people around, the ones inside drinking, they're making so much noise. This blonde ... why is she looking at me like that? Who's that bearded man smiling at us from inside? Why is this balcony moving?

I'm spinning and put my hand on the blonde woman's waist to steady myself.

'Oh, J,' she says drunkenly. 'You want me again, don't you? You want that second fuck? For old time's sake?' She moves my hand from her waist to her ass. She kisses my mouth and it's a taste I remember always having desired *and* always having had. She kisses my mouth and puts her hand on mine, forcing it to squeeze her ass. *'Oh, J,'* she bites my lip and in that bite, her tooth punctures my flesh and a single drop of blood stirs inside my mouth. In that single drop is my entire life. Bela. Epiphany. My mother and father. Emma. They all come back to me.

I break from her lips. 'What was the name of the film?' I tremble.

'What?' she says, piqued that someone's stopped kissing *her*.

'The film ... The silverware factory set...'

'Oh,' she says and returns to kissing my neck. 'Who cares, Little J?'

Her hand slides down my front until it finds my crotch. 'Just don't tell my boyfriend...'

I take her shoulders. 'What was the name of the film?' I shout and shake her as if doing so will rattle this memory of hers to the ground, where I can scoop it up and push it though my ear into my mind. *'What was the name of the film, you stupid whore?'*

And Jordan, she begins to cry.

'What was its name!'

'*Four Men*,' she sobs. 'It was *Four Men*.'

44

Rewind

'*What if we're all the bad guys?*'
  '*Who is truly good? You?*'
  '*Momentous events are sparked by free will and petty motivations.*'
Four Men is a dialogue-driven movie about four people who wake up trapped in the same room together. Two of them are handcuffed and there are two extra sets of cuffs on the ground. There's a pad of paper on the floor with directions written on it. In a shallow box on a rollered conveyor belt they find a set of keys and a cell phone with a dead battery. The kicker for these four men is that no one can remember who they are or how they got there. But they all smell gas and one of the handcuffed men has a gun.

And a line of dialogue says, 'You had it all wrong.'

A line of dialogue says, 'Fear makes us do all sorts of bad things.'

A line of dialogue says, 'Sometimes the crazy ones are the right ones.'

After I released my grip on Jordan, after I ran past Phineas and out onto the Promenade de la Croisette, I went from DVD stall to DVD stall. By the fourth one I started to fear I wouldn't find it. Then I saw one last stall on the opposite side of the Croisette. Its location was relatively poor as most of the foot traffic stuck to the right side of the street. The DVDs were arranged by actor. This vendor, he had all her movies:

The Best Girl.
Before Dying.
The Mechana Effect.
Caribbean Dawn.

All but the one I needed.

'*Four Men?*' I said.

'Ah, I keep that under "Donald Diamon" since he was the main star,' the vendor said. 'Let me see if I still have a copy.' He flipped through the Diamon section. 'Most people don't know that was Seabring's first role. She played an extra in the background during one of the flashback sequences in the second act. You must be a big fan if you know she's in it.' He pulled out the DVD then took my money and nodded towards the photos of her he was selling. 'Man, what a looker, huh? How'd you like to hit that?'

In my hotel room I sit on my bed, barely breathing as I watch the movie play out. The film consists primarily of close-ups of the characters and the items they find. In the first act the only medium and long shots you get are when you see the characters' flashbacks – when they suddenly remember something based on an item they find in their wallet or on a shelf or wherever. And then we get to it: the flashback scene of the middle-aged father. The one where you see his fifteen-year-old daughter in the background. Jordan Seabring's first foray onto celluloid. It lasts all of eight seconds.

After each flashback, when the camera returns to the present you get to see more and more of the room where the men are being held. And even though I've never seen this movie before, I've seen this room dozens of times. They're in a silverware factory. The factory is abandoned. Teaspoon after teaspoon rusts in boxes on roller conveyors. Forks dangle from strings overhead. Three furnaces fill the room in the far corner. Their mouths gape, revealing long extinguished insides. Behind them, scorch marks make permanent shadows on the brick walls. The floor planks are stained dark.

A line of dialogue says, 'Memory is tricky.'

It says, 'The mind finds ways to protect us.'

It says, 'Are you sure what you believe is true?'

I pause the screen and such a strain comes over my chest. Bits and scraps of thoughts swim around in my head. They stir in my mind as if shaken in a snow globe. And, as if they've only been playing with the idea of coming up for air, now the tiniest little scraps decide to break the surface.

Rewind.

I'm seventeen. My father and I are at the wrap party for *Four Men*. The party is being held on one of the lots at the old Imagination Studios. People are laughing and smiling all around. The extras are all huddled together in one corner, nervous excitement on their faces, hoping for the chance to talk to someone who might further their career. Phineas is there. So is Roland, only at this time he's going by the name Rolin. And, unlike the other people at the party, he looks a little worried.

Standing by a lighting rig Matthew and my father whisper to each other, grinning masters of the universe. On the other side of the room there's a girl around my age. She's an extra named Jordan. And my father approaches her and speaks briefly. Then he points at me. And Jordan, she walks over, smiling. She asks me to come with her to get something from the dressing room.

In the dressing room we sit on a couch. She looks nervous as we chat about nothing for twenty minutes. I'm nervous too. She's beautiful. She's got Hollywood written all over her.

On our way to the party tonight, my dad told me he had a special gift for me. 'A gift that will make you a man,' he said. And it doesn't take me long to realise that Jordan *is* that gift.

'OK, let's do this,' she says abruptly. 'My parents are picking me up in thirty.'

She takes off her top. And her breasts are magnificent – as the first breasts you touch always are.

'Take your clothes off,' she orders.

I do.

'Lie down.'

I do.

We don't even kiss. She pulls on my dick until it gets hard and she climbs on top of me. And *this* is where I lose my virginity. From underneath her skirt, she slides her panties to the side and puts me inside her. And she rides me like a toy pony. And ninety seconds later, I cum and Jordan climbs off me and plops back on the couch, annoyed and a little disappointed.

'I'm not sure if that counts,' she says. 'It was so quick.'

And for some reason, I want to cry. For some reason, this doesn't feel right.

'Well, let's go again,' she says. 'I want to make sure I get the part.' And she looks at my penis. 'Go on, get hard.'

I say, 'I can't.'

'Fine, I'll do it,' she says and takes my penis in her mouth.

Suddenly there's a commotion on the other side of the dressing-room door. Someone's screaming. Then the door bursts open and a black-haired girl in a light-blue dress runs in. She's crying and scared and shaking like a whipped animal. 'Oh! My! God! Get out!' Jordan screams, and the girl with black hair darts through a side door.

From the hallway, Rolin's voice shouts, 'She's in the dressing room!'

I'm so petrified that someone I know will see me naked, I take off out the side door, too. It leads through a prop room and out to the studio back lot. And I run in the night, exposed, across the back lot. I run and run until I come to a small building. Inside it's a set. And I stand in the middle of this set, naked. Shaking. Crying. I'm not who I was before this night. I feel wrong.

The set is made to look like a silverware factory. The oil that stains the floorboards is paint. The silver forks that dangle from the strings are really made of plastic. And from the left set wall – the one that's constructed to look like the tin siding of a shack with cracked, yellowed windows – the silhouette of a girl runs past. And I hide. Naked and shaking I crawl into one of the big furnaces that look like it's cast from iron, but really it's just moulded polystyrene, and I curl up inside. I cry.

And then I see her. The girl from the dressing room. She's fourteen, maybe fifteen years old. Her frame is petite and doesn't fully fill the dress she's wearing. Her face is small and round. Her hair, pulled back tight around her head, is black like a raven's folded wing. Her skin, white as cream. And her left ear – now it looks like a piece of her lobe was torn right off.

I want to shout, 'Over here! Hide over here!' But I don't. I'm too scared. So I just watch. I watch as this girl looks around frantically. I watch as the black soles of her pale feet give up. They won't carry her anymore. And I see more silhouettes run past the cracked, yellowed windows, the ones that are made from glazed sugar stained with coffee so they look older. And from my hiding place in the polystyrene furnace, I see Rolin enter. And then Phineas.

They claw at this poor girl like hawks attacking a prairie rabbit until she collapses to the ground. And she struggles on the paint-marked floor; she screams as she's beaten into restraint. And, as this poor girl is held to the floor, another man enters the set. Rolin and Phineas spread the girl's legs as this new man forces his hand into her privates. His movements are so rough, so powerful, that each gyration of his arm rocks the girl's entire body on the floor. And as the girl howls, this man takes his hand from between her legs and beats her on the face. As she bleeds from between her legs, the man orders Phineas and Rolin to drag her away. Then the man stands up and wipes his hand clean.

The man, he's my father.

45

The Secret History of Epiphany Jones and I

There's a shark in my bed. He's got a bullet hole in his head. Then he's gone, and Emma is in the bed. She's pale and sick and has cancer. Rachel stands in the corner, her red anime hair glowing. 'Come to me,' she says. Then she's my father. 'This will make you a man, Jerry.' And my father becomes LaRouche, who becomes the shark, who becomes Emma.

All of them are popping in and out around the room. I sink next to the nightstand and press my eyes shut. 'Please leave me alone,' I cry. 'Please...'

But they keep coming. Even with my eyes closed and my hands over my ears, I hear them. 'Stop this! Stop! I didn't ask for any of this.' I open my eyes and throw the bedside lamp at my father. And the figments popping in and out, they're more rapid now. Sometimes three are in the room at once. Now Epiphany is among them too. Emma is standing beside her.

'Please, Emma, please. Make them go away.' But it's Epiphany who walks over and places her hand on my shoulder. And when she does, all the other figments vanish – like they did with Bela. 'Shh. It's just you and I, Jerry. No one else is here.' And that's when I realise that this is the real Epiphany; the flesh-and-blood little girl my dad dragged off the silverware factory set. She's got a butter knife in her hand and the hotel room door behind her is ajar.

Epiphany sees the image of the silverware factory frozen on the TV screen. She sees the gun I tried to murder her with sitting on the nightstand. She reaches towards it, but instead of taking the gun she sets the butter knife next to it.

'Why are you here?' I shake. My whole body feels as if it's broken.

It's several moments before she answers. Then she looks at me with her green eyes and says, 'Because, for once, I listened to my own voice.' She takes another moment before cautiously adding, 'I didn't kill your friend. You need to know that. You deserve to know the truth.'

No. I won't believe it. She had to. She had to. There was no one else. 'You're trying to mess with my head. You're trying to trick me,' I shake.

'No, Jerry,' she says softly. 'No more lies, no more tricks.'

'Why'd you run, then? On the street, why'd you run?'

'When I discovered you in the bar, I was going to tell you everything, but then my–' She stops herself. 'I suddenly *knew* you had a gun. So I ran.' I'm looking at her, unable to utter a word. 'Jerry, when you held that gun to my face ... I had not seen that much pain in someone's eyes since they took my daughter from me. That is when I realised that you and your friend – you and she are as much victims of trafficking as my daughter and I, and all the others are.'

And before I can ask what she means, she says, 'You didn't kill Nico on that pier in Veracruz.'

'I did.' It's like I've just been kicked in the gut. 'I saw him lying, bleeding.'

'But not dead,' she says.

A cancer of remorse invades my stomach. I know what she's going to say. And now something I wished I could have taken back for the longest time, I cry that I didn't actually do.

Epiphany tells me what happened after I jumped ship in Porto. How she woke the next day. How she figured I'd need to hide in Porto until I knew what I was going to do now that the videotape showed nothing. She had Abdul phone different places to see if I'd rented a room. After a few days of being unable to find me, she knew she had to go on to the house outside of Seville without me. But she arrived too late. The girls had been moved. The only one left in the house was the madam. She was Russian, just like LaRouche. And this madam, after some 'very firm discussions', she revealed that there were twelve girls – all special order – all moved to Cannes the day before. The madam told Epiphany that one of the girls had even been kept there, unspoilt, for almost twelve years, aging like a fine wine for just the right occasion. This year was that right occasion. At Cannes, Matthew would be hosting an exclusive party that required only the purest treats.

So Epiphany, she dragged this madam from the house and tied her to a wretched tree that had died this spring in the unusually extreme Spanish heat wave. Then Epiphany went back into the house. It was minutes before she returned carrying a burning cloth wrapped around a stick. Fear came to the madam's eyes and she pleaded with Epiphany. She told her she had taught her daughter the mother tongue. That she had cared for her like her own.

Overhead, the sun was so relentless that, as Epiphany burnt the house to the ground, the flames hardly added anything to the searing heat of the Andalusian air. And Epiphany, she stubbed out the torch and told the woman that she knew it wasn't entirely her fault – this life of hers. 'But let's see if God sets you free before His sky consumes you.'

Now knowing exactly *why* her voices had said she needed me, Epiphany returned to Porto. But when she found me that day on my way to the farmers' market, Nico had found her. By that time he had tracked us to Portugal. As she stood behind a watermelon stand watching me, she and Nico saw each other at the same moment. She fled and Nico pursued. Her flight eventually led her to an alley where she hid. This alley, it was full of cats that seemed to crawl all over her body, making her invisible in the dark as Nico ran past. Then, as Epiphany remained hiding in the alley – desperate and scared that Nico had already gotten to me – 'as fate would have it', I walked by with a pumpkin in each hand.

And after our confrontation in that alley – after I left with my remaining pumpkin, after I told Epiphany everything she believed is wrong – she realised how mad she had sounded, because she had been so shaken by coming so close to finding her daughter in Spain and then by seeing Nico alive in Portugal. And Epiphany remembered the night in Mexico when she and LaRouche spoke at the kitchen table while I was lying in bed with a freshly stabbed back. LaRouche had tried to explain to Epiphany then that, though she understands so readily what she must do because the voice of God speaks to her, other, more secular, individuals would easily mistake her passion for madness.

So Epiphany tracked me to my apartment. She knew she needed to explain everything then, rationally and in full, if she had any hope of getting me to help her. That was when Paulo saw her outside at four in the morning. Epiphany feared that any man by my apartment at four in the morning might be working with Nico, so she fled. But she returned a few hours later and crept past the sleeping Paulo, up the stairs past the candlelit vegetables. But instead of finding me, she found Nico sitting in the kitchen – and Bela already dead in the bedroom. Instantly she knew Nico didn't travel to Portugal just for her. And Nico then understood that Epiphany wasn't with me anymore; that in fact she was looking for me herself. Nico leapt at her. Epiphany shows me where his ring cut her cheek. But she fought back and fled out the back window onto the roof.

'He followed me. I managed to lose him. But by that time I couldn't wait any longer for you. I hadn't heard my voices in days. I needed to get to Cannes,' she says. 'When I arrived here, I disguised myself in case Nico followed. And he did, Jerry. He's here. Every night I've been going to the bars to find someone who could help me get into Matthew's party. I've seen him at the Majestic.'

For moments I say nothing. It's almost too much. Nico. Alive. Here. I swallow, 'He put the cover over her in bed. Moved her to make it look like she was sleeping – waiting for me.'

Epiphany presses her lips together. 'Nico is a cruel man. Cruelty comes in many forms.'

I think I've reached that point now – the point where even though you want to, you just can't cry anymore. Minutes pass as we sit in silence. Then Epiphany, always one to ruin a good thing, looks at the frozen image of the silverware factory on the TV again. She says, 'There's more you need to know.'

I open my mouth, but nothing comes out. I don't have the strength to tell her I don't want to know about my father.

Epiphany waits until my eyes catch hers. 'When I was held by,' and she mercifully says *Matthew's people*, 'you can not imagine what it was like. We were moved from apartment to apartment in the city at regular intervals so as not to attract attention. We were never allowed outside. Our flesh became white. They required us to exercise on a stationary bike so our bodies kept nice. If they thought we had put on weight we were made to stand naked on a scale. If the scale showed more than a kilogram gained since our last weighing, our diets were limited; our rapes increased "for exercise". We were nothing more than prized thoroughbreds they wanted to keep looking good for their enjoyment.'

And here Epiphany's mercy at sparing the details disappears. Here she speaks between her teeth.

'For three years we were forced to service them and for three years, since your father took me in Mexico, I hadn't heard my voices. I prayed every day but they remained silent. But at fourteen ... I became pregnant and everything changed. My voices came back to me,' Epiphany smiles crookedly. 'The three-year abyss was only a test to see if I remained faithful to them. When Matthew and your father found out I was pregnant it was decided that I would have the child.' Epiphany, she shakes her head. 'With all the horrible things they did, they still had a twisted view that they were moral, upstanding Christians and that abortions were out of the question. It was the only thing they ever did that I was thankful for.'

Epiphany tells me that she was separated from the other girls during her pregnancy. She was moved to a nicer private apartment in the city where the girls were taken when Matthew or one of his people wanted a night alone with them. A back-door doctor with crooked hands delivered the baby. But Epiphany didn't even get to hold it. She screamed as it was taken from the room. The doctor came back with a bucket of water and a cloth. 'Clean yourself up,' he said.

Epiphany was locked back with the other girls after her pregnancy. Some of the girls were new. The new ones, they would clutch and hold on to the others as Matthew's men came to drag them out. 'We would huddle in our small apartment, only a bathroom and an exercise bike and mats on the floor. Sometimes a man would come around to do our makeup. He was allowed to rape the others as payment. The girls who had their makeup done knew they were in for a hard night.' Epiphany's eyes burn. 'One of the men was limp. He couldn't take us, so instead he photographed us as we were violated. He got off on capturing rape in black and white, salivating like a dog with each photograph.'

I think I'm going to be sick. I worked with him for so long. He dated my mother. And it hits me. That's why my mom had El Captain™. Roland couldn't get it up.

Epiphany tells me that, out of all the girls, she was never allowed to be photographed.

I say, 'Why?'

'I was the prized one,' she says. 'Men are territorial over their property.'

But Epiphany knew the power a young body could have over a man and she promised she would never tell anyone he photographed her if he would only tell her what happened with her baby. So Rolin, he told her that her child would be kept until it could be 'of use'. It was only then that Epiphany understood she had had a daughter. And Rolin, he took his photos.

Epiphany was determined not to let the same hell happen to her daughter. She began causing trouble. She would try to get the other girls to revolt – but this only got the girls beaten. So she tried something else. Even though they were treated no better than livestock, sometimes the men would become attached to them. They'd talk to them and tell them their worries and fears like they would to a normal girlfriend. There was one man in particular who was obsessed with Epiphany and she, well she used the oldest torture in the book: she became aloof. She hoped mentally mind-fucking this man would get him to have her shipped back to Nico for a new girl. It would be easier to escape in transport than in LA. But her plan backfired. The man started blaming her for his increasing unhappiness and only raped her more to 'teach her to love' him.

But then, on a quiet night in June, three of the girls and Epiphany were brought to the studio lot. There was an orgy with Matthew, Phineas, Donald Diamon and my father. And on this night, her voices spoke to her. They said 'pay attention'. And as the orgy progressed, Epiphany noticed a blinking light tucked away on a shelf. And at that moment what Epiphany understood more than anyone was that kinks never stay the same. They only grow. They only mutate.

When the orgy finished, while the men were discussing whether to move the girls that night or leave them until the next night, Epiphany crept over to the blinking light. It was just a small digicam – the kind that records video to SD cards the size of a postage stamp. Where a photo used to suffice, Rolin now needed moving pictures.

She knew instantly what she had. That tiny little card she took from the camera showed the most powerful man in Hollywood having sex with little girls. It was the best bargaining chip she could hope for. Not only for her freedom, but her daughter's as well. But first, she would need to escape.

The next night was the *Four Men* wrap party and, as I was being introduced to Jordan in the dressing room, Rolin was coming clean to Matthew and my dad about the missing SD card. Matthew was furious. Epiphany could hear the shouting from the room the girls had been locked in since the night before.

Matthew, Phineas, Rolin and my father each took one of the girls separately to demand they give back anything they took. The other girls were confused, but Epiphany knew what the men were looking for. It had been hidden in her vagina for the last twenty hours. When my father demanded Epiphany submit to a full cavity search, she ran. She ran into the dressing room where Jordan had my dick in her mouth. And as Rolin shouted from the hall, she fled out the back door, through the prop room and out across the dark studio back lot.

But, like all studio back lots, the walls were high to keep people out. So Epiphany, she ran across the lot until she came to Matthew's office. The office was lined with paintings and one of those paintings was a Van Gogh. She didn't have much time. She heard someone outside and, fearing she was about to be caught, quickly slid the SD card into the top of the Van Gogh, between the canvas and the support frame. She picked up the phone as my dad burst in so he would think she was trying to call the police. He lunged at her, grabbing her earring along with the phone. Her cartilage stretched until it tore. Blood flowed down her neck. That's when she ran again. She ran until she came to the silverware factory set where I had hidden.

And, after my dad forcefully checked her genitals, after I climbed out of that polystyrene furnace and got dressed, still trying to understand what I had seen, Epiphany managed to escape anyway. As she was marched back across the back lot, a lighting van was leaving. The driver of the van, he saw the three men and the beautiful young girl with the bleeding ear and thought nothing of it. This was a movie studio set, wasn't it? And Epiphany, her ears began ringing so loudly. Her voices told her she must run ... *now*. And she did. She ran like she never had before. She ran past the lot's security gate as it opened for the truck to pass through. She ran in her bare feet into the warm California night.

The last time anyone from Matthew's group saw her was later that night. She was still running. This time through a subdivision. And, as if by fate, she ran in front of a car. Our car. My dad, he was so shocked, he lost control of the Explorer and we crashed into a tree. As the horn blared, Epiphany stood outside the wreck and watched my father slowly bleed. And, despite the crying from someone she could only assume was his son in the passenger seat, she took that accident as a sign that God was just.

After the incident at the wrap party, after the accident, after my mind suppressed its imperfect perceptions of the world because it couldn't deal with what it had seen, Matthew closed the lot and moved his studio to its existing space. He also didn't risk having girls in America anymore. He kept them out of the country from then on. And for twelve years, Epiphany wondered if she would ever see the painting, or her daughter, again.

During those twelve years, Epiphany went from country to country, searching. She lived on the streets at times; other times she worked odd jobs here and there. Travelling like a vagabond for that long teaches you how to survive. It teaches you cunning. It teaches you how to steal. It teaches you how to fight. Then one day her voices told her to return to Mexico to look for LaRouche. And LaRouche helped her. She told her she thought her daughter might be in Spain. But, as Epiphany was about to set off, her voices stopped her. They told her to go to Chicago instead. Her voices had helped her stay alive for this long, she didn't dare disobey them even though she had no idea what could be in Chicago.

And in Chicago, Epiphany slept on Lower Wacker Drive for weeks, waiting for a sign. Then one night, a man with long, silvery hair who was sleeping on the streets offered her a bit of his old newspaper to feed her fire. And this newspaper, it had an article with a photograph in it. The photograph showed Matthew's Van Gogh along with Rolin – only now he was called Roland – and two other men. Epiphany knew then why she'd come to Chicago. For a second time, her faith had paid off. She tore out the photograph and kept it with her.

Epiphany began scoping out the museum. And, being a pretty girl, she became friends with one of the construction men working on the renovation. He let it slip that the security cameras would be inoperable three days from then. If he had been a smarter man, he would have noticed that, not only did he not see Epiphany after that, but he also didn't see a copy of his blueprints for the museum again.

And on that cold April day, Epiphany stood outside the coffee house across from the museum as she prayed and hoped that the SD card would still be beneath the canvas.

In the museum, Epiphany slipped right past security and walked to the lower level, where the blueprints showed her the photography studio was. It is there, her voices said, that she would find the painting on that day and at that time. And her voices, they've never been wrong. She walked in to find Roland standing in front of the Van Gogh, talking into a video camera. She asked where the SD card was but Roland swore he didn't know. Then behind the camera she noticed it in the card reader on his desk.

And it hits me: the memory of that day. I remember being in his studio. He was fingering the painting like he found an invisible pimple on it and then suddenly he seemed distracted. Then he rushed me out of the studio. That's when he must have prised the card out from under the canvas and checked to see what was on it.

But Roland had deleted the contents as soon as he saw what it was. And for Epiphany, it was too much. She'd finally found her bargaining chip but this impotent little man had erased it. She threw the empty card at Roland, who was cowering now. To Roland, Epiphany was like seeing a ghost.

And, just as she thought there was no hope, Epiphany, she saw the newspaper clipping framed on his desk. The same clipping she had torn out. And like everyone before her, only after looking at it a second time did she notice me, huddled at my desk in the back of the photograph.

'Why does he look like him?' she asked. 'Who is that man?'

But Roland was already in hysterics.

So Epiphany snapped the leg from the tripod that held the camera and asked Roland my name again. And Roland, seeing the point of the jagged tripod leg in Epiphany's hand, he screamed my name at her while pleading for his life. And that's when the videotape went dead.

Roland told her I was my father's son. He told her I usually take my lunch at the coffee shop across the street. And as he spoke, Epiphany saw his tongue ring and remembered how that tongue had salivated as he took photos of so many girls. And, before she knew it, she'd put the tripod leg through his eye.

Quickly Epiphany formulated her plan. She placed the small Van Gogh between a *Sun-Times* she took from Roland's desk and began to leave. But her voices stopped her. They told her to grab the videotape as well – *'It is essential.'* And as simple as that, she left the museum and crossed the street to the coffee house where a man caught her eye. That man was sitting on the floor of the coffee shop, covered in vomit. She waited by the museum back across the street so she wouldn't startle me. She waited until I got into a cab. She followed me and, when I left my apartment to return to work, she broke in and left the painting on my couch – her original plan to blackmail me into coming with her.

So here we are. That's why all this has happened. That's the secret history of Epiphany Jones and I.

On the TV in the hotel room I stare at the paused, flickering image of the silverware factory for minutes as I try to speak. Whenever I do, nothing comes out. It's just, what do you say, you know?

'Jerry–'

'But, when I first met you,' I blurt, 'I mean … in Chicago, you said you'd been looking for me for twelve years–'

'I'd been looking for a way to get my daughter back for twelve years. You just happened to be that way,' she says.

And as I sit on this floor with her, as I connect all the dots in my head, my exhaustion turns to anger. I'm angry because there are some people you never like. You never like the person who tells you your spouse is cheating on you. You never like the person who tells you he's heard the boss is going to fire you. You never like the person who shows you your dad is a sex-trafficking rapist. And above all you never like the person who tells you the guy who murdered your love is still out there and you chased the wrong person to France.

And these people you never like, you want to hurt them the way what they've revealed has hurt you. So you attack them any way you can. You tell them that all the above may be true, but their voices are still bullshit. God doesn't talk to them. They could have known every-thing they do, done everything they did, without divine intervention. You unleash all your anger at your father and your mother and your whole fucking life against them.

And as I curse her, a terrible chill seizes me. As I curse her, my head begins to tingle like fizzy soda.

And Epiphany, she looks at me and says, 'Jerry?'

And as I curse her, my vision goes cloudy with black spots.

And Epiphany, through the black spots, she's looking at me like my body is doing something I'm not aware of.

'Jerry?' she says again.

Blackout.

It's dark in the room. My clothes are soaked in sweat. Bela's hand touches my forehead. 'You have a fever,' she says. 'It will pass. By morning it will pass.' I nuzzle her hand down to my lips and kiss it. Her hand is so cold.

The nightstand light comes on. It's not Bela's hand. Epiphany sits beside me on the bed. She doesn't know what to make of me kissing her hand. Her cold, cold hand. Not like Bela's hand. In Epiphany's other hand is the bracelet Phineas gave me.

'It fell from your pocket when I moved you to the bed,' she says. 'It's...'

'The ticket to Matthew's party,' I say. 'It's tomorrow.' Let me go back to sleep. Let me go back to Bela.

But, no. 'My daughter, Jerry–' And I look at her and I know what she's going to ask. Questers don't rest. That scratch on her face makes her look more like a warrior now than ever. It's the scratch she got in my apartment in Porto.

The one given to her *by Nico*.

'What you said about Bela being a victim of this whole trafficking thing–' I shake my head. But just as I thought, that look she had on the pier – that one-dimensional, doesn't-see-anything-else look is back. 'I don't see how this is going to work.'

'Please Jerry,' she squeezes my hand, 'this once, take a leap of faith.'

And in my mind, I see Nico.

He's standing over Bela's body.

His hands are squeezing Bela's throat.

'Fine,' I say, 'leap of faith.'

46

Time to Party

'What's her name?' I say.

The pause is so long, I don't think she's heard me. Finally her voice, sounding almost ashamed, answers, 'I don't know.'

We're in the Carlton Hotel's boutique. It's two in the afternoon. We have two hours before we're supposed to take a taxi to the address on the back of my bracelet. I'm on one side of the curtain and Epiphany is on the other.

I take a moment before replying. I say, 'How will you know which one she is? How will she know who you are?'

'We'll know,' she says.

I almost don't recognise her when she walks from behind the maroon curtains. Her raven hair is tied up tight and she's wearing this white little number. It's right out of the 1920s. Just like in *The Great Gatsby*. The dress is what you'd expect to see people wearing at those elegant outside summer balls during the tea dances of the Jazz Age.

The woman who runs the boutique walks over with a blonde wig and helps Epiphany put it on.

'Oh, don't worry,' she says. 'Your girlfriend isn't doing anything the other girls aren't.'

I'm not so sure about that.

'It's always easier to wear a wig than do your own hair. The wigs will stay styled all night long.' And I watch as the blonde Epiphany makes sure the long wig covers her mutilated ear.

Back in the hotel room I put my tux on while Epiphany fidgets with her dress in front of the bathroom mirror. The smashed lamp that I threw at my father's figment lies just behind her white heels.

And I can't help but feel like this is the end. Like my life is on the last reel and there's nothing beyond today.

Epiphany's put together a sort of plan. This is a 'plan' in the loosest sense of the word, though. And when I tell her that, she says, 'Trust me.'

The plan, it entails me approaching Phineas while Epiphany mingles in the crowd and getting him to tell me where the girls are.

'He's not stupid,' Epiphany says. 'The way you said he was asking you questions – he was shocked to see you here. He wants to see how much you remember; if your father told you anything. Why do you think he gave you the invite to the party so easily? He wants to get you close. He wants to find out why you are here.'

'Why?' I say.

'Phineas was always a nervous person. He always worried about what others knew. The guilty are always fearful.'

'And if he knows I know?'

'He is going to know you know,' she says. 'Because you will tell him. And you will tell him you want to get in on the family business.'

So that's why Epiphany believes her crazy voices told her to bring me along – because I can convince my father's old child-molesting colleague to point to the room where his boss stores little girls. And just like that he'll tell me. And just like that I'll report to Epiphany, who will slip in and find her daughter and we'll get out without anyone knowing we are stealing a little abducted girl back.

But I don't argue. Because that's her 'plan'. But me, well, like everyone in this world, I've got my own plans.

And besides, despite her being a constant reminder of what my father was, I'm still glad to have her with me right now. When she touched my shoulder last night, all the figments in the room vanished. She can keep me grounded, like Bela did. She can keep me grounded until I've done what I'm going to do, and then I don't care what happens to me.

'Leave it,' Epiphany says as I glance at the gun. 'There will be security checks.' She clasps a floral pearl choker necklace around her throat. 'How do I look?'

She asks this not like a real girl would – not meaning if she looks pretty or just to fish for a compliment. When she asks, 'How do I look?' she means, 'Can you tell this is me under here?'

And she is beautiful, Epiphany is. Not a natural Bela beautiful, or a fake Jordan Seabring beautiful, but beautiful nonetheless. She's beautiful how a raven is: silent, mysterious; its whole body covered by black shadow – like someone dipped a dove in tar to conceal its true form. And as I button my jacket and Epiphany checks her wig one last time, I feel like I'm getting ready for the prom I never had – only this prom, it's Satan's Ball.

The taxi drops us at the address marked on the back of my bracelet. A man at the door asks, 'For Matthew's?' He looks like he's some techno DJ. He leads us through an empty club, past the kitchen, and out the rear door into the alley.

Epiphany asks the man if he works for Matthew.

'No,' he says.

Right answer, I think.

He tells us that Matthew rents his place for one day each year – along with some other places around town – so stars can be met by drivers in private, without the chance of paparazzi seeing them. 'I envy you though,' the DJ says. 'The celebs that show up here – man, it must be one effed-up party! It's fucking wild, right?'

I look at Epiphany, who is looking somewhere else. 'You have no idea.'

We speed along the French coast in a black Bentley. The driver either doesn't speak English or has been told not to talk to the guests. Epiphany and I aren't talking either. We both have too much on our minds.

We're different things to different people. Your family may love you and tell everybody you're the most wonderful man in the world, but your employees may loathe you and tell everyone that you're Satan's right hand. The guy who's heart you broke when you cheated on him thinks you're a manipulative bitch, but the homeless person you gave five dollars to thinks you're a gift from God. The thing is, in a way, everyone is right.

To me, my father, before last night, he had been a good man who had a hard life. To Epiphany, he was a monster who was sent by Matthew to collect her. Both are true. Different people live in all of us. What my dad took part in with all those girls – the only way to describe it ... well, how do you describe it? 'Wrong' doesn't begin to cover it. I wish I knew why he did it. Maybe after everything that happened to our family – after losing a daughter, and a son getting fucked up, and your marriage slowly dying – maybe it was easy to give into something that made you feel anything other than the hurt you drowned in on a daily basis. It was a way to cover the pain. It was what I did with television and my fakes, taken to the next level.

Epiphany's staring out the window, watching the trees speed by us. In the reflection in the window she looks more pale than usual, as if someone has just given her really bad news. There's a single tear that falls down her cheek. And I think about all the stuff that my father's done and that she's done and that I'm about to do.

But out of all the bad shit Epiphany and I have done to each other, the one thing we have in common is love. We've both lost people we've loved. For me it was Bela and Emma. For Epiphany, it's her daughter. And I look at her and think of her daughter and think of what my father did. How many men raped her after my father collected her from Mexico? I wonder what it's like not knowing who fathered your child? And her ear. That's a direct result of my dad. I wonder, Would a son's apology make things any better?

But then I think of why I'm going to this party. Who I'm going to find. What I'm planning to do.

So no, I know no words can be spoken that ease the pain we feel.

Epiphany quickly wipes the tear from her cheek. *'What?'* she says with her eyes.

I don't know how to ask why she's crying so I say anything. 'In Porto, in the alley, you kept mentioning some "awakening". I didn't know if you knew what you were saying...' She doesn't answer. 'Forget it, it's not important.'

Epiphany, she holds her gaze on me as I look back out my window. 'It's the name some of the madams gave to special events. Events like this, when girls would be saved for months for a certain occasion. They called these events "awakenings", because that was when the girls would first realise what their lives would be like from then on.'

As the Bentley curves along the road, the trees break and the view gives way to the Mediterranean. We come to a town where a sign says ANTIBES. As we drive along the coast little piers jut into shimmering blue coves where rowboats hover in the crystal-clear water. At the tip of the peninsula that forms the southernmost part of the town our driver makes a left and we climb a steep road, where our car joins a line of cars. The road becomes a circular drive as the caravan gets closer to Matthew's villa. The villa is beautiful. Something only the obscenely rich could buy. It's a white, three-storey baroque château that has two wings on either side. In the green lawns there are fountains and gardens and palm trees and sculpted hedges. At the top of the drive the rich and famous have their car doors opened for them, and they proceed to drift towards the villa's entrance as if the promises of fame and money and power itself were calling them home.

Our car is one length away from having its door opened for us. Then, as if now is the time to say her last words, Epiphany says, 'Yana.'

I say, 'What?'

'If I could have named my daughter, I would have named her Yana. It's a name I remember from my childhood. A beautiful name.'

Then she says, 'Remember it.'

Our car comes to a stop. Epiphany's breath shallows. I can almost feel her heart beating. She's waited for this day, planned for it for so long. We look at each other in the safety of the car one more time. She takes a deep breath as the door is opened. A man in a black suit greets us as we step out of the Bentley.

'Very welcome, Sir, Miss,' the man says, scanning the bracelet's barcode. He points down the white-gravel walkway. 'Follow this path to the entrance hall, please. From there, if you keep walking through the grand foyer and go out the back, you'll come to the gardens. Mr Mann would like guests to know that, besides the second and third floors of the west wing, the entire house is open to them and he hopes you'll enjoy it.'

We join the crowds and walk through the grand foyer and out the back to the party. We walk arm in arm like this party of the year is just another ordinary day in our stellar, fabulous lives.

Out back, the garden's grounds are manicured to precision. Flower-beds dot the greenest grass I've ever seen. Every ten feet there's another stand where a bartender will pour you any drink you want. A live orchestra plays 'Everybody Loves My Baby' on the stage overlooking the banquet tables that are already set for dinner. The plates are real china. The glasses are real crystal. The three knives, three forks, and two spoons on either side of every dining set are real silver tipped with real gold.

Unlike the other party, this one is what you imagine when you think of the lifestyles of celebrities. Besides the two life-sized statues of characters from *The Princess of the Sands* (one of Jordan's princess character and one of her evil stepbrother king, holding his big Arabian sword), there are no other signs that this is a party to celebrate Mann's latest blockbuster. To Mann, this party is a personal treat – an indulgence in power. And indeed, I know the only reason the two statues are here is because Phineas is like my father, and there's never an inappropriate time to shill your boss's product.

The gardens end at a cliff that overlooks the blue Mediterranean, where the yachts of the super rich float like rubber duckies. In the distance you can see the red-rocked mountains of France as they curve around to meet Spain. Above the mountains there are rain clouds forming.

There's got to be at least a hundred power-players mingling out here. It's easy enough to point out the stars – some of the hottest ones from today are here: the fat comedian whose heart should give out under his four-hundred-pound weight any day now; the gansta-rapper-turned-action star; the child television actress who's started making indie films so people will take her seriously. And where you have stars, you'll have their agents. Agents are always easy to spot because, no matter what they're doing, they'll always have one eye on their client – their cash cow. Yet, despite some of the biggest names in Hollywood being here, it's evident just how exclusive this party is.

'Is Harvey here?' an action star asks.

'Weinstein wouldn't even know about this party,' a man from the Mouse House answers arrogantly.

But there's only one person I'm interested in finding.

'We need to find Phineas,' Epiphany says.

When we stepped out of the car, I half-thought that she just might lose it right then and go running off to find her daughter. But no, she's as calm as ever. I, on the other hand, start to lose my nerve when I notice three men in grey suits patrolling the lawns. Their arms are big – the-size-of-my-thighs big. Their dark glasses and earpieces sit snugly on their muscled faces. And as if brute strength weren't enough, they've all got holstered weapons.

'Private security,' Epiphany says.

Imminent death – even when you expect it – always has a way of bringing out the coward in you. And I suddenly remember we could have brought the gun. Despite what Epiphany thought, there ended up being no security check. The gun would have made this much, much easier.

'This is insane,' I mumble.

Epiphany locks her eyes on mine and squeezes my arm tight. 'Stick to the plan, Jerry. It's going to be fine.'

'Plan?' I hiss as my nerves go. 'So we do have one? Because getting Phineas to tell me where the girls are is more of a best-case-scenario than a plan.'

Epiphany unlinks arms with me and graciously accepts two glasses of champagne when a roving waiter offers them on a silver platter.

'I mean, let's hear it then – *the plan*,' I say. 'Because when I saw the bodybuilders with their guns, I got worried.'

'Calm down, Jerry. You know what happens to you when you get worked up,' she says, like she's my mother, then hands me one of the glasses. 'My voices will tell me...'

'This is ridiculous,' I mutter.

'Stop thinking how ridiculous it is and start asking yourself whether or not you believe this will work. That's why it's called a *leap of faith*, Jerry.'

A leap of faith would be a lot easier with Paulo's gun.

Epiphany says, 'You are afraid. Feel it, then let it go.'

I refuse her the dignity of a reply.

She says, 'Trust me.'

She says, 'Now keep an eye out for Phineas.'

I scan the grounds. I don't see him anywhere.

'We should split up,' she says. 'It will be easier to find him. Besides, Phineas wouldn't mention anything about the girls in front of your date.'

I nod and watch Epiphany as she crosses the lawn, her blond wig shimmering in the sunlight. And then I hear it. 'Jerry! Jerry!'

And Jordan Seabring, she almost knocks me over as she wraps her arms around my neck. She tells me how sorry she is about last night; how drunk she must have been, and how bad she felt that she made me run off.

And for the next twenty minutes, as I look out for murderers and child rapists, Jordan sits me at one of the tables with their actual silver silverware, and she tells me about how hard her life has been. How her parents pushed her into beauty pageants at the age of three. How they told her to win at any cost. *'Fame is immortality,'* they said.

'There are just so many demands to being me,' she says as we sit and she drinks a nine-hundred-dollar glass of Cristal. 'It's a hard life.' And, if you're a cynical fuck like me, you're probably thinking, how can a young, rich, beautiful star have a hard life? But everything is relative, right?

Why would a fifteen-year-old girl fuck a boy on command if she weren't brainwashed into believing fame was the only goal worth pursuing?

You might think that her money and looks bring her freedom, but she's as chained as any of us. She's twenty-seven now. And though she's not being shown the door yet, she's definitely being handed her hat. She knows this, so she takes uppers to get through the press events and keep that young sparkle in her eyes. She has surgery at least twice a year to improve parts of her body (*'December it was my hips. February, my ears, see?'*). And, though her life is immeasurably better than Epiphany's or mine or yours, Jordan's been ruined by what people demand of her all the same. She's not a real person anymore.

'Phineas has begun trying to get reporters to refer to me as "The Starlet" like they used to when I got started. He says it will make audiences think I'm young,' the twenty-seven-year-old says.

A few more guests trickle out to the garden, but I still don't see him anywhere. From the other side of the gardens, Epiphany stands flanked by some new admirers hoping to get lucky with the mysterious woman with blond hair. She's holding her champagne glass up to her lips as her other hand playfully tickles the choker around her neck. She gives a throaty laugh. Here she can't tell her suitors to fuck off like she did in the bar, so she acts polite, all while keeping one eye on me and the other on the look-out for Phineas.

Jordan laughs at something she's just said. 'But Hugh, he's forty and still has another good twenty working years in front of him! He wouldn't understand. Besides, he's so busy. You've heard Matthew signed him to three pictures? No one in the industry thought Hugh would agree, but he did! Forty million a picture!'

On the orchestra's stage a cymbal clashes.

In the crowd a supermodel dances.

And I look around and I look around and I look around and I don't see him anywhere.

'That's sixty million!' Jordan says.

I say, 'Look, Jordan, the people who work for Matthew come to this party too, right?'

She says, 'Please, call me Starlet.'

I say, 'I mean, it's not just for your kind, right?'

She says, 'Do you spell Starlet with one T or two?'

I say, 'I'll bring you a calculator and a dictionary later. But right now, is there a place here where someone who works for Matthew would be? Maybe a room where they all hang out?'

She says, 'Everyone here works for Matthew. We all owe him for something.'

And then my breathing stops cold. Across the lawn I see him. The one I've been looking for since we arrived. The only reason I came. And even from this distance he looks so tall, so built. His dark face is scratched. And as Nico turns to enter the villa, I see a patch of his thick black hair on the back of his head is shaved.

Epiphany was right. He's alive. He's here. And as I watch the man I thought I murdered walk around all alive, my whole body suddenly courses with rage.

At our table, Jordan's going on about how she's so happy to be with Hugh Fox, the number one Hollywood box-office draw, the man whose name attached to a picture guarantees the film a one-hundred-million-dollar opening. 'Just being with him has given my career the boost it needed after I turned twenty-five,' she gushes. 'And ... oh, who are you going to tell? Last night, after you left the party, Hugh showed. He proposed! We're getting married!'

Please shut up, I think. There's a man I need to kill. Again.

'You want to meet him?' Jordan says like a sixteen-year-old dying to show off her first boyfriend.

'Love to,' I say.

And as Jordan goes bounding off to find her forty-million-dollar-a-picture boyfriend, I slide a gold-tipped silver steak knife from the table into the sleeve of my tux and stalk across the lawn. I brush by agents talking business, celebrities dancing to jazz, and waiters dressed in their white penguin jackets, carrying silver trays. Just past the orchestra's stage I pause at the open doorway and peer into the grand foyer. It's filled with more waiters and bartenders, more agents and stars and publicists. Then through the crowd I glimpse Nico. He's climbing the grand staircase. Up my sleeve, my hand tightens around the steak knife's handle. For something I wished I could have taken back for the longest time, now I can't wait to get it right.

But out of nowhere I'm grabbed by the collar and pulled back into the garden. I'm pulled behind the stage the orchestra is playing a rendition of 'Blue Skies' on. As the jazz trumpets flare a voice breathes, 'No, Jerry. No!'

Epiphany slams me against the back wall of the orchestra's stage. She's dragged me here so we're out of sight of all the guests.

She says, 'We aren't here for him. This is for my daughter. *Just* my daughter.' Her eyes, they're like nails pinning me in place.

As a saxophone blows, I yell, 'He killed Bela! He killed her and he's here. He deserves this!' And my hand with the knife drops out of hiding.

Epiphany's eyes go wide. 'You're going to get yourself killed,' she says and grabs my wrist.

'Then so be it!' I grit through my teeth. 'But I'm not going to let him go without even trying.'

On the stage behind us a bassist is doing a solo and Epiphany, she says, 'Yes, you are.' She says this and twists my wrist. The way she's looking at me, it's like I'm supposed to accept her words as final, absolute decree.

In my head, through all the music from the stage, through all the noise from the guests, through all the pain from Epiphany twisting my wrist, I hear Bela call me *'my alleegator.'*

To Epiphany, I say, 'She was working with her dad at a bookstore, did you know that? She was saving money to come to the States. She wanted to go to school so she could become a journalist.' My eyes are wet as the orchestra goes into full swing. 'She was a good person, Epiphany. She was smart and she was kind and she was completely innocent. She didn't make any of the mistakes you or my father or I have. She was innocent in all this.' Pulling my wrist away from Epiphany's grasp, I say, 'This is for her.'

But Epiphany, she grabs my wrist harder this time. She gives it a firm twist and the knife drops from my hand into the grass. She quickly kicks it out of sight underneath the stage. 'No, this is all for you,' she says.

And it takes all I can to not lunge at her.

'Help me get my daughter, Jerry. *Help me*. Don't become me.'

We're both breathing heavily and several of the guests look at us standing behind the stage as they pass from the grand foyer to the gardens. On stage, the orchestra is now playing 'Let's Do It, Let's Fall in Love'.

'You think the loss is bad, Jerry? You have no idea what revenge is really like. The things I've done to people – the things I'll do today in the name of *revenge*. Every time you do it, it's like drinking poison. Your Bela is *dead*. There's nothing left to save. But my daughter is *alive*. She's here. That's the *only* reason we're here. You need to find Phineas.'

And this is where Epiphany's manipulation really comes out. The concern at the hotel, the looking after me. It was all an act to move her goals along. *Her* plans.

'What about me? What about what I need?' I yell. It feels like every blood cell is exploding beneath my skin, like every cell is dancing to the beats of the orchestra. Epiphany tightens her grip on me until I lower my voice. 'What about losing my job and being framed for murder? What about my mom hating me? What about being stabbed and thrown off a dock and thinking you've killed a man? What about losing the love of my life – the only *real* thing I've ever known?' My voice quivers, 'What about *me*?'

And, as if she were a god speaking to an ant, Epiphany, the Quester, the Devil, the only-one-focus girl, she says, 'What about you?'

What. About. You.

'Fuck you,' I say and push against her so hard the stage almost shakes. A group of publicists from inside the grand foyer peek out the door, but neither of us is their client so they go back to their drinks. But one of the guards in the grey suits has seen our skirmish and approaches us. I raise my hands, signalling *I'm done*, and walk into the villa. Epiphany won't stop me. She won't risk the guard asking us to leave.

I'm here to do what I'm here to do. Epiphany is on her own.

47

Coming Attractions

I dart up the grand staircase, past more celebrities drinking and mingling, admiring the Oscars and Emmys displayed around the foyer. 'No, after you win one, your career goes to shit,' an Academy-Award-winning actress admits to a teen star. 'If you're a woman, that is. It doesn't happen to the men. But then you start your own clothing line. Branding yourself is where it's at.'

I pause mid-staircase and look over my shoulder towards the garden's entrance. Epiphany has followed me, but she stops and turns away when someone says, 'Just the person I was hoping I'd see.' I turn to see Phineas smiling at me from the top of the stairs. 'I wondered if you would come.'

I feel sick when I take his outstretched hand in mine.

'Jerry, are you all right? After you ran out of the party last night, I became worried.' He grins, 'I know Jordan can be a handful, but...'

'I've just had a lot of personal problems lately,' I say, looking around for Nico.

'It is a nice house,' Phineas says, misreading my glances. 'Come. Let me give you a tour. It will give us a chance to talk.'

We climb the grand staircase to the second floor. A personal tour is perfect. It'll let me look for Nico and keep Epiphany away at the same time. Phineas apologises for not finding me sooner, but he says he was dealing with some last-minute technicalities with an important guest. 'You know how temperamental these actors can be. Once they get famous, they lose all patience. When they want something, they want it yesterday.'

As we walk I look for anything I can use as a weapon. Nico's built like an ironhorse train. I'm going to need something a little stronger than my fists. Phineas and I are in the second-floor gallery now. It's a good fifteen feet to the ground below. I wonder, *Is it hard to push someone through a window?*

'Matthew designed this villa himself. It's been featured on countless home shows, you know. You should see the view from the rooftop deck – it's remarkable.' And as we look at the Monets and the Picassos and the Chagalls that hang on the walls, I say, 'Does Matthew own all these paintings?'

Phineas chuckles. 'God, yes, and many more. He probably doesn't even remember all the pieces he owns.'

My throat tightens. 'Did you hear about that theft at the Art Institute in Chicago?'

'No,' Phineas says, with slight confusion in his voice. 'But you know people in our business, if it doesn't relate to Hollywood, it doesn't matter.'

Surely the museum would have notified Matthew of the missing Van Gogh? But then I think, how could he know about the SD card? And the painting was recovered in less than a day. And then I remember what Donald told me once: any art theft is dealt with by liaising with the insurance companies. As powerful and busy as Mann is, chances are they don't have a direct line to him. One of his assistants at the studio probably deals with all his philanthropy work. And even if his assistant did bother him about this, would he even suspect Epiphany was involved? Would he bat an eye if the police told him I was a suspect? Would he even remember me?

We make our way to the third floor, passing the cinema and entering a type of movie memorabilia ballroom. Where the second-floor gallery was dedicated to fine art, this one is dedicated to Hollywood pop. Huge posters from Hollywood's past hang on the walls. *Casablanca. Breakfast at Tiffany's. Citizen Kane.* Under a glass case there's the blaster gun from *Blade Runner.* There's the golden statue from *The Maltese Falcon.* There's the headdress Elizabeth Taylor wore in *Cleopatra.* It's like being in one of those Planet Hollywood theme restaurants. Only this one has actual celebrities roaming about, laughing, talking business, looking self-important.

Beside us a Disney actress asks her handler how best to avoid the questions interviewers love to ask about the rumours she's still a virgin; that she's still saving herself for that one special person.

'What are you, twelve?' the handler says to the fourteen-year-old. 'Did you get into this business yesterday? I don't care if you've just won a MTV Movie Award. When someone asks if you're a virgin, you lie and you say "yes" and talk about the importance of your virginity whenever you can. People will see it as an obstacle and that will make you all the more desirable.'

The Disney actress nods her head.

'And always have your mouth open,' the handler instructs. 'No, like this. Always open your mouth a little and purse your lips out, like you're perpetually blowing on an invisible cup of hot tea. It will make people think of sex without making you look slutty.'

The Disney actress blowing on a cup of invisible hot tea says, 'OK.'

'Trust me,' the handler says. 'All this will help sell your television show and your movies and your albums. It's all about building a personal media empire. It's all about strategically stitching together all the pieces to build affinity around the content. But forget about that. That's marketing stuff. That's why you have me.'

And from the other side of the ballroom, a voice shouts, 'Has anyone seen my fian–' then stops abruptly and says, 'I mean, has anyone seen Hugh?'

Phineas hears my groan. 'Jordan is a handful,' he says. 'Come this way, let's escape to the roof. The view is magnificent.'

It's almost six in the evening now and the sun is still hovering above the sea. The Mediterranean's blue-green waters stretch endlessly beyond the cliffs. The rain clouds over the mountains in the west have moved closer, but the breeze is slowing their approach. Jazz music drifts up from the lawn. Bela, she would find this whole party silly, but she would love the view.

I scan the gardens below. We've been through the whole house. Where's Nico? What if he's left? And where's Epiphany? And now that I think about it...

'I haven't seen Matthew yet,' I say.

'He's probably dealing with some last-minute details for tonight,' Phineas says, and then stops abruptly. 'Jerry, if you do see him, I'll ask that you not approach him. It's not that he wouldn't show respect to his friend's son – he's just quite *particular* about these parties. I haven't told him I've invited you. I'd rather stay on his good side.'

'No problem. I understand.' I give him a wink. My wink, it's a warm-up. It's a way to fake confidence; to pretend you aren't a coward. Then I take a deep breath and, taking the biggest leap of faith in my life, I say, 'But I need to be honest with you.'

Phineas, he raises his eyebrows.

'There's a man here – an Italian named Nico. I need to talk to him.'

'I'm not sure–'

I'm not sure is never a good sign. So I rattle through Epiphany's 'plan' in my head. I cut him off and tell Phineas that I came here with ulterior motives. I tell him that I've known about Matthew's parties for some time – that my father told me everything the night before he made the deal with Jordan Seabring.

And the look in his eyes – the guarded suspicion – I can tell Phineas is wondering where I'm going with this. So I apologise and tell him I've been less than honest. Forgive me. Those personal problems I mentioned? I've just gotten out of a bad marriage, I lie. I've come to the festival to party and to forget, I lie. I tell him that when he offered me the tickets, I thought, *What better way to party than to experience the off-limits*? Just like my dad liked to do.

'Just like you like to do,' I say.

And Phineas considers me with a look of guilty astonishment for a moment. But then he lets out a laugh – it's a weird one; a mixture of apprehension and relief, as if he's flip-flopping back and forth between believing whether what I've said my intentions are, and not.

And then, finally, 'Just like your father,' he smiles and holds my gaze.

He begins to speak again, but stops when a group of guests spill onto the rooftop deck with us. Phineas beckons me to follow him and, as we walk down the stairs back to the third floor, he insists we speak in whispers.

'I'm confused,' I say. 'Doesn't everyone here know about this? Isn't that why they're all here?'

Phineas shakes his head. 'Why do sons never really listen to their fathers? No Jerry, this isn't a free-for-all. The people who are here, most of them come because it's the most exclusive party in Cannes. They come for the bragging rights. Besides, to turn down an invitation from Matthew Mann is certain to doom your career. But the real treats, shall we say, they are for a select few only.'

Phineas and I move through the movie memorabilia ballroom on the third floor, past VIPs who are drinking and eating and laughing, past the movie posters and the props in glass cases. A group of people exit the cinema and one of them gushes, *'Matthew's best movie ever! Dare I say, even better than Revolution?'* loud enough for everyone in the room to hear.

'Come, we need privacy,' Phineas says. We make our way down the stairs until we're in the art gallery again. It's still too crowded for Phineas's taste so we walk through the gallery and pass through to a small library at the end of it. I haven't seen this many books since Emma's hospital room. At the back of the library there are a pair of stained-glass doors. When Phineas opens them, the only thing I can say is, *'Jesus Christ.'*

Literally, there's a life-sized statue of Jesus Christ in front of me. Matthew Mann, he's built a chapel in his villa. And Phineas, ever the showman, loves the look of surprise on my face. 'The floor is made of imported granite. The statues are originals from Renaissance Italy. That cross there is over a thousand years old. The slabs come from a synagogue in Poland that was torn down by the Nazis after the start of the Second World War.' Phineas knows what I'm thinking. 'Excessive, right?' he laughs. 'Look, I wouldn't dare say it's a show he puts on because, well, I know he really believes.' He pauses for a moment.

'I mean, he was so worried about your father after Emma died. We all were. But Matthew made him read the Bible – he honestly thought it would help.'

It stings to hear Phineas say Emma's name. What would he have done to her if given the chance?

'But,' Phineas continues, 'this *is* Hollywood. *Everything* is for show in some way. And as I've said, this villa has been featured on countless home shows. Christians are a built-in audience. You appeal to them and they'll spend their money on your products. So it never hurts Matthew to publicly declare how profoundly it affected him when he realised Jesus Christ was his saviour.'

Phineas falls silent for a moment. He hasn't brought us down here just for privacy. The look on his face – the way he regards this place – he's come down here to think about my proposition. He looks at the statue of Jesus. *What should I do?* Phineas seems to think. But the statue, it wears a face that says, *Like I have the answers.*

'You know when your dad first came to me telling me he wanted to solidify your future career, I thought it was a horrible idea,' Phineas says. 'I told him not everyone would be open to our lifestyle – even his own flesh and blood. But your dad was worried about you. He said you were spiralling down after your sister's death, like him, and he needed to put you on a path.'

'Path?' I say.

'He wanted to give you something to do. Let you start building a career so you wouldn't waste your life in front of a TV,' he says. 'But Hollywood is competitive, and if your dad was going to use nepotism to get you in with Mann, we both knew you would eventually need to find out about the girls. So I came up with a sort of test for you and Jonathan agreed. We decided to give you Jordan as a gift and, if you were amenable to her, we would let you into our world and start prepping you for it.'

Poor stupid, beautiful, dumb Jordan.

'But then there was the accident,' Phineas says, omitting all the details that go with it.

'So this Nico guy: can he hook me up?' I say.

Phineas shakes his head. 'Nico is just a middleman, Jerry. He's a trafficker. A thug. He's here to transport the girls back after tonight's event. It's not like he takes orders for girls from just anybody – no offence. You're lucky you didn't approach him about this. He probably would have beat you to death before asking questions.'

I give my best 'surprised' look. *Nico, dangerous? Wow, dodged that bullet.*

'This batch, Jerry – this batch I picked just for this party. Most are virgins,' he says, standing next to a statue of the biggest virgin of them all. 'All of these girls – they're beautiful specimens. All between five and fourteen.' He speaks like he's in ecstasy. 'There are twelve of them, for thirteen guests. No one but those thirteen guests, Matthew, Nico, and I, know about them.' I furrow my eyebrows. 'There is a producer,' Phineas explains. 'His wife likes to watch while he has his way with the young ladies.'

A sickening feeling rises in my gut.

'Jerry, I don't want to get into trouble, but I want to help you out. I understand how life can get you down and sometimes you need a pick-me-up. And you've never experienced a pick-me-up like this. You may think you have but you've never experienced pleasure until you've experienced one of them.' He says this like he's recalling sampling a fine wine. 'The real show, it doesn't start until ten, and even though I can't let you have one of the girls – not tonight anyway,' he smiles, 'well, we are all part of the movies here. How about a preview of the coming attractions?'

48

Passages

Phineas nods and smiles at the multitude of guests as we make our way to the first-floor foyer. When an Oscar-winning actor asks where the host is, Phineas grins, 'He's the puppeteer making sure everything at his little party runs smoothly for your enjoyment. You'll see him for the toast at dinner!'

As we pass two famous directors drinking martinis, one says, 'Have you seen that pale blonde? Stunning!' The other answers, 'She could give Seabring a run for her money! I wonder who she's signed with?'

I look out at the garden from the foyer's floor-to-ceiling windows. I haven't seen the stunning pale blonde since she slapped the knife out of my hand.

Phineas leads me through the foyer, past a bar in the back of the room, to a roped-off set of stairs. 'Quickly,' he says as he moves the rope aside. We climb the stairs until we come to the second floor. 'This is the west wing, Jerry.'

It's quiet up here without all the guests and the small talk and the clinking glasses. There are four doors on either side of the hall and a large, nude pastel painting hangs at the end. The painting, it's of a girl who is crouching down in a big tin tub. A jug full of water sits next to her on a small wooden table.

'It is called "After the Bath, Four" by Edgar Degas,' Phineas says. 'It's worth more than twenty million. That's a good thing, too. No one would dare touch it.' And to my utter shock, Phineas pulls the Degas painting open like a door. 'I told you how Matthew designed this house personally? This is one of the reasons why. Go on, get in.'

Phineas follows me through and pulls the painting shut behind us. Inside, dim red lights barely illuminate the passage we're in. It's no more than three feet wide. The ground is padded in thick foam. Two-by-four support struts run diagonally from wall to floor. The passage extends in either direction before making right turns with the build of the west wing. Phineas gives a quiet chuckle when he sees my mouth hanging open. 'The rich, what they do to keep themselves entertained.'

'What is this?'

'This is a secret that only Matthew, I, a few others – and now you – know about.' He explains that this passage runs behind all the rooms in the west wing as he leads me in one direction, our feet not making a sound on the foam padding. And I can't help but think of playing Clue with Emma. These passages are exactly like the secret passages in the board game.

Around the corner, where the passage turns left, rays of light shine through double slits in the walls. The slits, they're peepholes. Each pair look into a different room. The rooms are all empty, but they're as richly decorated as the rest of the house: expensive paintings, lush furniture, mini-bars. I lean in to look through the third peephole, placing my hand on the wall to steady myself from rocking on the foam padding.

'Careful!' Phineas hisses as he pulls my hand from the wall. 'That's a doorway too. It opens a painting on the other side. There's one room on this side of the wing that has an opening and one room on the other side.'

I try to hide my look of astonishment at all this. And Phineas answers before I even have to ask. 'Matthew likes to watch,' he says. 'He enjoys it more than anything. None of his guests know. Sometimes he even sits back here and films them – in case he has trouble with them down the road.'

I can tell that the look on my face doesn't instill a lot of confidence that he's made the right choice by showing me all this. That's when I'm reminded that I'm supposed to find this all wonderful. 'Whatever gets you off, right?' I say, and Phineas grins like we're in some boys' club together. 'My dad always told me how he loved the different girls–'

Phineas quickly stifles a loud laugh and slaps me on the back. 'Jonathan could be a real braggart! But no Jerry, I'm sorry, even fathers embellish sometimes. He wasn't quite *Rico Suave*. Jonathan only ever used one girl. A gift from Matthew to help him get over his depression. A real stunner, too. Looked like a young Audrey Hepburn.' He shakes his head. 'I would have loved to have a piece of that one, but no one else was allowed to touch her.'

And suddenly a shriek of laughter comes from the room we're standing behind. We peer through the peepholes. In the room Matthew Mann, his fat, roly-poly back towards us, gropes a woman in his arms. The woman, she's wearing a white, tea-dance-twenties dress and her hair is a golden blonde.

What the hell is Epiphany doing?

Phineas whispers, 'Looks like he's found another actress who wants a part. Let's give them some privacy.'

We quietly traipse along the thick foam padding, carefully stepping around the two-by-four struts supporting the passage walls. But in the dim red light I trip over a dark-blue plastic bucket left over from the passage's construction. The contents of the bucket – some loose nails, a small hammer, a roll of duct tape – all spill onto the floor's foam padding.

Phineas signals for me to be more careful, then turns and continues making his way down the passage until we come to the corridor behind the rooms opposite from where we were, the ones on the other side of the west wing's hall. What Phineas doesn't see in the glow of the dim red light is that I've picked up the small hammer and slipped it into my pants pocket. When I find Nico this could work better than the steak knife would have.

Then I notice that, on this side of the west wing, there's a small ladder at the end of the passage.

'We don't want to be moving the girls through the halls in front of all our guests,' Phineas says when he sees me looking at the ladder. 'But I didn't bring you back here for an architectural tour. I promised you a show.'

'I thought it didn't start until ten?'

'Remember how I said stars think they deserve anything they want when they want it? The big enough stars, you have to accommodate them.'

Phineas nods towards the slit of light protruding from the wall we're behind. 'Careful,' he warns. 'That's another door you're standing in front of.' Through the peephole, the room on the other side is lined with framed movie posters of Matthew's films. On either side of the room are plush couches and chairs and, directly opposite the peephole, is a sofa like a shrink would have – one of those leather ones with the long backrest. On either side of the shrink's sofa are small tables, each displaying a golden Oscar statue.

But the main attraction in this room is the man in it. He's the most recognisable star in the world.

He's the star who has three blockbuster trilogies under his belt.

The star who's done comedy, thriller, action and indie, all to critical acclaim.

The star whose box office receipts exceeds six billion gross.

And this star, from the other side of this wall, he's staring right at me.

'*Variety* said we would never get Hugh Fox to sign with us,' Phineas whispers one peephole over. 'They had a point. How do you sign someone who's worth more than God? What could you possibly offer him? *This* was part of the contract.'

Through the peephole Hugh Fox curls his finger in a 'come here' motion and a girl walks into view. The girl, she must have been right below my peephole. Her hair hangs to just below her bare shoulder blades. It's a dirty, dark-blonde colour, but only because it's summer. It's the kind of hair that goes brunette in the winter. Emma's used to do the same thing. She's wearing a spaghetti-strap dress with a white-lace top that becomes flat as it flows to the tops of her knees. A little pink see-through frill pokes out a few inches below the end of the dress. Her legs, like her arms, are thin and tanned. Pink flip-flops cover her feet.

Next to me, one peephole over, Phineas whispers, 'The rest of the girls will be dressed for tonight in beautiful white communion gowns Matthew has picked out, but Fox wanted something a girl might wear to her sweet-sixteen party.'

Through the peephole, Fox orders, 'Turn around.' And the girl, she turns like she's a model on display. She's beautiful, the little girl is. Her teeth are a bright white and a light-pink gloss gives her lips a nice shine. She's definitely not sixteen – *maybe* fourteen. But those eyes, they're caked in eyeliner. She could very well be younger.

And through the peephole, the biggest star in the world drops his pants followed by his black briefs. Then he takes something that looks like a leather strap from his shirt pocket and twists it over the top of his penis and under the bottom of his scrotum. And as he strokes his penis, he tells the girl, 'I want you to call me "daddy". Now get on your knees.'

And the little girl, she kneels.

'Go ahead, grab it.'

The little girl places her little tanned hand on Fox's penis. Her small hand makes his dick look that much larger.

'Ask me if it's a lollipop.'

My stomach churns.

'Is it a lollipop?' The girl says in pretty good English. Hugh Fox stops stroking his dick and glares at her. 'Is it a lollipop, *Daddy*?'

And I vomit in my mouth a little. The acidic taste burns my throat, but I swallow it. I turn to see if Phineas has noticed my disgust. But Phineas, in the next peephole over, hasn't noticed me at all. And suddenly, looking through the peephole next to mine, he begins to breath heavily.

And in the room a muffled, bubbly voice says, 'There you are!'

And behind the wall, Phineas says, 'Oh, shit.'

Phineas says, 'Oh my God.'

I turn back to the peephole.

In the room, the bubbly voices says, 'I've been looking *all over* for my fiancée–'

And here's the thing: if you're gonna rape a little girl, lock the door.

Jordan, the Starlet, she says, 'Baby?'

She says, 'Hugh?'

She says, 'What are you doing?'

And through the peephole, I see as she raises her hands to cover her mouth, but she's unable to utter a cry. It's one of those cries that won't come after the realisation that your forty-million-dollar-a-picture boyfriend is about to get head from a tweenager.

Hugh Fox spins around, knocking the little girl to the ground. The cock ring has made his balls go a shade of blue. 'Jordan!' he squeaks. And as the Starlet begins to cry, as she runs from the room, a little scream escapes her mouth down the hall. Fox quickly pulls his pants over his bulging penis and tells the little girl to stay put; he'll be right back. 'Daddy will be back with your lollipop,' he cries madly as he runs out the door.

And behind the wall with me, Phineas is running down the passage now, running back the way we came like his ass is on fire. 'I've got to handle this!' he yells. 'Close the painting on your way out!' And even in the red glow of the darkened passage, the back of his neck is a pale white.

When I look back through the peephole Phineas is dashing past the room's open door. He shouts to someone in the hall, 'There you are! Take the girl back to the others!' And the little girl in the room, she just sits on the floor, drawing imaginary images on the carpet with her finger.

Then all breath leaves me as the man Phineas shouted to enters the room. Through the peephole I see his face is marked with scars from a fight. His six-and-a-half foot figure dwarfs the little girl on the floor. Those large hands – those murder weapons – take the little girl's face and he says, 'You've been such a problem, haven't you?'

And behind the wall, in my hand, I'm gripping the hammer I took.

And in Nico's hands, the girl, she's smart enough to remain quiet as he fondles her head with those meathooks. The ones that bruised Bela's neck. The ones that crushed her windpipe. And Nico says, 'You've caused me so much trouble. You know your momma is here looking for you?'

Momma?

He says, 'She gave me all these, your mother,' and rubs the scar marks on his face.

He says, 'Do you even know what a mother is?'

And Epiphany's daughter, she doesn't reply.

Nico shakes his head. 'Fuck the commission. Let's see if your virginity is worth all the trouble and money they paid to keep you all these years. Get on the couch.' Like a trained dog, Epiphany's daughter gets off the floor and sits on one of the plush couches. 'Face the wall. On your knees. Bend over.' And the girl, she does all this. Nico flips up the bottom of her dress, exposing yellow panties.

From somewhere out in the hall someone laughs or cries, or both. It's hard to make out from this side of the peephole.

In the room, Nico checks over his shoulder. 'Wait there,' he tells Epiphany's daughter. 'Don't move.' He leaves the room and while he's out, the girl does exactly what he says: she waits, kneeling on the couch, facing the opposite wall, dress hiked around her hips. She's as trained as can be.

My face is pressed firmly against the peephole. I place my hands on either side to steady myself on the foam padding. But the passage door makes a creak as it gives way a little bit under the force of my hand, and the girl on the couch – Epiphany's daughter – she looks in my direction. But I stop myself from opening the door. I resist the surprisingly strong desire I have to save this girl. So her face turns back towards the couch, then it turns towards the door leading to the hallway.

And me, with the hammer in my hand, I realise this is my chance, my perfect opportunity.

And I want to tell the little girl, Epiphany's daughter, that I'm sorry, but life isn't fair. We've all got our own problems. We've all got our own shit we need to fix. You aren't mine.

When is a man most relaxed, most distracted, most vulnerable? When he's shooting his load into something.

This will level the playing field. This is how David can sneak up on Goliath and bludgeon him to death over the head.

But in my head, a battle begins to rage. It's a battle of doing what's necessary versus doing what's right.

In the room, on the couch, Epiphany's daughter, she sways. It's hard to stay kneeling for so long.

And in my head, the battle; on necessity's side is almost every victim who's ever lived shouting, 'Save her and you give up revenge!'

And in the room, on the couch, one of the girl's little pink flip-flops has slipped off her foot, but she leaves it on the ground. She doesn't dare move from the position Nico has ordered her into.

Look, I'm sorry she has to be the sacrificial lamb, but this is for the greater good. This isn't just for me. It's for everyone who Nico won't be able to hurt in the future. This is for justice. The justice you have to make when God or life won't give you any.

But then in my head, on the other end of the battlefield, I see Emma. One little girl standing against the legions of necessity. She doesn't speak to me, or prod me to join her side. Even if she did, her tiny voice would be drowned out by the onslaught of the cries from the hordes that challenge her. Emma, she just stands on her lonesome.

In the room, on the couch, Epiphany's daughter wobbles. Tears roll down her cheeks at the realisation that the horror she has been bred for is about to come to pass.

In my head, I say to Emma, *If I open this passage door, if I try to rescue her, I give up my chance to surprise Nico from behind. He's so much stronger than me and I give up the only chance I have of overtaking him.*

'It's for Justice!' the legions of necessity shout.

And Emma, on the other side of the battlefield, she stands there against the whole world. A rock of conviction in a place where men believe in nothing and scoff at all things.

Behind the peephole, my throat tightens.

My grip on the hammer tightens.

But...

Damn it.

'Come on,' I call, and open the passage door. 'Hurry!' I say to Epiphany's daughter.

And there it goes – any chance of me getting the jump on Nico. He'll come back. The little girl will be gone. There will be another manhunt like there was the night of the wrap party.

I'm hanging halfway out the passage door, beckoning the little girl to follow me in, but the girl doesn't move. She just keeps looking out the hallway door.

'Come on!' I say again.

Then a chill engulfs my body.

A voice says, 'Perro.'

It says, 'I hoped I'd see you again. I'm just surprised it's in this room.'

Nico stands in the doorway. That's why the girl stayed put. She could see him coming down the hall.

His large hand touches the top of his skull. 'I owe you something,' he says, biting his teeth together.

And I see LaRouche, gap-mouthed.

'Run,' I shout at Epiphany's daughter. '*Run!*' But she stays frozen on the couch, one flip-flopless foot dangling off the end.

Nico laughs. 'Run where? Your little secret passage? Where's she going to go from there? Where are you going to go, perro?'

He takes a gun from beneath his jacket and motions me into the room.

He says, 'You can drop the hammer.'

And I do.

He says, 'No, on the *other* side. Pick it up and leave it in the passage.'

So I do.

He says, 'Now seal the passage.'

And I close the painting shut.

Now he says, 'See this?' and quickly shows me the back of his head. Where his hair has been shaved, several stitches lace his skin. 'You almost killed me that night.'

'I wish I had.'

Nico clicks his tongue. 'Don't be rude, perro. You've already been such trouble.'

I curl my fists.

'Easy, perro. Who has the gun?' Nico chides. 'You need to learn not to be a troublemaker. Now me, I do not like trouble. I thought I proved that to you in Mexico when we made our deal. I was willing to let you go. But then you did what you did, even after I explained I just needed to get rid of Hanna to protect my business. But your decision, you made me follow you to Porto. I had no choice.'

'You killed her.'

'It was one person, perro. A bitch in heat,' Nico says. 'She was just a penalty for what you did.'

And I lunge at Nico and he swings his gun at me and I feel a tooth crack as it hits my jaw.

'Down, perro. Down!'

I scamper back towards the wall, clutching my jaw in my hand. One tooth cracked. The pain is unreal and that's just one. I have thirty-one left for him to crack.

Nico, he's saying, 'After I killed your friend, I went to my storehouse in Spain. And what did I find? My caretaker tied to a tree, almost dead from the Spanish heat, and my house in ruins. Hanna had burnt it down like she did my orphanage.' He pauses and shakes his head, then he steps towards me and swings his gun again. On the other side of my mouth I hear another crack.

On the couch, the little girl, Epiphany's daughter, she pretends like she's not seeing any of this. Me, I'm crying.

Nico is saying, 'My caretaker, she told Hanna the girls had been moved to Cannes.' He grins. 'I left her tied to that tree, you know? I left her suffocate in that heat. I don't like when people talk.'

And outside in the hall it sounds like someone laughs or screams again and Nico, he puts his gun back in its holster underneath his jacket and waits to make sure no one walks by. When no one does he picks up one of the gold Oscar statues from one of the tables, like it's good to mix up what he's hitting me with.

'Really, you brought this on yourself,' Nico says, flipping the Oscar statue around in his hand, feeling its weight. He looks a little disappointed. 'You know, when Matthew said that Phineas told him he saw you in the bar at the Carlton I was surprised. I had thought you separated from Hanna in Porto.'

'I'm here for Bela,' I grit.

'Of course you are. Bela. That was her name, yes? Beautiful.' Nico laughs. 'Hanna is rubbing off on you. Both out for revenge for your own reasons. And here I thought I taught you business sense, perro. But if you had learned any, I guess it would have occurred to you that I couldn't let Hanna threaten any future deals, so after I left Spain I had to come to Cannes and embarrassingly explain to my valued client that an old friend of his might show up and, if she did, I would take care of her, I would set things right. Free of charge. I don't like having to give freebies. Freebies make me want to break mouths.'

And he hits me with his fist.

'What I was surprised to find out was that Matthew knew who you were when I told him your name. He knew about the "murder" you committed at the museum, but he was alarmed to find out that you had been travelling with Hanna. He was even more alarmed when a few nights later his man Phineas told him he had seen you at the bar.'

And he hits me with his fist again.

'We weren't sure Hanna would find us, but once he knew you were in town he ordered Phineas to invite you places, to see if anyone was travelling with you,' he says.

Against the wall, I'm crying, my jaw hurts so bad.

On the couch, Epiphany's daughter, she's still kneeling and not hearing any of this.

Nico clicks his teeth together and rubs a finger back and forth over the edge of a coffee table in the room.

'Matthew isn't as foolish as Hanna's presence here suggests she believes he is. He knew if he had Phineas invite you here, at the very least he could have me tie up one loose end – and at best he hoped you would bring Hanna as your guest if you were still travelling with her, knowing she would come for her daughter. Why waste energy searching for the two of you when we could get you to come to us?'

Nico clenches his first and I wince, expecting another punch. But he smiles when he sees my terror and unfurls his fist without striking me.

'Matthew, I like him very much,' he says. 'He is like me: take charge; use people until they can no longer offer you anything. Not like his stupid man Phineas, who doesn't realise everything that's going on around him. He doesn't know Hanna is here. He doesn't know why Matthew wants you invited places. Like most, he is weak and afraid to challenge the leash. He takes orders from his master because he's too afraid of what might happen if he questions them.'

This time Nico's fist hits me for real.

'I really wish Matthew would tell me to get rid of him, too. Maybe after Matthew is done letting Hanna think her little disguise fools him he'll let me take care of Phineas as well. Right now he's letting Hanna think that he's like other men; that the promise of sex will get him to tell her anything she wants. But once he's used her, he's going to do what he should have done years ago.' And here, Nico turns to Epiphany's daughter. He says, 'He's going to have me kill your mommy.'

In his hands, Nico flips the Oscar statue around. Those large hands. Those meaty weapons. I'm trembling like a leaf. 'You killed Bela. You didn't have to. I wasn't with Hanna any longer. I had left her,' I say through the pain in my mouth.

'Not my problem, perro. You had reneged on our previous agreement. You were dishonest! Worse, you left me for dead and even stole my money, like a petty thief.' Nico looks at Epiphany's daughter then back to me. 'You know, Matthew ordered me to kill you. But I like to think I'm a forgiving man. Of course, I took from you already. But that was for your betrayal in Mexico. You still owe me for the money you stole.'

'It's gone.'

On the couch, Epiphany's daughter, still leaning on her elbows and knees, her body wavers.

'Do not move!' Nico shouts and points the Oscar at her like a baton. 'Do not move or I will beat you like never before.'

The little girl stifles a cry and tries with all her might to steady her body.

'The money is gone? Of course it is. You have no discipline.' He places the Oscar back on its table. 'But, it's your lucky day. You have a choice. I can give you a new smile and then kill you, or,' he simpers, 'you can fuck her.'

The little girl, her body acts like it's heard nothing, but her eyes tell a different story.

'You can fuck that bitch's daughter and walk out with the same mouth you have now. Please take the second choice, perro. It will be more pleasurable for both of us,' he grins. 'Before Matthew has me put a bullet in her head, I would love to tell Hanna that you fucked her daughter to save your own ass.'

Nico's cruelty, Epiphany was right about it. On the couch, the little girl's eyes, Epiphany's daughter's eyes, they fall to the floor along with some teardrops. She's just an object in a world run by sick men.

But hey, we all have our own problems.

And feeling all the pain in my mouth, I say, 'I walk out?'

'You walk out – and this time you never let me see you again.'

'You'll just let me leave? Just like that?'

'I'm a man of my word. Unlike you,' Nico says.

I look at Epiphany's daughter. The tears have dried on to her cheeks. 'I'm sorry,' I say. Then I tell her to bend over the couch. 'No, the one by the table there.' I point to the shrink's sofa, the one next to the table where Nico has set the Oscar down.

Oscar statues, you think of them as such Hollywood inventions, but they're made in the good ol' Midwest. The mould was originally cast at a foundry in Batavia, Illinois in 1928. The statues, they're 92.5 percent tin and 7.5 percent copper. The gold plating is added after they've been moulded. I know this thanks to years of watching *Access Hollywood*.

I unbuckle my belt and Nico moves closer to me, his eyes appreciating a cruelty only he can orchestrate. And as I flip the little girl's dress up, I place one hand on the table for support as I lean over her. With my other hand, I unzip my fly.

The Oscar statue, it's officially called the Academy Award of Merit. It depicts a knight holding a sword standing on a reel of film with five spokes. The five spokes, they represent the five original branches of the Academy: Actors, Directors, Producers, Writers and Technicians.

Nico, I can feel him grinning over me as he waits for me to penetrate this little girl.

The Oscar statue, this blunt instrument of gold-plated britannium on a black metal base, its final weight is eight and a half pounds. Eight and a half pounds of solid metal.

So you'll excuse my surprise when I grab the statue and I swing it and it shatters like a porcelain vase as it connects with Nico's face. In my hand, all that's left is a fractured part of the Oscar's black base.

And the thing about Oscar statues is that, during the Second World War, to support the American war effort, they were made of plaster painted gold. After the war ended they were traded in for real tin and copper and gold-plated britannium ones. The old plaster statues, like this one, they're quite a collector's piece. Which is probably why it's in Matthew's possession.

And the thing about these rare plaster Oscar statues, they won't get you out of a jam.

They won't make a dent big enough to crack a human skull, to haemorrhage a brain.

They just break and crumble and sting, like a really harsh slap in the face.

And as Nico howls in pain, I find my voice. 'Run!' I yell at Epiphany's daughter, 'Run! Now!' But she runs, of all places, back through the passage door. And, as Nico reaches for his gun, as I hold the shattered golden statue in my hand, I realise my bravery is all used up.

49

Lemon Meringue

The thing about being a coward your whole life – or at least since you were twelve, the night you ran into the Hollywood hills before you were supposed to save your little sister's life – it makes you a fast runner. I was out the door before Nico had a chance to pull his gun. And when someone is hot on your heels with a gun pointed at your back, well, you don't run with a destination in mind, you aren't looking for a finish line – you just *run*.

Because if you do find that finish line, you're most likely dead.

Another thing about running for your life, when you're a coward like me, you're too afraid to look back. You're too afraid to turn around to see if you've outrun anything. It's like being in the ocean and being too afraid to put your head underwater because you don't want to know if a shark is coming up to eat you from below.

But, like everything in life, sometimes shit just gets in your way. I'm in the second floor art gallery now and it's packed with people. The crowd, they make it really hard to run for your life. So here, I kinda just mosey for my life. I slip past the waiters serving hors d'oeuvres on silver trays and I mosey.

I mosey by a comedian talking to a supermodel about the weather in front of what is probably Monet's greatest work ever ('Looks like it's going to rain.'). I mosey past a *Teen Beat* pretty-boy heartthrob being hit on by the manliest action star of the 1990s. I mosey by a forty-five-year-old Country-Western singer giving breast enhancement tips to Disney's latest sixteen-year-old cash cow.

Then I stop moseying and dare to look around. And see? I see Nico enter the other side of the gallery. He's clutching his head in one hand and with the other he quickly slips his gun into his waist when he notices how many celebrities have moved inside.

I bound up the central flight of stairs to the third-floor ballroom, where a crowd of celebs drink and pick at food from long buffet tables. They look more at home here, among the movie posters on the walls and the props in glass cases, than they did in the art gallery. And as the stars smile and laugh, as they nibble caviar and slurp raw oysters and drink the Dom Pérignon, I wonder who among them is part of the other twelve? Who among them are here to diddle little girls?

Against my better instincts, I dare to look back again. Nico, he glares at me, handkerchief blotting a little dribble of blood on his forehead as he walks up the stairs. I start towards the cinema, but stop as I realise there's no better place to kill me than in a darkened room full of self-obsessed celebrities admiring their own images flickering on the silver screen.

As Nico reaches the landing I notice a giant-sized Epiphany staring at me from the wall behind a dessert table offering sweets the size of your head. But then I realise it's not really Epiphany. It's just, well, with her face with her hair all up like that, she looks a lot like her now that I think about it. It's the original movie poster for *Breakfast at Tiffany's*. The one with Audrey Hepburn standing in a black evening gown, black gloves, big diamond necklace, cat around her neck. That one. The one with the red and blue and yellow borders.

Right by Audrey's hip is a bronze door handle. Without looking over my shoulder again to see how close Nico is to killing me, I slip through the door and lock it shut from the other side.

And, *shit*.

Literally. There's a piece of shit floating in the toilet. In magazine photos stars are so glossy clean it's hard to believe they have assholes like you and me. It's even harder to believe that they forget to flush.

There's a light tap at the door.

'Uh, one minute,' I say. The turd bobs gently below the surface in the toilet bowl. 'It's a big one!'

'My friend, let's not make this hard, OK?' Nico says through the door. 'I know it's you in there, perro. Let's not be silly. There's no way out.'

And he's right. It's either back out the door or through the window. And the garden is three storeys below.

You know how you tense every muscle in your body when you're holding in a fart? So you don't make a sound? That's what I'm doing.

Through the door, Nico says, 'Fine, I can stay out here all day; there's so much great food.' His voice dampens when he says, 'You *must* try this meringue, my friend.'

I walk past the green-marble basin and cabinets with gold finishings, past the free-standing bidet, and I wiggle the bathroom window back and forth, the one that looks out to the gardens and the Mediterranean below. The window, it's triple-glazed. Weighs a ton.

'What are you doing?' Nico's stuffed voice asks through the door as I strain against the weight of the window. 'It's over, perro. You tried. But even that little girl knows how this ends. She didn't even run. She just hid behind the wall. She's back with the others now. Be like her, perro. Accept this.'

'Open, open, open,' I say to the window.

A short thump comes from the other side of the door.

The veins on my temples flare. 'Come on, open, please,' I ask nicely. On the other side of the bathroom door, the thumping quickens.

Inside, I say to the window, 'Come on, open you sonofabitch. Open!' And with a loud screech, the windowpane shudders up.

I'm halfway out when the bathroom's lock gives. And Nico, he slips in and quietly kicks the door shut with his heel. In one hand is his gun and in the other is a huge piece of lemon meringue. Seriously, it's massive. I've seen softballs that were smaller.

Nico waves his gun and I crawl back into the bathroom. And, taking a bite of his massive meringue, he slides a tall metal trashcan underneath the door handle.

He says, 'OK, perro. That's two chances I've given you. Now, I need to kill you.'

'What are you going to do?' I say. 'Shoot me with all those people right outside?'

'No,' he says, taking another large mouthful of the meringue. Then he uses his gun hand to open one of the sink drawers and places the gun inside. 'I'm going to strangle you, just like I strangled your girlfriend.'

'And where are you going to put my body?' I say, like I'm the smartest guy on the planet. 'You can't exactly toss me out the window. Not with all of Matthew's guests outside.'

'Underneath the sink,' he says, tapping on the cabinet with his foot. I say, 'I won't fit.'

He says, 'I'll make you fit,' and takes another bite of his meringue.

Nico, he's got that smug grin on his face, the one that says, 'All the power in this room belongs to me. Let me finish my meringue; I'll kill you in a little bit.'

He takes another bite from his massive Swiss dessert and, with a full mouth, says, 'Please just don't scream like your little Portuguese girlfriend.' *Munch, munch, munch.* 'What was her name? Bela?'

My body shakes to hear him speak her name.

Nico shrugs. 'She was beautiful, perro. She was. That's a girl who could have made a man like me a lot of money.'

My chest heaves.

'She begged me not to kill her, you know?' *Munch, munch, munch.* 'She offered me her body. She opened her legs and begged me to take her if I wanted – anything so I wouldn't kill her.'

'You're a liar...'

'Am I, perro? Perhaps. Perhaps not.' He raises his eyebrows and frowns his lips. 'But you know what is the absolute truth? And this I swear on my dear mother's grave. Don't you wonder how I found you? In Porto?'

He lets this question hang in the air between us. As it lingers there, I remember the night before Bela ... Paulo told me a man had come around asking if anyone had rented the flat. At the time I thought it was Abdul – but now I know it was Nico.

I say, 'You saw through an old man's lie.'

Nico laughs. 'Wrong again, my friend! I went around the city looking for where you might be staying, but the old man, he lied for you – and he lied well. *I believed him* when he said a German couple who had already left had rented the flat.'

Nico motions with his hand for me to make another guess. When I remain silent he shakes his head in disappointment. He says, 'The thing is, I gave you a chance to punish her and you didn't take it.'

Munch, munch, munch.

'After Hanna fled from me in that market I thought I would never find her again. But, as fate would have it, I was leaving this nice little bar late one night. It was almost four in the morning, and who do I see walking down the avenue? Hanna. I followed her until she came to a small street where she stopped outside a café and peered towards the second floor.'

My heart drops into the ice pit that is my stomach.

'And, believe it or not,' Nico grins, smears of meringue caking his teeth, 'believe it or not, perro, she actually began talking to herself. She said, "Please, Michael, let Jerry believe me".'

Spasms run across where my heart used to be. Epiphany – if she had left me alone...

'"Let *Jerry* believe me". Nico smiles widely.

If she had left me alone ... Bela would still be alive.

'Now some man scared her off after that, but I knew she would come back for you. So, I waited because two for one is always a better business decision. After I saw you leave your flat a few hours later, after you spoke to the old man and he dozed off, I snuck up the stairs. I was going to wait for you – for both of you. Just imagine my surprise when I found the oddest thing: a beautiful woman lighting candles inside vegetables.'

'You murdered – '

Nico shakes his head. 'I didn't murder anyone, perro. I fined you like any businessman would for breaking our deal in Mexico.'

Munch, munch, munch.

'If it matters to you, she did fight back. She sprayed me in the eyes with perfume. It was all over my hands when I wrapped them around her beautiful neck.'

'You put her back in the bed...' I tremble. 'Made her look...'

Nico shrugs. 'Presentation counts.'

I open my mouth but nothing comes out for a moment. Then, 'I'm going to kill you...'

Nico shakes his head. 'No you aren't, perro.' He looks at me with condescending eyes. 'You're not because I gave you a chance to punish Hanna like no one else could and you chose to hit me over the head with a statue instead. She led me to your girl and you couldn't even fit together the pieces. You're like a child.'

Munch, munch, munch.

'So, why do you run? What do you have left? Hanna will be dead soon. You should hear the moans coming from that room. The last one was practically a scream.' He licks his lips, dabbing up some crumbs of meringue. 'And after Matthew's enjoyed her, he'll call me. I'll finish her.'

I don't flinch. I see Epiphany, tied to a stake, being burnt alive like Joan of Arc.

'Exactly,' Nico says. 'Why care about her after she led me right to your girl?'

His meringue, it's down to the size of a baseball now. *Munch, munch, munch.* He takes another bite, halving it.

'I've worked hard and want to enjoy the party,' he says between full lips. 'So, I'll be merciful. I'll make this quick,' and he pauses to stuff the remainder of the lemon meringue into his mouth, 'like I did with your whore.' *Munch, munch, munch.*

Crumbs from his stuffed mouth fall to the floor. They spill from his lips and land with the sound of boulders in my roaring ears. My body trembles as I watch his big, stupid, lemon-meringue grin split like a crack in the earth. There's a sudden quaking in me – a tremor of anger and hatred and rage and regret. Then an explosion follows of such force it could level a mountain to dust.

In the movies, if you hit someone square on the nose, you'll push its cartilage into their brain, killing them instantly. But this is real life, and that magnitude of anger you feel boiling up inside you? It can rarely be focused into anything useful. As I lunge at Nico, my punch misses his nose – misses his entire face. My fist lands on his shoulder as my feet trip over one another and I fall into him, taking us both down to the stone porcelain floor.

He lands on his back and I fall on his chest. It's like a barrel, his chest is. I scramble to my feet, intent on grabbing for the gun he's placed in the drawer, but as I do, Nico stays on the floor. The big veins in his thick neck bulge fat like bloated worms.

There's a banging at the door. 'Hey, come on!' a sassy voice shouts from the other side. 'You've been in there forever!' I heave breaths and my body sweats as the banging continues. Nico hasn't gotten up yet. Crumbs from the lemon meringue dot his mouth. His lips, they're a shade of purple. And this is where he begins clutching at his throat. This is where he starts to wriggle on the floor.

That last half of the huge meringue, it's lodged in his throat.

And Nico's face begins to turn an ever-darkening shade of blue. Sweat breaks out on his forehead. He makes odd clicking noises as he scratches at his Adam's apple. He would dig through his skin if he could. That's how bad it feels.

'There's a line out here, you know!' the sassy voice shouts through the bathroom door. 'You've got thirty seconds! Do you know who I am? Thirty seconds! One, two...'

And I count with the sassy voice. 'Three, four...' I count with the voice and watch a powerful brute wriggling around on the stone porcelain floor like a clubbed baby snow seal.

'Fourteen, fifteen...' Nico's hand clutches at my ankle.

'Twenty-six...' A horrid smell fills the room. Nico's shit himself. His body has relaxed every muscle – even his sphincter – in a last-ditch attempt at salvation.

'Thirty!' the sassy voice says. 'Let's go!'

On the bathroom floor, I squat by his side and Nico, his hand skims my chest. It pulls on my shirt. His eyes look wide into mine with desperation; with total submission; with absolute acknowledgement that I'm the only one who can save his life – me the coward; me the dog. He tugs my arm – my hand. He begs my hand to follow his to his throat, to use it to lift his death sentence. His hand dances and dances, his fingers tickle my tux, but me, I just slap it away.

Nico's eyes swim with surprise and horror that someone like me can so calmly sit by a man's side and watch him die. And weaker than before, his hand begs again for my fingers to pry the meringue from his throat. But again, I slap it away and watch Nico's shock until his face is the colour of a blueberry. I watch until his wriggling stops. I watch until his eyes are as lifeless as a shark's.

And that's how it ends for the terrifying and cruel Nico. The monster who trafficked girls all over the world. The murderer of my love. Killed by a Swiss dessert while wriggling in a pile of his own shit.

And I wait for it ... the relief.

'What's going on in there?' The voice from the other side of the door yells. 'What's all that noise? Are you ... are you having sex?'

The relief that doesn't come.

'Someone get security! Matthew wouldn't want something as base as sex in a public toilet happening at his party! Get security!'

Matthew's thugs with their guns and their thighs like tree trunks will shoot me dead once they've seen I killed Nico. I make for the bathroom window again. But before I'm fully out, I stop. Soon the room will be filled with security guards and men with bloated bladders, and, well, I'd hate for anyone to think *I* did it. I turn back inside. I walk past Nico's dead body. His expensive Italian shoes butt against the base of the toilet. That big piece of celebrity shit bobbing around the bowl? I give it a flush. I'm not gonna be blamed for that.

50

Freefall

Bela baby, I did it. He's gone.

And I wait … I wait crouched on the windowsill. The six-inch width of the ledge to either side of it not as frightening as what isn't happening inside of me.

'He's gone,' I say aloud. As if voicing it will carry the pain away in the breeze that flows past me.

But the only thing that carries up here are the notes from the orchestra playing three storeys below.

The pain's still there, inside me. The emptiness. The loss. The hurt.

And I know the pain, it's still there because of Epiphany. Nico said she led him right to Bela. Epiphany's as responsible for Bela's death as he is. The devil. All of us are insignificant collateral damage in her world.

She's like a goddamned cancer, Epiphany. You do the chemo, the carcinogenesis meds regimen, the bone-marrow transplants, the cell scrapes. You just want to stop hurting, so you do all that stuff, but Epiphany, it lays in you, dormant, slowly eating away at you. You think you've beat it. You hope. You dare to believe. But when you have Epiphany there's always something more. Something hidden. She's leukaemia and she's devouring you from the inside out.

Behind me, back in the bathroom, there's a loud scraping of the tall metal trashcan across the stone porcelain as someone forces the door open. Gripping the inside edge of the windowpane I slink my way across the ledge, out of sight of the window. As I release my hand from the window's edge, the windowpane shudders as it slides shut with a loud bang. That's when I reach my hands toward the sky like I've found Jesus. It looked like I could grasp the upper ledge of the roof deck, but my fingers come centimetres short. The best I can do is brush the bottom of the deck's ledge with my fingertips. I glance back through the window, hoping I can crawl back into the bathroom, but a security guard stands over Nico's body. I see him mouth 'What the hell?' as he pulls his gun from its holster.

I retreat from the window's view, balancing on my little ledge, three storeys above the garden, pressing my back against the wall of the villa. I'm spread-eagled, trying to balance on a ledge the width of a VHS tape, as my fingertips press against the bottom of the roof deck in an attempt to stop my body from wobbling.

The wind is picking up speed. Towards the red mountains that curve in the distance the storm clouds have moved closer. Now they block out the sun, causing the sky to form a premature grey-orange-purple dusk. I scan the villa to see if there's a way in through another window. Towards the east wing I see nothing, but when I look towards the west wing, that's when I see a group of girls – young girls – all huddled in a window on the third floor. They're all taking furtive peeks into the garden below. And one of the girls, from this distance she looks like–

I crane my neck for a better view and my heart fires wildly as my body caves outward as gravity tries to pull me from the ledge. I pivot my hips back, desperately trying to regain equilibrium. Every inch of my back tries to bond with the wall behind me. I swallow hard, only having narrowly avoided falling three storeys to my death. I try to be as still as a gargoyle, sucking in my gut, flattening myself against the wall. But the damned wind, it isn't doing me any favours. As the storm approaches, it blows my body hard. If I stay here I'm going to fall.

Three storeys below me, the orchestra plays 'Ain't We Got Fun'.

To my right, there's a drainpipe no more than a foot from my ledge. If I can reach it I can use it to climb to the deck above.

But stuff like this, it all looks way easier on TV. As I stretch my hand towards the pipe, my foot slips and I career sideways. The only thing that keeps me from going splat on someone's trombone is my tux sleeve. It's caught on a retainer holding the drainpipe to the wall. My jacket shreds as I desperately wrap my arms around the pipe. I stretch my foot towards the window ledge, but my weight causes the drainpipe to buckle. A rivet pops from the wall and the pipe bends like a straw. My feet dangle in the air. I kick wildly, searching for traction. Then I glimpse a surface below my soles. I press my toes onto the crown moulding as hard as I can.

So here I am, arms wrapped around a crooked drainpipe, toes clawing crown moulding, leaning like the Tower of Pisa over gardens filled with the most recognisable people on the planet. And man, the thing about stars is they never look up. They never look up because they know they're the ones to be looked up to. There is nothing above them. That's why not a single person below notices a man in his tux hanging on for his life three storeys above the ground.

But I'm not alone up here for long. Above me on the rooftop deck, the most famous actor in the world has stepped onto the ledge. Hugh Fox. The forty-million-a-picture man. The actor that likes to fuck little girls. The guy who likes to be called 'Daddy'.

A voice cries at him. It begs him to get down.

'Please, baby, just come to me.' It's the Starlet's voice.

'No!' Hugh cries. 'My career will be ruined when this gets out!'

'I didn't see what I thought I did,' the Starlet's voice lies.

'No. No, you'll tell people about this! It'll help your career. The coverage you'll get for turning me in–' Hugh looks towards the cliffs. His spittle, carried by the wind, mists my face. 'I'll be destroyed. I'll go to jail! Worse! I'll never get a major role again!'

And this is where Hugh does a triple-somersault off the rooftop. And on his way out of this world, he notices me hanging to my drainpipe. And in that space between free-fall and the ground, Hugh automatically flashes me that beautiful smile of his just in case the man hanging from the drainpipe has a camera with him. Then, splat.

Jordan appears at the edge of the roof. She screams and tears flood her eyes. And even from all the way up here, you can see the blood begin to pool around Hugh's body below. He's more a work of art in death than he ever was in life. Looks like a Pollock. Nice use of red.

Below, the orchestra stops playing. A group of publicists stare at Fox's body in stunned silence. Some of the partygoers in the garden begin to scream.

'What the hell is going on in this place?' a voice says. The security guard, he's forced the bathroom window open. Fox's is the second body he's found in five minutes. But just as the guard thinks he's seen everything, now the most powerful man in Hollywood comes trotting into the garden like he's in a one-legged race. His pants circle his ankles and a bloody hand is cupped over his balls.

'Help me!' Matthew Mann screams, 'Someone help me!' Then Epiphany bursts into the garden. She's lost her blonde wig and tiny blood bubbles dribble down her cream-white chin on to her cheap tea-dance-twenties dress.

There's such a stinging in my chest. The walking cancer. The terminal disease. *You led him to Bela.*

Below me, in the gardens, the crowd scatter like bowling pins at Epiphany's approach. Epiphany rips the fake Arabian sword from the hand of *The Princess of the Sand*'s evil king statue and, like the reaper, she stalks through the bed of lilies where Matthew Mann has collapsed. She swings the sword wildly at someone who attempts to help him up. She's scarier than death, she is. The blood that trickles from her mouth, it's all come from Matthew's penis.

And a celebutante faints.

A muscle-bound action hero screams like a little girl.

A conservative talk show host flees with a falafel balanced in one hand and a drink in the other.

In the bathroom window next to me, the security guard says, 'I left South Central for *this*?' and then disappears.

Above me, from the rooftop deck, a teardrop from the Starlet hits my hand. Is she crying over losing a fiancé or over how much his death will affect her career?

Below me, three security guards approach Epiphany, guns drawn.

Just shoot the bitch. She's got a plastic sword, for God's sake. Shoot her and put us both out of our misery.

A searing pain flashes through my shoulder blades. I press my eyes shut so tight I see red between my lids. And Bela, I see Bela.

The pain trails off and I open my eyes. Over by the circular gravel drive, you can hear limo after limo speed away.

Back below me, one of the security guards is down. Epiphany must have done something. His arm shouldn't look like that.

Another teardrop hits my hand. Jordan Seabring. The beautiful blonde actress again. The Starlet. The non-fiancée. So many names for one person. As I watch her cry, she reminds me of Bela. It's because of their lips. They both have full lips. But one's were real and the other's are due to three collagen injections a year.

Back on the ground again, the second guard is down. Epiphany hovers over Matthew like the angel of death. No. Not the angel of death. She hovers over him like a fallen saint. A misguided Joan of Arc. She fights fearlessly because she believes she has God on her side. She fights with one purpose, one goal. Her own.

Ask her, 'What about what I want? What about me?'

She'll answer, 'What *about* you? You don't matter.'

Fuck Epiphany.

The Quester.

The Devil.

And as I speak Epiphany's name in vein, pain sparks through my body like hellfire. Hanging from my drainpipe, I try to think of anything else to block the pain, but my biceps still spasm. My fingers lose all feeling. My body is done. I'm done. I crane backwards as my hold on the pipe begins to slacken. Below, the last guard on the lawn is down. The prop sword is sticking out of his throat. And Epiphany? Epiphany and Matthew have both disappeared.

My feet slip from the crown moulding, sending my body swinging away from the villa.

Jerry, this is your life.

These are its final seconds.

The last of my fingers slips. As my body enters free fall, time virtually stops. It's like you're given a slight stay of execution to take in the wonderful world that wasn't. And, after blaming Epiphany one last time, I fill my mind with thoughts of Bela and Emma. And I even see Emma. She's watching me from that window in the west wing. And even though I know she's only a figment of my imagination, brought on by the inevitable onslaught of my imminent death, it's nice to have someone you loved with you when you're about to die. You'll understand what I mean one day.

And, as Emma stares back at me from that window in the west wing, someone appears by her side. Someone appears by her side ... and takes her hand.

Oh God.

This person that takes her hand, it's Phineas.

His words, they echo in my mind: *Jonathan only ever used one girl ... A real stunner ... like a young Audrey Hepburn ... No one else was allowed to touch her.*

This figment of Emma I see? She's not a figment at all.

She's Epiphany's daughter.

And I say, *'Please–'*

As my body speeds on its collision course with the ground, I pray.

I say, *'Oh, Saviour, please–'*

I pray to Epiphany that she does what I was never able to. I pray that she saves my little sister.

51

Hanna

The landing feels exactly like it does when you wake from one of those dreams where you're falling. The unrelenting speed. The beats of your heart as you plunge. The sudden stop that jolts you awake.

Of course, there are differences too. A femur breaks. A rib cracks. I look to my side and there's an ulna sticking through torn flesh. Everything goes black.

'Damn it! How many people are going to jump off the roof today?' a voice is saying in slow motion.

Another voice, it takes on regular speed as I open my eyes. 'My God! My God! Whose *bone* is that?' a guy holding his shoulder says.

I'm looking up towards the sky. The drainpipe sticks out from the side of the villa. It sways in the wind. Massive, angry storm clouds float overhead.

I'm jumbled on a pile of bodies in the garden next to the abandoned orchestra's stage. The bodies belong to the group of publicists that came over to see what a suicided Hollywood star looks like, all splattered on the ground. They're the only reason I'm alive. They broke my fall. One publicist holds his arm as another helps him from the ground. The guy with the ulna sticking out refuses to move. It's a moment before I realise that none of the breaking or cracking belonged to me. I pick myself up and the guy below me screams as I grab his leg to steady myself.

'Who are you?' the publicist holding his arm says.

'He's not my client. Who cares?' the shoulder guy answers. 'Where *is* my client?'

'Can we focus here?' the ulna publicist grits from the ground. You can see his marrow dribble from his split bone. It looks like dried meat sauce. 'We've got to decide who we need to pay off to make this go away.'

Priorities.

All around us people are running and screaming and looking guilty.

When I stand it feels like the whole world is moving. The sky is grey as clouds swirl and a loud wind howls from over the cliffs. The tables in the garden slide like they're pucks on an air-hockey table. They slide, then pause and slide again, before completely blowing over on the lawn. China dishes and crystal glasses and food and real silver silverware go everywhere. Even the statue of the princess has been knocked over; she's landed between her evil stepbrother's legs. How embarrassing. The Party of the Year is a disaster. Celebrities flee like children as their PR handlers shout at them. A martial-arts hero pushes a Best Actress winner to the ground and dives into her limo, which speeds down the gravel drive without her.

I hear thunder, but it's only in my head. I look up to the third-floor window, the one in the west wing, the one where I saw Emma. There's blood on the pane now.

My head reels. Emma? No. Not Emma...

In my mind it feels like it's a cold November night in California. I stumble into the grand foyer. I catch a glimpse of myself in one of the large mirrors. My tux jacket is shredded where it caught on the drainpipe's retainer. My face is beaten.

On the grand staircase there's blood that dribbles up the stairs. I follow it to the second-floor art gallery.

'Did you see the gun she had against his head?' a woman shrieks as she passes me on her way down the stairs.

'The gun?' the man guiding her by the arm says. 'Did you hear her say she was going to *pull* the rest of his cock off?'

My head thumps like someone's put a pressure cooker inside it. Every floor of the villa is in chaos. Public relations people bark orders at their celebrities like they're scolding five-year-olds.

'You were never here!'

'*You had the stomach flu and couldn't make it!*'

'*We're going to have to release a sex tape to get the public interested in something else! We'll anal it if we have to!*'

The celebrities, some look more culpable than others.

The trail of blood continues to the third-floor ballroom, which was once buzzing with Hollywood's hottest stars feeling self-important and admiring all the movie props that sit in glass cases. Now the room is abandoned. One of the buffet tables has been knocked over. Food is everywhere. A horrible smell emanates from the corner of the room by the *Breakfast at Tiffany's* poster next to the bathroom door that's been forced open. It's the smell of Nico's shit.

My head throbs. The window. It was on the third floor – this floor. I race from the ballroom to the west wing. But this floor of the west wing, it's just another gallery. A very narrow gallery. Where the room should be, the one that owns the window where the girls are, there's a wall. Muffled screams come from behind it. The wall, I pound on it. I yell, 'Emma! Emma!' I don't know what else to call her.

I claw and pull down every painting in the hall. None of them are hidden doorways. Then a muffled shriek comes from behind the wall. And me, I see myself sitting in the cold Hollywood hills on that November night. I see myself letting Emma die again.

I dash back into the ballroom, past the cinema. Maybe the roof? I start towards the stairs leading towards the rooftop and that's when I notice them: a pair of legs wiggling from behind the tipped-over buffet table. He's lying right underneath the poster of my dad's favourite actress.

'Phineas!' I yell. I kneel by his side. I clutch his shoulders. 'How do you get to the girls?'

On the *Breakfast at Tiffany's* poster there's a streak of blood running down from Audrey's knees to just behind Phineas's back. His white shirt is cranberry red. His head lolls side to side as he speaks. He says, 'It's her, you know? Jonathan's girl. She's here...'

I ball my shredded jacket into his stomach to try to stop the bleeding. 'Phineas, please. I need to get to the girls. My sister. How do you get into the room?'

'I was in the room ... She came in and shot me. Not going back,' he says with a far away look in his eyes. 'Came up here to hide.'

I say, 'Please...'

He says, *'Epiphany* ... after all these years...'

'Phineas, please. The girls—'

Phineas's eyes are bleary. 'Your dad gave her that name, you know? Always called her *"my little epiphany"*.' He gurgles a little laugh. 'I thought it odd, but Jonathan said that's what she was to him – an epiphany. He said he realised that she was saving him from a life of hurt.'

'Phineas—'

'When he had brought me in he said that when he first found out what Matthew was up to ... noticing really young girls at private parties ... he confronted him. But Matthew made him feel complicit. So instead of going to the police ... he tried to *manage* the situation. He told me, "I was trying to keep the girl problem under control".'

My throat tightens. 'Phineas, how do I get in to the room? Is it the roof?'

Phineas's face pales. 'No room on roof...' His eyes shift. They look like they're staring at something only he can see.

'When I told Matthew I met you in the bar, he told me to lie to you and not reveal that he asked me to invite you here.' A laugh of shame weakly escapes his lips. 'He was being so secretive ... I feared he might be thinking of giving you my job, like your dad always wanted.'

A succession of quick inhalations shakes his body.

'This world keeps you paranoid about everything,' he says. 'But the thing about all this – the most frightening – everything we've done ... I can't remember when it stopped bothering me.' He breathes deep. 'It's troubling how quickly you can get used to anything... join in on it, especially when the people around you think nothing of it.'

'Phineas—'

But Phineas, he doesn't speak after that. He doesn't breathe after that either.

My whole body feels like it's being attacked. Like I'm losing to that

November night again. Thoughts swirl in my brain like snow in a globe. I look at Audrey on the movie poster. Her face is so confident, so knowing. Her eyes look to the left as an orange cat balances on her shoulder.

Then it hits me.

Phineas said he came *up* here to hide from Epiphany. He came *from* the room.

I follow the trail of blood with my eyes back to the staircase. The blood going to the third floor: it was Phineas's, not Mann's. All that snow swirling in my head, it freezes in place now. I know exactly how to get to the room.

I race back down the stairs to the second-floor art gallery. Sure enough, there's a trail of blood leading towards the west wing where Hugh Fox was. I enter through the Degas painting and stumble along the padded passageway until I find the ladder I saw earlier. Its rungs are wet now. The dim red lights mix with the liquid's true colour, making it look like maple syrup.

I climb the ladder until I'm on the third floor. The ladder leads to a platform the size of a phone booth. I press against every wall until one of them gives. The room I stumble into has racks full of clothes – everything from evening gowns to nurses' outfits to Sunday church-wear. Beneath the blood-stained window, the one that overlooks the garden, Matthew Mann mutters incomprehensibly, his pants still down around his ankles. His penis sits at an odd angle on his thigh, barely attached to his groin by a thin flap of skin. Just out of his reach is the gun Epiphany took from one of the security guards – the gun she shot Phineas with when she forced Matthew up here.

'Jonathan's son...' Matthew says, when he sees me.

He's dying from the blood loss.

Hiding between the racks of clothing, behind the tables full of makeup, are little girls in various stages of dress. Some already sport the gowns that resemble what you'd wear to your First Communion service. The girls – the older ones, they look like robots. No expression. No emotion. It's the younger girls – the seven- and eight-year-olds – that's where you see the despair.

I look around wildly. Where is she? Has Epiphany taken her? Then I hear a sniffling and pull a rack of clothes out of the way. Behind it, in the centre of the room, a girl is clutched in Epiphany's arms. This girl, she looks like she's just gotten the shock of her life. And Epiphany, the look in her eyes is the look of twelve years of longing, twelve years of pain, seeping away.

'My baby,' she cries. *'Mojo dorogaya malishka, bog soedinil nas vodno celeo.'*

I've never heard her speak Russian before.

I stare at my sister like it's the first time I've seen her; like she's not the same girl Hugh Fox had in that room. I want to grab her tight, just like Epiphany. But I don't. My hands are covered with blood from the ladder. I don't want to scare her any more than she already has been. And as Epiphany embraces her – my sister lets out a tiny smile. And I crack. Pools of water form in my eyes. I see so much of Emma in her now.

'Why didn't you tell me?' my voice breaks the air.

Epiphany wipes her red, puffy eyes. I think it's the first time she's noticed I'm here.

'Would you have believed me?'

I shake my head, but I know Epiphany already knows my answer.

Somewhere in the background, Matthew Mann mutters, 'My cock...'

Epiphany whispers to her daughter, *'Eto tvoiy brat.'*

Matthew mutters, 'You bitch...'

'Brat?' her daughter says. Epiphany nods and my sister looks at me. Epiphany's just told my sister who I am.

I don't know what to say. I stare at her with dopey eyes and smile the kindest smile I can.

'My cock, you bitch,' Matthew yells. This time his voice is so loud we all turn.

The gun is in his hand. It wavers between Epiphany and my sister. Matthew's face flushes with fury and vitriol. The raw chill that seizes my body lights up every nerve in it. And in a moment of fear and hope, love and redemption, I push Epiphany to the ground and snatch my sister from her arms. I clutch her to my chest and spin around, using my entire body to shield her in its embrace. I squeeze my eyes shut. The sound of the shot is deafening. And in this instant everything, my failure with Emma, my cowardice in the Hollywood hills – everything is absolved. This sacrifice is the second chance I've always needed. And my sister, I feel her heart beat against my chest. And as I wait for the bullet to sting my body like a molten bee, I smile.

And even though time feels differently in intense situations, causing dramatic events to slow for the person experiencing them, the sting has still not come. I force my eyes open, suddenly fearful that physics has failed and the trajectory of the bullet has curved around me and hit her. I pat my sister's body. I push my fingers through her hair looking for a wound. She's in shock, but her body is fine. Then I feel my chest and my stomach and my back. There's no wound anywhere.

Behind me, Epiphany stands upright, facing Matthew. There's not a mark on her.

But as I've said before, guns act differently when they're around Epiphany Jones. And I breathe a smile. I smile because this is a genuine miracle.

'We're fine,' I whisper with relief to my sister as I kiss her forehead. 'We're fine.'

I turn to Epiphany. She's still facing Matthew and I begin to wonder what she'll do to him. She's already grabbed the gun from his hand and thrown it clear across the room.

'We should get out of here,' I say. 'Call the police. Let them handle the other girls.' I look at my sister. 'But we need to get *her* out of here now.'

But Epiphany, on the side of her little tea-dance-twenties dress, a dark blotch grows.

'Epiphany?'

She turns to me. She smiles slightly. The front of her dress looks like a red ink blotter. And as she collapses, I hear myself stammering *'No, no, no...'*

Behind her, Matthew Mann is saying, 'Got, you ... bitch ... my cock...'

Then there's a scream and, Matthew Mann, he's begging me to stop. I don't even remember starting. I'm straddling his stomach, beating his face with my fists. His begging only causes me to thrash harder. I pound his face even after a knuckle cracks and a sharp pain splinters through my hand. Spasms run across my face. I beat him for what he made my dad become; for what he's done to my sister; for Epiphany. When it hurts too much to hit anymore, I club him with the bottom of my joined fists like I'm hammering a stake into the ground. Matthew struggles to raise his meaty hands to my face. He pleads with me to stop. '*Please*,' he gurgles, blood pouring from a gap where some of his front teeth used to be. Only then do I catch a reflection in the window of the looks on the girls' faces. Only then do I relent. And only when I relent do I realise how hard I'm crying.

On the floor, my sister, she cradles her mother's head in her lap. Tears stream down her young face. But Epiphany smiles. She smiles as she strokes her daughter's cheek.

I scuttle to Epiphany's side. My hands lap around the pool on her damp stomach. And through her crimson dress, I find the entry hole right next to her belly button.

'*Bitch*–' Matthew gurgles. The window behind where he lies clatters as grey clouds and wind and rain mix with the stormy sea.

I say, 'Epiphany–' and apply pressure. My finger tries to plug the hole in her stomach. It's so tiny, the hole is. It's no wider than a pencil. How can this much blood be coming from such a little hole?

Again, behind me, Matthew mutters, '*Bitch*.'

I think, '*Saviour*.'

He mutters, '*Devil*.'

I think, '*Godsend*.'

He mutters, '*Whore*.'

I scream, 'Shut up!' and I swing my blood-soaked finger at him, smattering droplets across the floor. 'Shut up!' I snarl. My voice is so frightening the other girls in the room stifle their sobs. And Matthew, his eyes fall to his side, like an old man in a nursing home afraid of punishment.

Epiphany's bleeding isn't stopping. I wipe tears from my face, staining them with her blood. 'Epiphany, we gotta get you out of here, OK?' I look at my sister. 'Can you – can you put your hands where mine are?' I show her. 'We need to stop your mom's bleeding. I need to call an ambulance.'

And my sister, she nods her head hesitantly.

'You can do this,' I smile through blood and tears. 'You're strong like your mom here, OK?'

'O-OK.'

'Good. See how my hands are? Just put yours like mine when I move–'

But Epiphany, she rests a pale hand on my bloody ones before I can remove them. 'They say I can go now, Jerry,' she smiles weakly. And her eyes, they're wet too.

'No.' I shake my head. 'No–'

'They say I can go...'

I swallow hard. 'Don't listen to your voices anymore–'

It's not up to me, her smile says.

'But, your daughter–'

Her daughter fights against tears. She's dealing as best as she can, but it's so much for a child to take in: a mother, a brother, freedom.

'You need to stay for your–'

'Sister, Jerry. *Your* sister,' Epiphany says, stroking her daughter's face. Then Epiphany, she looks at me and says, '*You* need to take care of her now. That's why you're here. My voices said you need to be the one to look after her. That's why I couldn't let you take the bullet. It's her brother that she needs...'

And a dam bursts inside me. Seventeen years of repressed pain and loneliness and guilt flow from my mind like a thunderous river. I don't try to block it; I don't try to hurry it. I let it surge through my body; I feel every part of it. Pain, regret, anger, hate. I feel them all – in an instant. The teasing and bullying at my grade school; the fighting between Mom and Dad; the self-hatred over Emma's death. More comes. Being laughed at behind my back by my co-workers; the loss of Bela; the hatred of Nico; the revenge that burned in my chest. The years wasted looking at porn; the anger at my mother for cheating on my father; even something as small as the anger I felt over the raise they gave to Roland instead of me – I feel it all flow out of me. And as the torrent ebbs, as the feelings slow to a trickle, my soul feels lighter than it has in two decades – like someone's taken the Amazon River and sprayed me clean of the planet's worth of mud that's been caked to my body.

I look at my sister and when I do, Epiphany's eyes glisten and she smiles. And I swear she can see what's happened inside of me. I swallow and take a breath. 'How long have you known?' I lose my voice for a moment. 'How long have you known you were going to die today?'

'Since the ride in the car this morning,' she says, a tear escaping her eye. 'They told me you wondered if it would help me if you apologised for your father,' she smiles weakly. 'Then they told me what was to happen to me. They said this was always the plan.'

I shake my head in regret of everything I've ever thought about Epiphany. I say, 'Why didn't you tell me, in the car?'

And Epiphany, she says, 'Because sometimes we need to discover things in our own time and on our own terms before we can believe.'

And the tears I have left, they aren't of pain or hurt. They're tears of gratefulness to this strange woman who came into my life. I squeeze her hand. I say, 'I'm sorry I doubted you.'

But Epiphany, she doesn't need apologies. 'Talk,' she says as her voice begins to falter.

She knows I understand the request. Despite being the ultimate believer, it's still frightening, death is. Just like Emma, she wants a familiar voice by her side.

'Your name,' I begin, 'is Hanna...' Epiphany smiles and her green eyes flash one last time. Then she turns to her daughter and takes her small hand in hers and places it on her chest.

And on this stormy day, in this secret room, as eleven other girls huddle in the corners, as Hollywood's most powerful man lies dying on the floor, I speak to Hanna – a girl who heard voices from God – as she looks into the eyes of her daughter, a daughter she's fought for twelve years to find. I recount our origin – our story. I tell Hanna about Emma, and how her daughter looks like her. I say how I can tell she's just as strong as her mother, and just as kind as Emma. And I tell her about the dreams I used to have of her and how, in those dreams, I knew she was the *Deliverer*, and how I finally understand what that means. And I talk and talk and talk until Epiphany Jones joins her voices.

Acknowledgements

No novel makes it to the shelves by the writer's will alone. You are only holding this book because of the cumulation of the work of a number of people, whether direct or indirect; whether they know it or not.

Thanks to my family, who didn't question (too much) the wisdom of me leaving a six-figure job to become a writer.

To Harriett Gilbert, I would not be where I am today had she not accepted me.

To Jonathan Myerson, tutor turned friend, who encouraged my writing, uncannily, at the times I needed it most.

To Jessica Ziebland, David John, and Toby Minton. Quarterly dinners with my writer buddies keep me sane.

To Luke Dormehl, for contacting me out of the blue that one morning.

To Harriet Poland, Henry de Rougemont, and my agent Maggie Hanbury for believing not only in the novel, but in myself as a writer.

To Martin Fletcher and West Camel, for their extraordinary editorial insights.

To Karen Sullivan, my wonderful publisher who is, no doubt about it, the hardest working person in the industry.

To Jose Farinha, who lets me fuck off when I need to.

To John Ames, whose existence brings relief that my weird thoughts aren't mine alone.

To Charles Gentry, who seems to scoff at everything, but liked the manuscript.

To Jo.

Finally, this book would not be possible without a number of shitty things happening over a lifetime. We only ever hope for the good, but sometimes it is suffering that propels us forward. Only when it has passed can we be thankful for what it's revealed.

IF YOU ENJOYED *EPIPHANY JONES*, YOU'LL LOVE ...

PAUL E. HARDISTY

'A stormer of a thriller - vividly written, utterly
topical, totally gripping' PETER JAMES

THE ABRUPT
PHYSICS OF
DYING

ONE MAN.
AN OIL COMPANY.
A DECISION THAT
COULD COST HIS LIFE

SHORTLISTED FOR THE CWA JOHN CREASY DAGGER AWARD
PAUL E. HARDISTY

THE
EVOLUTION
OF FEAR

BETRAYED.
A PRICE ON HIS HEAD.
IT'S EASY TO SURVIVE.
UNTIL THEY THREATEN
HER TOO...

'A solid, meaty thriller –
Hardisty is a fine writer and
Straker is a great lead character'
LEE CHILD

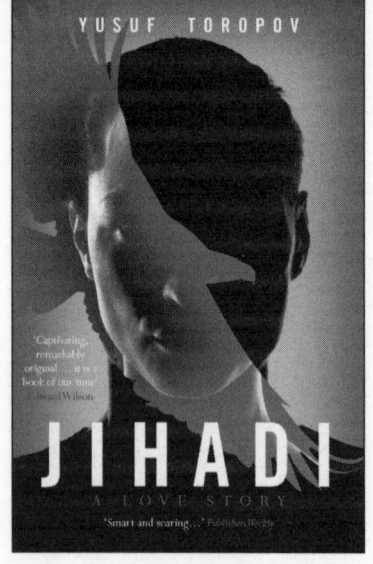

YUSUF TOROPOV

'Captivating,
remarkable
original ... it is a
book of our time'
Joan Wilson

J I H A D I
A LOVE STORY

'Smart and scaring...' Publishers Weekly

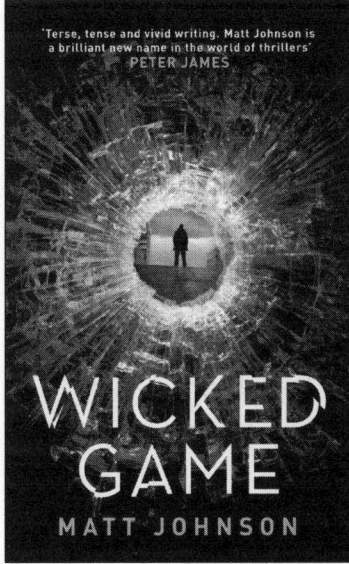

'Terse, tense and vivid writing. Matt Johnson is a brilliant new name in the world of thrillers'
PETER JAMES

WICKED GAME

MATT JOHNSON

'A wonderful, original voice – McCall Smith with a dark edge and even darker underbelly' PETER JAMES

Deadly Harvest

MICHAEL STANLEY

THE DETECTIVE KUBU SERIES

THE DEFENCELESS

BEST FINNISH CRIME NOVEL 2014

'A taut and provocative thriller with a raging social conscience ... cements Kati Hiekkapelto's position as one of Scandi-noir's most exciting and important new voices' Eva Dolan

KATI HIEKKAPELTO

'A NORWEGIAN
CHANDLER'
JO NESBØ

'STAALESEN IS ONE OF
MY VERY FAVOURITE
SCANDINAVIAN AUTHORS
AND THIS IS A SERIES
WITH VERY SHARP TEETH'
IAN RANKIN

GUNNAR
STAALESEN

WE SHALL
INHERIT
THE WIND

INTERNATIONAL BESTSELLER

STAALESEN IS ONE OF
MY VERY FAVOURITE
SCANDINAVIAN AUTHORS
AND THIS IS A SERIES
WITH VERY SHARP TEETH
IAN RANKIN

'A NORWEGIAN
CHANDLER'
JO NESBØ

GUNNAR
STAALESEN

WHERE ROSES
NEVER DIE

INTERNATIONAL BESTSELLER – OVER 2 MILLION COPIES SOLD

'Hauntingly beautiful' CLARE MACKINTOSH

'Thoughtful, atmospheric and deeply immersive, it wields an
almost mesmeric power over the reader' HANNAH BECKERMAN

in
her
wake

A perfect life ... until she
discovered it wasn't her own

Amanda Jennings

COMING SOON FROM ORENDA BOOKS ...

'Chilling, atmospheric and hauntingly beautiful ... I was transfixed'
AMANDA JENNINGS

THE BIRD
TRIBUNAL

AGNES
RAVATN

THE
EXILED

'A taut and provocative thriller with a raging social conscience ... cements Kati Hiekkapelto's position as one of Scandi-noir's most exciting and important new voices' *Eva Dolan*

KATI
HIEKKAPELTO

'Antti Tuomainen is a wonderful writer. His characters, plots and atmosphere are masterfully drawn' *Yrsa Sigurðardóttir*

ANTTI
TUOMAINEN

THE
MINE

DEEP
DOWN
DEAD

STEPH BROADRIBB